T0208951

PURE FYRE

KRISTALYN A. VETOVICH

BALBOA.PRESS

A DIVISION OF HAY HOUSE

Copyright © 2019 KristaLyn A. Vetovich.

All rights reserved. No part of this book may be used or reproduced by any means, graphic, electronic, or mechanical, including photocopying, recording, taping or by any information storage retrieval system without the written permission of the author except in the case of brief quotations embodied in critical articles and reviews.

Balboa Press books may be ordered through booksellers or by contacting:

Balboa Press
A Division of Hay House
1663 Liberty Drive
Bloomington, IN 47403
www.balboapress.com
1 (877) 407-4847

Because of the dynamic nature of the Internet, any web addresses or links contained in this book may have changed since publication and may no longer be valid. The views expressed in this work are solely those of the author and do not necessarily reflect the views of the publisher, and the publisher hereby disclaims any responsibility for them.

The author of this book does not dispense medical advice or prescribe the use of any technique as a form of treatment for physical, emotional, or medical problems without the advice of a physician, either directly or indirectly. The intent of the author is only to offer information of a general nature to help you in your quest for emotional and spiritual well-being. In the event you use any of the information in this book for yourself, which is your constitutional right, the author and the publisher assume no responsibility for your actions.

Any people depicted in stock imagery provided by Getty Images are models, and such images are being used for illustrative purposes only. Certain stock imagery © Getty Images.

Print information available on the last page.

ISBN: 978-1-9822-3919-0 (sc)
ISBN: 978-1-9822-3921-3 (hc)
ISBN: 978-1-9822-3920-6 (e)

Library of Congress Control Number: 2019919547

Balboa Press rev. date: 11/25/2019

PROLOGUE

"A dream? What do you mean, you had a dream? What's so strange about that?"

Ness sighed heavily. "I don't know, Mom. It was different. There were these two dragons, and they fought each other, or they started to fight, but before anything happened, the blue one was essentially torched."

Her mother responded with a blank stare and a slow nod. "Mm-hmm, that's quite the vivid imagination you've got there."

"Imagination?" Of course her mother would dismiss it so condescendingly. After eighteen years, nearly fifteen of them with a blazing crystal to match the golden light of her father's and proving she was destined to become the royal liaison to the people of Condel (once her father was ready to pass the responsibility to her), Ness had hoped she'd be treated with some amount of respect when she shared the dire message laced in her dream.

"Mom, I'm telling you, something is going on." Ness sat heavily at the round wooden table in their modest yet quaint home and took in a deep breath to calm herself. "I'm just saying it was really strange. It felt different from a normal dream." She paused, knowing she was about to bring up a sore subject, but also aware from experience that she couldn't stop herself from trying one more time to make her mother understand. "It felt like, I don't know, like maybe I could do something about it."

"Without one, I can be whatever I choose, while yours has narrowed your mind to a single, unnecessary purpose." He leaned closer. "You have my sympathy."

If Ness hadn't embarrassed herself enough already, she'd have lunged at her brother then and there, but she didn't need to cause any more problems. One day, they would understand. Until then, she could always tell her father when he finally returned from his meetings at the castle.

Ness frowned, looking at the dusky light streaming through the kitchen window. The streetlamps would light soon; it was nearly time for dinner, her father's favorite part of the day, a nonnegotiable communion with their family. But Darian was taking much longer at the castle than usual.

CHAPTER 1

This was unheard of and possibly insane.

Eofyn stood in the throne room—his throne room, though he felt he'd never quite grown into the grandeur of it—staring at the crystal that hung around his fiancée's neck. He'd just been receiving updates on the state of the kingdom when Lissa had entered with the first rays of the sun stretching through the wall-length window of the throne room, as if to greet her personally. Her face was not as bright or warm as the sunbeams, however, which was Eofyn's first note of concern. She stumbled two steps into the room, caught her balance, and sheepishly approached them. The door closed behind her with a thud. She glanced back at the door and then looked at Eofyn and his advisers, who waited for her explanation.

Tucking a strand of caramel blonde hair behind her ear, she inhaled, smoothing her hands down the front of her pale blue gown with the exhale. "Sorry to interrupt," she said, still a little too hurriedly, "but I've had an odd dream that I feel strangely compelled to share."

Eofyn knew Lissa was a rational woman. She had a keen sense to separate nonsense from necessity. Her healing ability extended beyond physical mending. She could balance the mind and the heart as well, healing wounds of all sorts. Therefore, she was always well balanced herself. To see her at all flustered made Eofyn's stomach roil.

"What is it, Lissa?" Darian, the people's liaison of Condel, asked, using his abilities to ease the rising tension in the room. He approached her and placed a gentle hand on her shoulder, the pulsing green light from his crystal offering its calm to her.

Lissa gave a small nod of gratitude before crossing the hall with him to join them, her footsteps echoing across the vast, marbled room more than usual.

She stared into Eofyn's eyes, almost pleadingly, but he had nothing to offer her but an apologetic frown. She sighed. "I do realize how this will sound, and I apologize," she began.

Eofyn and his two companions waited.

"In my dream, there were two dragons."

Eofyn's heart began racing. It would have been bad enough to mention just the one dragon, but two? His eyes trailed to the window and found the great statue of Swelgan, Condel's patron dragon, its back turned on him and its eyes on the city, as if to shun Eofyn's poor rulership.

"They did not duel each other," Lissa amended quickly.

Relief washed over their faces, but she was about to mend that as well.

"Yet the blue dragon did fall." Her final words tumbled from her mouth like a ten-ton weight, and Eofyn nearly fell with them.

Never in history had someone of Lissa's talent class had prophetic dreams. She was a healer, not a seer. Seers weren't even a class. They only appeared in legends and children's stories, yet what she had witnessed in her sleep clearly stirred up a foreign blend of emotions in her, and she wrung her hands. Fear and anxiety were not the most common sentiments in the kingdom of Condel. There were, in fact, talent classes to help with those. Condel was a place of happiness and contentment, where the people thrived with grace and ease with the help of their crystals. Even nightmares were uncommon. So why Lissa, and why now?

"Swelgan," Darian said, breathing heavily.

"But that's not possible," Pyram, Eofyn's closest advisor and best friend, said, a pulse emanating from the flame-red crystal around his neck. "It's been centuries, millennia, since the dragons have animated. They have all but faded into legend."

"Don't be so naïve, Pyram," Darian said, his shoulders tense with a frustration that never reached his face or his tone. Darian always put kindness first, a father to all who surrounded him. Of course, Eofyn noted, that may have been because Darian was one of the eldest members of staff, especially since the passing of Eofyn's father. Flecks of gray speckled Darian's trim, black beard, which he now stroked in thought. "We've all noticed the Fyre weakening throughout the kingdom. The people are losing their confidence in their crystals, and their strength has been dwindling." He sighed. "It was really only a matter of time before it came to this."

Eofyn felt Lissa's steady gaze on him while Darian and Pyram averted their glances to the floor. He knew they had all overlooked this problem, in part out of sympathy and patience for his adjustment as king. It had been nearly a year since his father's passing, and Eofyn had heard nothing from the otherworld of Bryta, an ability that had been the birthright of every reigning monarch of Condel.

Eofyn did not wear a crystal as the others did; with his ability, he should not have needed one. He should have inherited his talent, the Pure Fyre, the moment his father's life ended, but Bryta remained silent. The prince had never felt prepared for the role of being king, and his motivation to activate his gift quickly faded. This only supported his theory that he was unworthy of receiving it. And so his crown remained in its case in his father's study; his more regal garments went unworn. He favored the more common, if somewhat refined, style of a linen shirt with an embellished vest, wool pants, and practical leather boots—a velvet jacket only when ceremonially required, similar to the way Pyram preferred to dress. To all who entered, there was no king in this room, only castle staff.

That was not good enough for his people. They needed a leader, and they needed the guidance from Bryta that they'd had under King Arisan's rule. Eofyn was failing them, and rather than doubt their beloved king, they doubted themselves and the power of their crystals.

Eofyn had overheard Darian mention the depletion to Pyram before, when they thought he wasn't listening. It was Darian's job and his talent to promote confidence in the kingdom, but the people were nearly beyond his help, even the children who had not yet blossomed in a particular field. Their crystals remained untouched by color, but their hearts filled with the unsettling doubt that had now blanketed the kingdom, even if their minds could not yet comprehend the reason.

As the oldest in the room, Darian was the most qualified to say what the other nonroyals could not, yet still Eofyn cringed when Darian accepted the responsibility. "Your Highness," Darian began, bowing at his stout waist with the utmost respect, "we haven't seen the dragons come to life in all of recorded history, but the legends were passed down precisely. And while Miss Lissa's dream could simply be a product of hearing the story throughout her childhood, it could still well be true."

Eofyn tore his stare from the marble floor and moved to give weary reply, but Darian interrupted: "I understand you already know this, but I'm sure you're also aware that we need to act. The dream was likely a blessing, and we'd better not ignore it."

The anger that had crept onto Eofyn's face fell away as he caught himself. He looked at Darian, the slightest glimmer of hopelessness in his eyes, and let his gaze fall back to the floor.

He heard Lissa clear her throat and glanced through his curtain of brown bangs to see her offer Darian a sympathetic smile before they both turned to Pyram, Eofyn's closest friend and advisor, who had been employed as an orphaned child by King Arisan himself. Pyram had grown up as Arisan's second son, and there was no one Eofyn trusted more than him. Lissa begged Pyram with a subtle tilt of her head to use his bond with Eofyn and make the king listen to reason.

Pyram blinked and opened his mouth to argue, but he acknowledged her point with a lift of his slender eyebrows.

He leaned toward Eofyn's ear, close enough to speak softly and ease the embarrassment that the young king already felt. "Fyn," he said, speaking the nickname only he was permitted use, "I know this is rough, but you can handle it. You know what to do. Trust yourself."

Eofyn tightened his jaw, but Pyram persisted. He clapped a lean hand over Eofyn's shoulder for support. "You're the king. It's in your blood to always get it right."

Eofyn cast an angry glance out the wall-length window at the front of the hall. There, sitting at the top of the alabaster stairs that overlooked the kingdom, sat Swelgan. The idea of this stone dragon actually coming to life put a tense crease between his eyes. Eofyn wanted to blame the dragon for the trouble that was to come because the only other option was to blame himself. He took in a breath to refocus on the others and tried to imagine what his father would say in his place.

"According to legend," Eofyn said, his voice not nearly as firm as his father's would have been (his father had boasted a broad chest and a voice that boomed and rumbled like thunder; Eofyn, by stark contrast, inherited his late mother's sleight frame and softer tone), "the dragons only move when peace must be swiftly restored. Condel is not perfect at the moment," he admitted with a nod to Darian, "but we have done nothing to shake the balance of all of Curnen." He paused as if to force away the words he'd have to say next.

His father would never have hesitated.

"Then the problem must be under the eyes of the other dragon. It must be in Gaernod."

Although they all must have known it was coming, Eofyn's words still made the others flinch.

"Well, so much for simple," Pyram muttered.

CHAPTER 2

Spyre thought it fishy several days ago, when King Afor organized an army of soldiers and marched out of Gaernod without a word, but he assumed it to be another pest control mission. Probably an issue with the elves. They were always testing their boundaries.

But when his older brother Ryne, along with the king and the rest of the battalion, hadn't returned after two days, the likelihood of an elfin skirmish became slim, and after a week, Spyre began to think Afor was up to something.

No one else around town seemed bothered by the mysterious absence of their family members, however. Gaernod was an every-man-for-himself kind of kingdom, but Spyre would have thought the people would still care about the missing hands not being around to carry their weight. Timepieces kept nothing but silence without the cooperation of every cog and spring, and while Gaernod had never been a well-oiled machine, with so many people absent from their jobs and homes, the kingdom was a few screws short of a pillory.

Yet Afor kept control over the people of Gaernod by threatening their livelihoods and keeping it in their best interests to do his will. Still, it was a living for those involved. Survival, even at a hefty cost, was better than the alternative.

But that's just stupid, Spyre thought for the first time. The words in his mind surprised him a little. It had never occurred to him that the ways of Gaernod should be questioned, but now that it had, he felt strongly about the subject. No one person should have so much influence over an entire kingdom. At least no one person like Afor. Gaernod was filthy and failing. Shopkeepers sod their wares out of carts because they couldn't afford the overpriced storefront shacks that lined the mucky streets. Money was hoarded rather than traded because no one ever felt secure enough to spend. Investments were the only way to be sure your worth couldn't be so easily stolen from you. The economy of Gaernod was broken and corrupt, and a great deal of the blame belonged to its king.

As Spyre's boots sank into the street's miscellaneous substances, including but not limited to various wastes from the shops (and other things that everyone contributed to but no one saw fit to clean up), his nose hardly registered the pungent cocktail of sewage and rotting goods. Instead, his mind wandered to things unknown, one of his favorite subjects. His brother Ryne hated him for it, but Spyre never could resist an experiment, be it social or mechanical. Today, curiosity—and a fair bit of stupidity, it would turn out—led him to attempt something that no one in Gaernod did if they could avoid it: he made eye contact with another person, a husky but not overly threatening-looking shopkeeper.

The burly man caught Spyre's glance. There was a boyish fear about him that contrasted his particularly large stature, and he quickly shifted his gaze, as was customary, but when his eyes flicked back to get a better look at what should have been Spyre's profile, the shopkeeper's defenses engaged. He stepped in front of his goods and glared, his hand slowly moving underneath his leather apron to the belt around his thigh, making no attempt to conceal a rather pointed dagger.

"What are you looking at, blue eyes?" the man spat, calling attention to another trait of Spyre's that stood out from the rest of the people in Gaernod. It was an insult, and it felt like one every time someone used it against him.

On second thought, Spyre gave a hasty, crooked smile, followed by a curt nod before picking up his pace and hurrying on, despite the difficulty of pulling his boots out of the grime with each step.

Once he was a safe distance away, Spyre turned to see the grumbling man return to his cart and count his goods. He realized there were two things he couldn't understand: why the people of Gaernod continued to live their lives in bitter selfishness, and why he had never noticed or even bothered to care about it before.

He sighed as he finally approached the small cottage he and Ryne had built years ago on the farthest hill of Gaernod, near Tweogan Forest, where no one would dare disturb them. Spyre trudged through the split-jam door, which he had thought was a nice touch, but had eventually nailed shut at his brother's insistence. He threw his bag from his shoulder onto a table strewn with pieces of wood that would eventually become anything requested of him. Woodwork was an uncommon trade in Gaernod; the preferred material was metal. It was sharper, shinier, more lethal. But there was the odd request for a handle repair or a table or chair. Spyre even made a set of kitchenware once.

He took any orders he could get to pull his weight and contribute to the household, designing contraptions to make everyday chores simpler. He'd created things like a chain reaction machine that set the table and a pressure switch that shot a pellet from a slingshot into a precarious block of wood, knocking it onto an air pump to stoke the fire, which was lit by a combustible pebble of his own design, set to explode a few seconds after a rough impact, like tossing it into the woodpile. All this while he continued his work across the room, never leaving his chair. He would eventually have to reset the wooden block, but the system worked well enough, though he hoped none of it broke anytime soon. He had misplaced most of his plans for the devices. He was a bit scatterbrained that way. Not that it often mattered. What he created in his spare time never really amounted to much in the appreciation of his kingdom.

In fact, he thought, *it wasn't enough.*

He glanced out the window and noticed for the first time how very inviting the lonely-looking gate to the city of Tweogan seemed. It was a simple stone arch over a patch of grass with mud on the Gaernod side and a dense forest beyond. Maybe it was the peaceful lure of nature that he found so attractive. Or maybe it was the lack of people who would threaten him for his eye color. He looked back around his meager home, just the main room of wood on all sides and a small closet where Spyre kept quietly to himself whenever Ryne happened to be home for a night or more. He turned again to the portal to freedom outside. His foot slid toward the door.

No, he thought, *that would be stupid*. He caught himself, sitting down at his workbench. *The elves would sooner tear me apart than feed their families, and I can't even fathom what the trolls would do if I managed to reach the Aforthians.*

Spyre rested his chin in his palm, but it wasn't long before his head turned toward the door again. His fingers drummed against his jaw. He could feel the tugging in his chest. He knew he would end up leaving. His mind had already made itself up without his consent.

Only thirty minutes had gone by since the first rogue thought on the street, and suddenly, Spyre couldn't imagine spending another day in Gaernod. Ryne could easily manage without him. He wouldn't even mourn the loss of his brother, probably wouldn't bother questioning it, just like the rest of the people in the kingdom.

That left one problem.

Outside Gaernod, there was only one other place where humans lived. Crossing all the settlements of creatures, who would not be happy to see a human of Gaernod, would leave Spyre in even more trouble once he finally reached the kingdom of crystals. They would not accept him in Condel. Spyre had no special abilities, no background with them. He was, in fact, their enemy, and journeying to live in Condel would be the most treasonous act imaginable. If Afor ever found out …

Somehow, though, it seemed worth the risk. There was no explanation for it, but Spyre knew he should leave. He was no more welcome in Gaernod than he would be in Condel, so he had nothing to lose.

But this was just lunacy.

It would take days to get to Condel, if he survived the journey at all. Frustrated, he looked down at the table and saw his carving knife next to a large piece of wood whose fate had yet to be determined. Somehow, he felt he could relate.

He let out a relenting growl.

"Fine."

He grabbed a big satchel from a hook on the wall and stuffed it without thinking. Food, a blanket, a spare set of clothes, his knife, and that strange piece of wood were all he felt compelled to take with him. Without a second thought or even a moment to take one last look at the house that had never been a home, as evidenced by the lack of furniture, fabric, or keepsakes of any kind, Spyre made for the gate, not planning his next step or guessing what might lay ahead as he passed the ancient stone dragon, Cuman, which guarded it.

For once, and with the worst timing in his life, Spyre wasn't thinking at all.

CHAPTER 3

"I know this all seems very urgent." Eofyn heard Pyram attempt to take the edge off the panic rising in the room. "But let's make sure we're not jumping to conclusions here. Is there any way the dream could mean something else? Maybe the dragons are symbolic of something."

"If I may." Lissa placed a hand at her collarbone, ever graceful and composed. "My dream felt incredibly real. The dragons seemed to wholly consume my senses, and while their battle may be symbolic of the two human kingdoms, I felt as though they were also speaking to me." She looked away. "It sounds so foolish."

Her eyes closed, and she tipped her head back.

"I have this awful sense of foreboding, as though fierce trouble is at our doorstep, and time is running out."

Eofyn stepped forward, even the small step echoing in the sparsely furnished hall, and raised a finger in thought. "But there's yet another mystery," he said, pointing his finger at the girl. "Lissa has a healer's crystal, so why is she suddenly able to prophesy? The crystals have never given the gift of foresight. Why now, and why her?"

"She is the most talented healer in the kingdom," Pyram suggested. "And she has stature. Maybe she was chosen because of her soon-to-be-royal position."

Eofyn shook his head. "No, talents are not discriminatory. Status has never been a factor in the measure of a person's ability."

Lissa cleared her throat, as if to remind Eofyn that she was still in the room. "I don't think it has anything to do with my talent. It probably came to me so I could tell you." Her delicate hand rested on Eofyn's shoulder, releasing the tension that had built there with the soft blue light of her crystal. Then she paused, cringing slightly.

"I, well, I don't suppose you've had any signs or possibly whispers …" She took a nervous breath. "… from Bryta? Perhaps …"

Eofyn dropped his shoulders, feeling sick to his stomach with guilt. Careful not to appear angry, he pulled his shoulder away from Lissa's touch, more disappointed than frustrated. He walked to the massive window that displayed the lustrous city of Condel like a living painting and leaned against it with one arm, sighing.

"No. Nothing. Never." The shame of it overwhelmed him, bubbling in his stomach as though it might spill onto the floor. He squinted through the effort to force it away. "I just don't seem to be able to—"

"You are the heir to the legacy," Pyram said, interrupting him. "It will come to you."

For as much as Eofyn appreciated Pyram's efforts, he couldn't bring himself to believe it. There was only a year between Eofyn and Pyram, but Eofyn respected his faithful guide and guardian more than anyone else, save his father. Pyram was like a physical link where the Fyre wouldn't provide a magical one. It had been Eofyn's father who had taken Pyram from a homeless life, destined for nothing but hunger and solitude, and appointed him as Eofyn's knowledgeable companion: not a father or even a brother, and not even too close a friend.

Pyram could go from being a gentle servant to the rough, blunt street boy he'd been before King Arisan had saved him from a group of guards he'd been trying to steal from. Since the passing of the former king, however, Pyram had primarily been Eofyn's best friend. He had the knowledge of both the castle and the real world beyond its walls, and Eofyn knew Pyram would never lead him astray.

But perhaps it was too much this time. Even Pyram must have had doubts about Eofyn's ability to inherit the link to Bryta and the sage counsel of the otherworld. The gift, which had been with his family for generations, seemed to have finally skipped one. Eofyn was unworthy, as his lack of decision continued to prove, but the time for excusable indecisiveness had just fallen away. Bryta or no Bryta, Eofyn was the leader of Condel, and his people needed him to be his father now. Eofyn straightened and turned back to the others, lifting his chin and trying to look like a king.

Darian stepped forward, a request for permission in his half-bow. Eofyn nodded for him to speak. "There hasn't been a battle in several thousand years. What we decide today will be the model for future generations as well," he reminded the king. "I can send someone to keep watch at the gate, so at the very least, we'll have some sort of warning when it begins."

"And what are we expecting it to be?" Pyram asked, arms folded across his chest.

"The red dragon is a reference to Gaernod," Eofyn decided, almost sounding like Arisan. "With my father gone ..." He paused, collected himself, and continued, "Afor has probably been plotting an attack all year. There will be an attack, and it will be a brutal one. He's been waiting patiently for this opportunity." Eofyn looked away, his stomach churning in self-loathing. "It shouldn't have taken a prophetic vision to see this coming."

Pyram frowned. "We can't dwell on that right now," he said pointedly, drawing Eofyn's eyes to him. He turned to Darian. "Who is your quickest messenger?"

Darian considered for a moment and then grinned. He held up a finger and closed his eyes. After a few moments, he opened them and smiled, waiting.

It wasn't long before the sound of running feet echoed through the hall. A young man trotted through the great door, indigo crystal glowing as it bobbed up and down with his pace. He came to a stop in front of Darian, looking expectant.

"What can I do, sir?" he asked in a voice that had barely reached maturity.

Atelle was small for his age in height and in stature, delicate and pale, with a youthful fascination ever-present on his face. He was one of the youngest on the castle staff. His talent for telepathy was somewhat rare and proved useful for sending messages more quickly than delivering them by foot.

Darian said, "Atelle, go to the outside wall and send word if anything ... unsettling happens to appear on the horizon."

Atelle frowned in confusion but gave no comment. He nodded and turned to scamper away.

"Atelle," Eofyn called out quickly.

The walnut-haired boy stopped and turned, more questions on his face.

"Keep yourself low, would you? Stay safe."

Atelle looked more than a little frightened, but he quickly recovered, gave a firm nod, and ran off to do his duty.

"He's so young," Eofyn lamented as Atelle drew out of earshot.

To add insult to injury, the teenager handled the responsibility much better than his king did. Eofyn watched the door after the boy left. It was time to make himself useful. The impatient pressure in his chest continued to build, but he had no outlet. There was no plan; there was no way to prepare. He knew what the kingdom needed from its king, but he was incapable of giving it. For that, Eofyn truly hated himself.

Unable to contain his frustration, Eofyn turned to the others and said, "I need a moment to … to try … something."

He strode out of the room, leaving the others to stare after him and hope, for the kingdom's sake, that he managed a miracle.

Eofyn paced in his quarters, a round room lined from floor to ceiling with oak bookshelves and ornately framed portraits; alongside the grandiose carved fireplace were two velvet-cushioned chairs to read in. Of course, Eofyn never used them. He wasn't much for reading, and the backs of the chairs were too straight for him to sit comfortably.

"Why?" he demanded of the portrait of his father, who would have sat comfortably in one of Eofyn's tall chairs for how proudly he held himself.

He was every inch a king, with pronounced, angular features and soft, forgiving blue eyes. His hair had turned snowy in the later years, but in this portrait, it was still dark, with streaks of gray that suited him rather than aged him. Even his flaws had served his father well.

"Why did you do this to me?"

The portrait remained silent, staring back at Eofyn with a gentle smile. Eofyn resented that smile. When he was younger, it had erased his troubles many times, but now he needed answers and guidance, and that empty grin was giving him neither.

"Just a hint," Eofyn pleaded. He looked down at himself; he'd give anything for even a whisper of advice on how to turn it on, or whatever he was supposed to do to make the Pure Fyre work. He glared at the picture. "Where are you?"

If there was a Bryta and people continued to exist there, then why wouldn't his father talk to him? He'd been patient. He'd waited an entire year, but in that time, everything had only gotten worse.

He hated his next thought, but it was one that continuously plagued his mind. He stared into his father's painted eyes and finally admitted, "I'm starting to think it was all a lie."

It felt horrible to say what he had been afraid to think for months now, but what other conclusion could he draw from what was happening around him? He felt deserted and inadequate, and in the solitude of his chamber, he could finally let it out, but he also knew he was letting his father and his entire kingdom down by giving up on his inheritance.

Could the entire history of Condel be nothing more than a fantasy they had deluded each king enough to believe? All their wisdom and guidance provided by the so-called Pure Fyre may well have been their own keen instincts and not from some otherworldly source.

They may have been too humble or too unwilling to disturb the people's belief system to admit it. Maybe the monarchs had never been capable of wielding crystals and created the legend of the Pure Fyre to compensate so they wouldn't lose their throne. Either way, Eofyn saw no point in dragging it out now that the situation had turned dire. For the first time in history, Condel needed the guidance of Bryta for something life-threatening, beyond natural causes. What a time to discover that there was really nothing there.

But maybe just one more time, he thought to himself, turning to his father's portrait, trying to preserve his respect for the king now passed. He moved to the nearest comfortable chair and sat, placing his hands on his knees and closing his eyes, focusing on deep, cleansing breaths.

"I need guidance. I need your help," he implored, not sure who he was asking. "Please, for the sake of the entire kingdom and maybe all of Curnen, help me." His hands clenched into fists, and he waited, barely breathing.

Two agonizing minutes of silence.

Five minutes—a lifetime of empty air.

Nothing came to him.

His fingernails pressed marks into the heels of his hands.

Eofyn assumed, if there was a Bryta, they would know the gravity of the situation, but maybe they needed to hear him say it. Whatever their conditions, he received nothing.

He shut his eyes tighter, digging deeper for the answer, but scolded himself for not finding it.

He glared at his father's portrait. The steady smile seemed to have faltered. Eofyn knew a painting couldn't do that, but the hints of disappointment he could read on his father's face was enough to make him believe that much.

On top of being incapable of his divine right, Eofyn was also wasting time. Bryta clearly did not intend to contact him now, if it ever did. It was time to decide on his own what the fate of Condel would be.

He returned to the hall where he had left the others, to find the room cast in an orange glow. Swelgan loomed larger in this dusky light. The setting sun highlighted every angle of his stone scales, ancient yet unweathered over the countless years. Swelgan's usually stoic expression turned sour and brooding with supernatural judgment. The shadows of night curled out and away from the dragonlike talons stretching over the throne room in an eternal, subtle grip on Condel's seat of power. It sent a shudder down Eofyn's spine.

In the long shadow of the dormant dragon stood Eofyn's companions, huddled in a silent meeting.

The door closed, echoing through the stillness of the hall. Panic hung in the air; fear was suffocating them. Lissa, Pyram, and Darian turned in sync to face him.

Before they could arrange their faces to ask, Eofyn shook his head and replied, "Nothing."

"Well, then." Pyram picked up Eofyn's slack and took the positive initiative. "It's a good thing Condel has its most qualified people in charge, isn't it?" He stepped up to his friend and put a strong hand on his shoulder. "Fyn, we can do this. How long have we trained, imagining we might get the chance to be heroes? Now we're being called. Let's respond, shall we?"

Eofyn smiled at the reference to their childhood games of running through the streets of Condel, pretending to vanquish evil thieves, modeled after Pyram's own exploits before living in the castle with wooden swords and strong lectures. With such a peaceful history, they'd never imagined evil looked as bleak as this. Eofyn's father had done well keeping the wretched truth from everyone.

Eofyn's smile faltered so miserably no one even noticed the attempt. To recover, he nodded his agreement. Then he faced Darian. "Any news from Atelle?"

Darian shook his head. "No, thankfully. But that could change at any moment."

Eofyn rubbed his temples, trying to pretend that the situation was not so grave. He followed the impulse to walk through a secret door in the large window of the hall, and the others followed. They gathered next to Swelgan and gazed at the lazily winding streets of Condel and the shopkeepers closing their windows or pushing their wagons home for the night. Straight lines put too much focus on the destination and not enough on the journey, so his father had told him. Here, the people of the kingdom could be mindful and reflect as they strolled along the winding streets and canals.

The design was not as suitable for a crisis as it was for personal growth, however. Escaping the city would be difficult, and there was nowhere outside of the city walls for them to run to. Eofyn pictured his people fleeing the kingdom that had stood peaceful for centuries and felt guilt creep up on him once again. He forced it down.

"It's probably best to alert anyone with crystals attuned to defense," Eofyn thought out loud. "We've never been a kingdom of warriors, but anyone who can contribute somehow would be useful. Atelle will give us a bit of warning. That's good." He looked across the shingled rooftops of the kingdom. "But why would my father leave us so vulnerable?"

The others stared at him, with nothing to offer but sympathy in their eyes.

"My father spoke with Afor more than anyone would care to know," Eofyn revealed. "They sent messages through my father's connection to the Pure Fyre." If that's really what it was, he kept to himself. "That only made Afor bitterer. My father must have realized that Afor was preparing for this. Why wouldn't he take some sort of precaution for his people?"

The sun finished setting, and the crystal lamps that lined the streets eased into glowing. Eofyn watched the others' eyes widen as they scanned to the streets in shock.

"Well, that's not great," Pyram mused.

The lights of the streets were the same as the crystals that enabled the abilities of Condel's people. They shone brightly every night as long as the people believed they would, but tonight, each lamp had the glow of a firefly, leaving the streets cast in shadow.

"The Fyre is going out," Eofyn said, breathing heavily.

Darian shook his head low. "I tried not to notice," he confessed. "I thought I was just overreacting. I never dreamed that this was possible, but I didn't realize the people were feeling this conflicted and scared." He looked away. "My daughter did, though. I think Nessa felt this coming. That girl's crystal would glow a thousand times stronger than mine if radiance were a measure of talent." He frowned at the weak glow of the lampposts. "We should've listened to her."

Eofyn didn't turn at the news that perhaps this could have been prevented. His mind was preoccupied instead with the reality that Darian's teenaged daughter seemed better suited to lead his people than he, the son of a long line of capable kings and queens. Perhaps the Pure Fyre hadn't vanished. Perhaps it had simply sought out a capable host, and that wasn't him.

CHAPTER 4

Spyre had to laugh. The area outside the city gate was somehow less muddy and filthy than the ground inside. His boots didn't squelch when he walked. It made him feel like he had lost a weight he'd been carrying his whole life of trudging through the slurried streets of Gaernod. What did that say about its people?

He headed as directly east as he could whilst weaving through the trees. Slowing his pace to navigate the woods had frustrated him at first, but he realized he was in no hurry. He was likely traveling across most of Curnen, only to be turned away. Maybe he'd be smarter to just keep going straight into the unexplored land of Tir, beyond Condel, and live there in solitude.

He laughed again. That would be suicide.

He peeled himself out of his thoughts for a moment and realized how dark the woods had become over however long he'd been walking. The smart thing to do, he felt, would be to make camp for the night. He'd had an impressively successful day. Why spoil it by getting lost in the dark?

Spyre rummaged in his bag and found the wool blanket he had been wise enough to pack. He grabbed the edges and allowed the blanket to float to the cold ground. At this point, his sense of pride in his resiliency frayed. He had forgotten a second blanket. This one protected him somewhat from the chilled dirt, but the air still had an advantage over him.

He looked around the mossy glen, searching for resources but finding nothing practical. There must be something around him he could use.

On the other hand, if he turned around, he could be home by the middle of the night.

It was tempting. He looked back toward the direction he'd come from. His body was ready to move, but his will stopped him, and he involuntarily relaxed and sighed with disappointment. He cast his glance to the side and saw a cushiony patch of moss on a rather large tree he hadn't noticed before. It was dirty, but he'd seen worse. He was accustomed to a certain level of filth, anyway. The mud that squished between his fingers as he tugged the moss free from the tree didn't even faze him. He laid the moss on the ground and made himself comfortable, with his blanket as shelter.

Spyre closed his eyes, but to his surprise, sleep did not come immediately. His mind buzzed with doubts and concerns about what he had done and what he would do. He imagined he was now an outlaw of sorts, but on second thought, no one would really notice his absence. There was no thrilling danger, no glory, and absolutely no clue about why he had to go to Condel.

As the thread of questions ran on, the last strings of sunlight faded from the tightly woven canopy. The chirps of various bugs and scurrying of nocturnal animals waking for the night provided a strangely peaceful cushion of sound, and Spyre began slowly drifting to sleep, until he heard a branch snap under the weight of something heavier than a small woodland creature. Already annoyed, he opened his eyes to find another beady pair looking back at him.

"Ooh!" The small proportioned creature leaned backward but not enough to get out of Spyre's personal space. His brown eyes remained fascinated and fixed on Spyre.

Spyre blinked, waiting, but when the moment became too long, he broke the silence. "Excuse me, but do you mind?" he asked, his voice strained by his half-curled position on the forest floor.

Sitting back on his heels, the creature replied in a quick, chattery tone, "Not particularly. Do you?"

"Obviously." Spyre pushed the spindly limbed the newcomer away.

He should have expected to run into an elf once he immersed himself into Tweogan Forest. They infested the place, to put it in Afor's terms.

Spyre pushed himself onto one knee, bringing himself to the squatting elf's level. He gave the elf a once-over to decide how much of a threat the gangly creature might be. Looking at his round eyes and seeing confusion, curiosity, questions, but no trace of malice, Spyre figured he was safe enough.

"So what do you want?"

The elf's ears perked up, and he pointed to himself questioningly. Spyre didn't feel like stating the obvious, so he nodded, eyebrows raised in more condescension than was polite or necessary.

The elf allowed his heels to slide out from under him and plopped into a sitting position with a thud, his legs sprawled out before him. Spyre noticed how he, like many elves, resembled the woods around him, his arms and legs seeming to grow from his torso like branches of a tree. His hair topped his head in a shaggy mop like copper leaves, dry and brittle in the onset of winter. He tipped his head in the same manner a squirrel would as it sniffed the air for danger and looked a little bemused, resting one arm across his torso, the other arm on his first, and his chin in his palm like he had just forgotten something important.

"I expected you to be much fiercer," the elf admitted, poking Spyre's lean arm.

Spyre jerked away from him.

"You don't do much to honor the men who came before you." He didn't pause long enough for Spyre to inquire about those who had come before him. "Of course, perhaps you're not like them. You may have a class system. We have a class system. Oh, I just don't know. Is it really important?" He stared at Spyre, who couldn't figure out which statement to respond to.

"Probably not," the elf said, satisfied enough. "We might never know. My name's Faran, by the way. Do you have a name?" He scrunched up his nose. "Should I have bothered asking? You probably won't tell me, anyway. Oh, well..." He cast his sad glance to the side.

Spyre could only stare for a moment, not sure if the creature was finished. He felt almost sympathetic for the frazzled creature and decided he should try to address at least a few of Faran's wonderings.

"My name is Spyre," he began, organizing Faran's queries in his head. "And no, I'm not a warrior. We don't have much of a class system. It's basically just Afor and those below him."

Faran looked up at him with a mist of awe in his eyes. "Ooooh," he said, elongating the word. "That's interesting. So those soldiers are no more important than you are," he deduced, pointing a spindly finger at Spyre for emphasis. "But then, that doesn't mean you're important either. No one is, except for the Afor man." He shrugged. "Or I could be wrong."

"You're not," Spyre reassured him, disappointed by the truth in Faran's assessment.

"Are you sure?" Faran rested his cheek in his hand. "Maybe I'm not, and you're not, either. Have you studied your own politics?"

Spyre opened his mouth to tell Faran how wrong he was and to prove his qualification to speak on the Gaernod culture, but what if Faran was right? Afor could hide anything, really. Who was there to question him? Certainly no one in Gaernod dared, and the creatures outside the kingdom knew better, thanks to Afor's regular incursions to show them their place.

Spyre shook the thoughts from his head. It didn't matter now.

"Listen, do you need to take me to your king or anything like that, or can I be on my way?" The elf must have had some purpose for sneaking up on him while he slept.

Faran again looked surprised. "Talk to the king? The chief? I've never done that. I'm not sure if I'm allowed. I've never tried." He hooked a finger around his chin. "Although I was sent to retrieve you for interrogation."

Spyre nodded. Finally, they were getting somewhere.

"Does that mean I'll get to talk to the chief?" Faran asked. Before Spyre could answer, Faran looked away and asked, "Do I want to talk to him? He's a very stern man."

Knowing by their exchanges already the elf would only continue if uninterrupted, Spyre put a firm hand on his shoulder. Faran took in a sharp gasp, and his eyes shot to Spyre's hand and quickly back to Spyre. He gave no sign of a struggle.

"Can we get this over with, if you don't mind? I'd rather be on my way sooner than later," Spyre said. How bad could an elf king be if this was the character they sent to arrest someone?

Faran's jaw dropped as he tipped his head skyward to cope with Spyre's height as he stood. He nodded vigorously and stood up, the tip of his head level with Spyre's waist.

Spyre waited to see if Faran might decide to attack, but his drooped shoulders and slack arms proved the elf had no intention of putting up a fight. Such a tiny creature had poor odds of winning in combat against a taller being, anyway, and Spyre wasn't in the mood for violence. Not now or ever.

Instead, Faran stumbled into a fast stride, not looking back to see if Spyre was following.

With methods like Faran's, any of Spyre's remaining apprehension at meeting the elfin leader fell away.

As Faran pushed leaves aside and ducked under branches and loose hanging moss, Spyre took his time to observe the forest he'd always known but never visited. There were forest creatures everywhere. Birds and squirrels perched in the trees; mice and other rodents Spyre had never seen from the edges of Gaernod all watched him. None ran, but neither did they approach. The leaves barely even made a sound beneath their feet. It was eerie to Spyre, although he imagined it helped them to feel safe. Spyre was so involved in his surroundings that he nearly tripped over Faran when the elf suddenly came to a stop.

"What's wrong?" Spyre asked.

Faran stared at the sky, considering. "Well, there could be any number of things going wrong. I can only imagine. But we're here." He gestured with both hands at what looked to Spyre like nothing more than grass.

Spyre scanned the ground around his feet. "Well, where is it?"

Faran shrugged, swinging his leg back idly and kicking a rock with his toe like he was bored.

Then Spyre felt his stomach launch to his throat as the ground beneath them gave way. He gasped; his jaw clenched, his hands shot out to his sides to grab anything they could find, and he tightly shut his eyes for several seconds before he decided it was smarter to see what was coming. But all he saw was Faran, arms crossed, muscles relaxed, legs extended beneath him as though he were floating in midair rather than falling to the depths of the earth.

Fear gripped Spyre's chest, which he found more intriguing than terrifying. He'd never needed intense emotion in Gaernod. There was always the dormant caution at the back of his mind to protect him from Afor's decrees or the threat of other Gaernod people who felt it was time to expand their wealth to his homestead, but that was a dull sensation, at best. This was exhilarating. It consumed every part of him. Nothing resisted it. His mind and his body had finally agreed on an emotion, and they were pursuing it fully.

As his heart pounded through his chest, Spyre struggled to breathe, realizing that this particular rush of emotion was quite uncomfortable. His eyes darted to the still solemn Faran. In response, the elf quickly looked down and back up. A warning? Spyre knew too well he wouldn't get a direct answer from Faran, so he didn't bother shouting.

Fortunately, no bones broke as the pair crumpled into a pile of moss after what had only been a few seconds. As he lay there, Spyre noted that this was far more comfortable than the makeshift bed he had attempted to build. Part of him wanted to stay there, certain that sleep would not be a frequent player in his near future. But Faran had already leapt to his feet and was staring at Spyre in question.

Spyre lifted his head. "That way?" He pointed to the black tunnel behind Faran.

Faran turned toward the tunnel, held a contemplative finger to his chin, and then nodded.

Accepting that as good enough, Spyre got to his feet and dusted himself off, looking around. There wasn't much to see, just a bunch of moist, packed earth with roots here and there, and the moss patch that must have been deliberately placed to catch falling visitors, or prey, more likely.

"I believe this is the way." Faran's voice echoed. "Should be the right way. They may have changed it since yesterday; you never know."

"I bet you don't," Spyre muttered to himself.

Faran made no sign he had heard the quip.

"So what am I expected to do? What do they want to know?"

"Hmm?"

Spyre groaned. "You said they wanted to interrogate me. What do they expect me to know?"

Faran's eyes glistened and widened. "Oh, well, isn't it obvious?"

Spyre stared at him. He could feel a twitch in his left eyebrow.

"They want to know why your people came here and left," Faran explained, confusion on his own face to mirror Spyre's.

"What do you mean they came and left?" The forest circled the entire kingdom of Gaernod. Spyre had assumed Afor's army was on the other side, not that they'd gone straight through. That meant they were headed for the trolls' domain.

Faran gave a dramatic nod. "Your people of Gaernod came here, which is not unusual, and they threatened us, which is not unusual, but then they continued through and out of our woods without a single casualty on our part, which is most unusual."

Spyre agreed. It was suspicious. His theory, which he had been questioning since entering Tweogan Forest, was wrong. Afor wasn't out for the elves. He was moving farther away. That was bold of him. What business did he have with the creatures beyond the forest? They had nothing he could truly need. Which left only one option.

The realization hit Spyre just as his palm collided with his forehead. He wasn't escaping Afor; he was pursuing him. All the way to Condel, if Spyre's guess was correct.

The sound of Spyre's self-abuse startled Faran. He jumped and spun in the air, catching himself with uncharacteristic grace, and walked backward to keep an eye on the human.

"Why did you do that?" He leaned curiously to the side enough for one foot to lift off the ground.

Spyre threw an exasperated hand in the air. "Afor … He's—" He let out a frustrated sigh, wondering what in the world he should do now. "He's on his way to do something stupid."

Faran's head tipped to the other side. "And that's why you're here? To follow and stop him?"

"What?" Spyre's eyes grew wide. No, he had no intention of even trying to slow Afor's progress. Spyre sought liberation, not suicide. "Well, I'm—I mean, I'm not—"

"That offers some relief," Faran cut him off, turning to walk normally. "The elders would have likely put you to death as a punishment for your kingdom's trespasses. They might spare your life if you intend to save us from Gaernod."

This was news to Spyre. Faran had given no sign of his elder's intention to kill him, and that was not something Spyre wanted to walk into. Neutrality was now much less of an option.

Spyre squeezed his chest to contain a groan. Saving the world it is, then.

"Yes," he said firmly. "I came here to stop Afor, and save you and everyone else from his horrible … tyranny." His heroic tone faltered at the end, but surely Faran would spend too much time wondering if he'd heard the change in Spyre's voice to address it.

Instead, the elf's eyes lit up. Looking like a child at a solstice festival, Faran turned and continued to lead the way. Spyre let his shoulders slump. He reminded himself that choosing not to die now was only choosing to die later at the hands of Afor, but he followed, anyway.

CHAPTER 5

Eofyn panicked. It was happening. His sharp-sighted guards had spotted the Gaernod army in the distance. They would be here soon. Less than a day. And he had no plan. None at all.

He was alone again, in his father's old room, looking for inspiration and finding nothing but disappointment in himself. He had sent messengers; a handful of people with telepathic talents like Atelle had been directed to contact the head of every household and warned that unless they wanted to partake in a battle, everyone should return to their homes and try to stay hidden. No one else had stepped forward. They were essentially surrendering before the enemy had even arrived.

There was a knock on the door. Even with no hint of a connection to the Pure Fyre, Eofyn knew it was Lissa. The air of her presence and the gentle way she knocked was a rare, unmistakable magic in itself. What did she think of him now? He didn't have the strength to answer the door, but she was persistent. She knocked again, no louder than the last time. He didn't have the heart to turn her away, so he opened the door, reluctant to meet her glance. They stared at each other in silence as he awaited her reprimand.

But Lissa's features remained soft with compassion, a smile tugging at the corner of her mouth. "No one could have planned a defense on such short notice," she offered instead.

Eofyn almost wished she would be angry. He deserved it.

"And you are not the only one to blame for not noticing the signs. No one expected that Condel would ever face a threat or that we would lose our power."

She rested a hand on his forearm as he clutched the doorknob, dropping his gaze to the floor.

"Neither I nor anyone else blames you. I promise. I don't know what will happen, but we will find a way to survive it." She tilted his chin up, catching his eyes with hers, and added, "And to endure."

Eofyn reached out and cupped her face in his hands. "You are wonderful," he said breathlessly, ignoring how horrible it felt to see her acting like a better leader than he was.

She wasn't royal yet, but she was born for the responsibility, and she handled it with such grace and poise.

He kissed her forehead and whispered, "I love you."

Lissa's smile lit up her whole face, from her rosy cheeks to her glittering green eyes, as he held her at arm's length, strands of blonde waves falling from her shoulder to bob at the bodice of her lacey blue dress, which complemented her fair complexion. She brushed a hand across his cheek. "I love you too, Eofyn. We'll get through this."

He attempted a smile, but she had more to say.

"Though you really need to accept who you are soon, darling, or there won't be time to find a solution between your bouts of self-pity."

He blinked at her, surprised by her direct approach.

Her face softened again. "But I really do love you."

Eofyn almost felt a laugh bubble up in his chest when the disturbing presence of Atelle burst into his mind and made him step away from her, grabbing his head.

They're getting closer. We can all see them now. Darian told me to let you know, Your Majesty.

Even in his thoughts, Atelle sounded terrified. The Gaernods must have been closing in quickly. He had to choose his response with care. Lissa was right; he needed to get over dwelling on his failures and focus on his kingdom.

Atelle, it's going to be all right, Eofyn responded, trying to sound encouraging. *We are not likely to win this battle, but we will overcome them somehow. I'll find a way.*

There was no response. That was fine. Atelle was young, and Eofyn was probably the only one in the kingdom who was too numb to be afraid.

Lissa stared at him, patiently waiting for the news after he went still.

Eofyn rested his hands on her shoulders, wishing he could show her how much he cherished her. But there was no time, no space in his mind for anything save fear and panic and scrambling for options that didn't exist. "Afor will move through the city quickly," he said. "He'll be headed for the castle while his men ransack the town. We'll be on our knees by sunset."

Lissa wrapped her arms around him, leaning against his chest. "And what you're avoiding is the fact that Afor will come straight for you," she said, pinching her eyes shut as though she could already see it. "He'll have to dethrone you before he can secure the rest of the kingdom. He'll make an example of you."

Eofyn nodded against the top of her head as he pulled her closer. "Probably," he whispered.

Before he could confess his plan to meet Afor at the gate and spare as many homes as possible, Eofyn turned his head to the side with the odd idea that there was something more he could do.

"We can't stop Afor now," he said as the thoughts swirled together in his head, "but we have to be able to stop him later." Then the solution became clear. It was stupid; it wouldn't work, but it was the best and only option for his people.

"We need our strength back," he mused. "The people need to regain their confidence in their crystals."

His gaze dropped to Lissa, as she stared up at him, waiting.

"I need to find the source of the crystals' power. I need to go to Tir."

Lissa's eyes grew wide. "Sweetheart," she said with a hitch in her voice. "I know this is a time for firsts, but no one has ever been to Tir and returned. We don't know what is in that land aside from the endless sand. I admire your courage, but don't you think the kingdom needs you here?"

Eofyn shook his head and smiled. "No," he said, almost laughing. "I don't think they do. I think that anything I could do for them here, you can do better. Someone needs to get outside help, and we also need to make sure that Afor doesn't get what he's looking for."

Lissa's eyebrows knitted together, creasing her usually unblemished face. Eofyn wished he could comfort her, but he couldn't think of anything encouraging to say.

"I have to move quickly. They'll be here soon. It's probably best if I get a head start." He released her and moved to his father's dresser.

King Arisan kept a special closet of city-casual attire, and he always smiled when he wore it, something Eofyn had never understood before the role of patriarchy was passed to him. Now it seemed fitting, not just so it would be easier to escape from his city, but to remind himself that he was part of the city and not merely its figurehead.

He took enough clothing for five days and packed them in a satchel that hung from his father's four-post bed.

"You'll need food," Lissa whispered, leaning on the nearest bedpost for strength.

Eofyn saw her eyes glistening with unshed tears, but he continued tucking clothes into the satchel. He knew this was foolish, but it was the best chance they had. With the crystals so dim and morale so low, the kingdom might never recover enough on its own to resist Afor. "I have to do something."

Lissa shook her head. "I disagree. Your people need you here. You are their morale. No one has ever seen the source in Tir. What if you can't bring it back? It will still function for us just as well if you remain here and rally the people yourself."

"I've done a wonderful job of that so far," Eofyn scoffed. "I need to show the people I am as devoted to them as my father was. I need to go to any lengths possible for them. I am no source of motivation until I prove myself to be capable of it. Darian and even his daughter can help to lift the people's hope until I return with solid proof of their own power."

"They might interpret your leaving as abandonment," Lissa countered in a small, feeble voice.

Eofyn intertwined her fingers with his and stared at them, imprinting the warmth of her hand, then she squeezed his hand as though she never planned to let him go, and he led her out of the room. Regardless of the awful things that were coming all too quickly, he felt alive with the fact that he was finally taking action and doing something that felt right, very right. There were more preparations to make, but one was most important.

He halted and spun toward Lissa, holding their hands between them and searching her eyes. "Promise me, Lissa. Promise you won't tell anyone I'm leaving." No one could be responsible for knowing where he was going. They'd find out he was gone soon enough, when Afor failed to find him. Darian would reassure them that they'd understand once he returned.

Lissa opened her mouth to protest, but Eofyn hushed her. "I didn't want to mention this, and I know you've been avoiding it too, but what do you think will happen if I stay?"

Lissa's eyes glossed over, and she looked away.

"If Afor finds me, if I sit here and wait for him, the example he'll make of me won't exactly end in my favor." And the gift, even though it had skipped a generation, would be lost. If Eofyn were to accept the responsibility of who he was, he needed to preserve the future of Condel, and that meant keeping himself alive. He frowned. But he would most certainly not hide like a coward. He wanted to do something about this in any way he could.

"And you think you can spare your life by going to Tir?" Her voice was weak, but Eofyn could tell that she meant for it to be sarcastic, a tone she never used convincingly.

"I think my life has a better chance there, yes." He smiled, brushing a tear from her cheek.

Lissa's shoulders dropped. "I don't know."

"I do," he assured her. "I don't know how, but I do. You just have to trust me, and I know you can." He pulled her close to him and took a moment to appreciate everything she was to him. He tried to commit to memory her rose-scented perfume, how he felt when he held her, just in case this was the last time he would.

He understood how sudden this was for Lissa, not just the impending attack, but his strange burst of courage and confidence. Eofyn had never been this decisive, especially in this past year as king. He always thought everything through, almost too thoroughly. Thinking offered more time, and time was the only thing he could think of to bring him closer to Bryta, one way or the other. This decision was different. It had to be. Eofyn needed to learn to be spontaneous, and for once, he wasn't second-guessing himself.

Lissa followed Eofyn to the kitchen, where he wrapped loaves of bread in cloths and tucked them into his father's satchel. He did his best to be as prepared as possible. He was no seasoned adventurer, but he tried as best as he could to think of everything he might need. Eofyn was far from prepared, but time was not a luxury he had.

Atelle, how long?

Not as much time as I'd like, Majesty. They're getting closer to the gate. You can almost see Afor's smile from here.

Please let the others know they should ready themselves. I suppose we'll be calling them soldiers from now on.

As Atelle's presence eased out of the king's mind, he thought, *I have to get out of the city quickly.*

Eofyn turned to Lissa. "I have to go now. I'm sorry. I will get you to safety, and then I'll find my way around Afor's men." He kissed her. "I love you, you know."

Lissa kept her head low and didn't speak.

A rumbling tremor shook the castle.

Lissa spun toward the door. "What was that?"

Eofyn caught her shoulders. He could only imagine how that felt outside. He stared at the ceiling. The people would be in a panic. He looked at Lissa and grabbed her hand. "Come with me."

Lissa's eyes grew wide as she allowed Eofyn to tug her behind him. "To where? Tir?"

Eofyn laughed as he ran, adrenalin kicking in. "I would never allow it. I'm taking you somewhere safe." Darian's family sprang to mind; his wife was a nurturing soul. They would welcome Lissa and keep her safe and comfortable. "If Afor can't find me, he might settle for you. That's another thing I won't allow."

Eofyn led Lissa to a small window and strained to see the city gate. It had crumbled at the Gaernods' first attempt to breach it. Men in shining black leather, unlike anything worn in Condel, poured into the streets. There seemed to be at least half as many Gaernod soldiers as there were citizens of Condel. Through the stone and glass, they could already hear screaming. It pained Eofyn to know he should have prevented this, but he had to distract himself with the fact that he would fix it.

"Come on," he said, tugging Lissa away from the scene. "We'll use the canals."

The castle was not designed with an escape route, at least none that any recent king knew of, but it did have a side door. Eofyn used to pretend that he was a hero, sneaking out of the castle with Pyram to fight Condel criminals, even though there was very little crime to contend with. Eofyn felt nothing like a hero, and Pyram would not be along to support his crime-fighting efforts.

The door was simple enough. There was no combination or difficult lock. He only had to lift a wooden plank and push the door away. An alabaster canal wound along the side of the castle and branched off a few feet from the wall, one branch going down through the city and the other flowing down the middle of the staircase to represent the fount of Condel's life source. Another ran along the opposite side of the castle for the sake of aesthetic symmetry. Eofyn and Lissa would take the more discreet side canal.

Eofyn led his betrothed down and along the water past the castle walls. He tried to stick to the shadows, which was easy with the painfully dimmed streetlights.

The streets were empty as the king and his future bride ran toward the center of the city. All the citizens had received the notice from Atelle and the others in the form of whispers to their minds to remain indoors, but then Eofyn and Lissa heard another loud crash. Suddenly, the streets filled with people running toward the castle.

Eofyn and Lissa dove under a marble bridge to stay out of sight; he pushed Lissa against the wall while he peered around to see what happened. What he saw made his knees buckle. Smoke rose from the front of the city, and Gaernod soldiers, all physically fit and with sharp eyes keen to strike swiftly, were forcing their way toward the castle. No one was left in the streets or near the windows. At least they could take comfort in that. Though his people were suffering, Eofyn was glad he didn't have to watch, to his shame. He flattened himself against the wall next to Lissa.

"They're burning the city. Flushing everyone out." He squinted his eyes shut, trying to clear the image from his mind, even as the sound of screams and crumbling rock reached his ears.

"Eofyn," Lissa began. Her eyes were wild, yet the rest of her was relaxed and composed.

Eofyn watched her. The light of her crystal illuminated her features as she tried to calm them both. "Eofyn, he's doing it to scare you. He won't burn everything. Then he'd have nothing left to rule. He'll go to the castle and find you gone, and then he'll stop, knowing you aren't there." She took a deep breath. "You need to go quickly."

Eofyn ducked his head, pleading with any deity that would listen to make this all stop, but that was impossible. His head fell back against the stone wall. "Okay, but first I need you safe."

He fumbled at the buttons of his embroidered vest and threw it in the canal, allowing it to flow away downstream. Now he looked more common and less recognizable. He clutched Lissa's hand once more and gathered his courage before emerging from under the bridge.

But they had moved too soon. Eofyn jerked backward, caught in the strong grip of a Gaernod soldier as soon as he left the shadow of the bridge, and another soldier soon ripped Lissa from his grasp. Eofyn's arm shot out to reach for her, but the soldier slammed him against the wall, sending a dull buzz to his ears and a shock through his body.

The soldier held Eofyn by the collar of his shirt and studied his face; the king caught a glance of his royal garment floating away, grateful to see it disappear.

"Thought you could hide, did you?" the man growled, throwing Eofyn to the ground and pressing a boot to his chest.

The air escaped Eofyn's lungs as he tried to push the heavy boot away from him. Lissa made no noise, which confirmed for Eofyn that the soldier who grabbed her was stifling her.

"I think he was supposed to take this one to a safe house," the second guard said. "She's dressed too fancy to be with him. She must be from the castle. Is there a princess of Condel? Is that what you are, sweetheart?" he asked in a drawling voice with a crooked grin, moving his face close to Lissa's as she struggled to break free of his arm.

"Get off her," Eofyn snapped, straining angrily with the last of the air in his chest and trying to gasp for more.

The soldier ground his foot as if he were crushing a bug. Eofyn's ribs bent until he was afraid they'd break.

"Let's take her back to the castle," the first guard decided, studying Lissa's face. "She could be useful in finding that pathetic king of theirs. Afor will be glad to see us with her. There should be a reward for this one."

"And what do we do with him, then?"

Eofyn watched the first guard tip his head in consideration. He knelt on one knee, putting the bulk of his weight on Eofyn's chest. Eofyn squinted in pain at the soldier's lazy left eye, still fighting to breathe.

"What do we do with you, hmm?" The soldier patted a hand against Eofyn's cheek like he would a child. "Let's take him to the front. What do you say? Up for a little campfire?" he asked his comrade, laughing.

Eofyn heard Lissa attempt to protest, and the lazy-eyed soldier looked up at her. "Get her to the castle before Afor gets there. Give him some good news. I'll take care of the peasant boy."

The other guard muffled Lissa's screams with his hand as he dragged her away. The remaining soldier removed his foot from Eofyn's chest, but   the disguised king wished for a moment that the boot pressed on him more, as punishment for dragging Lissa into this and condemning her to whatever it was that she was being taken to. Why? Why did Bryta seem determined to emphasize his failures? Of course, he knew he was a terrible king, but now in trying to fix that, he'd failed to protect the woman he loved.

Eofyn took in a deep breath to refill his lungs, but the soldier cut him short as he lifted him by the collar, threw a knee into his gut, and shoved him against the stone bridge.

"So what's your preference? Front of the city inferno?" He sneered, pulling out a shining knife. "Or would you rather just end it now?" He braced Eofyn against the stone, squeezing his throat, and pulled his free arm back, ready to bury the knife into Eofyn's stomach.

Eofyn looked into the foreign soldier's dark eyes, waiting for the end, but then the soldier's eyes crossed, and his grip on Eofyn failed. He collapsed to the ground and left Eofyn standing confused until he looked up to see Pyram, shaking his head. He held a splintered plank of wood in his hand, Eofyn's soaked vest slung over his shoulder, and an incredulous look on his face.

"Fyn," he said in a monotone, his eyes hooded with disappointment. "What are you doing out here? Are you insane?"

Eofyn wilted against the wall, gasping. "That's still up for debate," he wheezed, looking down at the guard and kicking the knife from the man's hand.

Pyram led him back to the safety of the bridge. "Where do you think you're going?" he demanded.

"Oh, come on, Pyram. Do you really think I'd be any safer at the castle?"

Pyram seemed ready to argue but decided against it, waving his hand dismissively. "So what was your plan, then?"

Eofyn sighed. He didn't want to tell Pyram the truth. His friend would only try to stop him. But it seemed he had little choice.

"I'm going to Tir, Pyram. I have to find the source of the crystals and bring it back to prove to everyone they have all the power they need to resist Afor."

"Okay. Then I'm coming with you."

"No," Eofyn said, laughing at Pyram's predictable response. "No, you need to stay here. Pyram, they have Lissa. I need you to protect her."

"Darian can protect her," Pyram dismissed him. He gently grabbed Eofyn by the arm and began ushering him farther into the shadows, casting sharp eyes that reflected the orange glow of his crystal as it sprang to life to serve him in their escape. "Or anyone at the castle. They love her. They'll keep her safe. Afor has no reason to kill her. She's too useful to him alive."

Eofyn glared at his friend's blunt disregard for Lissa's safety.

"Fyn," Pyram said coolly, "Atelle heard your plan in your thoughts and warned me. I knew you were doing this. For a journey like that, you're going to need courage, which you've got, but it wouldn't hurt to take a little street smarts along with you." He held his glowing red crystal up, evidence of his cunning. "You need me. That's why your father took me in. If you leave alone, I've failed him."

Eofyn released a defeated groan. "I'm assuming you know the best way to escape the city?"

Pyram grinned. "You know I do." He gestured to the darkness to their left. "That way."

Eofyn heard the sounds of the houses being destroyed, and Pyram led him straight for them.

"If we go where they've already been, we're less likely to get caught," Pyram reasoned, but Eofyn dreaded the sight of what his lack of leadership had caused. He wasn't sure he could bear it. Why couldn't he have worked out how to use the Pure Fyre and have seen this coming?

As the city shook and crumbled, they ran to the source, hoping to slip by unnoticed. Eofyn had faith in Pyram's abilities, but with the crystals so dim, he wondered if Pyram's gifted instincts might falter. Pyram didn't seem worried, but it was difficult to tell his thoughts beyond his almost arrogant mask. Eofyn had always envied Pyram's confidence, but now he nearly feared it. The shouts of the Gaernod soldiers grew louder, the thunder of falling buildings broke his heart, but he pressed on and followed his friend, who never so much as blinked at the carnage.

But when they rounded a corner and saw the city square, even Pyram stopped in his tracks. What was usually a wide stone plaza, bustling with trade and entertainment, had ruptured and cracked in pure devastation. The people of Condel who hadn't abandoned their goods and tried to secure them before seeking shelter lay everywhere. The buildings surrounding the square were razed so flat they could see the demolished city gate from here. There was nowhere else to hide, and they were only at the edge of the war zone.

"We … we just have to make it to that canal there," Pyram decided, breathing heavier. "It flows out of the city to complete the flow back to the Sea of Modwen. That's our escape. Just get past a few buildings, sneak into the water, and we're out." He looked from the wasteland to Eofyn. "Off to Tir then, right?" He laughed, empty and light, but neither of them could muster a smile.

Another shock shook the ground.

Eofyn shuddered. "We'd better go."

They ran to the next crumbled building, and another after that, keeping their pattern scattered to avoid attention. Eofyn kept his eyes on the horizon to avoid the sight of arms lifelessly exposed from beneath the rubble and of broken pots and glass from all the art that had been destroyed along the Gaernods' barbaric march for the castle. Would they destroy the castle too? Would Eofyn's home be subject to the same malicious treatment? Then again, why wouldn't it? What made him so important that he shouldn't share in his people's loss?

Lissa's terrified face flashed in his mind, and he wondered if he already had.

When they hit the last building, they crouched down among the pile of rubble and checked the path between them and their escape. There was no living person in sight.

"Uh oh …"

He spun back at Pyram, terrified at what might cause him concern, especially when his talents were already working to guide them to safety. "Uh oh, what?"

Eofyn spun around to see a soldier leering at them as he approached with a black orb that appeared to be on fire. Eofyn stared back at him, unsure if running was their best option.

The soldier drew back his hand, preparing to throw the flaming ball. "Something new to you, hmm?" he asked, sneering at the shock on their faces and showing his yellow teeth. He tilted his head to the side.

Pyram's red crystal blazed, but he visibly fought his instinct, until finally he shook his head, saying, "Nope, we should definitely run." He grabbed Eofyn's shirt and ran off with the king in tow.

The soldier threw the ball. It bounced just behind Pyram and Eofyn. Eofyn looked back just in time to see the black ball explode.

Flames redder than Pyram's crystal enveloped Eofyn's vision as the heat seared his face. The shock wave picked them both off the ground and sent them flying ten feet into the air.

Eofyn felt a yank on his shirt as he and Pyram spun off in different directions. Eofyn landed hard and felt his head smash against a piece of what had once been someone's home. He saw blurred swirls of red and orange, felt more searing heat before Eofyn accepted that he had failed.

And taken his closest friend with him.

Eofyn's eyes opened to a blinding light. He had expected as much. The stories of dying always talked about light. Perhaps he'd been wrong about Bryta. Maybe the light from the other world had finally come for him.

But the light wasn't above him.

Eofyn allowed his vision to adjust and realized that there were only dark, gray clouds rolling above him, but then where was the light coming from? This could not be Bryta; even now, he couldn't make contact.

He couldn't move. Several ribs were definitely broken, and the skin on his arms, legs, face, and chest stung from the burns he'd suffered in the explosion. The air carried a metal tang that he could taste as well as smell over the scent of burning wood. He could only shift his eyes to take in the surrounding area. Judging by what he could see, the night had ended, but his surroundings were the same. Glancing to his side, he could see many unwelcome things that made him never want to open his eyes on his fallen kingdom again, but he followed the urge to look outward toward the castle.

Eofyn could not strain enough to see the castle itself, but what he saw baffled his senses. Among the gray blanket of clouds, there was one perfect circle of light. It must have been his imagination, but he watched the light begin illuminating the ruined part of the kingdom. He tried to tilt his head, but it wouldn't move. His peripheral vision would have to do, and he thought he might faint from what he saw.

The light moved over those who had fallen the night before. It paused over a man who had perished, but the man suddenly stood up, smiling, and then he disappeared.

The pattern continued, and it occurred to Eofyn that he should try to identify one of the spirits as Pyram. He wanted to find his friend standing and looking relieved of all burdens the way these poor souls did, but he wanted more selfishly to find Pyram alive, even if that meant he was injured. He dreaded each moment but found it utterly beautiful at the same time.

In time, the light passed over Eofyn. He lay there, resigning himself to the fact that he had fallen before he'd had much of a chance to start.

He looked into the light, expecting to see something comforting that would make his passing a more welcome event. Maybe his father's face.

But the light did not take him. He felt its warmth spread over his body, bringing pressure in more bones than he could keep track of. The burning sensation of open wounds faded away to blend with the comforting warmth of the glow, until he took a deep, full breath. The light had healed him, and now it left him behind.

With Eofyn mended, the light moved on to the next unfortunate—yet somehow fortunate—soul, and Eofyn could leap to his feet. He ran after the beam of light, trying to see if it would lead him to Pyram.

When he finally caught sight of his friend after several false alarms, he slid to a halt. The light was almost upon Pyram's still form. Eofyn couldn't breathe. The light paused over Pyram and held its position for what seemed to Eofyn like an eternity. Finally, the light moved away, and the hole in the clouds swirled closed. But Pyram remained.

Eofyn looked around. No one else stood around him. He ran to Pyram, who stared at the sky in awe.

"Pyram? Are you okay?" He reached out his hand.

Pyram took his hand with a firm grip and stood. He regarded Eofyn with wild eyes. "Did you see that?"

Eofyn smiled and dragged his friend into a firm hug.

"I'm glad to see you're okay," Eofyn said, "but we'd better leave while we still can."

Pyram nodded, dark hair still wild and a devilish grin stretched across his face. "Yeah. Yeah, let's go."

They picked their way through the ruin, staying low to the ground. When they reached the canal, they turned toward the castle for the first time. It seemed untouched, to Eofyn's guilty relief, but the Gaernod army hadn't left a single structure standing in the first quarter of the city and along with the main winding street that led to the castle stairs. It was as if they'd dragged a massive rake behind them on their march, destroying anything they came in contact with; houses, statues, and bridges all lay in piles of stone and wood. The cobblestones of the streets were pulled up and dipped in places where more of those exploding balls had clearly gone off. Everything was horribly quiet, and the castle was still. Eofyn and Pyram had no way of knowing what was happening within their home, but it couldn't be good.

Eofyn noticed a glow of red to his left and found Pyram thinking.

"I think we should get going," he said. "Look." He pointed to a figure emerging from the dust.

It was the same guard who had pinned Eofyn to the bridge. From this distance, it looked like the Gaernod had no left eye at all. He was smiling. The reward for returning Lissa must have been rich. Eofyn forced himself not to think about it.

"Come on," Pyram said, tugging Eofyn's shoulder until they were both squatting next to the canal. "We'll make everything right, but first we've got to find that source of yours."

Still staring at the guard, Eofyn nodded and reluctantly followed Pyram as he leapt into the knee-deep water. It was freezing, but Eofyn was too numb to care. They trudged along the only clean thing left in Condel and passed underneath an arch in the wall that marked the edge of the city.

Eofyn followed Pyram out of the canal and onto the green grass. The world beyond Condel showed no sign of the apocalypse that had taken place inside. There were flowers, and the clouds out here were pure and fluffy in the darkened sky. It was so perfect, it made Eofyn feel queasy, and it didn't go unnoticed.

"Use this," Pyram advised, giving Eofyn a focused stare. "Concentrate on what you'll do to fix it," he said, lending Eofyn some of his strength through his flat, clear eyes.

Eofyn wanted to reprimand him. It seemed outrageous, and the guilt of allowing himself to feel happy was overwhelming, but he was adult enough to realize that he was only angry because Pyram was right.

"Well," Eofyn said with a sigh. "No map necessary, huh? We know the way to Tir."

Pyram let out a single laugh. "Yeah, we do. Let's get this done. We'll be the first people to go to Tir, see the source, and come back to talk about it. Sounds good to me."

"If we manage to accomplish all of that," Eofyn added.

What they were doing was suicide, but going back was practically the same thing. So they headed north to Tir, trying to think of it as just another childhood game.

CHAPTER 6

"So you actually think I can do that?" Spyre asked the elfin chief incredulously. He kept his hands folded at his front, aware that the chief's guards were ready with their sharpened sticks, and what a slow and painful death it would be if he made them nervous enough to use them. His brain, however, was not so composed. "Are you crazy? One person against the whole Gaernod army and Afor." He held up a finger for emphasis, keeping it low enough so as not to seem threatening. "And then I'd have to get the Condels to trust me after I get around Afor and hopefully beat him to their kingdom. That's a lovely dream. Really."

"It is a difficult idea. I don't know how you'll manage it," the chief admitted, hands folded over his round, exposed stomach. This was not a chief who led with action. Then again, with Faran as Spyre's first impression, none of the elves seemed particularly driven to action. "You have quite the journey between Tweogan and Condel, but you won't be alone, will you? We'll send Faran to help you to your next step."

Faran had seemed to be in a daydream since they'd arrived at the elfin court. His eyes were wide as saucers, soaking in every inch of the earthen room, but Spyre knew he would be filled with infinite questions. His ears perked up, and he looked around.

"Me? What am I doing?"

"I won't repeat myself," the chief said. Where Faran was short and lithe, the chief was taller, shoulder-height on Spyre, but he was rotund, with stubby legs and a portly face. Clearly there was no shortage of foodstuffs in Tweogan, at least for their leader. "The two of you need to be on your way. We've loaded your pack with more rations to last you a few days. We don't really expect you to succeed, but elves can't leave the forest. What other choice do we have?"

"Well, I could think of a few," Spyre said. "Starting with, why can't *you* go if you're so concerned?"

The chief laughed. His voice was really too deep for such a small creature. "It is not my path, whatever my path is. Only humans can traverse the different regions of Curnen. I don't know why. Besides, I did not receive the call to leave my land, but you did. You are the person who is meant to do this, don't you think?"

Spyre waved his hands in front of him. "You're reading too much into this," he countered. "I left on what was probably more of a tantrum."

"But do you plan to return to Gaernod?"

"Not a chance."

"Then you must go somewhere."

"Yes, but—"

Except there was no but. Spyre had nowhere else to go. The chief was right. That was annoying. Spyre tried to think of a good retort, but nothing came to him. He couldn't admit that his leaving Gaernod had anything to do with fate's design, but he knew it left him no option to return.

"Okay, fine," he surrendered. "I guess I'll give it a shot, but the army is way ahead of me. They'll beat me there."

The chief leaned forward. Spyre couldn't help noticing how his throne conveniently sat several steps above the average human eye level. Afor must have left a more lasting impression on elfin culture than Spyre suspected. He almost laughed, but this was definitely not the time.

"They'll almost certainly beat you there," the chief agreed.

Almost certainly, Spyre noted. This was the land of indecisive answers.

The chief continued, "You'll have to find the Condel king and help him overthrow Afor, won't you? His name is Eofyn, if the rumors are true. He'll probably need your help."

"What can I possibly do to help him?" Spyre threw his arms out to his sides. "He's the one with all that magic stuff. I don't have a crystal strung around my neck." Spyre drew an imaginary loop over his chest for emphasis. "He doesn't even need that. He's super-crystal. What do you expect me to do?"

"I don't know." The chief shrugged. "Fate brought you out of Gaernod. I assumed you'd know what to do. But if you don't plan to be of use to Curnen, then I suppose maybe we could do something else with you." He regarded Spyre over steepled fingers, lifting an eyebrow.

Spyre didn't wait for the chief to decide. He would use the elf's indecision to his advantage. He reached out and grabbed Faran by the back of the collar, pulling him to his side. "Looks like we're going on an adventure, buddy." He looked Faran in the eye. "You know the way, right?"

Faran opened his mouth, but Spyre stopped him.

"Sure you do. Come on, let's get started. No time to lose."

He dragged Faran toward the doorway, and the elf didn't object, gazing around with owlish eyes as if to choose his actions based on the reactions of those around him. They strode back down the tunnel they had come through, leaving the cavity of earth behind them.

Spyre turned around and called, "Worry not, Elf King. I—uh—I've got this under control." He pushed Faran ahead of him and followed the stumbling elf through the series of tunnels that led back to the surface.

When they emerged, Spyre gave Faran a small shove just to knock him off balance. Faran looked up at him, wide-eyed.

"Next time," Spyre said, pointing at the short creature, "be more descriptive about what you're getting me into."

Faran looked at him. "Sorry?"

"I could've used a bit of a briefing. You should have told me what your chief was expecting, what the plan would be, if there even was a plan—which there isn't."

Faran shook his head. "I had no idea what the chief was like. I don't think I've ever seen him until now." He turned away to search his memory, but Spyre couldn't take it.

"Is there anything you do know? You never have a straight answer. There must be something you're sure of."

Faran considered him, and Spyre was starting to think his eyes were always that wide.

"Is there anything you are sure of, Gaernod man?"

Spyre smiled as he meant to recite a list, but as if the universe had suddenly smacked the faith out of him, he could think of nothing he was truly certain of. He looked back at Faran.

"Are you at least sure of the direction we need to take to get out of the forest?" he asked sheepishly.

"Do you want the most direct route or the safest?" Faran asked.

Spyre didn't want to have to think anymore. Being around the elf was confusing him even further. He remembered his brother ranting about the tediousness of elves before, but this was ridiculous. Had Spyre not heard the stories from Ryne, he might have suspected the elves blank expressions and ceaseless questions were a trick, but even the Gaernod army preferred to avoid the forest and the elves within for this very reason. Their childlike curiosity was endearing but unchecked.

"Let's just take the quickest way, and we can both get back to our lives."

Faran shrugged and said, "If that's what you want." He looked left and then right. "I think we have to go this way," he said, heading off to the left.

Spyre sighed, hoping his guide had at least a small clue about where they were. Spyre knew where he would end up, and he wasn't looking forward to it. He had seen the maps of the lands that made up Curnen. Between Gaernod and Condel lay a whole mess of realms with plenty of cranky creatures that would be only too happy to knock them around. If he ever made it away from the elves, he would have to deal with trolls. He'd never seen a troll, but based on what he'd heard, he wasn't in for a pleasant meeting.

"Why did you pick the fastest way so quickly?" Faran interrupted Spyre's thoughts. "Aren't you worried about the danger?"

Spyre chuckled. "What could possibly be more dangerous than being here in the first place? I've got no clue what I'm doing, and I've got nothing to lose."

"Nothing to lose," Faran repeated thoughtfully. "If you have nothing to lose, then you must have nothing." It looked as if something occurred to him, and he frowned at Spyre, making him both annoyed and nervous.

"And if you have nothing, then what are you searching for? Something? What something? How can you know what something you want if you have nothing?" He stopped walking to stare at his open hands, and Spyre, mind numb with confusion, stopped with him.

Drawing his conclusion, Faran dropped his hands and looked up at Spyre. "You'll end up lonely, desperate, and probably dead."

Faran continued walking, but Spyre gaped after him. That was the most certain thing he'd heard the elf say.

"Thanks for that motivating speech," Spyre muttered once Faran was out of earshot. He caught up with Faran with a few long steps, wondering if the confusing little elf might be right.

CHAPTER 7

Eofyn and Pyram hadn't run into any trouble. They were still a while away from Tir, but Eofyn wondered if he could have spared Pyram the journey. Granted, it had only been a day, but it had been a very uneventful one. They were sitting around a campfire built by Pyram, though Eofyn liked to imagine that he could have done it.

As Pyram stoked the flame, preparing to cook the food that Eofyn had brought, he smiled. "This brings back old memories," he said, an air of laughter in his voice. He glanced up at Eofyn, nostalgia in his eyes. "Don't get me wrong, living in the castle is great, but this life …" He sighed with content. "It was pretty sweet too."

It had never occurred to Eofyn that life on the streets could be considered sweet. He had always assumed it was hard, depressing, and lonely. Pyram had never told Eofyn much about his time on the streets as a young child, but by the look of it, he couldn't have struggled much.

"More freedom and less worry?" Eofyn guessed.

Pyram tipped his head to the side, staring at the fire. "Well, not quite. The freedom only lasted if you hid from the guards and everyone you had to steal from, and the worry only went away if you'd found a really great hiding spot for the night.

"It wasn't the freedom, Fyn. It was the excitement. I miss the adventure. The stuff we used to dream about." He grinned at Eofyn. The shadows cast across his face from the glow of the fire made it look almost wicked. "This is it. This is what we always imagined. We get to be the heroes, save the kingdom, crush the bad guy." He brought his fist down into his palm, eyes glowing as they watched the dancing flames.

"You're trying to dull my guilt again, aren't you?" Eofyn accused. "Am I supposed to overlook that the bad guy is here because of my mistake?"

"You're supposed to realize that there's nothing you could've done," Pyram argued. He spread his arms to the open world around them. "Just because something bad is happening doesn't mean it's your fault. No leader is actually fearless, Fyn. Even your dad had worries, but he handled them."

Pyram nudged Eofyn with his elbow. "You know, you're doing exactly what he would have done in your shoes."

Eofyn narrowed his eyes and looked at Pyram. "Are you kidding?"

Pyram shook his head with a shrug. "Without a connection to Bryta—and not for lack of trying—your father would have had no warning, and he would have been in this exact situation." He smirked. "He wouldn't have had me, though, so you're kind of lucky."

Eofyn could have argued about the horrible things that were happening in Condel without him, about how he'd abandoned his future wife into the arms of a tyrant, but following Pyram's line of thought, he realized if Afor had apprehended him, there would have been no one to restore Condel. Without the hope of rekindling the Fyre, the people would lose their abilities, and Eofyn represented that hope. He didn't feel qualified for that kind of mantle at the moment. He hoped the people would find comfort in Darian and Lissa in his stead.

"I wonder how Lissa is doing."

That killed the optimistic tone.

"Lissa is a very strong woman," Pyram reminded him. "She'll be fine. Not even Afor can break her spirit."

Eofyn smiled. He did love Lissa, with all of his heart. She could handle herself, and he fully believed that, but it didn't negate his right to worry about her.

"You worry too much," Pyram said, as if reading his mind. "Everything will work out. It's going to take Afor more time to figure out what we're up to. When he does, we'll have trouble, but the closer we get to the source, the more power we'll have."

Eofyn seriously doubted that would be the case, but seeing as it didn't yet matter, he nodded anyway.

Stars speckled the sky as the sun set like it would any other day. They could still see Condel, a diamond in the distance. Eofyn couldn't tell by looking at it that it was a kingdom under siege. It still looked majestic, especially to Eofyn, who had never seen it from afar. It shone white as alabaster, though Eofyn had never noticed the city walls were such a clean color from the inside. It felt strange to look at the place where he had spent every second of his life, his home, and not recognize it.

He turned away from the city, and the pulsing red glow of Pyram's crystal caught his eye. Pyram and the others were fortunate. They all had crystals, concrete proof of their abilities. Eofyn had nothing and no sign of his special powers to prove to him he was truly a king of Condel.

He wondered if the crystal made the man. He hoped not. It hadn't in his father's case. And who made the crystals? Legend said a family who was searching for somewhere safe to live and grow discovered them. They traveled among a group from their ancient kingdom in search of something better and stumbled upon the crystals, which magnified their natural talents.

Over the millennia, the crystals honed only one skill in a person. Perhaps that was a sign they had always been losing their effectiveness. It was possible that Eofyn was just the first of a new generation that would have no ability. Maybe the crystals didn't last forever. Whatever the reason, it was no excuse for his own ancestors, descended from the leader of the wandering family's clan, who had not needed a crystal from the beginning.

Eofyn's ancient grandfather had known something that those who relied on crystals did not see, and he had passed that knowledge down, but why not to Eofyn? Was all this part of some cosmic design, as Pyram suggested? That didn't seem fair. Eofyn couldn't see the purpose behind such an idea, although there was a lot that he could not understand. Maybe this was just one concept among many that would elude him. It was difficult to dwell on but also to ignore.

"Still on that guilt trip?" Pyram's voice shattered his thoughts. "Or have you started your pity party already?"

Eofyn's brain caught up with his ears. "What?"

"I don't mean to be disrespectful to the king and all," Pyram said, laughing, because they both knew those sorts of rules did not apply to him, "but I know that look on anyone, especially you. I must say, you're doing better, though."

Eofyn ducked his head and forced a laugh. "Must be."

Pyram laid back against a rock. "It's understandable. You don't just get over something like this, which is why I recommend denial, crazy as that sounds."

"It's a valid point," Eofyn admitted, nodding and staring at the fire. He sighed, clearing his mind and preparing to convince it of something he knew wasn't true.

This isn't my fault, he told himself, mesmerized by the flickering flames. *I couldn't have prevented this. It's some sort of divine plan that no one can explain. Yeah, sure it is. No, focus. It is. It makes sense. It's the only thing that makes sense. And I'm going to make it okay. I'll find the Source of the Fyre and fix everything. Somehow.*

He leaned back, using his satchel for a pillow, and gazed at the stars. He had never seen so many. The lights of Condel had always been too bright. He glanced back at the kingdom. It should have been glowing. Condel was famous among the other realms of Curnen for its glow when seen from a distance, but that was no longer the case. The city looked average, if a little majestic.

Guilt clutched at Eofyn's heart.

It's not my fault. I'll make it right. It's not my fault …

CHAPTER 8

It was all Afor's fault. He had to march off and take half of Gaernod with him. Now Spyre was not only picking up after his mess, but he also had to find some way to stop him. That was not as simple as the flighty elves seemed to think.

He followed Faran, who had already taken them in four circles, thanks to his lack of fortitude. Spyre cocked his head as Faran bent over a small sprout of a tree, inspecting it with a finger curled around his chin.

"Hmm, I think I've seen this tree before." Faran stood up straight and looked around as Spyre rolled his eyes and dropped his pack on the ground.

"Well, since you and the twig are so well acquainted," Spyre said, "why don't we camp out here for the night?"

Faran looked blank for a moment and then fell into a lotus position in the grass next to the seedling.

Spyre nodded and absently reached into his pack, pulling out the piece of wood and knife from his worktable. He held both in his hands and poised the knife to carve. Staring at the blank piece of wood, he could think of nothing he should do with it.

"Tomorrow may not be easy," Faran commented out of nowhere.

Spyre glanced up at him and back to the wood, using the tip of his knife to carve a small notch in it. "Nothing is ever easy," he responded.

He picked at the wood with his knife, a little angry and a little anxious. Part of him didn't want to stop for the night. The woods didn't feel safe, but he reminded himself that nowhere was safe anymore. He had always imagined that there must be somewhere in the world that was safe, regardless of the rest of the nations' feuds. He had always imagined that place was Condel.

How was their infamous pacifism working out for them now?

But it didn't have to be unsafe there. It sounded ridiculous, but maybe, oh, just maybe he really had followed some sort of calling. How else could he explain it? Time would tell, but having nowhere to go wasn't acceptable to him. Spyre didn't want to just wander around for the rest of his life. He wanted something constant. It hadn't even occurred to him that he could simply run from the task given to him by the elves. Maybe that was more proof that he could save Condel, and after all, if he saved the kingdom, they would be more likely to welcome him than to turn him away. Perhaps Afor had accidentally given Spyre an in with the gifted kingdom.

He smiled, still gouging notches in the wood. *I bet I can do this. If it was fate that took me out of Gaernod, then fate should keep me alive until Condel is safe, and I've at least got somewhere to stay. I'll settle for a house of sticks, if I have to.*

Tomorrow, he would start early. With the help of Faran—surely, the elf would find some way to be useful—Spyre would navigate the dangers that the little creature expected. The fears of a timid elf were nothing Spyre needed to worry about.

Spyre laid back against a sturdy tree and allowed himself to drift to sleep, imagining he was in a safe and comfortable home in Condel, rather than on the muddy forest floor.

CHAPTER 9

The house could not possibly fit any more people. It was the only one left standing within a hundred feet, and Ness's parents had seen fit to take in everyone put out by the invasion, as if that was the top priority and all they could do. Her father had made it home safely, but his work continued as he scrambled to serve and save anyone he could find and bring them into safety once their house had stopped shaking and the air had gone still.

Ness felt the need for a bigger plan with a bigger impact. She also needed to get away from her noisy, nosey neighbors.

As she maneuvered around the crowded kitchen, every open space was filled with someone wrapped in a blanket, a towel, even spare drapes, and she yet couldn't help noticing that the conversation had segued from the horrible invasion and how many dishes had been lost to how mature Ness had become. And how very single.

"Do you know, Elene," Gesamne, the city's matchmaking talent who dressed herself like she belonged in the castle, all royal purple robes with gold lining, said to Ness's mother, "your young Ness is getting on a bit. She'll soon need a husband." She leaned toward Elene, tapping her round nose with a chubby finger practically dipped in red nail polish. "I could consider her, if you'd like."

Is business really that slow? Ness fumed to herself.

Ness's mom looked disappointed. "Not just yet, Ges, but thank you. Ness is only eighteen. She's got plenty of time. I want her to be comfortable with herself and her path before she enters into a relationship. Marrying too soon can do horrible things to a girl's self-esteem. Ness is making her way just fine for now."

Parts of her mother's statement flattered Ness, but others offended her. What was wrong with her self-esteem? And Ness knew her path, even if her mother didn't like it, but she focused on the compliments, relieved to have deflected Gesamne's advances for now.

Ness felt a tug on the back of her sleeve as she passed by. She caught her footing and stumbled backward to meet the eyes of her captor.

"What do you have to say, Nessy?" Gesamne asked, still clutching Ness's sleeve.

I say, Ness thought to herself, catching the words before they could reach her mouth, *if you call me "Nessy" one more time, I will spill hot tea all over you.*

"I haven't met anyone that I'd particularly enjoy spending the rest of my life with yet, Gesamne," Ness responded frankly, "but thank you for your concern."

"Oh, don't be silly. We have who we have in the city." Gesamne stretched her shoulders behind her, the chair creaking beneath her as she pressed farther back than necessary. "The lads here are your only options, so you'd best take a liking to one before they're all spoken for. I can think of several suitable young men for a spitfire like you."

"Really, that's all right." Ness unclenched her gritted teeth. "I have plans I'd like to see through before I settle down."

Gesamne leaned back in her chair, a condescending, knowing look in her eyes. "Ah, yes, you and your little desire to save the world. I'm sure I've got someone for you." She looked to the side in thought for a moment.

Ness just wanted to walk away.

"In fact, I have. A handsome young man assigned to the king's guard. He would complement you well. He's exactly your age."

"That's really all right." Ness's temper rose to a simmer. No member of the king's guard was even close to prepared for a true fight; she'd seen them occasionally when she accompanied her father to the castle. They were placeholders to make the city walls look more official, in her opinion. None of them had their heart in protecting Condel. They'd never needed to. It had been a cushy job until today.

"Oh, darling. Don't be a fool." Gesamne spread her hands with a smile. "What more worthy man to find than one who seeks to save mankind? Hmm?"

Ness snapped. *Oh, we're rhyming now, are we? Okay, sure. Let's rhyme.* "But love and fancy fall from fashion when with a man who lacks compassion," Ness spit back, sharply tilting her head to the side.

Gesamne straightened herself, smoothing her skirt with fidgety hands. "You'll need someone by your side eventually, young lady. I suggest you find him before all the young men have overlooked you."

"That's enough, Ges," Elene intervened just as Ness's jaw dropped to retaliate. "You're the best at what you do, but you can't fight timing. Ness isn't as ready as she wants to be when she finds someone. It's her life."

Ness turned to her mother and said, "Thank you." Then she moved her gaze to Gesamne, gave her a curt nod, and walked away before her temper got the best of her again.

She headed for her room but was snagged yet again on her way to the stairs. At the tug of her sleeve, Ness turned around, ready to scold Gesamne like a child. But it was her father who had pulled her aside, resting his hands on her shoulders and searching her face in concern.

"Ness? Are you doing okay?"

"What kind of question is that, Dad?" Her frustration seeped through, along with her impatience. "I'm sorry, but we've just been taken over, and we just let it happen. Who do you think is going to save us?"

Darian gathered his daughter into his arms, resting his chin on her head.

"It won't be long now, Ness," he whispered, his voice muffled by her hair. "You might find that it will be too soon. Just give it time."

Ness scoffed. She knew she wasn't as wise as she liked to think and that her father probably—almost certainly—knew more than she did, but the impatience was too unnerving for her to understand him now. As far as she was concerned, she had no time to give. She needed to take action now. She couldn't just sit around serving coffee and tea, especially not with Gesamne lurking around. It was time to take matters into her own hands. Even if the king had left with a good reason, the kingdom needed someone to watch over it. She would gladly fill that position.

"You're right, Dad."

Her father smiled sadly at her before heading downstairs.

Ness mentally put together the most practical outfit she owned. There were several factors to consider, and she would leave nothing to chance. Her wardrobe needed a few alterations, but she knew her mother would forgive her once she proved herself.

She went to her closet and pulled out a dark blue dress. It was plain except for two lines of simple gold stitching around the quarter-length sleeves and waist. She held it against herself and took a pair of shears from her dresser, cutting a notch in the skirt on each side at tunic length. Then she laid the dress out on her bed and removed the skirt less than skillfully, leaving an uneven hemline, but that didn't matter.

Next, she rummaged in her drawers for the black undergarment that kept her warm on cold days. This was autumn. It would be necessary, but the long legs of the suit would have to moonlight as tights for her purposes. She donned the suit and tunic, masking them with a skirt to appear less conspicuous.

What she saw in the mirror made her beam with excitement as she pulled on her rugged knee-high boots. Tonight would be a good night.

It was dark. Very dark. The city had never been this dark before. It was perfect.

Ness's mother had arranged a bed for everyone to sleep, delegating Ness's bed to none other than Gesamne, upon the matchmaker's request. She said a few nights in Ness's room would give her a better sense of the girl's personality so she could better find a match for her. Ness wanted to run to her room and lock the door, but her mother's firm arm blocked her way. It was just a good thing that she was already dressed.

Her allocation for the night had been the kitchen floor. Not comfortable, but she wouldn't be using it, anyway. She only had to make it out the door, and it would buy her a few hours of a reconnaissance near the castle.

At the moment, she lay still on the floor, waiting to hear deep breathing coming from the rest of the room. She shared the kitchen with a few neighbors, none of whom she'd ever known affectionately, and with her brother, Losian. As far as she could tell, he had dozed off more than an hour ago.

The coast should be clear.

She slowly climbed to her feet, staying low to the ground and using the kitchen table for cover until she was sure she was the only one awake in the room. She took a few crouched steps, analyzing her roommates before rising to her full height. Slowly, she crept for the door, feeling a strong sense of pride, until …

"I'm telling Mom." The whispered threat was unmistakable.

Ness didn't even turn around. "Go back to bed, Losian." She sighed. "And mind your own business."

The thirteen-year-old stood up defiantly. "And what do you think you can achieve out there?" he asked, arms crossed, sounding just like their mother. "You'll get yourself caught, if your childhood is any example."

"Are you seriously bringing up cookie jar demerits right now?" Ness hissed incredulously, turning around to face him and glancing around for signs of the others stirring awake.

"If you show no aptitude for something, you shouldn't pursue it." Losian looked down his nose at her.

"Then you're in for a rough life without even having a crystal for talent, aren't you?" Ness shot back, hands moving to her hips. This was one attack strategy she was familiar with.

"Shut up, Ness," Losian snapped, reverting to the impudent boy he was.

"You can have all the quiet you want for the rest of the night," Ness assured him as she moved back to the door.

"You'll get yourself killed, you know."

She rolled her eyes. "Will not. Just go back to bed." She looked at him sharply, pointing a finger. "And don't tell Mom or Dad."

Before he could respond, she slipped out the door.

Ness felt invigorated. Finally, she felt like she was making a difference. She skirted along the outsides of homes and buildings, drawing nearer to the castle, not sure what she'd do when she got there but hoping that something would come to her. Books and legends always promised that impulses had a funny way of working out, didn't they? She would see.

The streets were unusually clear for a hostile takeover. The Gaernod soldiers must have felt secure enough with the idea that there would be no resistance to focus solely on the castle. That played to her advantage, for now. When she got to the castle, there would be more planning to do, but that was still some distance away. For now, she would use this exhilarating feeling as a guide to boost her confidence and sharpen her senses.

She felt light on her feet and swift, moving along the unbroken back streets as if she'd prowled them every night, when in reality she had never navigated through Condel in darkness. The crystals had always kept the streets lit, until tonight. She had to feel along the rough, cool stone walls for a corner before she saw it, and that only made her feel even more like an intrepid vigilante.

As she closed in on the castle, she cast a quick glance over her shoulder to check that no one followed her, and she saw it: the devastation that had come the day before. Ness's knees grew weak, and she stumbled into the dark shadow of a larger house, eyes still glued to the scene.

She had heard the crashes and screaming, but everyone she'd known well had shown up at her door for sanctuary. It hadn't occurred to her that others might have felt a more devastating loss. Who else was housing refugees to distract themselves from the now-empty chair at the kitchen table? Ness could feel the sting of tears threatening to fall as the reality hit her of how many people of Condel were experiencing the horrors she had, in her ignorance, dared to consider exciting. She paused, allowing the revelation to sink in. The people in her kitchen had lost everything. Yes, they distracted themselves by sticking their noses in her business, but if she could help keep their minds from suffering more over their losses, was that not the very service Ness was born to provide? She paused to process how much her father's job entailed. It wasn't simply convincing the people to be proud. It was lifting them up when they couldn't find their pride. This night, more than ever, Gaernod made it seem almost impossible to find confidence or even faith. They had taken everything.

For as tall as this venture had made her feel, her brother had gotten something right: They could capture her. The Gaernods were heartless, and they would not spare her on any conditions she could propose. She was just one of many to them, nothing special, and certainly not a hero. She had to take this more seriously.

She grasped her dimly glowing crystal, feeling the warmth of its light and taking comfort in the wisdom that seemed to pour out from it. First, she had to acknowledge that what she was doing was for the people and not for the sake of adventure. She nodded. Understood.

Second, she had to realize that she was not living a lie, and for as big as this journey would be, it was her destiny. She could do it, somehow. Her crystal was about faith and knowing the morale of others. She was well-seasoned in believing in herself, and she used that as a foundation for knowing when others were affirmed in their own faith and when they weren't. She had been groomed for this day, regardless of her talent's passive nature. She only had to trust her instincts. And her instincts were urging her closer to the castle.

She allowed the scene of a destroyed Condel to imprint itself into her mind as a reminder of what she was about to fight for and to remain humbled before she turned away from it and walked the steady slope toward the castle. Houses would dwindle now, and soon she would have to rely on the landscaping of the castle yard for cover.

She crept around the final house and scanned the castle grounds. There were no gates. Who would have thought they'd need them? Beyond a border of shrubbery, there lay only ancient trees and statues, but they would have to do.

She took a step out to make a quick rush for the nearest shrub but immediately flattened against the house again when she heard footsteps, accompanied by two voices. She did her best to steady her breathing.

"We didn't even need to come along," one whiny voice said. "If anyone steals my crops while I'm gone, Condel won't be the only one under attack."

"Eh, the king is still missing. That might be some excitement for you, if Afor needs to send someone else to go after him," the second, deeper voice said indifferently. "Since you lost him the first time you captured him, I'm surprised Afor didn't either kill you or send you straight after him. But it was Ryne who got that mission, wasn't it? At least he brought in the queen." The man laughed at his comrade.

Ness peered around the corner of the building just in time to watch the first soldier punch the second squarely between the eyes. The second man's eyes focused on the first's fist as he fell to his knees and then forward, face in the dirt. His partner gave him a good kick before continuing on around the corner of the courtyard.

Ness felt enraged. How could they treat each other like that? If this was how they were to their own kinsmen, then what must it be like to live in Gaernod? How could they ever find compassion for an outsider? Thank goodness they hadn't found the king. They would have brutalized him. Still, Ness wasn't sure if that was enough of an excuse for him to run, but their ruthlessness had given Ness a window of opportunity, and she accepted the cue with little hesitation.

With the second guard unconscious, she took her chance and ran for the thick shrubs, diving into them with little grace and trying to find cover while checking to see whether the Gaernod men still blocked her way. It made her heart sink to see that no one stood watch outside of the castle itself. Her path was clear.

Had Condel really been so easy to take? She couldn't bother with disappointment now. The pebbled way to the castle steps was open for her to take, and at the least, if someone was waiting for her, they would never expect anyone to be foolish enough to use the front path. So, by doing the foolish thing, she was being wise. She would go with that for now.

Remaining low to the ground, Ness made for a large tree. She paused and made sure the coast was still clear before scurrying to another tree. Next she found refuge in the shadow of a statue. It stood tall, polished, proud, not nearly as old as the nature in the courtyard, and she knew whose image it bore. She looked up into the benevolent eyes King Arisan, a man she'd admired deeply. She could still see the pale blue of his compassionate stare overlaid on top of the white eyes of the statue. It didn't do his kindness and strength justice.

"Boy, are we missing you, Your Majesty." She shook her head, heaved a sigh, and ran for the base of the grand staircase, crouching at the newel of the left railing.

The stairs were clear, so she scaled them, so low to the marble she could use her hands for speed and support. She kept her near-crawling stance until she reached the base of yet another statue, which stood only ten feet in front the vast glass window of the throne room. This one was much larger than the late king's. It surveyed the entire kingdom from its perch at the front of the castle with a stern glare, like it expected trouble on the horizon. The base itself had three layers, and she climbed those as well, knowing her next step. She knew which statue this was too, and it was about to become her perch. The entire wall behind it was made of glass, and it exposed the throne room to the city. There was no possible way for her to continue without being seen, but there was also no better vantage point.

As she neared the top of the statue, she pulled herself up to find that she was now face to face with Swelgan. Looking into the dragon's narrow, discriminating eyes, she tilted her head.

"Shouldn't you being doing something about this?" she asked the glorified hunk of rock. "I thought you were the great protector of balance. What is taking you so long?"

Unsurprisingly, Swelgan gave no response. Ness shook her head at him and continued to the top of his head, where she lowered herself as close to the stone as possible, pressing herself against the dragon's forehead for cover and peering around one of his curled horns. From here, she could see into the throne room, the place, she assumed, that she would one day know well, once her father saw fit to retire and pass his responsibility on to her. But the throne room was filled with the wrong sort of people today.

Afor sat comfortably on the main throne. He was everything Ness would have expected of a heartless tyrant, judging from the back of his head: dark hair, slicked backward over a growing bald spot he couldn't hide from a bird's eye view, bony shoulders pressed almost up to his ears with tension, and a long, prominent nose that she could see even at this weird angle. He slouched in the throne, the queen-to-be as demure and composed as ever at his side, in spite of the evil she now shared space with. Ness felt the anger ready to erupt inside her, but she reminded herself that this excursion was about collecting information, not taking action. Not yet. She felt her body tense as she forced herself to sit and listen to the muffled voices. By the look of it, Afor was the one doing most of the talking, with no participation from Her Majesty. The words were impossible to make out, but Ness could see that Afor had plenty of men with plenty of weapons. It was safe to assume that the conversations were one-sided, but at least the future queen was alive. Afor showed no care for excessive violence. He seemed rather content, probably waiting for word from his agent—what had the soldier called him?—Ryne. Whoever that guy was, she didn't like him.

She waited a moment longer, feeling like she must be able to gather some valuable information from their conqueror, but the room seemed strangely inactive. Then something in the corner of the room caught her eye. A young man with chains on his wrists entered the room, carrying a pillow. Ness leaned forward as far as she could. She recognized him. Her father had introduced her to him while he trained him during his first days at the castle. It was Atelle. His eyes, wide with terror, darted between Afor and Lissa, and then took in the various soldiers in the room, never settling on one person for more than a moment, as if someone would lunge for him if he didn't keep them in his view.

Soldiers on either side of Atelle urged him forward with their swords, pushing him to his knees when he reached Afor's feet. He held the pillow close to his chest until encouraged to do otherwise by a sword to his throat that caused him to lean backward, extending his arms and moving the pillow to within Afor's reach. Atelle's eyes were round and glistening as he focused on the blade. Ness could see by the queen's relaxed shoulders and dipped head that Lissa did not blame him for his actions.

Afor leaned forward and picked something from the pillow with two fingers. Ness's jaw dropped as she watched him place a crystal around his neck. It had the faintest glow, but that it had a glow at all was terrifying. Afor was not of Condel. There was no way he should be able to wield the power of a crystal. Only citizens of the blessed kingdom could manipulate the crystals. What had he done?

Ness looked around, wondering if there was any way she could sneak into the castle to find out more. Not from this angle. And if she went anywhere but backward, they'd notice her.

I really need to plan this out more next time, she thought, drumming her fingers on Swelgan's head. *But at least I know something important.*

King Eofyn was being followed, and she seriously doubted he'd taken anything to defend himself with, except for Pyram, and Afor had somehow found favor with the Fyre. How had he managed that? She needed to see what else she could gather from Afor and his legion, but that was impossible tonight. She would need rest if she planned to keep up appearances at home while still having enough energy to investigate at night, and she needed to find a better angle into the castle yard that would give her a better vantage point of the throne room. She would find a way into the castle if she could.

She slowly crawled back down the dragon statue, one foot at a time. When her shoe reached Swelgan's snout, she accidentally overcompensated and missed her foothold. With a gasp, she slid crudely to the ground with a graceless thud and a soft involuntary yelp; Swelgan's snout caught her stomach on the way down. Someone could have heard that, and suddenly her heart raced.

She leapt to her feet and raced for the castle's boundary, not willing to stop to check for the guard, but the second guard was still unconscious, face down in the dirt. She hurdled over the man and ran for her street, not stopping until she was safely inside her own door, and not seeing the Gaernod soldier slowly lift his head as she receded into the city.

CHAPTER 10

It was cold. And damp. And cold.

Why was darkness always so cold? Eofyn couldn't even dream of sleeping, though Pyram seemed to have no issues. He lay next to Eofyn, nothing between him and the ever-moistening dirt, and he slept peacefully. Eofyn grumbled and rolled over, realizing that he was jealous of Pyram's natural ability to simply survive.

It was laughable. Eofyn had always heard people mention how envious they were of the royal talent when he was a child. Back then, he had been proud, knowing one day he would inherit that most coveted talent, but he felt no rush to collect it. Now that the time was here, Eofyn noted the irony of coveting Pyram's abilities.

There had to be something to it. For Pyram, it was just natural. He knew what to do without even trying. For Lissa, it came in signs and signals. It was clear when it was time for her to use her healing powers, and she called them forth with a few deep breaths before reading symbols in her mind to solve people's problems.

Darian had a more difficult task. He relied on his own feelings and had to decipher whether they were the collective feelings of the kingdom or just last night's roast. For each of them, it was instinctual. It happened when they needed it. How could Eofyn's abilities be any different? Perhaps he hadn't recognized his cue from Bryta yet. Perhaps he was overlooking it. All he needed was one sure sign to prove he was making contact, and he would know henceforth beyond a doubt when he was receiving wisdom and when he was on his own.

Eofyn sat up, staring at the dwindling flame of their campfire. *All I need is a sign.* He let out a deep breath. *Just give me one sign you're real or here or at least that I'm not a complete failure.*

He waited.

Some kind of animal scurried in the distance, and a breeze blew through his hair, but there was no sign. No beam of light shone over him, as had happened earlier to everyone who had fallen the night before. The sky did not open up to prove that they had heard him. He was alone. The disappointment was overwhelming, but he had to find another source of hope to keep him going.

Once I find the Source of the Fyre, everything will be clear, he told himself. *Maybe the answer is waiting for me there. Maybe it's just not the right time.*

He repeated these words to himself until his mind eased, and he lay back down. He did not sleep. Instead, he imagined what the source could be and who would be there to illuminate his rightful path. Clinging to this dream, he waited for morning.

CHAPTER 11

Another day dawned, and Spyre was feeling pretty good. The longer he was away from Gaernod, the less connected to it he felt. It was liberating. He had risen with the sun, which was unlike him, but he knew he had a long journey ahead. He wasn't even out of the woods yet. His small companion was still curled up affectionately next to a tree, but Spyre was ready to go. "Faran." He nudged the elf with the toe of his boot.

There was no reaction.

"Faran, come on. It's time for us to go," Spyre urged. "If we get going early enough, maybe we'll get through the woods before anything dangerous even wakes up."

"Danger never sleeps," Faran said, still unmoving. "Or perhaps it does, and I've just never seen it." His eyes popped open, already fixed on Spyre with childish awe. "Have you ever seen danger resting?"

Spyre sighed, rubbing his forehead. "No. No, I haven't. But it might just be early enough for us to find out. Come on, let's get going."

Faran sprung to his feet with ease and stared at Spyre, waiting for orders.

Spyre stared back at him. "What? I'm not the one who lives here; you are. Which way do we go?"

Faran frowned and looked around, scratching his head and ruffling his already messy brown hair, which glinted with almost metallic green highlights in the sun's scattered beams.

"Hmm … I think … that way." He slowly pointed toward his best guess, but that wasn't good enough for Spyre.

"No offense," he said, dropping his pack to the ground and walking over to a sturdy-looking tree. "But I think I'd like a second opinion."

He stood at the base of the tree and planned the climb in his head. He grabbed the first branch and pulled himself up to it until he could stand on it and reach for the next one. He carefully picked his way up through the branches until he finally reached the canopy of the trees.

There was no way he could stand on the last branch, but he guessed he wouldn't need to, if his arms were strong enough. He took hold of the final limb and pulled himself upward until his arms were fully supporting his body and he could just barely catch a glimpse through the thick leaves. Fortunately, the Aforthian Mountains were easy to spot, and they were directly in front of him. Not the direction Faran had pointed to. He lowered himself back onto a sturdy branch and climbed back down the tree, leaping to the forest floor once he was close enough.

"That way," he said, pointing toward the mountains.

Faran tilted his head. "Are you sure?"

"Yes, I'm sure," Spyre grumbled. "Let's go."

Faran willingly followed him, still tapping his chin in thought. "I don't know why, and I'm probably wrong, but I think this is a bad idea."

"You think everything is a bad idea," Spyre noted.

Faran smiled with an agreeable nod. "That's true, isn't it?"

Spyre shook his head and led the way through the trees, keeping as direct a path as he could toward the mountains.

"So, the trolls. Have you ever met them?" Spyre asked after a while.

"I don't believe so," Faran answered. "Though I may have. Aren't they rather large?"

"Rather," Spyre said dryly.

"I believe I did meet one once, but fortunately, we could only stare at each other. She was at the base of the mountains, and I was in the trees."

Spyre frowned. "She didn't come after you?"

Faran shrugged. "I'm sure she would have if she could have, but our boundaries keep us safe. From the trolls, at least."

"Why is that?" Spyre remembered the chief mentioning something about boundaries before, but that had been low on his list of priorities at the time.

"I suppose you wouldn't know," Faran admitted. "There is a natural law—I don't know what the explanation behind it is—but it prevents us from crossing over any borders. I am an elf and will only ever know these woods. They," he gestured ahead of them, "are trolls, and they will never pass beyond the mountains on either side. But you," he glanced at Spyre, "you and your kind are free to come, go, conquer, or kill as you please." He looked forward, frowning. "I don't know why that is, either."

Spyre felt ashamed that his people were measured only by violence. "I didn't come to kill anyone," he said, not sure if he was reassuring Faran or defending his own pride.

"Which is why you're still alive," Faran said with a nod. "But the chief had been talking of a change in the wind. Said something important was about to happen. Then you showed up, and what else was he supposed to think?"

Spyre was about to speak when Faran's eyes lit up.

"There's the mountain." He bent over and pointed into the distance. "You see, it's a bit gray now where it had been green. The rocks are approaching—well, we're approaching them. Wouldn't you say?"

Spyre considered arguing that the craggy mountains looked more charcoal to him as they became visible through the thinning trees, but that would only lead to a significant waste of time while Faran questioned his eyesight.

Instead, he asked, "Do you ever just say something and assume you're probably right?"

"Should I?" Faran blinked up at him innocently.

Spyre could only shake his head. "Oh, brother."

"I haven't seen the mountains in a while," Faran continued, oblivious. "And the sooner you get there, the sooner I can go home in peace, I hope. It won't take long to get there from here. I think we might save time if we move faster; might that be right?" He looked at Spyre, but before he had a chance to answer, the elf was off.

"What the—" Spyre barely had time to think before Faran was nearly out of sight. He took off after him, wondering how such an indecisive creature could be so speedy at the same time. The urge for self-preservation did funny things to elves, apparently.

Suddenly, Faran stopped and gazed around, a stunned look on his face. *There,* Spyre thought, *he's confused again. That'll at least slow him down.*

But as he got closer and Faran turned in an unnatural motion to look at him, Spyre knew something was wrong. He tried to slow down, but he was already upon the elf. With a wet gulp, Spyre felt his legs sink into the muck of a bog. Faran had only sunk to his knees. Now they could see each other eye to eye.

"Oh, this isn't good, is it?" Faran asked, frowning at the surrounding mud. "I had forgotten about this. It used to be a river, I think."

"That's a safe bet," Spyre snapped. He tried kicking his legs to find anything solid he could push himself off of to try and reach the more sturdy ground, but he might as well have been floating in midair, though that would have been much more pleasant and less restricting on his legs. "How do we get out of it?"

Faran tilted his head again. "Good question. I don't know. I would have to say we're probably doomed. I don't think we can escape. We'll eventually starve, and that'll be that, unless the wolves find us, of course. That's always a possibility."

Spyre raised his eyebrows at him. "You're kidding, right?"

Faran hadn't even looked around. And he lived here; how had his people survived at all without knowing how to get out of a swamp when there was a massive one right in their forest?

"We don't come this way. It's too dangerous," Faran said simply.

"And you didn't tell me this, why?"

"I wasn't sure if this was the direction we were heading. You could have been leading us to the safer path, for all I knew."

"The safer path," Spyre said, deadpan. "And which way was that?"

"I don't know. But it isn't this one, is it?" Faran rested his chin in his hand, considering.

Spyre had to count to ten. He let out a deep breath. "Okay, so we need to get out of here. Let's look around and consider our resources."

He glanced around them. It would be easier for Faran to escape, since he was lighter. If Spyre could lift the elf out of the muck enough for him to move quickly, he might be able to get to the shore of the old river and help Spyre free himself. He leaned as much as he could to look behind Faran so far he would have fallen over if he weren't stuck. And then he saw something.

"Faran," Spyre said casually, trying very hard to cling to his dwindling patience.

Faran turned to him. "Hmm?"

"Would you mind explaining why you told me there's no way out of here when there is a sturdy-looking rope tied to a tree right in front of you?" Spyre pointed to the rope, which hung from a tree branch at the edge of the muck. It was lightly frayed, but not weather-worn the way it should have been if no one had come this way recently, as Faran indicated. This rope was a product of Gaernod and a sign of their passing through the forest on their march to Condel.

"Oh," Faran said, looking at the rope. "You know, I can't be sure."

"Don't you think it would be a good idea if we use it?"

Faran shrugged. "Perhaps."

"Grab the rope, elf," Spyre scolded, staring at Faran.

Faran's eyes grew wide, and he quickly snatched the rope from the top of the bog, holding it up as if to ask what he should do next.

"Now, pull yourself out," Spyre coaxed, nodding to the old shoreline.

"Are you sure?" Faran tipped his head, frowning. "Because I—"

"Just do it."

Faran quickly put one fist in front of the other, kicking his legs like a child learning to swim until he was safely to the edge of the riverbed. He spent a long moment assessing his situation, and Spyre nearly shouted at him to just pull himself out already, but Faran's good senses seemed to come to that conclusion just before Spyre lost his patience. The elf crawled onto the more solid land with a loud squelch as he pulled himself out of the suction of the swamp. Once free, he stood and then looked at Spyre for further instructions, mud-caked from the chest down.

Spyre put out his arms, sinking another half-inch. "Please, throw it here."

Faran stared at the rope and then at Spyre, gauging how much force he'd have to put into it. Spyre bit his tongue. Shouting at the elf to just throw it already would doubtlessly lead to a long series of misguided throws, which Spyre neither had the time nor the patience for.

He waited until the elf made himself somewhat comfortable with the idea of throwing the rope, swinging it, presumably to gauge heft and distance, or at least that was Spyre's hope. After Faran stretched the length of rope in front of his face and inspected the twist of fiber for the third time, Spyre loosed a low growl for attention. Faran perked up at the noise and tossed the rope in a startled jerk. It landed five feet out of reach, and Spyre nearly buried his face in the mud just to end the misery there, but Faran tried again, then again, and finally on the fourth try, the rope fell just within Spyre's reach.

He loosed a relieved sigh and eagerly stretched to his limit and pulled himself out of the mud, inching toward the shore as Faran sat and watched in fascination.

When Spyre finally collapsed onto the firm land, arms and core burning from the strain and heart racing from the adrenaline, Faran commented, "That was interesting. You must be stronger than I first thought because I honestly didn't think you could do it."

Spyre rolled onto his back, waiting for his heart beat to return to normal. "You know, that's not helpful at all."

"Shall we continue?" Faran sprang to his feet.

Spyre tilted his head to see the elf standing above him. "Sure. That's a fantastic idea." He rolled over and pushed himself up to brush off the dirt from his pant legs but realized how hopeless it was.

Once Spyre was steady, Faran nodded at him, smiling.

"This must be the way. If this is how the Gaernods came through, then this must be the way." He took a few steps forward, and Spyre was just about to follow when the sound of a soft shink reached his ears.

Spyre's mind raced. The elf stopped short at the sound, and Spyre knew they were in trouble. An image of one of his contraptions sprang to his mind. It was a hunting device he had used to avoid actually entering the woods. Without a second thought, Spyre ran toward Faran, knowing what would happen next.

Below the grass and leaves, and now Faran's foot, was a trigger with two blades that cut a string when Faran had stepped on it. The string led to a hollow tree, where it kept a rock safely suspended until the blades had cut it. The rock fell, knocking down a pin. The pin had held the string of a bow that now loosed an arrow through a small hole in the tree directly in front of the trigger, set at about elf height.

Faran turned to Spyre in what seemed like slow motion, his eyes slowly widening. Spyre ran toward him and leapt into the air as he heard the twang of the bow's string. He threw his arms out and pushed the bewildered elf out of the way, but just a little too slow.

Time returned to normal as a sharp pain shot deep into Spyre's left shoulder, barely missing his neck. He fell to the ground, tensing from the pain but still able to ask himself the important questions: how had his device gotten here? Why was it made into an elf trap? What had his brother done?

Breathing was difficult, the world was out of focus, and Spyre couldn't move through the pain. He laid there and watched the clouds roll by until Faran leaned into his line of vision.

"Are you okay?" The elf tilted his head inquisitively.

Are you serious? Spyre thought.

Faran tapped his chin, shaking his head. "You're not okay."

"Excellent guess."

"I'll get you help," Faran declared, suddenly assertive. He looked around and seemed to see something. He ran away from Spyre, shouting, "Help! You've got to help him. Just believe me."

Now that's interesting, Spyre thought, as his eyes grew too heavy, and he simply let go.

CHAPTER 12

Well, Eofyn thought, *here we are.*

Tir was even stranger than he had imagined. While Condel was a pristine, white city on a lush patch of grass at the edge of the Laefa Pinewood, behind it and only a surprisingly short distance away were the white sandy dunes of Tir. The sand glittered in the rising sun like all the crystals of his ancestors had been ground to dust and laid to rest here.

"Well, it's really … sandy, isn't it?" Pyram said at his side.

It wasn't even midday yet, and they had found the edge of the charted world.

"But where do we go from here?" Eofyn asked, cueing Pyram to work his magic.

Pyram held up a finger and narrowed his eyes at the desert, concentrating. His crystal pulsed as he looked around. After a short moment, he pointed forward. "That way." He casually walked off, leaving Eofyn in awe of his confidence.

Sure enough, a few yards into the hot, white sand, they came upon a stone partially buried in the dust, but obvious enough.

Upon seeing it, Pyram dropped to his knees and scooped the sand away, glancing over his shoulder at Eofyn and gesturing that he should help. Eofyn blanched before taking the cue and clumsily digging around the stone. It was taller than he expected, requiring them to brush away roughly a foot of sand before they could read the inscription on the tablet. When they had uncovered the full message, the men sat back on their heels to read.

"A straight path has yet to earn its bends. What you seek is before you."

They looked into the distance, and sure enough, there was a temple, nearly the color of the sand, looking like a mirage in the heat. Its boxed edifice rose to an impressive height in the middle and was framed by two smaller square structures on either side. From this distance, there was no sign of decoration, no glitter of gold reflecting in the sun, no shadows betraying any sort of carving in the face of the building. It stood alone in the expanse of the desert, its size speaking enough of the majesty within. That would be the house of the Source of the Fyre.

"Well, that's simple enough." Eofyn looked to Pyram for confirmation.

Pyram squinted into the distance. "You can see it? Wow. You've got good eyes." He leaned forward but shook his head. "Forward it is, I guess."

They continued in silence for a time. Eofyn noticed the wandering look in Pyram's shifting gaze. His friend was giving him more time to come to grips with his situation, seeing as his denial had not yet set in properly. Eofyn wondered how that was even supposed to happen at all. How can you just ignore tragedy? But he couldn't control the situation any more than he was already doing, so maybe he should continue to distract himself.

"So legends of Tir tell of ... what, exactly?" Eofyn broke the silence casually. "I don't remember being taught much about it. Was there more to the legends that you heard in the town or through the castle? I never even thought to ask."

Pyram tipped his head and shared what he knew: that Tir was said to be the land of the Fyre's beginning and that Eofyn's ancestor had somehow made it here and received his gift. Legend said the people didn't receive their talents at first, until they settled in Condel, where there happened to be a mine full of crystals, the one underneath the castle still used today.

When they happened upon the mine, the crystals glowed, and Eofyn's however-great-grandfather had told them the crystals were theirs for the taking. With that success, he became king, and the people built his castle over the mine to protect the crystals from people like the

Gaernods, who never received the Fyre's blessing because they weren't there when the gift was given.

Pyram took a breath and looked into the distance where the temple stood. "I guess they built that temple too, but I've never heard of it before. I had no idea what to expect when we got here."

Eofyn nodded at Pyram's nutshell account of the past few thousand years. At least they would be blindly entering the temple together.

They continued on toward the structure, which loomed large over the landscape. From here, Eofyn could tell that there was little done to ornament and commemorate the importance of the temple. Perhaps they hadn't known then that this new power would lay the foundations for an entire thriving civilization. Maybe they too had taken it for granted. Perhaps it had come to them too easily, and only those overlooked by the blessing could understand how very precious it was. Eofyn found himself wishing the temple were more decorated, that it had been given the credit it was due, but in the end, he supposed, it was just a lonely monument to a bygone era. The future was more important. Maybe he would return to the temple and rededicate it once they saved Condel.

Pyram threw a glance over his shoulder and loosed a deep breath. "If we step lightly, we can probably make the temple by nightfall," he said, a spring in his step at the idea. His crystal burned bright as it bobbed against his collarbone.

Eofyn, too, liked the sound of a night indoors. He smiled at his friend, wondering what the temple was like on the inside. No one had seen it since his early ancestors had built it countless years ago.

"You know, it really is amazing how simple it was to get here," Pyram pointed out. "I don't understand what was always so threatening about Tir. Were people just always discouraged by the legend that no one comes back? I mean, maybe no one ever returned because no one actually bothered to come here before."

"That's a good point," Eofyn admitted. "No one really cares to leave Condel. We've always had everything we've needed."

Pyram's face took on a wistful look for a moment. "I suppose," he said, "but I've always wanted to see what's outside of those white walls. We don't know anything except for what we can see and what our maps from who-knows-when show us. If you think about it, the world may not even look like that anymore, depending on how old our sources are."

"You would want to get out," Eofyn said with a smile. "You never were strong at sitting still or sticking to a routine."

Pyram grinned.

"Eh, you kept things interesting enough." Pyram gave Eofyn a friendly nudge.

Eofyn rubbed the back of his neck, smiling. "You know, it never occurred to me to apologize. I assumed living in the castle would be a step up for anyone, but you are more of a city person, aren't you?"

"I enjoy an adventure," Pyram replied, correcting him with a pointed finger. "Growing up in the castle definitely fit that. No regrets here, okay?" He gave Eofyn a friendly punch in the shoulder.

Laughing, Eofyn stumbled forward a few large steps. He caught his balance, but with the next step, the sand beneath him collapsed. His momentum pushed him forward, but his foot insisted he remain stationary, and the two forces did not agree, leaving Eofyn on his hands and knees, sinking into quicksand.

Eofyn gasped, eyes widening as he tensed every muscle.

Pyram was already crouched at the edge of the unstable sandpit. "Don't do a lot of moving, okay?"

Eofyn looked up at him with a disdainful glare. "You can't possibly know what this is," he said, talking through the panic rising in his chest. "How would you know?"

Pyram remained calm in crisis, as usual, taking his time to weigh his answer. "I don't sleep that well. Once I learned how to read, I used to sneak into your father's more private historical documents for an interesting book."

He responded to Eofyn's shocked and confused expression by quickly explaining, "There are more legends about the world than just the ones about Tir. Back in the old days, there were tales of some nomadic group that passed by Condel and shared information with them. They talked about sand that would swallow you up if you let it overwhelm you. Theories suggest that those nomads were the ones who eventually colonized Gaernod, but the fallout between the kingdom and the nomads happened after they talked. That's when the nomads noticed our crystals and got upset when we couldn't share with them."

His speech had almost made Eofyn forget the gravity of his current situation, until there was a soft hissing sound, and he subsequently sunk into the sand another few inches.

"Whoa," he said as the sand suddenly brushed his chin. "Did they happen to share how to get out of the sand?"

Pyram closed his eyes, as if rereading the texts behind his eyelids. "Can you maybe roll over?"

Eofyn raised an eyebrow at him. He lifted his chin, too aware of the sand slowly creeping up his chest but unable to do more than twitch his legs under the pressure. "Won't I go under if I try to move more?"

"If you're on your back, you won't go down."

"Oh, sure. That makes complete sense," Eofyn snapped as the sand reached his neck.

"I'm open to suggestions," Pyram countered, "but how long are you willing to wait?"

Eofyn released a frustrated sigh as he pulled a hand out of the sand, sinking a little farther. He tried to control his breathing to keep his nerves at bay as he slowly rolled onto his back.

"Flat like a board, Fyn," Pyram encouraged. "You can do it. Just get yourself closer to the surface, and I can pull you out without getting stuck myself."

It both impressed and relieved Eofyn as his body floated to the surface of the sand when he applied Pyram's advice. He sighed, laying back and relaxing the tension in his chest and arms. With a plop, Eofyn was nearly free from the suction. Pyram took his pack off of his shoulder and tossed the strap to Eofyn, keeping hold of the pouch. Eofyn needed no instruction to grab the strap and allow Pyram to pull him to where he could free himself from the pit. He knelt, covered in sand, and gathered his wits.

He looked up at Pyram and said, "I think we should go around this. Do you maybe have a stick or something?"

Pyram understood and held up a finger as he fished a stick out of the satchel (he had kept it for kindling). "How about I stay near the edge?" he offered with a laugh.

"If you insist," Eofyn replied, smiling.

Pyram helped him to his feet with a frown. "It's weird, though. The records said this stuff was only in forests where there's more water in the ground. Wonder what's down there."

Eofyn shook his head in response, not caring to find out.

They continued around the sandpit, gauging the edge of the quicksand by running the stick along the surface around them as they went.

CHAPTER 13

"Take him." It was Faran's voice, but it couldn't be. It sounded too sure of itself. Spyre tried to open his eyes, but the world was a blur of light and his own eyelashes.

"What? Why would I do that?" Spyre didn't know this new voice. It was rough and far too gravelly to belong to an elf. Who had Faran found in the woods?

"Because he's here to help us, but now he's hurt. Dying, probably, don't you think? Save him. The mountains have the healing water. We know they do. You can save him."

"Help us?" the newcomer scoffed. "He's one of them. What kind of lies did he feed you?"

"He's not like them," Faran insisted.

Spyre was touched to hear the timid, indecisive elf stand up for his sake. Where was this confidence before?

"Take him. Revive him. If you don't believe me after you've spoken to him, then you can kill him, but you have to save him now."

Okay, Spyre was less flattered now.

"Listen," the gruff voice said, "you're out of your mind if you think for one moment that I … Okay, I understand. Give him to me."

Spyre noted the change in the voice, how it had gone from angry to soft. He wanted more than anything to open his eyes and see what was happening to him, but as a pair of muscled arms lifted him from the firm forest floor, Spyre's mind surrendered to sleep once more.

When he finally regained consciousness, he felt awful. He knew he was alive; the pain made that clear, but everything else was questionable. Where was he? Well, he was no longer on the forest floor. This was harder than that. What had happened? Oh, right. The arrow. How did his design get there without him installing the trap? His brother. There was no other option. He must have gotten some sweet compensation for that one. Could Spyre move? Maybe. Did he want to? No.

He remained still, trying to build the gumption to even consider the situation he was in. And where was Faran? That little elf would have made all sorts of noise if he were around. And since he wasn't, did that mean that Spyre was no longer in Tweogan? Faran had told him that the creatures of the lands between Gaernod and Condel had to remain in their own realms, so the next step in his path to the blessed kingdom put him in the Aforthian Mountains. He hadn't mentally prepared for this stop yet. Maybe he should just play dead.

"You've rested enough," came the same voice from before, except it was angry again. "Open your eyes, human."

That sounded inviting. So Spyre was in the company of trolls now. They weren't known for their propriety. To obey, or not to obey?

"You're lucky we kept you alive this long. Get up."

Spyre received a pointed kick to his ribs that took the wind out of his lungs. Instinctively, he sat up and glared at his host. He winced at the ache of his next breath, clutching his side through the dull pain. The troll, a tall, muscled creature closely resembled Spyre's own brother, Ryne, if Ryne had been covered in a thin layer of wiry black hair.

"And what did I do to merit your fine hospitality?" Spyre asked with a sweep of his arm to the rocky overhang they were huddled under, a small fire burning nearby. It occurred to him that he may want to adjust his attitude as he noted the prominent muscles that rippled over the troll's mostly exposed body. He wore only a pair of worn leather pants stretched over trunk-like thighs the size of Spyre's neck.

"You'll feel it in a second," the troll responded. "Now, get up."

Spyre kept his eyes on the troll as he rose to his feet, supporting himself on the stone wall with his left arm and nearly falling back to the floor as a pain sharper than anything he'd ever imagined shot down from his neck to his fingertips.

"Ow!" He seethed, clutching his wounded shoulder.

The troll laughed. "Something you'll have to get used to," he said. "We patched you up, but nothing we have could heal you completely."

"Did you even try?" Spyre asked indignantly, rubbing his arm.

"Hey, an arrow shot you." The troll folded his bulky arms over his muscled chest. "We have mineral water with healing properties, but nothing in nature can fix a wound that deep. You will have a weak arm for the rest of your life, but you're still breathing, aren't you? Be grateful."

Spyre narrowed his eyes and looked down to see the damage of his shoulder. What he saw made his jaw drop. "The arrow is still in there. Didn't it occur to you to maybe take it out?" The base of the arrowhead was still sticking out of his shirt. At least they'd been kind enough to remove the shaft of the arrow.

"It has serrated edges," the troll said flatly. "Taking it out would probably kill you. But," he sighed, "if you insist." The troll reached out for Spyre's shoulder, but he jumped back against the wall.

"No." He composed himself with a deep breath. "No, that's okay. I'll live."

"You're welcome for that."

Well, technically … "Yeah, thanks." He cradled his left arm and glanced back up at the troll. "So do I get a name? Or am I not privy to that kind of information?"

The troll narrowed his eyes in suspicion. "You first. You're the one out of your bounds."

Spyre gave an arrogant laugh, attempting to match wits with the muscular creature. "Apparently, I'm the one without bounds, but I see your point." He shrugged. "My name is Spyre." He gestured across the crackly fire to the troll, waiting.

"Dugan."

"Okay, then." Spyre got to the point. "What's next?"

Dugan's mouth elongated into a very thin version of a smile. "Come with me."

He left the room, and Spyre just stared after him. He quickly glanced back and forth, as if someone should be there to back him up, but he knew he had no choice but to follow Dugan, so he did.

They must have been inside the mountains because there was no sign of the sky or grass or even fresh air. Just gray rock, dry dirt, and a damp, musty smell in the torch-lit dark. As he followed Dugan through senselessly winding tunnels of stone and earth, Spyre realized that he wasn't exactly in the mood for an audience with the troll king or chief or whatever he was. He only wanted to sleep and perhaps pity himself over the piece of metal that would forever be lodged into his shoulder.

But that wasn't in the cards for him as Dugan suddenly grabbed his good shoulder and shoved him forward through an archway and into a rather large, rounded room. It was a cave within a cave, with feeble excuses for torches in the walls. Spyre didn't do much looking around. He was too preoccupied by the mass of muscle and musk presiding over the room, sitting on a throne of rather large animal bones on top of a stone platform in the rocky cavern. Spyre's stomach flipped, and he wondered if this was how Faran felt standing next to a human: tiny, weak, and breakable.

Trolls were tall, but this one must have been their alpha male. He had a grayish tint to his tightly muscled skin. His face was stern, and every feature, from cheekbones to chin, was prominent. Half of his hair was pulled back, while the rest draped along his shoulders, and he wore only a tattered pair of leather pants. His hands, curled around massive skulls at the front of each armrest, pulled him forward as he noticed Spyre's arrival.

Dugan positioned Spyre directly in front of the alpha and forced him to his knee. Spyre winced as he went down, almost every move affecting his left shoulder. He kept his head down, trying not to let the trolls see his pain.

Alpha stood and stepped forward to the edge of a stone platform, bringing his feet within Spyre's line of sight. When Spyre saw the leather boots, he took a deep breath and looked rebelliously up at his host.

Alpha looked at him, glaring for a moment. "Name?" he asked Dugan.

"Spyre, so he says."

Spyre and Alpha locked eyes.

"We brought you here," Alpha informed him, "because the elf said you wish to help us. Therefore, you will remove the hand of Gaernod from these mountains, or you will face punishment."

Spyre was surprised. He'd forgotten the Gaernod camp that Afor had set in the mountains to force the trolls to be their guardians, an unnecessary precaution against a Condel invasion, but Afor took no chances and loved the thought of dominating the muscled brutes.

Alpha did not seem to appreciate Spyre's thoughtful silence. "What do you have to say for yourself?" he demanded loudly.

"I miss the elf," Spyre muttered flatly, looking to the side with a frown.

Alpha angrily kicked Spyre's knee, landing him face down in the dust with only one arm to help himself back up through the sharp pain. The troll walked away from him, but Spyre could still hear his whispered conversation with Dugan. By the glances and sadistic gleam in their eyes, he had a feeling he was meant to overhear.

"Is he worth it?"

"He made it out of the kingdom and through the woods, sir."

"Not much of a feat, with Afor gone."

"True."

Spyre heard a low laugh.

"What have we got to lose? Take him to the camp. If he doesn't die getting rid of them, he can go."

Spyre really didn't like the sound of that, but the next thing he knew, a hand gripped the back of his shirt and yanked him backward. He could not catch his balance as Dugan dragged him out of the room and threw him up against a wall outside. Pain seared through him, but Spyre was more irritated by his mistreatment than he was by the arrowhead.

"What is the problem?" Spyre hissed through his teeth, not wanting Alpha to come out of his chamber.

"You're a Gaernod. What about that isn't a problem?" Dugan growled in response, matching Spyre's heated tone.

They engaged in a staring battle, neither one wanting to be the first to back down. After about thirty seconds, Spyre got bored.

He rolled his eyes and said, "Can we get this over with, please?"

Dugan glanced over Spyre suspiciously before he harshly released him.

"Follow me. And don't get ahead of yourself." He poked Spyre in the chest with such force that he fell back against the wall.

Catching himself and glaring at his captor bitterly, Spyre gestured for the troll to lead the way and followed.

CHAPTER 14

They had increased security at the castle. Ness was flattered.

But she had, thus far, eluded them. She only had to bypass the two guards, who marched opposite each other now, at the main entrance to the castle grounds, and then she had to avoid the lone guard who stood near Swelgan. No problem. However, she had added a scarf to her night-watch ensemble to cover her face. She couldn't allow them to identify her and, as a result, her family.

Ness had devised something of a plan after her first night of gallivanting through the now-broken and eerie city: she needed an inside man, but she didn't want anyone to be at risk, and there was only one person who could safely tell her where to go and what to do without getting herself killed. Someone whose crystal gave them the gift to speak without talking. She closed her eyes on her kitchen floor and focused on his name, pushing all else out of her mind to reach out to the telepath in the castle.

Atelle.

She waited.

Atelle.

He- hello? Who is this? He sounded scared. Ness's anger at Afor flared.

Atelle, this is Darian's daughter, Ness. Do you remember me? Are you okay?

I'm, I'm okay. He paused. *Yes, I'm fine. What can I do for you?*

They haven't hurt you, have they? Ness pushed.

No, no. I'm fine, he insisted in the accommodating tone she'd heard him use when she visited the castle. Atelle was young, but he handled his work like a professional. *They make threats, but they don't seem to be very interested in me as anything more than a servant.*

Ness hated the sound of that. Atelle had always been so gentle. He wasn't meant for something like this, and she was about to ask more of him.

Atelle, do you think you could help me with something?

She waited, giving him the chance to decline, but he offered no objections. She continued.

I'm trying to gather information about what Afor is up to in the castle. I'm not asking you to spy on him for me. I only need help getting into the castle safely. Do you possibly know of a secret entrance I could use? He's up to something, Atelle. He has a crystal, and it's glowing. That can't be good. Will you help me?

Of course, Miss Ness. I'd be happy to.

Ness was a little stunned. That was easy. Atelle had become too submissive, but this was for the good of the kingdom, so she didn't comment.

Perfect, she thought to him. *When is the best time for me to get to the castle?*

There was a moment of pause as she assumed Atelle considered their options.

Around eleven. That's when they gather in the throne room for their meeting. I can't imagine what goes on in there.

And so at eleven o'clock, with everyone securely nestled in their makeshift beds, especially Losian, who'd given up arguing with her, Ness slipped out into the night. There was a blend of fear and familiarity this time. She knew the way, but she also knew the danger. Then again, she reminded herself, that meant she could find ways to avoid the danger. This time, for instance, she wouldn't approach the castle from the front window. She arrived at the side causeway over the small canal that split around the castle, where Atelle was waiting. He hurried her in and pressed a gentle hand to her back to quietly urge her into a broom closet in the corridor.

"What is it exactly that you're planning to do? You could get yourself killed," Atelle reminded her.

Ness rolled her eyes. "You sound like my brother," she replied. "I need to find out what Afor is up to. I've seen him with a crystal, and every night the glow of his crystal is getting brighter, and our lights are going out. He's sucking away our power, and I need to know how. I can't do that from outside."

"Well, you can't do it from inside, either," Atelle whispered worriedly.

His green eyes caught the soft glow of Ness's crystal as her natural ability rose up to calm his insecurities. He glanced at the crystal, startled by the strength of its light, but then he smiled. His shoulders lifted, and he took on some of his usual proper and trim posture.

"How do you plan to get close enough to hear his conversation? That's a heavy door to listen through."

"Yeah, but don't they have any servants in there with them?" Ness offered. "You've gone in there before."

"They don't let me stay for long. They know what I do," Atelle pointed out as he grasped his crystal tightly.

Ness sighed. "So no maids or servers?"

Atelle tilted his head to the side, admitting, "There is one serving girl; they call her in to bring a tray of drinks for the men. She has a talent for good health. They say she has been very useful to them, but I'm not sure what they mean."

Ness fumed with anger. "I know what they mean." She looked at Atelle gravely. "She is a perfect power supply for his crystal. Having her right there regenerating herself to death is giving his crystal a significant boost; its power is coming from us."

She leaned against the wall of the closet, shaking her head. There was only one option. "Swap me in for her."

Atelle's eyes grew wide. "You must be joking," he protested. "Miss Ness, if he is draining people, and most of all those nearest him, I can't allow you, a civilian, to go in there. I wouldn't even know how to make that happen. You must find another way." He crossed his arms over his chest and looked away from her.

"Liar," she accused. "Even I can think of a way to get in there, but you know more than I do, so it would be really convenient if you'd help me out here. Please," she added as an afterthought, remembering what her mother would say of her manners and catching flies with honey or some nonsense.

Atelle didn't smile in agreement, but neither did he glare at her persistence. He considered Ness with a side-eyed glance and then sighed in surrender. "Okay, I'll help you, but please be very, very careful. I don't know how I'd ever face your father if—"

Ness nodded at him, smiled reassuringly, and asked, "So what's the plan?"

Atelle looked down, regretting what he was about to do. "I can go in with you at first, but they will send me away. We'll tell them that Lorette has succumbed to illness. Please maintain an air of naivety in their presence, as we're not supposed to know what they're up to."

It surprised Ness that he handled this so professionally. "Play dumb," Ness confirmed. "Got it."

"I'll escort you in, but is it wise to make them aware of your gift?" Atelle asked.

She shrugged. "I'm sure they'll love the irony."

Atelle pinched the bridge of his nose, closing his eyes and taking a breath. "Also, please try not to allow your … boldness to play a role. Just remain quiet, listen carefully without being obvious." He put his hands on her shoulders, looking her in the eye, and added, "And try to stay strong."

Ness took a deep breath, nodding at him. She covered his hands with hers, smiling to reassure him the way her father would do with an apprehensive citizen. "Let's do this."

"Your father is going to kill me."

"You're a teenager who talks like a thirty-year-old. They can't afford to lose you," she said, laughing, but he didn't join her. "Okay," she said in a much more serious tone. "Suit me up."

Atelle nodded after a pause, lowering his shoulders, and said, "Follow me."

They slipped out of the closet, and Atelle gripped her hand firmly to lead her down the hallway to the left and down a few stairs. Soon they were in the kitchen. A few maids gave curious looks as they noticed the new face, but none dared to question anything. Knowing would only incriminate them later.

Ness tried, unsuccessfully, to make reassuring eye contact with the frightened maids. She followed Atelle to a cabinet where he pulled out a simple tan dress and an apron. It was so plain and uniform. She had never known the castle to be this way.

"They're new since Afor arrived. He had the seamstresses make them," Atelle said, answering her thoughts. She looked at him and frowned. "Sorry; it was quite a loud thought, and I hoped I could maintain your good impression of the castle as it should be."

Ness nodded. "I understand." She held up the dress. She supposed she could make it work. "I guess I should go put this on. Give me a minute."

"They'll be getting thirsty soon," Atelle warned.

Ness retreated to a particularly dark corner of the room, not too concerned with decorum since her outfit would easily remain concealed beneath the servant garb. She slipped the dress over her suit and tunic, feeling more secure knowing she was prepared to run, if necessary.

Costumed and ready to go, Ness emerged from the shadows, looking like a castle servant under Afor's brutal influence. She offered Atelle a reassuring smile, but he only looked pained.

"Hey!" A loud voice from the top of the stairs made everyone jump. "Where are our drinks?"

"Pour the ale," Atelle said urgently to one of the maids.

She did not speak or make eye contact. She gave a small nod and did as he told her.

From an adjoining room, a young girl around Atelle and Ness's age emerged. She looked pale and weak. Her deep-blue crystal glowed dimly in the dark kitchen. Lorette. As she drew closer to Atelle, holding her hands out to accept the tray of drinks, Ness could see the bags under her empty, blue eyes and how sallow her cheeks had become.

"Not tonight, Lorette," Atelle whispered, taking the tray from the maid and out of Lorette's reach. "You take tonight and rest. You may have to continue again tomorrow, so make tonight count and recuperate. Ness will take your place in the throne room."

Lorette looked confused but acquiesced with little hesitation. Instead, she turned to Ness, taking her hands into her own and whispering, "Thank you," before retreating back to where she had come from before someone could change their minds.

Atelle passed the tray to Ness, who took it clumsily. "Don't spill it, and don't speak," he advised. "I'll introduce you. Just act as meek and even frightened as possible. They prefer that."

"That shouldn't be terribly difficult," Ness admitted, exhaling heavily as she tried to prepare herself for what she was about to do.

Atelle nodded. "Follow me, and I'll tell them what happened. I'm sure they won't be too bothered." He turned and headed up the stairs.

Ness trailed carefully behind so as not to spill the ale.

When they emerged from the kitchen, a Gaernod soldier was waiting for them, arms crossed impatiently. Ness saw him, caught his eye, blanched, and averted her eyes, but Atelle continued forward. He, too, avoided eye contact, but he spoke with confidence.

"Sir, I do not doubt that your keen eyes have noticed that this," he gestured behind him, moving nothing but his arm, "is not the normal maid who serves you. I apologize, but she has fallen ill. Her crystal has nearly ceased to glow, and she is taking tonight to replenish her strength to better serve you tomorrow and onward." He took a steady breath. "This girl is of good health and can suit your needs. I sincerely hope you will accept her as a worthy substitute."

The soldier stepped closer to Ness; she could smell decay on his breath as she kept her eyes pinned to the floor, trying not to tremble too noticeably. He curled a finger under Ness's chin and tilted her face upward. She did her best not to gasp but allowed her fear to show in her eyes as the soldier inspected her face, smiling wickedly.

"What does she do, then?" he asked Atelle, not taking his eyes from Ness.

"Equally useful to Lorette," Atelle said carefully, "she has a talent for maintaining confidence, not only her own but also the faith of the entire kingdom, promoting our assurance in our crystals." He lowered his head.

The soldier's eyes flashed with excitement. "So if she were to falter," he said, making Ness grow slightly weak, "the rest of the kingdom might suffer as well?"

Atelle closed his eyes, steadying his breathing to avoid letting his anger show. "It is possible, sir," he mumbled. "They would have no reassurance to their doubts and fears."

Ness could see bits of food stuck in the soldier's teeth as his smile grew. She had to stop herself from recoiling in disgust. "She's perfect," he mused. "Why have you been hiding her?" He gripped Ness's arm with his rather large hand and tugged her out of Atelle's reach. "Come on, you," he said to her. "You've got a job to do."

Ness had to focus on keeping the full glasses of ale upright as he pulled her back toward the throne room. Was this really what she had wanted? Was she prepared for this? Too late now.

The soldier pushed the large door open, and Ness was overwhelmed by the size of the room and most of all by who sat in the king's chair. Not even King Eofyn used that chair. In the minds of nearly everyone, it still belonged to King Arisan, out of respect for his still-recent death, and seeing Afor in his place infuriated Ness, but she had to remain calm, if not fearful.

The soldier led Ness to the base of the throne platform, where she finally glimpsed the future queen. Lissa sat quietly, wearing a simple black dress, either at Afor's request or out of mourning. Likely both, Ness realized. The future queen stared at her folded hands, probably ashamed and heartbroken, though her face looked blank and almost peaceful in Lissa's almost ethereal grace.

"We've got a new servant girl," the soldier announced, shoving Ness forward so she stumbled and had to catch her footing.

Ness had never been good with balancing a tray, and it annoyed her that this guard was making it so very difficult. Rebellion threatened to show on her face, but she swallowed it down.

At the sound of the news, Lissa glanced up and caught Ness's eye. Ness had met Lissa before outside of the castle, when Lissa had still been as much of a civilian as Ness. She saw the spark of recognition in Lissa's eyes and hoped she offered a steady, reassuring gaze in return.

Lissa glanced in every direction, ensuring that she was not being watched, and mouthed, "What are you doing here?"

Ness did not have the luxury of responding. She replied with a calm, collected face.

"What happened to the old one?" Afor asked suspiciously, rising from the throne.

"She was weak." The guard laughed. "This one's better anyway, my lord. Her crystal glows for assurance, and not just her own." He raised his eyebrows suggestively, and Afor caught the message, raising his own brows in excitement.

"The kingdom?" Afor asked, his voice high with the prospects as Ness focused her surfacing glare to the marble floor.

The guard at Ness's side nodded, smiling. Afor returned it, wagging a finger at him. "There may be a reward in this for you." He looked at Ness, and she stared up at him, seeing no remorse in his eyes for the disaster he had caused. He gave a firm, approving nod as he looked her over and said, "Now, get her to the side, and let's begin."

The soldier dragged Ness to stand next to Lissa's chair. When he released her and moved back with his king, Lissa reached up and touched Ness's arm, eyes fixed on the Gaernods. Ness was not telepathic like Atelle, she couldn't initiate a mental conversation, and neither could Lissa, but Lissa's message was clear: "I'm sorry. Be careful. There's nothing I can do."

"To business," Afor said, ignoring the Condel citizens in the room. He reached into the pocket of his elaborate robe and pulled out a chain that slowly revealed a crystal, glowing a toxic shade of greenish-yellow. The sight of it alone caused Ness to falter.

What is that? she thought, but she did not have to wait for an answer. Afor had noticed her reaction.

"Ah, so it's getting stronger," he said, rising and casually walking over to her. He dangled the crystal in front of her face, and her eyes involuntarily fixed on it. "This," he said in a hushed voice, "is my crystal, but how can that be?" His words mocked her thoughts. "How can a Gaernod king have a crystal? But look at the glow." He grabbed her chin with an uncomfortable jerk of his hand to stop her from averting her gaze. "Look at how bright it is. Have you seen one of your crystals glow this brightly? Ever?"

She hadn't. Tears threatened her eyes. Her head throbbed. She shut her eyes against the dull pain.

Afor touched the crystal around her own neck, and suddenly, Ness felt as though she was being stabbed in the chest. She stood stiffly, not making a sound despite the pain. "Yours, my dear, is quite dim," Afor commented. "I expected more."

Tears escaped from the corners of her eyes, streaming down each cheek and racing to the floor. She wished she could escape from herself, too, just leave her body and fly away from this horrible place.

Drawing nearer, Afor held her crystal next to his, making Ness's head feel like it was splitting in two. She dropped the tray she had been holding. Glass shattered, and the deep amber ale spread across the floor.

"I am stronger than you," Afor continued, his breath on her face. "I am stronger than your entire kingdom, and I am certainly stronger than your pathetic king." He laughed harshly, clutching both of their crystals in his fist. "Wouldn't you like to feel the power of a crystal this bright? Wouldn't you like to feel strong? Not even Arisan gave you that, did he?"

It couldn't be true.

"Why do you all resist me when I can show you how to become this strong in your own gifts?" Afor lamented to her.

Ness couldn't hold back anymore. She shook her head ever so slightly, just wanting this to stop, and Afor noticed. He grinned and brought his mouth next to her ear. A disgusted chill rand down her spine.

"I can make this kingdom thrive," he whispered. "I can give your people a figure to look up to instead of that worthless king you've got now. How can you have confidence in someone who ran away as soon as he saw me on the horizon?" He watched her weave in place as she lost her strength. "I have power. I am stronger. I will win—"

"No," Ness said, breathing heavily and losing her composure.

"—and this is real."

"No." Her crystal flickered. It darkened for seconds at a time, draining her.

Afor stepped even closer. She could feel him in front of her. "Your kingdom was built on the lie that you were unique and that you were chosen to be the strength of this world." He spit the words out like poison. "But I prove all of that false. My very presence weakens you all. Everything you thought you knew is wrong."

"No!" she shouted desperately as her crystal gave a final burst before extinguishing completely. Her legs gave out, and she collapsed to the floor, weak and numb. A shrill tone rang in her ears, scattering her thoughts and leaving her feeling empty. She caught movement out of the corner of her eye and shifted her gaze to see Lissa gasp and try to get up to help, but a fierce glare from the soldiers put her back in her place.

Afor stepped away from Ness's quiet form, laughing. "Gentlemen and lady," he said, giving an exaggerated flourish to Lissa, who looked horrified. He gestured an arm to Ness, crumpled on the floor. "I give you the state of the kingdom. Good news." He looked down at Ness and smiled. "It has—literally—fallen."

He held up his crystal, and his smile turned to a grimace. "Look at that," he said, gazing at the glow of the crystal. It shone like a small star in the room. He looked back down at Ness. "We need to use her more often." He spun to Lissa. "Get her back on her feet. She needs to regain her strength. We'll do this again tomorrow."

Lissa jumped at the chance to rush to Ness's side, tears of guilt in her eyes; she placed one hand on her forehead and the other on her heart, focusing her healing energy as her blue crystal blazed to life.

It wasn't long before Ness's eyes felt less heavy and her mind cleared enough for anger to replace the confused glaze over her eyes.

"Excuse me, Majesty," she whispered.

Lissa leaned back onto her heels, eyes wide.

Ness stood slowly, ensuring that her footing was firm. Afor's shoulders straightened, as if he could sense her movement, and he turned to face her. He seemed somewhat impressed with her strength until he saw her expression.

"You," Ness said between pants of breath, "are not my king. You are not my master, and you are definitely not more powerful than we are. You are a liar and, apparently, a thief."

She glanced at the fiery crystal in his hands. "I will never follow you, and no one will believe in you enough to let you win." Her anger fueled her audacity. "Arisan was a great man, and his son …" She knew she couldn't pause for too long. "His son is doing his best, and he will come through for us; if there is one thing I believe in, it is my people and this kingdom."

She stepped closer to Afor, violating his personal space. "We will bring you down." She scaled him with her eyes and gave a short laugh, stepping back and spreading her arms out to her sides. "And I'm going to help make that happen."

Afor's face contorted into an awful grimace. Ness had never seen true hatred until this moment, and her instincts took the hint.

"Kill her," the Gaernod king hissed.

Ness saw the guards come at her, and she ran; staying to fight was out of the question. She moved past Lissa and suddenly knew her only option. Swelgan loomed outside the dark window like a silent guardian. In this moment, for all the doubt she had regarding that stupid stone dragon, she had to believe he was leading her well now. She didn't know how she would do it, but she knew what she had to do. She ran toward him.

The guards hadn't expected resistance, and it gave her a few extra seconds as they corrected their paths to pursue her. They would corner her at the window.

She would have to remember to apologize to the king later.

She crossed her arms over her face and ran as fast as she could, crashing through the glass and earning a few gashes on her forearms, but she didn't feel a thing. The Gaernods stopped in their tracks as the shards from the huge window rained down around them. Ness kept going past the dragon and ran down the steps, escaping into the night.

The guard on duty at the castle bounds came running at the sound of shattering glass, but Ness lowered her shoulder and caught him unawares, breaking past him as well. Once she turned the corner and entered the maze of houses, she knew they wouldn't bother chasing her any farther. It would be easier to search the castle for a snitch than to scour the kingdom for a girl. Her heart broke for Atelle and the maids. They would be the first to face questioning, but Ness hadn't thought this far ahead, and she couldn't think of anything in the moment but the safety of her kitchen. She darted through the streets and hesitated at her front door, only to keep from charging in and making a rattled scene.

Ness nearly slid onto the kitchen floor, lying down and covering herself so that, if anyone happened to look in the window, they would only see another congregation of refugees. But her heart still raced; she knew she wouldn't be sleeping tonight. She clapped a hand over her mouth to quiet her erratic breathing. What if she had ruined everything? What if they knew where she lived, who she was? What if they tortured Lissa or Atelle for information? Would they protect her, or would they give her away? In either case, someone Ness knew was going to get hurt.

She'd never forgive herself.

CHAPTER 15

Spyre was in a camp. It was much more official than what he and Faran had set up before. They had settled into a ditch in the mountainside with a tent made of animal skin. A fire lit the tent, and Spyre was whittling to ease the tension of Dugan's incessant staring. The block of wood had become rounded since Spyre began toying with it. Grooves spiraled from top to bottom.

"So you think you can do it?" Dugan asked, breaking the silence that had lasted for hours.

Spyre looked up at him, eyebrows raised, face still unamused. "Do what?"

"Get rid of the Gaernods," Dugan clarified with a huff. "Take them down and get them off this mountain."

Spyre laughed a little, shaking his head and staring at his art project. "I have absolutely no idea. I hope so, for my sake, right?"

Dugan glared disapprovingly. "How can you be so calm about this? We've been trying to get your people to leave for years, and here you are saying you have no plan, but you still seem perfectly at ease. What's your secret? Are you some great warrior or something?"

Spyre laughed more. "No way," he said. "I'm just making this up as I go."

"Then why are you so confident?" Dugan eyed Spyre suspiciously.

"I'm not—I'm petrified," Spyre corrected him. Then he shrugged. "But I've made it this far, haven't I? There's got to be a reason, and if that's true, then I'm sure I'll come up with something, somehow."

"You're insane." Dugan leaned back against a rock. "You're going up against trained soldiers with no experience behind you, and you've got a serious wound. They won't miss that, you know."

Spyre set down his wood and knife to stare at Dugan. "What do you want me to say? 'No, you're right. I can't possibly do this. I give up.' And then what? You'll kill me. I'd rather get more time by at least trying, thank you."

"Good enough point, I guess," Dugan conceded, poking the flame.

"Yeah, I don't like it either, but this is my lot, it seems." Spyre took his frustration out on the piece of wood, carving deeper grooves into it.

Dugan grinned. "Yeah," he said. "So what are you going to do now? Think you can sleep knowing what's coming, or are you going to keep carving ornaments for your grave?" He nodded to Spyre's pet project.

Spyre humored him with a curt laugh. "I'm sure I can sleep just fine." To prove his point, he spread out his blanket and lay down, facing away from Dugan so the troll wouldn't see that he could not close his eyes.

What had he been so confident about before? How in the world was he going to get through this one? What kind of spirit of destiny did he really think would miraculously save him and deliver him over the mountains? Had he really thought that? It was a miracle he was still alive. And he had only just barely managed that. He had a serrated metal arrowhead in his shoulder to prove it.

I'm definitely going to die tomorrow, he told himself.

But wait a second here, another part of him reasoned. *If there's nothing helping me, how did I possibly make it this far? Trolls acting hospitable? That just doesn't happen. They prefer to bludgeon first and ask questions later. It sounds insane, but really, what other choice do I have?* He glanced to the side. *If there is something helping me along here,* he addressed the universe in challenge, *how about a good night's sleep, huh?*

Dugan threw water on the fire, and the tent grew quiet, still, and even peaceful.

Spyre darted his eyes from left to right, searching for some ethereal creature to be laughing at him from the corner of the tent. There was nothing.

Wow, okay then. Thanks. He tentatively closed his eyes.

Morning came with no alarm or rude wake-up call from Dugan. Spyre awoke of his own accord, feeling refreshed. Why was that? He sat up quickly, rubbing his sore shoulder, and looked around. Dugan was staring at him, a fire started and some strange meat roasted and nearly prepared to eat.

"What's this?" he asked skeptically, wiping the sleep from his eyes.

Dugan smiled craftily. "Last meal, I suppose. Thought I'd at least give you that."

"You're really helpful, you know that?" Spyre muttered, maintaining his cynical attitude.

"Well, you don't have to eat it," Dugan said, reaching for the food.

"No," Spyre said, lunging forward. He cleared his throat as Dugan paused, eyes gleaming. "You can leave it. It's okay. Thanks, even."

Dugan sat back and crossed his arms as Spyre grabbed at the food, nearly expecting it to be a trick, but the troll didn't move.

"You're welcome. Get your strength. You do not understand what you're up against here, even if you are from Gaernod."

Spyre looked at him as he reached for the meat that was frying over the fire, not caring what it was and wondering what could be worse than the soldiers he had in mind. He knew his brother, and he knew many other soldiers that Afor employed. They were brutal and emotionally unattached. They would kill without a thought and sleep straight through the night. So he gnawed the gamy rodent and ignored the dryness in his mouth.

"So I suppose I'm in this alone?" Spyre asked when he'd finished the last of his portion, deciding against a second helping.

"Well, you can't think I'm sticking my neck out." Dugan laughed at Spyre's expense, not looking in his direction.

But then Spyre noticed something. "You're afraid," he realized in disbelief. "You're petrified of them. A troll, all muscles and brute force, is afraid of a few human soldiers." Now it was Spyre's turn to grin.

"Shut up," Dugan growled, silencing Spyre. He looked away, fidgeting.

"So you're having me do this because you've exhausted your options or because you've never tried?" Spyre questioned, narrowing his eyes for any tells on the troll's face, but Dugan didn't look at him, and that answered Spyre's question.

The trolls could talk, but they couldn't act. Spyre was a last-ditch attempt before giving in completely. So this was not a death sentence but more of a desperate call for help, albeit a rude one. They were quietly depending on him. Their anger was a simple mask of pride.

Spyre now smiled warmly at Dugan. "Okay." He caught Dugan's attention. "I'll help you. This will end today. Then I'll be on my way, and you can be on yours, and no one ever has to know that your kind was ever anything less than dominant."

Dugan merely grunted, but Spyre chose to interpret it as thanks.

"What weapons will you use?" Dugan asked, but Spyre just shrugged.

"I don't have any weapons," he confessed. "I don't even know what I'm up against here. Do you think I expected any of this?"

"Fool," Dugan muttered, intending for the man to hear.

Spyre laughed. It wasn't like he could really argue. This whole journey seemed foolish, but the foolish thing and the right thing were the same in his case.

"So I guess we should go check out the competition." Spyre pushed himself to stand, ready to move on. "Then I'll be better prepared to come up with something. What do you say? Can we get closer?"

Dugan looked at him, thought for a moment, and sneered, "You may have to come up with something quicker than you think, but I can get you close, yeah."

Spyre didn't like the sound of that, but he knew he had little choice. He gestured to the entrance of the tent, refusing to show fear but not willing to take the lead yet. "Go ahead."

Dugan nodded with a small grunt that was not as threatening as his previous ones and left the shelter. Spyre followed, trying to convince himself that the trolls had exaggerated the extent of the soldiers' wrath just to make him sweat. He knew the soldiers had weapons, but the sight of another Gaernod might throw them off, if they were human enough to pause before resorting to violence.

What could he tell them? That he was a messenger? He was coming from the wrong direction for that. That he wished to be a new recruit?

Pathetic, but maybe. He would have to wait and see what, if anything, came to him.

He followed Dugan a few yards up the mountain, until the troll abruptly halted without warning. Spyre bounced off of Dugan's back, and his mind registered the danger before his mouth did.

"What's the problem?" he whispered, peering around Dugan's broad form.

He pointed upward, and Spyre's eyes moved from Dugan's face to the area he was pointing to. There they were: Spyre's kinsmen. There were two nearly identical grunts with metal-plated armor on their chests, legs, and arms, with helmets made of hard leather covering their heads and faces. Afor must not have thought the trolls were worth more than that. Maybe this wouldn't be so bad.

"They don't look that intimidating," Spyre whispered.

"Of course they don't," Dugan snapped. "You think we couldn't handle a few humans?"

Spyre looked at him with innocent, round eyes. He glanced up to the guards and back at Dugan before hesitantly saying, "Well, you haven't, so—"

"It's not the soldiers, you idiot," Dugan snapped at him. "It's what they've got protecting them. Look closer. You might catch a glimpse of it."

"I don't see why you can't just tell me," Spyre said, shaking his head as he turned back to the soldiers. Then he saw it, like a dark boulder rolling across the landscape. It was lumbering and huge. Spyre gasped.

"Tell me," Dugan said, "how would you describe that to someone who's never seen it?"

Spyre's mouth opened to respond, but there were just no words. The creature was a small mountain in itself, covered with brown fur and beady black eyes, with no trace of soul behind them, only bloodlust. A soldier of Gaernod in animal form. "Wha—what is that thing?"

"It's a bear," Dugan said bluntly. "It's the last one on this mountain. They used their weapons, and they killed the others. This one was a cub, and they raised it to recognize their uniforms so it won't attack them, but it goes after just about anything else that moves."

"So why don't you take that one down the way they took out the others?" Spyre asked, trying to make sense of everything. "Where are your weapons?"

Dugan stared hard at the ground.

Spyre dropped his hands to his sides and said, exasperated, "You don't have weapons. How do you not have weapons?"

Dugan glared at him defensively. "Where do you propose we get the material, human? Where should we get wood strong enough to build spears? Where do we find metal to make swords? There might be metal in this mountain, but how do we get to it without having at least one pick?"

Then Spyre remembered and felt guilty. "Oh, that's right. You can't leave the mountain on either side."

"When they need more supplies, they go wherever they need to get materials, build their weapons, and return," Dugan explained bitterly. "We are bound to the mountain. All we have is stone, which means we either throw rocks at them or something equally useless, or we hide."

"Well, there's an easy solution to that," Spyre said.

Dugan raised a cynical eyebrow at him, trying but failing to look disinterested.

"I can get you some wood from Tweogan. I can cross the borders, and maybe, if you promise not to kill them, you could offer the elves a deal. They can give you wood. You can give them stone." He responded to Dugan's sardonic glare by mirroring it. "Everything they have is made of wood and mud. It's not exactly built to last. They wouldn't need much, and neither do you. It's as easy as rolling a log, or in your case, rolling a boulder."

Dugan narrowed his eyes, not buying it. "You would do that?"

Spyre laughed. "What other options would you propose? I'm sort of at your mercy here. I'll help you, and you won't kill me. I consider that a win." He flashed a cheesy smile, trying to persuade Dugan to trust him. "Come on. The elves are no threat to you, and I don't have forever."

Dugan narrowed his eyes at Spyre.

"Okay," he said brusquely. "But I'm taking you to the border, and I'm keeping an eye on you."

"I honestly prefer that," Spyre replied. "And I like the idea of getting out of here. Shall we?" He turned for the downward slope of the mountain, still looking at Dugan.

Dugan gave a single, firm nod, and they quickly left the area. He moved much more quickly down the mountainside than Spyre could. Spyre stumbled and tripped after the troll, sliding on loose rocks where Dugan seemed to surf on them.

Spyre attempted to take mental notes on Dugan's expert movements as the day progressed. The way he stepped in the right places to avoid pieces of shale from sliding out beneath him, the angle of his feet to cope with the steep gradient of the mountain, but it always ended with him losing his footing entirely. He'd slide for a few moments before catching his heel on a more solid rock and somehow regain his footing. He imagined it was a matter of core strength, which he lacked but which Dugan had in spades. When the mountain leveled out around midday, Spyre had too much momentum from a recent slide. Inevitably, he tripped and slammed into Dugan's back. The troll looked back at him, eyebrows raised at Spyre's novice efforts.

"We have to stop meeting like this." Spyre strained as he gathered himself.

Dugan stepped to the side. "This is where you get off."

Spyre peered around him and saw the dirt abruptly transition to grass. He stepped around the troll and crossed the boundary into Tweogan Forest, secretly enjoying being out of Dugan's reach and yet only a few feet away from him.

He looked at Dugan and said, "You can stay and wait if you want. It shouldn't take me long to find a few sturdy branches for spears and such." He scanned the woods, already building things in his head. "I've got a few relatively simple ideas."

Dugan said nothing, but Spyre liked to imagine that he saw a flash of gratitude in his eyes. He decided not to think about the troll's eyes on him as he walked away, seeking out trees with the right size and strength of branches. Then Dugan's attention shifted to the ground in fascination. How long could a man of any species stand around watching grass grow?

On second thought, if you don't really get to see grass that often …

He chose an old, sturdy tree, knotted and thick at the trunk, with branches to spare from what must have been centuries of lush growth. It would be perfect. He looked around, trying to find a way to climb it. He saw a stone, and if he stretched himself, a branch he could pull himself up to. He stepped on the rock and reached, but his fingertips only barely brushed the tree limb. He exhaled, staring the branch down, knowing which of them would most likely win in a fight.

He jumped. Didn't make it.

He bent his knees and jumped higher. Almost. He needed a better grip on it, or maybe …

He slung his bag off of his shoulder and set it onto the rock. It should have been sturdy enough to support his weight long enough for him to grab the branch. He stepped up, but the bag slid out from under his foot, and he landed flat on his back on the forest floor. Several yards away, he heard Dugan laughing.

"Great," Spyre muttered. Not the best way for him to reassure Dugan that he could outsmart or outmatch his own people.

Fed up with trying to outsmart nature, Spyre just took a running start and leapt onto the rock and up toward the branch. Finally, and fortunately, he got a firm grip on the branch. As the weight of his body hung from his shoulders, he flinched, but he had made it. He could just picture Dugan's face. He smiled and swung his legs around the branch to pull himself up, relieving his wounded shoulder.

Spyre sat on the branch and inspected the tree, reaching a hand out to touch it thoughtfully, imagining what he could do with its resources. His mind filled with blueprints and designs, and he reached accordingly for the right-sized branches. There were arched and flexible branches, branches shaped just right for his plans, but when he thought of Dugan, he knew he needed something more.

He needed a long and sturdy branch, but this tree did not offer that, except for the branch that Spyre currently sat on. It was perfect, but there was no way Spyre could get the branch off of the tree without at least mildly hurting himself.

He looked to the Aforthian border. The landscape changed from forest to mountain with unnatural distinction. It looked as though someone had drawn a three-dimensional map. Was there magic to the way the lands of Curnen worked? Had anyone ever thought to study it? Spyre considered the priorities of Gaernod and the stories Condel and presumed not. If only he had the time to take notes and experiment.

Down below, Dugan was still watching him, hiding his confusion beneath a cynical mask.

Spyre didn't have the time to look for another climbable tree with the right branches. He had what he needed here. All he had to do was have the guts to get the job done. He sighed and shook his head at the tree trunk, knowing this would hurt. He broke off the more flexible branches and dropped them to the forest floor. Then he stood on his perch and grabbed another twisted branch above his head for balance, bouncing his weight on the bottom branch.

"Hey," a voice called, making Spyre nearly lose his footing and sending a sharp pain down his arm.

He looked down and saw a shaggy copper head and two chestnut eyes staring at him. He focused through the pain and realized it was Faran. He almost smiled at the familiarity of the elf's face.

"Why are you taking the limbs from this tree?" Faran asked. He looked at the branches around his feet and scaled his eyes back up the tree to Spyre. "Are you taking the limbs from this tree?"

Spyre sighed. "Yes, Faran. I'm taking a few limbs."

Faran's eyes widened. "But you're going to fall, aren't you?" Then he frowned. "And why do you need the branches? Weren't you going the other way?"

Spyre growled under his breath. There hadn't been enough time for him to miss Faran's circling questions. "Why do you ask so many questions?"

The elf stared back at him blankly, probably wondering if he had an answer to Spyre's question or imagining a query in response.

"Why don't you go talk to my new friend, Dugan?" Spyre suggested, already wanting to get away from the pestering elf. "He's right over there. He can't hurt you, so there's nothing to worry about. I'll catch up with you in a minute."

Faran looked stunned, spinning around to see Dugan staring with one eyebrow raised. He pointed at the troll, asking a silent question. Dugan raised a corner of his mouth along with his other eyebrow and nodded. Faran stepped lightly toward the troll, and they left Spyre to his work. Now they could sort out a resource trade, and Spyre could get what he needed so he could finally move forward with his journey.

He jumped on the branch. It moved but didn't break. He jumped again, to the same result. Rolling his eyes at his luck, he jumped three times in a row.

The branch finally snapped. Spyre did not have a good enough grip on the branch above to support himself, and his wound wouldn't allow it, anyway. He dropped to the ground and landed in a heap on the grass.

Faran and Dugan turned at the sound and broke into laughter together.

A bow. A few spears. Even a slingshot. Spyre impressed himself, but he couldn't say the same for Dugan a few hours later.

They were back at their camp in the mountains. The sun was just dipping below the horizon. Spyre was assembling as much of a variety as he could and hoping that Dugan was taking notes.

"You have animal skins, so you can use the leather for a slingshot, see?" Spyre wound the strip of hide around two ends of a Y-shaped branch he had shaved into shape with his knife, tugging on the leather with satisfaction. He passed it to Dugan. "Just pull, aim, and shoot."

"What about that?" Dugan asked, pointing to the bow and arrows that Spyre had made.

"Those are mine," Spyre cautioned. "I can teach you to make more."

"So you think these will kill the bear?" Dugan didn't seem confident. His tone had been nothing but critical all day.

"If you make those tips sharp enough." Spyre nodded to the stones that Dugan was shaping into arrowheads and spear points. "I think it'll certainly help."

Dugan smiled almost viciously. "Oh, they're sharp. Don't worry about that." The score of pride that Dugan intended to settle manifested as flashes of excitement in his eyes.

"Uh huh," Spyre drawled, not liking the fire in Dugan's stare when he thought about dismembering the humans at the peak. "Well, help me attach them to the arrows and spears, and we'll get this started."

They wound leather strips around the stone tips and fastened them to the sticks that Spyre had gathered and smoothed down. Spyre swung a spear over Dugan's head and sliced a thin tear into the tent they were hiding in. He smiled as Dugan ducked and glared fiercely at him.

"Good work," Spyre commended, proud to see his project complete. "It's definitely sharp."

They assembled the rest of the weapons and slipped them into their belts, each taking a spear and dividing the slingshot and bow. Dugan would wield the slingshot, because his arms were about the size of Spyre's entire body, and a stone needed more strength behind it than an arrow would.

Spyre ran a checklist in his head but realized there was no other way to prolong the fight. He sighed, wondering what he should do. He had a general idea of how to fight, how to aim a bow, and where the bear's weak points would be, but would the soldiers step in to aid the animal? What level of skill did they have at their disposal? He assumed it would come down to speed and precision.

"Okay." He exhaled. "Let's see how this goes."

He stood and left the tent, leaving Dugan to stare after him for a moment. Spyre was petrified. Trolls were one thing, but going up against his own people was far more intimidating. They would see him and crush him sooner than they'd want to crush the troll. Spyre was more than a pest to them; he was competition, a threat by every definition. But he had to do this. At least it would be a quicker death than the one the trolls would offer if he failed. Besides, he had made it this far. Why would fate stop him now?

Hold your breath, and keep thinking that, he told himself. He checked the bow and spear, making sure they were within reach, and stowed the arrows in his bag while Dugan led the way up the mountain until they were close to the summit where the soldiers and bear were.

"So the plan is to sneak up on them and get as close as possible before they notice?" the troll asked, hoping for more information, but he received a look of innocence instead.

"Well, they won't be expecting us, so why not?" Spyre noted. Who could argue with that?

Spyre followed Dugan up the mountain, becoming more aware of how many things he had never done. He'd never climbed a mountain; his legs made that clear after his exhausting day of physical effort. He had never built weapons of war before, which explained why he didn't think to bring a quiver for his arrows or the proper belt to hold a spear. Dugan had his weapons secured to him as if he'd expected to make them. But why would Spyre have expected to come up with a plan to get past the enemy?

Dugan stopped him with a solid arm. He nodded upward. Spyre followed his gesture and saw the bear prowling at the top of the mountain. It could probably swallow both him and Dugan whole, with room for seconds. How did they think they could get past that?

Time to think: *One arrow alone, no matter how well placed, wouldn't take it down. It would howl, then it'd come after us, and worse, the soldiers will know we're here. Will they watch for sport, or will they attack? What weapons might they have? They favor swords and close-range weapons, but they had a bow for the mechanism in the woods.* He stewed in frustration. Nothing was certain anymore. This was huge.

"You aim for the head, and I'll aim for the heart," he finally decided. "Confuse it, and injure it. Then reload and keep it up. We'll handle the soldiers if we have to."

"Great plan," Dugan said skeptically.

Spyre laughed nervously, in complete agreement with Dugan's sentiment, as he readied his bow.

They took aim and let fly. The bear hadn't been looking their way, so Dugan's rock hit the side of its head hard, while Spyre's arrow entered its chest area on an angle. The bear roared and reared on its hind legs. It was much taller than either Spyre or Dugan, a variable that made Spyre seriously reconsider this whole endeavor. He imagined that this was the point when the soldiers would take notice.

The bear stumbled around, looking for its attackers. Spyre set another arrow. Dugan took the hint and did the same with a large rock. They shot again. Now the bear had located them and ran swiftly toward them, sharp teeth on display. Spyre debated whether he should reload. He wouldn't have the strength for close combat, but Dugan would, and the problem of the guards still needed addressing. He decided.

"You take the bear," Spyre delegated.

Dugan shot him a wild glare.

"It won't be too hard for you now. Use your spear; use your arms." He steadied his heartbeat with a slow, drawn-out breath. "I've got the soldiers."

Dugan blinked at him, eyes wider than his strong brow could cope with, but Spyre was already skirting up the rest of the mountain. He quickly approached the Gaernod campsite, but they anticipated his arrival. As he neared the summit, he looked up to see that a rather large boulder had appeared above him. It teetered momentarily, cueing Spyre to move before it fell down the mountainside. Spyre jumped to the side and watched in shock as the rock sped past him.

"Look out," he yelled into the air, but Dugan was too preoccupied with the bear to look up.

He was on a very thin ledge that barely fit both him and the bear, and when the rock hit them head on, Spyre found himself staring at an empty ledge, horrified. Should he go back for Dugan? He looked up and saw another boulder looming. If he went back, he'd be crushed before he reached his accomplice.

He dove to avoid the next boulder. His heart nearly skipped a beat when it fell within a few inches of his left shoulder. He breathed heavily and then kept moving upward, making it to the peak just as the soldiers let another large rock fly. They looked at him, surprised that he had made it this far, and Spyre looked at them, surprised by something else.

Two. It really was just two soldiers, and an admittedly huge bear, that had kept an entire pack of trolls at bay. Clearly, the trolls had not made very many attempts to challenge the men, who had easily taken out the only competition they'd had on the mountain. Hopefully, bringing down the last bear would give Dugan some faith in his breed.

The two soldiers separated to confuse Spyre, but the joke was on them, because Spyre had no idea what he was doing anyway. They had swords. He had five arrows and a spear. His bow was useless at this close range, so it would be down to the spear. He clumsily reached back and pulled the spear from his belt and through the strap of his satchel, glancing back and forth between the soldiers as the sounds of Dugan's scuffle with the enraged bear erupted behind them. Shouts mixed with snarls and whines until it was impossible for Spyre to tell who was winning, the troll or the bear. He could only focus on his own situation: the soldiers skulking toward him. They balked when they realized through the visors of their helmets that it was a human who'd crested the peak to their camp, but that didn't slow them down too much. They drew their swords from their sheaths and ran at Spyre.

Spyre wasn't sure what to do, but he was very aware that two sharp points were rushing toward him at the same time. If he attacked one, the other would get him. He tried to take a fighting stance, but for some reason, he planted his foot on a loose piece of shale that slid from underneath him, sending his feet from beneath him and landing him hard on the ground as the blades pierced nothing but air where his head had been. He fell onto his back, sending a jolt down his shoulder that made him regret ever leaving the tent this morning.

The guards seemed amused as they looked down on him. Spyre glanced up, feeling more afraid than ever. He couldn't think quickly enough to decide who or how he should attack. Where was this fortune that fate was meant to be giving him? He looked into the eyes of the guard who now fell upon him, pressing a thumb into his injured shoulder and smiling as Spyre's anguished cry echoed through the mountains. The guard raised his sword in his other hand, preparing to skewer Spyre through the gut. He inhaled sharply, wondering if his life would pass before his eyes or if he should just close them.

But the soldier's glinting eyes suddenly went blank, and he crumpled to the ground like a puppet whose strings had just been cut. Dugan must have come to his rescue, but Spyre didn't have time to look around and offer his thanks. There was another threat to deal with. He pushed the lifeless man away from him and looked up to see the second angry soldier in mid-attack.

Spyre let out a yell as he instinctively reeled back, thrusting his weapon in front of him defensively, but the spear was longer than he thought, and before his brain could stop him, the pointed tip slid into the second guard's chest, smoothly finding its way out the other side. Spyre's jaw dropped, mirroring the Gaernod soldier's expression as he fell to his knees, only a few inches from Spyre's face, his own sword raised and primed to pierce Spyre's neck.

Spyre's eyes grew wider as he realized how close the blade had come to meeting its mark, but the soldier's face didn't change as the life slipped away from his eyes. The blood drained from his face as he slumped forward at Spyre's feet.

Gasping, Spyre awkwardly pushed away from the man, entangling himself in his own limbs until he hit a large stone and used it to stand, ignoring the pain where the stone had met the back of his head. Spyre looked around in shock to see Dugan tucking his slingshot back into his belt. He rolled the two guards over the ledge toward Tweogan and out of sight before turning back to Spyre.

"The … the …" Spyre stuttered, pointing to the drop-off. He stopped himself and took a deep breath, placing a hand over his rapidly beating heart, eyes closed. "The bear." He was hyperventilating.

"Gone," Dugan said, smiling victoriously.

"I …" He could feel how shocked his face looked. "I killed someone." He pointed to the ground where a few drops of blood had stained the dirt scarlet, making it look like powdered rust.

Dugan sighed, shaking his head. "You go through the world to make a difference for the better. For everyone's benefit," he reminded Spyre.

Spyre gaped up at him, surprised at his level voice.

"They wanted to destroy everything. They wouldn't have stopped, and they couldn't have been contained." He moved toward Spyre, placing a hand on his shoulder, careful to choose his uninjured arm.

Spyre stared at his hand, not missing the fact that Dugan was actually taking his weakness into consideration.

"You did the only thing that could have been done. Don't blame yourself for it, and especially not for what you must do by the time you're finished."

Dugan moved away, leaving Spyre to stare ahead and come to terms with the reality of what he was doing and how far he still had to go. He helped Spyre to stand and guided him to the other side of the mountain. They looked over the edge.

"Down there is the Cape of Eofot. Beyond that is the sea, and then you'll be very near your destination." Dugan turned Spyre to face him, holding him firmly by the shoulders. The troll sighed, his face more relaxed and eyes gentler than Spyre had ever seen them. "Thank you. You've done what we asked, and you can move on safely."

Spyre nodded and was about to open his mouth to respond, when suddenly Dugan gave him a firm shove and sent him tumbling down the side of the mountain, wide-eyed, toward the Cape of Eofot.

As he fell, Spyre could hear a deep, full-throated laugh.

There was much to see on his trip down the far side of the Aforthian Mountains, but Spyre didn't take in any of it. He was too busy trying to breathe and protect his head, not to mention his throbbing shoulder. He coursed down the side of the mountain, somehow avoiding larger boulders and drops. The slope wasn't gradual, and Spyre often found himself airborne, flopping down the mountain like a rag doll, because what else could he do? He hated Dugan.

Spyre hit a ledge, rolled, and dropped again. He finally came to a halt when he landed in a patch of grass, sending large clouds of pollen flying into the air. He stared at the misty sky for a moment, trying to compose himself and to breathe through his burning lungs, his ribs and back throbbing. He took his time lying on the moist ground. He didn't care where he was or how far he still had to go before he reached Condel. His body wouldn't respond even if he wanted to keep moving. This was too much for Spyre to take in.

"Intruder." A chorus of whispers sang on the salty breeze.

"Evil."

"Killed his own kind."

"Betrayer."

Spyre winced at the accusations that filled his senses, but at least he wasn't falling anymore.

He moaned and rolled onto his side to see a sandy beach and pale green reeds, but no one else was around him. It was silent apart from the continuing whispers. He didn't want to, but he knew he would have to get up and find out what kind of creatures he would encounter here. Beyond trolls, who posed a potential threat, and elves, who occasionally caused a headache for Afor, his people had never really cared about what other species lived in the world.

Spyre sat up and checked to see if he had any major injuries, finding he had twisted and bruised several things, but he seemed relatively fit to move. He stood shakily and looked around. There was nothing around him but tall, brown grass, gently swaying in a breeze that smelled of salt.

"Failure." The voices hissed again.

"Trickster."

Spyre looked around, trying to pinpoint the source of the voices. Were they in his head or on the wind? No, they definitely rose and fell with the breeze. Whatever these creatures were, they were soft spoken, and there were enough of them to fill a whole city. He heard males, females, even children, but there was still nothing but pollen around him. Spyre furrowed his brow, casting his eyes to the side as he realized something.

"Brown grass." He shook his head, confused. He didn't know much about botany, but he knew a bit about nature. "Grass doesn't give off pollen. Flowers do, and—" He looked around again. "Not flowers." He let out a puff of air, shifting his eyes to the things floating around him and muttering. "Okay. Not strange at all. What do I know, anyway?"

"Wasted time."

"Killed."

Spyre firmly planted his foot in the packed sand, looking behind him for the crowd of his accusers.

"Who is that, and what is your problem?" Spyre shouted at the air, frustrated in knowing the voices were right. He sighed, aware of how foolish he looked shouting into the air, but who was around to see?

"Murderer."

"That's not fair," Spyre objected. He looked around and noticed the pollen grouping together unnaturally. "Okay, maybe I'm not as crazy as I thought; that's definitely not pollen."

The specks of cloudy, fuzzy dust surrounded Spyre, whispering his every mistake into his ear.

This was ridiculous. He had to get to the sea and make it to Condel. He didn't have time for stupid specks of dust trying to tell him what he couldn't do right. He waved his hand and sent the nearest specks flying, but as he walked toward the beach, the dust caught up with him, badgering him relentlessly, and to make things worse, as the briny green water came into view, he realized that there was no method for him to cross.

He had hoped that Afor would have left a boat for soldiers like the ones on the mountain to cross if he needed backup in Condel, but no such luck. He tried desperately not to think that his only option was to go all the way back to Tweogan for more wood to build a boat, and he didn't really trust his ability to build a sturdy enough boat in such a short amount of time.

"You don't have the skills to make it," the voices all sounded at once.

"Have you rehearsed this or something?" Spyre called out, turning as the specks surrounded him.

"You've killed. You'll be killed."

"They won't accept a child of Gaernod in their city."

"You might have a problem with that boat issue."

"Afor has more power than you can fight."

"Whoa, whoa, whoa, wait a second," Spyre said, turning on the specks. "Which of you mentioned the boat?"

Among the cloud of dust, one bobbed up and down from the middle of the group. Just one? All those voices from just one creature?

"You?"

The speck stopped.

"Okay, the rest of you, go away." Spyre cleared the surrounding air with his hands. "I don't have time for your attitude. You." He nodded to the slightly more optimistic dust particle. "Come with me."

He turned around and walked, waiting to see if his little friend would care to listen to him. He smiled when he saw a flash of grayish white but took a step back when the dust sharply turned and headed straight for his face, stopping at the last second. Spyre raised his eyebrows momentarily before lowering one into a more skeptical expression.

"You've made mistakes in your time, haven't you?" the speck whispered in every tone of voice imaginable, from young to old and feminine to gruff.

"What are you?"

"We are wisps. And we don't like you."

"I'm not too keen on you right now, either," Spyre countered, "but I need help, and you seem somewhat reasonable."

The wisp remained silent.

"Do you have a name? Or are you all just one—" He moved his hand in a circular motion, as if stirring a pot, searching for the word: "consciousness, hive, colony, or cluster?"

"I am Soru," the wisp responded curtly. "We've seen what you've done. We know what you're doing, but are you really up to it?"

"Do I have a choice?" Spyre laughed.

"Yes, you do. You can still turn back."

Spyre was almost offended. He had convinced himself that he was destined to be on this quest or mission or journey or whatever history would call it, if it even remembered him, and this little wisp—Soru—was telling him he should forfeit with a voice that sounded like an entire kingdom was telling him to give up.

"I can do this, okay?" Spyre protested.

"It's not okay," Soru insisted. "As you've seen, this is real and should be taken seriously."

"I've figured that out, thanks," Spyre quipped.

"There is a boat."

Spyre's ears perked up. He looked at Soru. "What?"

"There is a—"

"You have a boat?" He looked around. He saw nothing but sand and water. "Where is it?"

"How are you going to save us if you can't even use your eyes?"

Spyre was getting angry. He wouldn't respond to Soru, and he definitely wouldn't be asking for any more clues. He would find the boat. He walked along the edge of the water, scouring for any hint of a wooden plank or a mast or just something. He searched until the sand relented to grass, still missing the boat.

The wisp was at his ear. "You've missed it. How have you even made it this far?"

Spyre bit his tongue and kept scanning the shore.

"And now you've wasted enough time that you have to face another challenge for your feeble intelligence."

Spyre nearly flicked the wisp. That would show it.

"The sun has set. Would you rather set out at night and sail for the day or sail at sunrise and face the night in the middle of the sea?"

"I'm guessing I'll be facing a night on the sea either way." Spyre matched Soru's condescending tone and stubbornly folded his arms. "What's there to be afraid of?"

"You're not prepared for this at all. Did you make it this far simply by wishing?"

"Do you mind?" Spyre said, turning on the little speck. He let air escape through his teeth. "Oh, fine. I guess I'll have to call it a day for now." He turned and headed toward the grass. As he sat down, pulling his blanket out of his bag, the wisps swarmed him.

"You're not prepared."

"They won't want your help."

"You're one of the enemy."

The voices filled Spyre's head until it seemed like he didn't have room for his own thoughts. This would not work, and from his experience with the other creatures of Curnen, he knew the wisps couldn't follow him onto the sea. He had to find that boat the weird one had mentioned. He'd swim if he had to. Maybe he could even make a canoe out of the dry grass. Would the journey really be so long?

He shoved his blanket back into his satchel and walked to the water, knowing what he would see. There was no sign of land in the fading light, but it was there somewhere. It would just be a long journey. He walked into the water, allowing the incoming tide to rush over his feet. The cold water was a new sensation, compared to water Spyre was used to. He'd spent his life in Gaernod with nothing but fresh, if muddied, water from a well. The sea was entirely different. Something he'd only heard about. It receded and then returned, and it fascinated Spyre without him knowing exactly why. He walked along the water, indulging in the peaceful feeling it gave him and loving how it put him in another territory where the wisps wouldn't follow.

"It would be nice," one of multivoiced wisps said from the edge of the water.

Spyre turned. It was Soru, he guessed.

"It would be nice to cross the sea."

"That's a rather genuine thing to say," Spyre commented, as he trudged through the water.

"You wouldn't know."

Instead of using words to express his anger, Spyre kicked at the water instead. He regretted this the second that his foot came in contact with something solid beneath the surface.

"Ow," he shouted, staggering backward.

"Oh, look. You've found the boat," Soru said. The speck had no face, but Spyre was sure it was grinning.

Spyre furrowed his brow in confusion. He looked down and kicked the hollow object among the matted seaweed and algae again. "What? That's the boat? It's underwater. How is that useful?"

"Well, it holds water well. Imagine how it'll do keeping water out."

Spyre laughed at how ridiculous that sounded. "I don't think you quite understand how this works."

"I don't think *you* do," Soru said. "I'm not surprised." The wisp moved back and forth, almost as if it was pacing. "The boat is only a few days old. It was among the boats that Afor took across the sea."

Spyre followed Soru with his eyes. "So what's it still doing here?"

The wisp was quiet for a moment. "Shortly after they set off, one of your men asked a question that Afor did not approve of. Afor decided that the soldier no longer needed transportation. The boat returned to us on the tide."

Despicable. Afor had killed one of his own people before even seeing the scale of Condel. Spyre wasn't sure if he was more enraged by Afor's blatant disregard for others' lives or by his arrogance toward Condel.

"If you have the strength to turn it over, which seems unlikely," Soru said, "you might find that the boat is just what you need."

Spyre ignored the parts of Soru's comment that weren't helpful and squatted next to the submerged vessel to feel for its size and girth in the water. It was twice as long and almost as wide as he was tall. The water inside made it too heavy for him to lift himself, and the wisps didn't appear to have any arms, let alone the willingness to help him. He would need something else. He looked around. Grass, sand, a few rocks at the base of the mountain. He could think of one option.

He went back to the mountain, a much shorter distance than what he and Dugan had walked to Tweogan. There were several sizable rocks he could stack under the boat on one side and inside the boat on another. That way, he could at least get some water out, but it would take time. He bent over and grabbed a few of the bigger rocks until a color he didn't expect caught his eye.

There was a straight, brown stick poking out of a small pile of rocks. It was his spear, and next to that was his bow, along with the used arrows, but he didn't remember having them when he'd tumbled down the mountain. They would have skewered him on the way down. Dugan must have thrown them down after him. He pulled the spear out of the rocks and saw the blood that remained on the point as he slipped the bow over his head and onto his shoulder, tucking the arrows into his satchel.

Rocks in the crook of one arm and the spear in the other, Spyre walked back to the water, trying not to let his anger at himself get to him. Wisps circled around him, commenting on the blood, but he kept his face stern and focused on the push and pull of the tide against the sand. He dipped the spear in the water and allowed the sea to wash away the evidence of his mistake.

Feeling slightly better, he went to the boat, stood in the water next to it, and placed rocks against the inside. He walked to the other side and placed one rock as a fulcrum, using his spear as a lever and using his anger to thrust it well underneath the boat. Glaring, he pushed down on the spear with both arms, feeling the boat budge just slightly. He held the spear in position and jumped, putting more of his weight on it.

The boat moved a little more, and the rocks he had set in it fell against the side, tilting the boat farther. He jumped again and freed the boat from the suction of the sand. One more jump, and the boat moved much easier. The rocks tumbled against it, and the boat rolled onto its side, emptying some of the water that had filled it.

Spyre caught the boat before it could fall backward and stuck the spear underneath it again. He was getting out of this place, and he was getting out now. He couldn't stand to be in the company of the wisps anymore.

"Do you imagine that you can escape who you are?" Soru asked from behind him. "Haven't you already proven that you are a true citizen of Gaernod? You killed without a thought."

"Stop it," Spyre shouted, still holding onto the spear but not moving.

He'd killed someone. He wasn't happy about it, but he did it to defend Dugan and the other trolls. He closed his eyes, making a promise to himself. If he could help it, it would never happen again.

"I will save more people. I won't let myself mess this up, and I'll use what I did to remind me of what I don't want to be." His head dropped, and his eyes closed tightly as the shame that the memory incurred overwhelmed him.

He sighed, pushing the guilt from his mind. "I won't let this kind of thing happen to other people. If it wasn't for Afor, this wouldn't be happening. What do you expect me to do when I meet him? Scold him and let him walk away, hoping he'll learn his lesson? I won't be like him, but I can't just do nothing." He turned his head, still not fully facing Soru. "You're telling me I have to save you, but what exactly do you want?"

Soru remained silent.

"Exactly. You want Afor gone, but you don't want to do it, so you think you can judge me." Holding the spear in place with one hand, Spyre turned to face the wisp. "What about you should make me want to save you?"

Soru dipped in the air for a moment.

"I will try," Spyre assured it in a softer voice. "But please, don't make this harder on me than it already is, okay? It's just not helping." With a final push, the boat flipped over, and the spear snapped.

Spyre grabbed the edge of the boat and dragged it back to land, where he could flip it right-side up without having to worry about refilling it with water. He checked the inside. It had plenty of space and two parallel planks for seating that could easily fit four people Spyre's size. The wood was still in decent shape, and there were no leaks. It could make at least one more trip. Spyre cracked a smile.

"The sun is set," Soru said from behind him, hovering at the edge of the water. "Will you still depart tonight?"

"Once I make a sail here," Spyre said, fishing in his bag for his blanket.

He scooped wet sand from the water and piled it in the boat's middle, sticking his spear in the pile and pinning his blanket to the spear with his two arrows. He would be at the mercy of the wind, but he was bound to hit the next coast, eventually.

"Do you require company?" the many whispered voices offshore asked.

Spyre paused. He turned to Soru. "You want to come with me?" he asked, slightly baffled. "But I thought you couldn't move from one realm to the other."

Soru floated past Spyre and out over the water. "The Modwen Sea is a middle ground. There is no restriction because it has no specified species. Wisps have gone to sea before, but the winds and tides pose a formidable danger to us, and none have ever returned."

"But with me you can make it?" Spyre turned his face away suspiciously. There had to be an ulterior motive here somewhere.

"Whispers tell of a forest where beautiful and graceful creatures live on the other side of the sea," Soru said.

Spyre's eyebrows rose in surprise. He had thought, and hoped, that Condel would be his next stop. What was this about another forest?

"The legend of them is too old to measure, but I have always wondered …"

"What creatures?" Spyre didn't want to think of what could be worse than trolls and wisps.

"They call them pinewood sprites," Soru explained. "They are peaceful creatures."

"I can see why you wouldn't believe they exist," Spyre said, noting the irony of peaceful creatures in Curnen.

"You could not last even a day among us," Soru noted. "Imagine belonging here. You left Gaernod for the same reason."

Spyre's wit failed him, and he fell silent. It would only be a few days, and it might be nice to have company. He looked at Soru and somberly nodded his agreement. "Yeah, why not? You can come along."

"But let me offer you some advice," Soru said almost immediately. "Your sail will require almost constant attention with nothing to keep it open and the sand needing to be re-soaked as it dries."

Spyre knew that.

"You should rest before you go. It will do no good to leave fatigued. I will tell the rest of my kin to leave you to your own thoughts. They will give you peace."

Spyre nodded his appreciation, sighing in relief. He stepped out of the boat and allowed himself to collapse on the sand. This would do. He wasn't feeling picky. It was a warm night; the sand was soft, and he was exhausted. He watched the wisp return to the others, and the specks dispersed from their cloud formation to blend back into the mist. Would they stay that way if Spyre slept? Was the paranormal force still at work to protect him, if it was there at all?

His body decided for him. Even as he tried to keep himself awake, he constantly found himself jolting out of dosing. Finally, he stopped fighting it.

CHAPTER 16

Eofyn and Pyram made it to the temple. Eofyn had to admit that he was excited to see what was inside.

They came to a strange, sheltered doorway with no obvious door, just three walls, the farthest with a peculiar indentation on it. Eofyn approached the far wall, running his hand along the strange T-shaped mark as if recalling a memory.

"What do you think it is?" Pyram asked him while checking over his shoulder for signs of the soldiers.

Eofyn laughed softly, distracted. "I thought you were the one with all the cunning."

"Hey, nothing I snooped around in back at the castle mentioned this stuff." Pyram turned his attention to the open desert behind them. If the Gaernods knew he was watching, maybe they would keep their distance for a while longer.

"Well, what do we know?" Eofyn asked, puzzling over the room. "The tablet at the border said what we seek is before us."

"The temple," Pyram said, as if it was that simple.

"Just the temple, though?" Eofyn turned to him as he spoke. He pointed at the hole in the wall, processing. "I think it could apply here too, but there's something off."

"Yeah," Pyram agreed, turning back. "Like what do we put in there to make the thing open up?"

"What we want is before us, but—" He thought about the rest of the words from the tablet and smiled at the memory of his father. "It's all about the journey." He looked to the sidewalls. "Exactly. See here?" He pointed to the walls where shallow markings could be seen if you looked for them.

Pyram saw the marking and looked to the opposite wall. "Yep, we've got one over here too."

"It looks like ..." Eofyn put his hand to the marking. It was a little smaller than his own, but it definitely was a handprint. "But how are you supposed to do both at once?" he muttered. Then he looked at his friend. Another idea his father had always held dear: never go alone.

"Pyram, you push that one. I've got this one."

Pyram nodded and placed his hand on the wall without hesitation. No result.

Eofyn furrowed his brow and absently slid his hand to the area around the print. "I've never seen so much dust in my life."

He brushed away the cobwebs and dirt that caked and coated the walls like a time-woven tapestry, and sure enough, he revealed a circular outline. He turned to see that Pyram had been watching over his shoulder. Pyram gave him an affirmative nod, and they each pressed their hands into the stone prints, twisting them in the direction that gave way, right for Eofyn and left for Pyram.

The stone creaked in protest, complaining that someone had disturbed its millennial slumber. Several thunks, and creaks, and sounds of rolling rocks followed from above them, and a small rope fell from a narrow hole in the ceiling they hadn't noticed before. At the end of the rope was an object that was long and thin, about the length of both of Eofyn's fists, and the top of it extended past its cylindrical base. It was ornately designed, but one thing was clear: it would fit the space in the other wall. Eofyn approached the key and untied it from the ancient string.

"Wait," Pyram blurted, earning a frown from Eofyn. "When we get in there," he said, "you realize that it will not be a direct path to the source. We will probably have to search the temple for quite some time."

Eofyn smiled at him, finally feeling confident. "I understand that, but we've done well so far. I feel like we can do this."

Pyram let out a disheartened sigh.

"Let's just ... take our time," he said.

Eofyn looked back at him like he was insane. "Pyram, I understand trying not to put too much pressure on ourselves, but this isn't a vacation. We need to find the source and get it back to Condel."

Pyram raised his hands in surrender. "All I'm saying is that we should be careful."

Those words never came out of Pyram's mouth unless they were about to be busted by his father's stewards, but those days were long gone. Pyram had always been quick to jump in headfirst, followed closely by his slightly more reluctant prince.

Eofyn looked at his friend, questioning with his eyes. Pyram responded with a tight-lipped nod, and now Eofyn knew what was coming. They weren't alone. He should have known by the urgent pulse of Pyram's crystal since they'd made it to Tir, but Eofyn understood now. He hoped Pyram could take some consolation in that. They would know what to do when the time came.

They moved into the darkness of the temple, guided by the light of Pyram's crystal. The first room was vast, with carvings on the floors and unlit torches on the walls. Torches, not crystals. Crystals weren't discovered until the old tribe settled in Condel, so they wouldn't have had crystals here. Maybe that was a smart idea.

Pyram lowered himself to his knees and inspected the carvings on the floor. "This is the story," he said. "Look, you can see right here." He laid his hand next to an image of a man kneeling on top of a pile of stones, face lifted upward as lines of light fell upon him. He looked at Eofyn, smiling crookedly. "It's like your first family scrapbook, Fyn."

Eofyn knelt next to him and stared at the stick figure image of his ancestor. It felt so strange to be in the place where it all began, where no one had been since. He felt an odd bond between his ancestor and himself, both looking for help to better their kingdom. His distant grandfather had found it, and Eofyn would follow in his footsteps, almost precisely. If all went well, maybe the source would inspire Eofyn's connection to Bryta to at last establish itself, as it had for his forebear.

He stood. Pyram had already risen.

"So which way do you think?" Eofyn asked casually, but he couldn't take his eyes off of the floor.

"Not the alcove near the exit, that's for sure," Pyram responded quietly, alluding to the location of the soldiers who had crept in behind them.

For the first time, Eofyn and Pyram desperately wished that, in all of their infinite wisdom, at least one previous king would have thought to build an army for Condel. They were defenseless against the trained men behind them.

"Uh …" Pyram said louder so that the soldiers wouldn't get too suspicious. He tapped Eofyn's shoulder and jerked a thumb to the rightmost door.

Eofyn nodded, and they moved toward the doorway at the right end of the room. It had been a good choice, considering there were only three doors in the main chamber: the entrance, to the right, and to the left, mirroring the puzzle at the entrance, and that suggested the same design.

What they sought would be in front of them, directly through the wall. All they had to do was take the journey through the halls to get there. There was no door in their way. They walked through into another corridor that curved into a long hallway. Clearly, this temple would not be a complex maze, which was good, but that also gave them less time to form a plan. Eofyn glanced at Pyram and could practically see the gears turning in his head. This would be interesting.

They followed the hallway in a quarter-circle, seeing only dust, cobwebs, and unlit torches. How had they lit them so long ago? Pyram's crystal flared, and Eofyn could only hope he'd had an idea. When they came to another doorway, Pyram put a hand on Eofyn's shoulder so Eofyn would let him pass through first, in case of traps or any other danger that might be waiting in the dark. He held his crystal out and quickly scanned the room before taking in its design. Pyram relaxed ever so slightly, leaving Eofyn to wonder why.

"Wow," Eofyn said breathlessly, as he stepped into the room.

In the chamber's middle was a replica of the same stone mound that had been in the drawings of the main chamber, but something that had not been in the mural was visible at the top of the pile. Eofyn approached it without waiting.

It felt familiar, like a family heirloom. He placed his hand on the stone first and felt a cool, calming sensation, as though everything finally made sense. He couldn't specify exactly what made sense, but his fears and panic subsided. He closed his eyes and inhaled more deeply than he'd ever been able to before.

"Is this it?" he heard Pyram ask behind him. He sounded edgy, as though he was hoping Eofyn would confirm the source so he could finally call out the Gaernods, or at least start running.

But that didn't bother Eofyn in this moment. He felt calm, almost wise, and somehow he knew. "No. It's not here."

Pyram's jaw dropped a little. Someone moved in the dust, and Pyram positioned himself by the wall. Based on their actions the night of the invasion, the soldiers would go for Eofyn first so they could disarm Pyram with a knife to the king's throat, but Pyram would fight them first. The shadows moved toward Eofyn, who remained entranced in the dark. Pyram reached up.

Eofyn felt strong fingers curl around his clavicle. His serene stupor shattered to be replaced by immobilizing pain.

"Fyn, catch!"

Eofyn could not open his eyes through the pain, but he could tell which direction the sound had come from. He raised his hand and felt something hit his palm. He curled his fingers around it just before it bounced to the ground and saw a flash of light before the soldier's grip on his shoulder vanished.

Free of the pain, he opened his eyes and saw a lit torch in his hand. But how?

Pyram flashed past him, lighting another torch from Eofyn's and running at the soldiers. He used the torch as a sword and thrust it toward their faces, sending them reeling, but it wasn't long before they regained their composure and drew their real weapons.

One guard threw a dagger that whizzed past Eofyn's ear, and he ducked behind the rock for cover, soon joined by Pyram.

Pyram grabbed Eofyn's shirt. "It lit because of you, Fyn. You're the heir to the Pure Fyre. It channels through you."

Eofyn couldn't process what Pyram was saying. His mind was still clouded, and he could hear the guards running for them. One slid around the rock and grabbed Pyram, disabling him with an elbow to the head and pinning his arms behind his back.

"You have it," Pyram muttered through the oncoming darkness that swirled his vision as he tried to kick his way to freedom, looking almost intoxicated. The second guard apprehended Eofyn, but he was too focused on Pyram's words to care.

"It didn't skip you," Pyram said; his voice was weak but desperate as his head dropped heavily to his chest, and his knees buckled beneath him. "Figure it out, Fyn. Figure it out."

The guards were dragging them toward opposite sides of the room, and soon Pyram was out of sight, and Eofyn felt the distinct sensation of a rock slamming into the back of his head before he, too, saw only darkness.

CHAPTER 17

"By the souls of Bryta, what is that?"

Ness shot up, clearing her grogginess as her mother released a string of profanities that would otherwise have burned the girl's ears. She rubbed her eyes and shuddered when the world came into focus to reveal Losian smiling at her like he had evidence for blackmail.

"I stand corrected," he said smugly. "You won't get killed out there. Mom will kill you." He looked over at their mother, who was pacing around the kitchen. "Right about now, I should think."

"What?" Ness snapped, becoming more alert by the second. She looked around and located her mother, who was finally turning her fierce gaze to Ness. She knew. "Oh. Oh, no, no, no." How did she find out?

"Ness," her mother said, staring at her, eyes fierce. "Ness."

Ness gazed at her, dumbstruck.

"Ness," she said again, scaring the girl more than Afor himself had the night before.

She could still feel a strange, cold sensation in her chest from when her crystal had shorted out, but her mother's wrath seemed much more dangerous right now.

"Ness." Elene was looking expectant now.

Oh, for the love of— "Yes, Mother?"

"What is this?" Her mother shoved a piece of paper in her face.

Ness leaned back to take the view in properly. Her eyes saw the sketched picture, and she read the words.

"Oh no," she said, breathing heavily. It was a wanted poster. They must have forced Atelle or one of the maids to describe her. Or they had Atelle send them telepathic image of her. What were the people left in the castle going through now because of her?

It sent a chill through her to imagine that the soldiers had been right outside her door, posting her picture across the kingdom. And her mother had found it. Now she was in trouble.

Her father entered the room. Her mother looked at him, nodding as she held the poster at arm's length. "Wanted for treason against the king," Elene announced from memory. "Breaking into the king's castle, manipulating the king's servants, infiltrating the king's private council. Oh, and they've apparently set a curfew, because you've violated that as well." She slammed the paper down on the table. "What have you been doing?"

"Elene," Darian intervened. "Try to stay calm. We don't want your stress to affect the baby."

Elene spun on him. "She's been sneaking out, Darian. Into the castle."

Darian slid a chair behind Elene and gently sat her down while Ness debated the consequences of breathing.

Darian eyed the poster from behind Elene. "Ness, what happened?" he asked softly.

Ness could hear the pain he was trying to hide, though he didn't seem surprised to discover her secret.

"I had to know more about why the lights are almost out, Dad," Ness explained in almost a whisper. She sat back, looking to the side, remembering. "And I found out more than I imagined. He's got a crystal, and it's bright as the sun."

She watched for a reaction from her parents. They were unmoved, knowing the worst was yet to be told. She sighed and braced herself.

"I had to know more." She explained to them what had happened the night before, reliving it and seeing it all happen again in her mind, including what Afor had done to her crystal.

Everyone's eyes widened in response.

"And when I pulled myself back together, I got a little mad. I ... may have possibly ... broken the window in the throne room," she finished, knitting her fingers together.

Elene's head fell into her hands as she nearly cried. Ness's face fell, and she had to look away. She hated to see her mother like this. Her father rubbed his pregnant wife's shoulders, trying to comfort her. His own face looked pained and even guilty, eyes shut against the news of his daughter with a dead crystal, but he didn't look Ness in the eyes.

Darian took in a deep breath and said, "You must get out there and take as many of those posters down as you can."

Elene quickly looked back at him, outraged.

"We can't have the people turning Ness in because they're afraid of what Afor will do, and she'll move faster than I can," he tried to explain. "It's still early. The sun's barely up. If she goes now, most of the kingdom won't have seen the poster at all, and the rest can claim they didn't." He looked at his daughter with sad eyes. "Go, Ness. Get it done."

Ness stood up, briefly revealing her pants before she quickly pushed her gray dress back down over them, wincing.

"Oh, how long has this been going on?" Elene moaned into her hands.

Ness looked at her father, wondering if she should answer, but Darian shook his head grimly. Ness frowned, ashamed of the pain she'd caused, and picked her way over the blankets on the floor. She quickly slipped out the door, grabbing a cloak as she went to do damage control.

Ness had finally taken down every poster. She'd been extremely careful not to allow anyone to see her, Condols and Gaernods alike. It would only have led to trouble, so after hours of peeking around corners and ducking away from windows, checking and rechecking every wall in the town, Ness headed home. The sun had long since set, and she slipped back into the house; her mother was waiting at the table. She still looked angry and drained.

"Mom," Ness said feebly, but Elene held up a hand.

"Did you get them? All of them?"

"I got them," Ness said, feeling ashamed. She waited for a moment, hoping it wasn't too soon to address the tension in the room. "Mom, I didn't mean to scare you. I just had to see what was going on. What if we hadn't figured out what Afor's up to?"

"What difference does it make?" Elene asked wearily, bringing her hand down on the table. "Ness, he made your crystal go out. Do you know what that means?"

Ness was only too aware of what that meant. She nodded, stifling the tears she'd been suppressing. She had been afraid, petrified. She'd nearly died. If Afor did that to her in just one night, what was he doing to the girl in the castle under constant exposure to his power?

"I know," Ness said delicately. But she wasn't sorry. "But Mom, now that we know, we can find out how to stop him. He breaks our wills. He's draining all of us. The lamps are basically extinguished. I was close to him, so it went a lot faster, but he's still draining me now. He's draining all of us. That's why our crystals are so weak." She pointed to the streetlamps outside the window to remind them. "We have to stop him. As long as he's here, he's stealing our power for his own crystal." She paused, knowing what would happen once she continued. "I need to keep watching him."

"No," Elene snapped, scoffing at her daughter's ignorance. "You're not leaving this house again."

"Elene," Darian protested softly as he came into the room. Ness noticed all their guests kept to themselves upstairs. She was sure her father had explained everything in the most diplomatic way possible.

"What?" Elene asked as she turned in her chair, resting an arm on the back of it and giving Darian the look.

"She was trying to help us," Darian offered feebly.

"She almost died."

"She knew how and when to get out."

"Darian, she crashed through the castle window," Elene retorted flatly.

Darian paused before giving an acquiescing nod.

"Mom." Ness stood firm, fists at her sides. "I was out in the kingdom all day. No one is on the streets, and there are hardly any soldiers. The only ones out there are just there because they have to look for me. They don't consider us a threat at all. We're just eating out of their hands. How can you be okay with that?"

Elene leaned toward Ness. "What you're forgetting, young lady, is that you're not the queen of this kingdom. Our king is probably on his way back to fix everything by now. Leave the kingdom to the king, would you?"

"Because he's done such a great job," Ness mumbled under her breath. She looked away angrily.

Elene visibly fumed. "Get to bed. I don't want to hear anything else about the castle or Afor coming out of your mouth."

Ness was angry, but she knew an argument with her mother could never end in her favor. She walked around the kitchen table and awkwardly organized her covers.

"Not there," her mother said.

Ness turned around, blanket in hand, staring at her mother, trying not to look as aggravated as she was.

"You're staying in my room, on the floor, where I can keep an eye on you." Elene gave Ness a stony glare that dared her to argue.

Ness's jaw dropped as she nearly took the bait to complain about how unfair her mother was being, but a pleading glance from her father silenced her. Her mother was only concerned, her father's face told her.

Ness admitted that losing her Fyre had been a serious problem, but she had recovered. She didn't know if she could do that another time, but she wouldn't allow herself to get into that situation again, either. She wanted to say something that would resolve the issue, at least for now, but there were really no words that made up for what she'd done, even if she didn't think it was the wrong thing. Instead, she kept her thoughts to herself and took her blankets up to her mother and father's room.

She entered the room and carelessly tossed her blankets on the floor; as she sat down, she thought she heard something.

Ness … Miss Ness, are you there? Oh, I hope you're all right.

It took Ness a moment to realize that she wasn't hearing anything in the room with her. She looked around for the source of the sound, but when the realization hit her, she focused.

Atelle? She stared at the ceiling as though Atelle was calling to her from the roof. *I hear you, and I'm fine. What's going on?*

What's going on? Atelle asked incredulously. *How can you be so casual? You're lucky to be alive, in more ways than one. Poor Miss Lissa has been in a panic all day. There are posters everywhere, even inside the castle.*

Inside? Oh great. There went her chances of getting back in. She threw down her pillow in frustration.

You want to continue? Atelle had clearly overheard more than she'd intended. *Forgive me, but are you feeling stable?*

Now you sound like my mom. She groaned.

She almost thought she heard Atelle sigh. *Miss Ness. You won't be able to get back into the castle. Afor has promised a reward to anyone who spots you and turns you in, and I can't take down the posters of you, or I'll be killed.*

They were both silent for a while as Ness sulked, looking out the window as the moonlight poured in.

What I can do, Atelle continued in a lighter tone, *is keep you informed on what is going on within the castle, and you can try to make some sort of impact from outside, if you must.*

Really? You'll do that?

Can I really leave you to your own devices? Atelle asked. *I'm doing this as a favor to you and to your father. I'll be able to keep watch over you while you watch Afor.*

Just don't tell my mom, and we'll be okay.

CHAPTER 18

Spyre felt it was finally time to leave this place. Things had to get better from here. If Soru was right, and the sea was the middle ground of Curnen, then maybe the creatures he'd encounter there wouldn't be so bent on putting him down. He had to admit that he was looking forward to a conversation that didn't include insults and fatal challenges.

The night had been a good one. He'd slept lightly, but at least he hadn't been sleeping just because someone had knocked him out. Morning mist saturated his clothes in a salty damp, but the bright of the sun behind the curtain of clouds was warming the air by the minute. He sat up, brushing sand off of his ragged clothes, ready to get that boat on the water. He saw Soru floating near the waterline. Either wisps didn't sleep, or this speck of dust was excited. He smiled, confident that Soru was ready to cast off.

Spyre hopped into the boat and checked his poor excuse for a sail, feeling fantastic. He had no idea what waited in this next forest, but the creatures there sounded nice enough, and as for whatever lay beyond that before he finally made it to Condel, he'd just have to handle it. He would get there. Hopefully, it would still be in one piece when he finally did.

He jumped out and pushed the boat back into the water. It floated, but he waited a few moments to double-check that there were no holes. It stayed afloat. Spyre smiled. Something was finally going according to plan. He finally had a plan. Compared to the uncertainty of yesterday, this was fantastic.

He didn't let himself think too much about the day before. When he felt the memory of the soldier's eyes creeping into his head, he moved to the back of the boat and looked to Soru, who was hovering just under the edge of the vessel, protected from the sea wind. Spyre cupped water in his hands and poured it on top of the pile of sand that would help to keep the sail upright. In truth, he was impressed that it worked so well. He looked back at Soru.

"So how does the wind usually behave? I don't have a paddle or anything."

He glanced back to the shore, scanning to see if there was anything he could use to build an oar, but there was nothing but sand, grass, and a few rocks. He still had his whittling tool and his blooming piece of art, but that wasn't big enough to use.

Soru rose and fell back quickly, like it was shrugging. "There is not much known about the Modwen. We will have to wait and see."

"Well, on that note of optimism, let's do this."

Spyre pushed the boat with a few steps and hopped in as it went out with the tide. He moved to the sail and held it open, feeling relieved when it swelled and propelled the boat forward. The plan was to sail as straight as possible, but he knew it was unrealistic to believe he could actually do so. He also knew his arms would tire of holding his sail open, but that was a small price to pay for getting a step closer to Condel.

He had to do whatever it took to get there in time to save their king. But really, that idea seemed slimmer by the day. Afor had to have made it to Condel by now, and Spyre couldn't think of a reason why he would keep the king alive. But he also had a gut feeling that all hope was not yet lost. None of it made sense, but neither did turning back.

The sea was choppy, but it didn't seem to slow the boat much. Spyre was actually enjoying himself as he struggled and adapted with the change of the wind. Sure, it was work, but the mechanics and the progress that came of it satisfied him. Now this felt like an adventure. He realized that what he'd been doing for the past few days probably counted as adventurous, but he hadn't really had the time to stop and think about it like that. This, the boat bobbing up and down over swells on the sea, felt like an enjoyable epic journey, even if they could still see land on the horizon behind them. That would soon change.

Every current, every second was taking him somewhere that he knew was better. He was leaving his part of the world and headed toward the other, the part that everyone knew was more privileged. It would be a sweet moment when he set foot on those shores.

Spyre looked down to see Soru still hovering below the edge of the boat. It was not exactly safe for the wisp to be any higher. It feared the wind. With good reason. It remained underneath a ledge that extended a few inches inward around the rim of the boat, but from there, Soru would miss the whole journey it'd waited its whole life to take. That didn't seem right to Spyre.

He looked around the boat for options. Deciding what he'd have to do, Spyre held the sail with his left hand, to spare his injured shoulder, and moved a part of the gunwale trim back and forth, loosening it from the rest of the boat. The wood was soft from being submerged at the beach, so the plank came loose rather easily, leaving its nails in the lower piece of wood. He tugged on them until they, too, came loose.

"Do you have a specific reason for destroying our means of transportation?" Soru asked, bobbing in the air where it hid.

Spyre, working on a second plank and two loose nails, just motioned with a sharp tilt of his head that Soru should wait a moment for the explanation. The nails came loose with the board this time. Spyre let go of the sail completely, and the boat lost velocity. He wasn't bothered. This wouldn't take long.

Spyre took the wood and nails to the rim that was still intact near Soru. He pulled his knife from his bag and broke both of the boards in two over his knee. He used the handle of his knife to hammer the first two halves to the existing ledge, another piece to the top, and the final piece to the back, leaving an opening that faced the opposite side of the boat. Kneeling, Spyre held out his cupped hands toward Soru. The wisp didn't move.

"Hop in, so to speak," Spyre said with a shrug. "I'll keep the wind away until you can get in your little cubbyhole."

Soru bobbed in what Spyre guessed was a wisp's gesture for hesitation but finally floated into Spyre's hands and followed his movements toward the new viewing box. It floated inside and didn't make a sound, but Spyre assumed that was just the way wisps gawked at things. Spyre smiled at it and went back to his sail.

"Thank you," Soru said stiffly a few moments later.

Spyre's smile grew wider. It was nice to hear something positive. Phrases like "thank you" weren't used much in the Gaernod culture, and the elves and trolls hadn't seemed too acquainted with them, either, but Soru had just slipped up. It had even sounded heartfelt, and maybe that was because everything it said came out in a whisper of countless voices, but Spyre took what he could get.

"So is it everything you'd hoped for?" Spyre asked, tugging on the edges of the sail to keep it inflated with the direction of the wind.

"We've only just begun to cross Modwen," Soru cautioned. "This isn't even a fraction of what the sea has to offer."

Spyre looked at the wisp, feeling intrigued.

"Whispers of violent weather patterns and mystifying creatures have often reached the shore of Eofot."

"Do you guys just have that keen of hearing, or are we talking legends here?" Spyre asked, one eyebrow raised as he leaned over the edge of the boat to get more water for his sail's foundation.

Soru remained silent for a moment before remarking, "The winds of the sea are different. Something about the water carries words on the current and back to our ears."

"I guess I shouldn't be questioning whispers on the wind with something like you right in front of me," Spyre admitted. "I mean, do you even have ears? You're a floating ball of fluff. I don't even know if you're a man or a woman, or if that even matters to you."

"I am neither," Soru said flatly.

"That's an answer I was hoping you'd keep to yourself." It begged the question of whether or not Spyre had only hallucinated the existence of wisps. He hoped not, seeing as he had otherwise just built a little house for his imaginary friend.

"Did you ever try whispering back?" Spyre asked, as it occurred to him. "All this time, you could have been passing secrets with that species you're looking forward to meeting." He looked at Soru for a response, but once again, the speck remained silent. Spyre really wished Soru had a face. He could never tell what the wisp was thinking.

"Are you sure you want to know?" Soru asked.

"Not anymore," Spyre replied shortly, looking back to his sail. "Though it might be useful every once in a while."

"Get used to not understanding things," Soru said harshly. "You're very far out of your element here."

Spyre frowned at the speck. "So I've noticed. And you don't seem very interested in helping. I know you don't exactly have hands to help with anything, but if you're going to be here, a little moral support wouldn't kill you. You could stand to be more civil."

Soru hovered lower. "I understand your point. This must be a difficult journey for you, and I'm sorry that your company has been so hard on you."

"No one has been worse than my own people on this trip," Spyre admitted, rubbing his shoulder and laughing at the irony. "They shot me with my own invention, tried to skewer me with a sword, and that's probably only half of what would have happened if I'd stayed in the kingdom."

"Perhaps you should consider no longer calling the Gaernods your people," Soru proposed thoughtfully. "You no longer live in their kingdom, you don't agree with their customs, and you don't affiliate with their people. I would say you no longer fit the description of a Gaernod, except for your physical appearance."

Spyre's eyebrows rose in surprise. He hadn't expected Soru to say something so positive, and he hadn't expected to agree with it so easily. Spyre was a Gaernod-born nomad, hopefully soon to be a citizen of Condel, but an uncomfortable thought occurred to him.

"What if I'm not accepted in Condel?" he asked, not to discount the faith and pressure all the creatures had put on him, but more because he realized that he did look physically different. His skin was slightly darker than that of the gifted people, who were rarely tanned by the sun, and his eyes, though not brown like other Gaernods, were a much darker blue than a Condel's. And he had no ability with a crystal. Would they consider him to be too much of a misfit? Well, that wasn't really something he could worry about now, was it?

A larger swell hit the boat, and Spyre planted his feet more firmly, holding onto the sail as it knocked Soru into the side of its alcove. Spyre looked around and noticed that the sea had in fact become rougher, and there were now dark clouds on the horizon.

"For some reason, I expected bright rays of sparkling sunshine to be coming from that direction," Spyre joked as he moved with the boat to stay on his seat. "The dark clouds are supposed to be behind us, aren't they?"

"Am I supposed to give an answer? I fear you'll lecture me on my attitude again if I do," Soru commented facetiously, but Spyre appreciated its wit. "Those clouds appear to be moving away from us. We won't catch up to them for quite some time."

Spyre looked at the wisp, liking its logic. Maybe it wasn't a storm. Maybe it was a sheet of gray clouds that just happened to make the waves more active. Nothing to worry about here. Nothing at all.

The sea was boring.

They spent an entire sleepless night on the water, navigating the waves toward the darkening clouds. There was no longer any land in sight, and Spyre wondered how he'd have the strength to continue for much longer. Modwen wasn't the largest body of water in the world, but it had separated the two portions of Curnen well enough throughout history. He estimated, and hoped, that he only had about another day of travel before he would see the blessed coastline.

Soru was becoming impatient as well. As far as dust went, Spyre was almost certain that Soru was exhibiting excitement. It was hard to tell because it kept to its little hutch to escape the wind, but Soru's silence and its tone when it did speak were signs enough.

"So what are you going to do when we get there?" Spyre ventured to make conversation.

"I should like to see a sprite," Soru confessed. "And trees. The trees sound magnificent."

Spyre furrowed his brow. "How do whispers on tides provide enough information for you to know all of this? I mean, I accept that they exist, but do you hear entire conversations or captain's logs? How old are these whispers?"

Soru was quiet for a moment, hovering, and Spyre wasn't sure if he was hesitating to avoid admitting that he didn't know or if there was a more weighted answer.

"They are only a few days old," Soru admitted. "They came from your men as they landed at Laefa Pinewood. The wind caught their reactions to the landscape, and we were able to understand them."

"So that's a wisp thing, is it?" Spyre asked, ignoring his feelings at the mention of Gaernod soldiers. "Wisps can hear sea whispers better than other creatures?"

"We live on the edge of the sea and always have. It has become instinct to interpret the whispers. You've known nothing like the wind of the sea, so naturally you won't hear its voices."

"Naturally," Spyre agreed flatly. "Well, if you hear anything important, feel free to let me in on it, okay?"

"I have been hearing things since we set off," Soru stated matter-of-factly.

Spyre gaped at it. "Well, what have they been saying? Are there still soldiers there? Should I maybe not have broken my spear? Why didn't you say this before?"

"You're overreacting," Soru said calmly. "There are no soldiers. It is the sprites."

"I thought you said they might just be legends?"

"Apparently, they are not."

"Well, what are they saying?" Spyre asked, emphasizing his words with frustration.

Soru remained silent as Spyre regained his composure. "They know we are coming," the wisp finally revealed. "They are waiting for you, and they want you to know you are nearing your destination but that you have much still ahead of you."

Spyre had gone from happy to frustrated in two seconds. "So Condel is close, but Afor's beaten me to it," Spyre surmised, more to himself than to Soru. "I'm going to have to fight him." The words felt so unnatural coming from his mouth.

"You knew that before you set to sea," Soru reminded him without sympathy. "They also want you to know you should take better control of the boat as we near the dark clouds."

Spyre looked up and realized that they were indeed catching up to the weather. He considered asking Soru to find out what was in the clouds, but he knew he'd see for himself soon enough. The clouds created a dense fog that Spyre couldn't see through, and he knew his navigation would become even more difficult. He splashed more water onto the sand in the boat, packing it tighter for added support on the sail. He heard no wind, but that didn't mean that it wasn't there. Apparently, there were also entire dialogues going on around him that he was unaware of.

They were entering the edge of the fog now, and it suddenly didn't look so gray. The threatening feel of it faded. Maybe it was just a part of the sea environment, a common product of atmospheric conditions. Who was he to question nature?

The wind died.

The boat slowed, idly floating deeper into the mist.

"I guess the conversation is over," Spyre remarked absently, glancing in every direction.

The water was still moving, but his sail had deflated. He released it, somewhat happy to rest his arms and his stiff shoulder. He went to the side of the boat and peered into the water. Not that the sea was dark, per se; it was more that Spyre couldn't see what was beneath its surface that bothered him. It was deep. Who knew what was down there, and they were dead in the water, at the mercy of the tide. He looked around the boat. There were no shadows, no other ships, which meant no other threats. They were alone.

"I think you can come out," Spyre said to Soru. "No wind here. You can get a pretty good look at it. Maybe even risk a skim of the water if you want."

Soru floated outside of its alcove, hesitating before going much farther, but it wasn't long before it finally moved to hover next to Spyre's shoulder.

Spyre looked at the wisp and smiled. "Everything you hoped for?" he asked with an air of sarcasm.

"Much more," Soru replied, unfettered, but Spyre had to laugh at the wisp's less-than-awestruck tone.

Soru slowly backed away from the edge of the boat. Spyre followed him with his eyes, frowning.

"Wait, what's the problem?" Spyre asked.

He got his answer a second later when, while his head was turned, a strong hand grabbed his wrist and yanked him over the side of the boat and into the water. He hadn't even had the chance to gasp for air before the water filled his lungs. Instincts stopped Spyre from breathing in any more fluid as the thing pulled him deeper into the sea. He didn't know how to react. He'd never had to learn much of how to swim.

His free arm clawed at the water around him, the salt of it burning his shoulder like fire, and his feet were kicking, but whatever had dragged him out of the boat was too fast. He looked down, only able to see a blue blur as his eyes stung. His head felt like it was about to implode from the building pressure. His lungs shared the constricted feeling as the air within them rose and escaped through his mouth and nose in small bubbles. Spyre felt weak and couldn't resist.

The creature suddenly turned and released his wrist, leaving him floating limply, but it was too late for him to try to swim. Fortunately, he didn't have to, because his attacker put two hands firmly on his chest, and together, they rocketed toward the surface. Spyre's cloudy eyes widened as much as they had the strength to before closing completely, a few tiny air bubbles still abandoning him, a pair of fierce, sea-green eyes imprinted in his mind.

Spyre was forced up out of the water and back into the boat, the scaled, humanoid creature landing on top of him with force. He was at the edge of consciousness, but the creature remedied that when his head met the bottom of the boat, jolting him awake and probably giving him a concussion. He opened his eyes to see the face of his abductor and his savior and, possibly, his soon-to-be-murderer.

The creature had the same fierce green eyes he'd seen in the water and dark blue skin with lighter blue lines running along its arms, legs, and torso in a pattern that resembled the tides; based on the soft lines of its oval-shaped face, this was a woman. There were gills on her slim neck and scales along her calves and forearms.

Spyre gasped for breath as he stared at his attacker, wondering where Soru was and why he had bothered to bring the cowardly wisp along in the first place.

With one leg on either side of Spyre, the creature lifted him by the collar and quickly dropped him so that his head hit the wooden planks of the boat yet again. He was already weak, and now he was even more dazed, but he did his best to give the woman a disdainful glare at her unnecessary assault.

"Are you going to ask for my help?" the sea creature hissed at him. She kept a tight grip on Spyre's shirt, occasionally shaking him for emphasis.

"What?" Spyre asked groggily. He was seeing double now. "I don't even know what you are. You tried to kill me. Why would I ask you for help?" He closed his eyes, focusing his strength. "But I'd love to ask you to get off."

He kicked his legs up and shook the girl's balance, tossing her to the side as he gracelessly rolled backward, feeling dizzy when he finally sat upright. His hand went to his head to stop the world from spinning. The girl's eyes narrowed. She shot forward and grabbed Spyre by the neck before he could focus. He gaped at her, trying to pry her fingers from his throat.

"What did I do wrong?" he strained through a blocked windpipe.

She shook him. "Where are the others?" she demanded in a husky voice. Spyre imagined she wasn't used to speaking above water. Did her people speak with words, he wondered, or had she learned them from the whispers on the wind as well?

Spyre could no longer support the weight of his head, and it fell to the side in her grip. "Other what?" He choked.

A little late, Soru emerged from its box and flitted in front of the creature's face. The blue girl blanched at the sight of the wisp, looking surprised but not loosening her grip on Spyre, who was taking on a blue hue of his own, growing weaker in her clutches.

The girl stared at Soru, visually weighing the situation. She looked curious, but her eyes never lost their aggression. She looked at Spyre, who blearily stared up at her, now limp in her grip and on the brink of asphyxiation, and then back to Soru.

"You are not human. Are you his hostage?" Anger flashed in her eyes again. She gave Spyre a firm shake, and its eyes crossed momentarily.

"On the contrary," Soru corrected her. "I asked to join his journey."

The girl's features softened from malicious to mild intrigue.

"You can let him go." Soru hovered closer to Spyre's drowsy face. "In his current state, he is no harm to anyone."

The sea-girl looked down at Spyre as if she had forgotten him and quickly dropped him like a hot coal. Spyre gasped for breath as he sank against the side of the boat. He opened his eyes slightly but decided it wasn't worth the effort to move; instead, he allowed himself to faint as his body regained its composure. Ryne had mentioned the seafolk when he spoke of his excursions with the Gaernod army, but Spyre never imagined they were this hostile.

The sea-girl watched Spyre intently for a moment before turning back to Soru.

"You are a wisp from the edge of the water," the girl said. Most of her ferocity had washed away.

"And you are a lady of the sea," Soru replied. "I am Soru, and he is a human of Gaernod."

The girl raised her eyebrows incredulously, glancing back to Spyre. "Oh, I am well acquainted with his people."

Soru hovered closer to her shoulder. "His people will have given you the wrong impression of him, as you can see."

Spyre moaned as he came to, opening his eyes to see the sea-girl and quickly backing against the side of the boat. His eyes darted between the two creatures, wondering if they'd formed some kind of alliance against him in the few moments he'd been unconscious. He scanned the girl, trying to decide what exactly she was.

"You ... you have fins on your ankles," he pointed out groggily. "And you're blue."

"You're pasty and a horrible swimmer," the girl snapped back at him.

Spyre flinched a little, expecting another attack.

"Why are you here?" she demanded.

"My name is Spyre," he began, sitting up stiffly. "I'm from Gaernod, and I'm trailing the soldiers from my kingdom. I'd like to try to stop them."

The girl's eyes widened just slightly, lit with a glimmer of awe and belief.

"What did they do to you, Miss—?"

The girl glanced away insecurely, a flush of dark blue rose in her pale, nearly translucent cheeks. "Rowan," she divulged hesitantly. "I'm one of the seafolk. Hence the fins." She held up her arms to reveal another set of fins at her wrists.

Spyre grinned at her sense of humor. She gave a wry smile back to him. He relaxed.

Rowan's smile faltered. "Your soldiers came here several days ago. The wind died inside the mist, and they asked one of my kinsmen for guidance to the blessed coastline. He went with them." She paused, turning her face away, the anger returning. "We found him yesterday on the tide. Now his skin is whiter than yours."

Spyre was getting tired of hearing stories of death revolving around his people. Anger was something he and Rowan now had in common.

"Sorry isn't enough," Spyre admitted, his jaw as tense as his tone, "but I won't do anything to your people. You can do whatever you want to. I'm just trying to catch the bad guy, although I think I'm just a little late." He glanced sadly at the still water around them.

Rowan seemed impressed. She nodded at Spyre, eyes scanning him as if reevaluating her judgment of this individual human. She cracked a sharp-toothed smile, which scared Spyre. She looked at Soru and then back to Spyre.

"I like you," she said pointedly. "I will help you."

Spyre blanched but quickly shook his head. "No," he said, quiet but firm. "I appreciate it, but no thanks. You and your people have had enough. I'll figure this out."

Spyre had already accepted responsibility for his people's actions, but Rowan shook her head at his words. "You'll die without me," Rowan said bluntly. "You don't know which direction your boat is facing, do you?"

Spyre responded with a blank expression.

Rowan nodded knowingly. "You are going the wrong way."

Spyre frowned at his surroundings as if they'd betrayed him, and she laughed.

"You need my guidance. It will not be too much farther from here. If you are willing to push yourself, we can be to the shore by midnight."

Spyre blinked at her in amazement. "We're that close?"

She smiled and nodded.

"We can be there by morning?" He looked to Soru as if he would receive an enthusiastic response. He should've known better, but that didn't sour his own excitement. He composed himself and looked back to Rowan. "You don't have to. Are you sure?" His voice betrayed his excitement despite his words.

Rowan rolled her eyes at him. "Fix your sail. As soon as we break the mist, the wind will return, and I don't want to be wasting my energy."

Spyre beamed at her and crawled to the middle of the boat to straighten his makeshift sail. Finally, he was getting somewhere. He patted the sand around his broken spear and soaked it with seawater. Then he looked around. He wanted to make this as easy on Rowan as possible to thank her for her help, so he weighed the sacrifices and decided it was okay to pour the contents of his bag into the boat to loop the strap around the bow of the boat so Rowan could pull them rather than push them blindly.

The sea-maid followed Spyre to the front of the boat and took hold of the bag's strap. "I will take you within sight of the coast, and then I will have to turn back. I cannot touch the dry sand."

Spyre frowned, confused. "I thought the ocean was a middle ground. If Soru could come with me this far, why can't you get closer to the shore? Not that I'm complaining—"

"I am a creature of the sea, and you're not mistaken," Rowan said, nodding grimly. "But the Laefa Pinewood is not a common ground. I cannot leave my realm."

Spyre didn't understand. He didn't see why these creatures could never know more than what they had. "But why can't you? What is so different between you and me?" He leaned forward, interested in hearing what Rowan had to say. He rested his elbow on the boat and placed his chin in his palm.

"You are not the same as we are," Rowan said, gesturing to Soru and herself. "We are creatures of our own instincts. We know how to survive in our own worlds and cannot adapt to others. But you," she added, looking coyly at Spyre, "you are a different creature. Your kind has traversed Curnen without restraint. No other species has discovered that secret. I don't think we are meant to."

"But that's not fair," Spyre mumbled, knowing it didn't matter.

Rowan smiled at him. "Is it fair that your king is destroying the gifted city?"

Spyre lowered his eyes. Rowan reached up and gently touched his face. He looked at her carefully.

"We are not the only ones to suffer, but you can ease at least some of the pain in this world." She smiled. "And I'm not complaining about my situation. I love the sea, and I love my people. I imagine your friend feels relatively the same." She looked past Spyre to the wisp.

Spyre followed suit, looking back at Soru for an answer.

"The Cape is my home, and the wisps are my people. If I were to live among others and not them, I would never feel at ease."

Spyre accepted that as good enough, but he wondered why Soru had been so eager to join him if that was the case.

Rowan got Spyre's attention again, putting her hand on his arm. "Do what you have to, Spyre. Something has called you to make a difference. Allow yourself to do it. No more questions."

She slipped back into the water, and the boat moved through the mist. Spyre watched as Rowan jetted naturally through the current. Her body was nimble and streamlined, and she cut through the water with a certain majestic grace. She bent and dipped with the current; the water seemed to worship her as it carried her along. She was perfect for her habitat, unlike Soru, who had quickly retreated to its box. He wondered what Faran and Dugan would do if they had to switch places. It was difficult to fathom, and Spyre couldn't shake the feeling that it wasn't fair. The people he had met deserved more, but what could he do about physical boundaries? There was one thing he could do for them, and that made his race to defeat Afor feel even more crucial.

Spyre spent hours in silence, staring at the sail and keeping it inflated to speed Rowan's pace. Being underwater, the sea-maiden wasn't particularly conversational, and neither was the wisp. Soru stayed in its cubbyhole and kept whatever it used to speak with shut. Spyre was bored again.

The sea was beautiful, and the wildlife and the blue of the water preoccupied his sense of wonder for the first five hours, but then it became monotonous. The water churned, the clouds were gray, the air smelled of fish, and the mist chilled Spyre through his clothes. At least now the sun had set, bringing him that much closer to Condel. So, so close, but the time was somehow slowing down. How had he sped through his journey up to this point without even a moment to think, yet now every dragging moment felt like an additional day? It was awful because all the questions he had been trying to keep from his mind were settling in.

How far ahead of him was Afor? He had left Gaernod a while before Spyre had, but Spyre secretly hoped that the trolls or the seafolk or even the sprites had provided some sort of obstruction to him. Unrealistic, he knew.

What had Afor done to Condel, providing that he had made it there, which was almost certain? He dared not let his imagination process that.

Was the king still alive? Would the king allow him to help, or would Spyre die as soon either Condel or Gaernod soldiers spotted him?

How would he even get to the castle? Were the people okay? And, most importantly, what in the world was he going to do about it? He had felt comforted by this whole guided-by-fate thing for most of his journey, and it was playing out fairly well for him, but what sort of divine inspiration could give him the upper hand with Afor? The man had renamed an entire mountain range after himself. What hope did a peasant craftsman have against a warlord? Granted, he was a warlord who had never had cause for experience, but that didn't make him any less vicious. Afor had mistreated the people of Gaernod for years, and he would be even less forgiving toward the Condels.

Spyre looked up, and for the first time in his life, he noticed the vastness of the glittering night sky. There were no trees, no rocks, and no mist to hide them. He glanced around at the water, noticing the light that reflected on it. It wasn't a dark night. He'd never seen a night like this. It amazed him. He hadn't expected the world to be so different here. Sure, he'd travelled quite a distance, but it wasn't like he'd crossed the entire globe. He couldn't help wondering how many more changes he would see before he even reached Condel.

Okay, that was enough brooding.

"Soru," he said, pushing his thoughts away. "What are you going to do once we get to shore?" That was at least a question he could learn the answer to.

"We shall find out soon enough," the wisp said evasively.

Spyre frowned. So much for answers. "You haven't thought about it, have you? Do you know if you'll be able to cross the shoreline, or is Rowan going to tow you back to Eofot?"

There was a moment of silence, during which Spyre was sure he sensed trepidation. He decided not to push it any further. He would know soon enough. It wouldn't do any good to pry into Soru's discomforts now.

"Hey, Soru. Do you happen to hear any whispers on the wind right now?" he said, changing the subject for the wisp's sake.

Soru shifted in the air. "A few," it responded.

Spyre sighed, wondering why the wisp wouldn't have told him. "Well, what are they saying? Do they know anything about how far ahead Afor is?"

"I don't think you'll find the information encouraging," Soru said promptly.

Clearly, it'd received this update some time ago. Spyre narrowed his eyes at the dust speck.

"He has been in Condel for a while now, almost as long as you've been traveling."

Spyre's jaw dropped slightly. That was worse than he had hoped for. He sighed, feeling frustrated, impatient, and helpless. Suddenly, the boat, the sea, and the stars just weren't appealing anymore. He wanted out. He needed to take action. But it was then that the boat came to a stop. Spyre looked around and went to the front of the boat; Rowan was no longer swimming.

"What's the problem?" Spyre asked, some of his aggravation seeping into his words.

Rowan raised an eyebrow at his tone. "I could feel you tapping your foot from beneath the water." She blinked slowly. "Will you permit me to ease your mind?"

Spyre shook his head. "No, I'm fine. Just get us there." He didn't want a supportive monologue. He wanted results.

"No," Rowan snapped. "If you let your anger get the best of you, then you will ruin everything." She reached a hand out of the water toward Spyre's face, shooting him a corrective glare when he stubbornly flinched away.

"You could not have known, but my people have quite a talent for serenity. I can share some of it with you, but I prefer to have your permission."

Spyre didn't like accepting help. He could feel the tension in his forehead as he mentally grappled with what he wanted and what he knew he should do. Finally, still frowning, he gave a nod of surrender. Rowan smiled wryly and gracefully slipped into the boat, kneeling in front of Spyre, who sat on one of the planked seats. She took a moment to catch his uncomfortable gaze, and when she did, he tried to look away, but when she put her hand on his cheek, his attention darted back to her.

She looked deep into his confused, blue eyes, leaning forward as if sharing some silent secret. Spyre leaned in, searching her eyes in fascination. There was a moment when their eyes locked, and time seemed to freeze. Something in the pit of Spyre's stomach told him that this moment was either very kind of Rowan or it was the merfolk way of luring their prey in for the kill. They held each other's gaze that way for several, strangely comfortable seconds, until Spyre's eyes suddenly rolled back into his head.

Rowan caught him and eased him down, laying him on the seat of the boat, still aware but not quite conscious.

Soru buzzed down next to Spyre's face. "What have you done to him?"

Spyre wanted to speak, to demand the same answer as Soru, but nothing came. He could barely form the thought to begin with. It wasn't an unpleasant feeling, though Spyre almost wished it were. No, he was fine. Relaxed to the point of paralysis, calm to the point of numbness. Imperturbable and free of any tension, even in his wounded shoulder, which dulled from a constant sharp pain to a throbbing afterthought.

"Relax," Rowan said, brushing Soru off. "He'll be just fine. I simply stilled his mind. He will sleep for a while undisturbed, and when he awakes, he will feel much better. I have moved the thoughts that caused his stress to the back of his mind." She hopped back into the water, gazing forward. "It won't be long now. We're close."

Soru retreated to its alcove and waited as the boat continued toward its destination. Spyre remained on the seat, leaving the sail unattended, but with the short distance that remained, he was sure it made little difference. He watch through half-lidded eyes as the wisp took in the view of the sea while it still could, occasionally checking Spyre's deep and even breathing.

A few hours later, Rowan stuck her head out of the water and called back to Soru, "I know we can't touch the shore, but we have to get him there somehow."

She peered over the edge of the boat at Spyre's nearly lifeless body. He tried to move, to reassure her that he could handle himself, but whatever Rowan had done to him held strong. She shook her head. "He won't wake up in time to swim, so that means we will have to get dangerously close. Are you willing to take a risk with me?"

"What use can I possibly be?" The sarcasm did little to mask Soru's trepidation.

"Don't be rude," Rowan scolded. "I will carry him to shore, so I won't be able to call the sprites to attention. You must call out to them and let them know we've arrived."

Soru bobbed in the air for several seconds. "I will do my best," it promised soberly.

Rowan nodded her appreciation and returned to her work at the bow, while Soru hovered in place, presumably listening for the whispers it'd mentioned before. Then Spyre watched as the wisp began to shudder in the air. Soru darted around erratically before finally zipping around the front of the boat to give a frantic shout in its many voices, "There is trouble ashore!"

Spyre watched the gray sky as the boat suddenly jerked to a halt. Something must've happened to Rowan in the water, but he couldn't guess what. All he could think was how peaceful the sky looked as he watched the clouds roll along. Soru darted across Spyre's vision and then back again, out and away from the boat.

That wasn't good, Spyre noted. Soru would get caught in the sea breeze if it wasn't careful.

Then the boat did the strangest thing: it moved backward, as though the sea were pulling it back toward the cape, but there would be no reason for that sort of pull unless …

The wall of water was upon him before Spyre's brain could piece together the clues that a wave was coming in. It came down on the boat with a mighty rush of briny seawater, and the world spun around, dumping him into the surf.

Without his good senses to protect him, Spyre's body continued breathing as though nothing had gone wrong, and water rushed into his lungs. Black crowded the edges of his vision. Before it took the rest of him, Spyre caught sight of Rowan, her eyes sharp with concern. He appreciated that, as compared to the fierceness she held in them just hours ago when she'd threatened to kill him. Now he could only assume she was saving him.

Again, like last time, Spyre felt himself forced up and out of the water, but this time, it was onto the soft bed of sand. Rowan bent over him, Soru at her shoulder.

She looked to Soru.

"They have heard me," Soru assured her.

"The boat is gone," Rowan said.

"I know." Soru sounded unusually passive and even peaceful, despite its urgent situation and the rising sea wind that came in on the tide.

Rowan stared at the wisp, her mouth a firm line and shoulders pulled back. "What will you do?" she started to ask, but as she finished, a strong gust came off of the sea, catching Soru in its current and carrying the wisp toward the coastline.

Rowan threw her arm out, tipping Spyre onto his side, and desperately called out to Soru, but she could do nothing. She was as helpless as Spyre watching Soru cross the border between the sea and land. The vapors that comprised its body scattered and lifted into the air, vanishing.

Tears landed on Spyre's cheeks, but they were from Rowan's eyes as they stared at the space where the wisp had been. A noise at the edge of the Pinewood drew her attention, and she looked horrified. With one last glance at Spyre, she threw herself back into the water and swam away. Alone and numb, Spyre allowed the darkness to claim him as he lay in the sands of the blessed land.

CHAPTER 19

Eofyn couldn't see. He wasn't sure if he even wanted to. The soldiers had come prepared. They must have followed them the entire way from Condel, and somehow, Pyram had known. In a time when all lights were going out, Pyram's hadn't faded from him. Eofyn respected that more than he could say, especially in his current predicament.

The soldiers, after apprehending Eofyn and Pyram, had kept them separate. They took Eofyn back to the main chamber. The guards had bound him and taunted him by melting the temple key over a fire and rendering it useless before throwing the key out into the sand. Then they'd blindfolded him for good measure and thrown him into the cramped alcove near the door.

They were with him almost constantly, no doubt expecting him to be contacting Bryta, but little did they know how they were wasting their time. Eofyn hadn't seen or heard a thing. Granted, he hadn't really tried. By now, he was almost completely convinced that, despite Pyram's ideas, the Pure Fyre had deemed him unworthy. Though that funny feeling he'd gotten at the stone pedestal in the other room had been strange, but maybe it was just the lack of oxygen.

He had felt happy and, even more impressive, assured. The source was not there, but that hadn't bothered him. Why hadn't it bothered him? It meant that this long journey that was meant to solve everything and help to redeem him to his people was truly for nothing. They had lost. The whole kingdom could very well be demolished already, for all he knew.

Eofyn sat quietly, head hung low, listening to the two guards shuffling around. Why hadn't they done anything? Couldn't they just get it over with already? What were they waiting for? And where was Pyram? Were they going to let him die alone in the dark? Perhaps he was nothing more than an accessory totem, but Eofyn felt awful. The person who had the most faith in him was bound and abandoned in a dark, ancient temple.

Eofyn, regardless of his own self-loathing, felt he owed Pyram the respect of at least trying to make a connection here. Maybe something about the temple would stimulate his gift. After all, this was where it was first brought into the world. He remembered the torch lighting as it touched his hand. That had been enough for Pyram, and Pyram would've known. His unfailing gift would have supported his theory.

He decided; he had to admit, it couldn't hurt more than his pride to try. He sat up against the wall, bending his legs in front of him so that his feet were flat on the ground, supporting him. He lowered his head and focused. He felt his eyes roll back, as if searching his own brain for something beyond his own consciousness. The darkness behind his eyelids grew deeper somehow. With the added cloak of darkness, a strange sensation bloomed in the center of his forehead, and something in his mind seemed to pull a curtain aside, revealing light and the vision of a misted void all around him.

Eofyn dared not breathe. In the farthest distance of his internal vision, he could see the smallest speck of white light. He felt as though he was dreaming. His body was comfortably heavy. His head smoothly rose and fell back to rest against the wall, lifting his face to the ceiling. The light remained. Eofyn heard nothing and felt at peace. It was the same sensation that had set upon him in the other chamber. His mind drifted to the object that had been in the stone of that room, but the white light quickly reclaimed his attention.

What is it? Eofyn asked himself, but even as he asked, he somehow knew.

This was the Pure Fyre. Before his eyes, as if a reward for his acknowledgment, the light split into three smaller orbs. Eofyn felt his brow furrow. What did that mean? The orbs lingered for a moment but returned to a single glow after a few seconds.

156

Is the source divided? Eofyn wondered, but something within him told him that was not the case. What then?

The orb drew closer to Eofyn, and he realized what it was trying to show him. The closer it came, the more obvious it was that the orb was not a single light but a bondage of three, with seams fitting them together. Eofyn was eager for more, but for whatever reason, this was apparently enough information for now, as the light ceased moving and slowly faded away, leaving true comfort behind.

Eofyn took a deep breath. Though the moment had been brief, at least now he knew the Fyre was real. Even better, the Pure Fyre was real, and it was within him. He could feel it in his soul, even though he still had much to learn, but he felt elated nonetheless. That his best friend might be injured or dead and that he had absolutely no means of escaping from the Gaernod soldiers bothered him significantly less, even though he knew he should be terrified. A foreign presence in his soul reassured him that something would reveal itself.

Eofyn's smile faltered slightly when a large boot kicked him in the ribs and knocked him onto his side.

"What are you so happy about?" a soldier asked.

All the joy from Eofyn's revelation fell away at the sound of his captor's voice. Just before they had fitted him with the blindfold, Eofyn had recognized the soldier to be the same man who had taken Lissa away from him. He would have known that twisted smirk anywhere.

"You will not survive this temple, little prince." His grin shone through his voice. Eofyn pictured that thin sneer from the night of the invasion in his mind and gritted his teeth behind a deliberately blank expression. "You wouldn't be smiling if you knew what we're planning for you and your little friend, but give it a few more days. You'll see soon enough."

Eofyn heard him walk away. His voice echoed as he said, "Afor wants you to know your kingdom is completely destroyed before we kill you. He said any of your people who haven't proven useful by three days from now will be burned up."

Eofyn glared regardless of the blindfold. Anger boiled up inside him, but he took a deep, soothing breath. Something would happen.

He couldn't find the Pure Fyre, only to lose everything. There was a reason. There was a reason for everything.

Wasn't there?

Eofyn felt like an amateur. He spent the next hours curled quietly in his alcove, ignoring all the discomforts of fatigue and hunger and other bodily functions for fear of drawing the attention of the soldiers and incurring their wrath. Instead, he focused on trying to get more information, something more concrete to help him get a better grip on his newfound ability. Why it had taken so long to finally emerge, he did not understand, but he had it now, and that meant that he needed it. Pyram had been right. And this was awesome.

After spending a life of normalcy, with the excuse that one day, he would be unique among his people, Eofyn had never imagined this. But this was not an easy gift. Like Pyram's and Lissa's, it was instinctual but needed precision of the mind. Eofyn could feel that there were voices, answers trying to get through to him, but he couldn't quite hear them.

What do I need to do? he thought, racking his brain.

A feeling came over him that made him wonder if he'd just asked the right question. The voices were no longer so urgent. He still couldn't hear them, but they now seemed more familiar. He focused.

What can I do?

There was a stillness that seemed to be intended as a response for him. There was nothing he could do, but there was still hope. He took a calming breath and nodded to himself.

What am I looking for?

He waited, and through the veil of his mind's eye, he saw two figures walking toward him, with another shadowy form trailing purposefully behind them. The shadow didn't make Eofyn feel threatened, so he decided that it must not have been negative. He considered the image, trying to discern its meaning.

Two people are coming? And ... what ... they are being brought here by you?

The image burst into a flash of yellow, and Eofyn's eyebrows rose above his closed eyes.

Understood.

He rested his head against the cool stone wall and smiled inwardly. Best not to let the guards know what he was up to. They were simply counting the hours and, by the sound, sharpening their swords, but Eofyn was doing his best not to worry. If the information he was receiving was true and not a figment of his admittedly desperate imagination, someone was coming, and he would be alive to see it. Otherwise, why waste knowing they were coming? The source wasn't in this building. Something important was here, but not the source. Eofyn desperately hoped that whoever was on their way needed his help, because if they didn't, then he had nothing to take from his vision but consolation for his failure.

And there was also Pyram. The two guards had been shuffling around Eofyn and arguing about who had the least tolerable family, the one with the wife or the one who lived with his weakling brother, since they'd put him here. So what were they doing with Pyram? If Pyram could have escaped from wherever they held him, he would have by now, so it was clear to Eofyn that his friend was trapped. Pyram didn't do well in confinement. He would get restless. If he made too much noise, the guards were liable to …

Eofyn's heart thudded in his throat, and he had to measure his breathing to calm himself.

Please, he begged whatever had shown him the hopeful images. *Please show me that Pyram is all right.*

Pressure filled Eofyn's forehead, and blinding light flashed behind his eyes until something strange happened. He was staring at a temple wall, but not the one closest to him. This room was drowned in darkness, and Eofyn felt himself in a seated position, free of bindings. This wasn't Eofyn's lens of experience, he realized. It must have been an answer from Bryta. This had to be Pyram.

Eofyn explored the feeling deeper, sinking into Pyram's consciousness to see the world as he saw it, feel what he felt, and share his thoughts.

Pyram was free to move around but couldn't see enough to go anywhere. He knew even if he could see, there was still no chance of escape, but at least he'd have better means of occupying his time if he had something to look at. He needed to light one of those torches.

He stood from the pile of rocks he'd been sitting on and held his hands out in front of him, waiting to feel a wall against his palms. It was several seconds before he bumped abruptly into the coarse wall of the chamber. He felt around for the mount of the torch and ran his fingers along it until he found his cone-shaped prize. He knew of one way to light a fire without the help of Eofyn's special gifts, but it pained him to do it.

He would have to break two stones from the cobbled altar, which had stood untouched and undamaged for thousands of years. If anyone were to desecrate it, he'd have thought it would be the Gaernods, but it would be him. He felt along the many stones for the loosest one, feeling like he should be apologizing. He found a loose stone and kicked it with his heel several times, until it rolled off of the pile. He listened for the direction where it landed and followed, finding it and picking it up before returning to the altar for one more. None of the other stones of the well-built pedestal felt loose, so Pyram regrettably knelt down and hammered the one that protruded the most with his first plundered prize, knocking the other from its housing.

With the two stones in one hand, Pyram sat and grabbed the torch, holding it upright between his knees. He struck the stones together a few times until they sparked on contact and held them up to the torch. It took several tries, but Pyram finally directed a spark into the torch, lighting it and the rest of the room as well. Even the dim light of the torch hurt his eyes after several days in complete darkness, but Pyram was never happier to be able to see.

He allowed his eyes to adjust for a few moments and finally took a stroll around the room, taking in its modest details. The walls were blank, but Pyram remembered that the walls hadn't been the canvas of choice in the first chamber. He looked to the floor. There was dust everywhere, so much so he could see the footprints that Eofyn, the soldiers, and he had left throughout the room. The dust had not been that thick on the altar or the walls, even though they had been there for as long as the floor had. Something about that didn't quite make sense to Pyram.

Why would more dust gather on the floors than anywhere else? It was a considerable amount, and it almost looked deliberate. He brushed some dust aside with his shoe, and sure enough, there was a line etched into the floor. Pyram's eyes widened with excitement. He propped his torch up against the stones of the altar and knelt on the floor, brushing the dust aside with his hands to reveal words written in an elegant calligraphy. It was suddenly clear to Pyram why their ancestors had built the temple in such a simple style. They had spent their time focusing on its message rather than its surface appearance.

Pyram continued to brush away the dust until he revealed an entire word: Source. He quickly broadened his range and wiped the dust away from nearly the entire floor until the whole message was revealed. Pyram stood and walked along each line, reading quietly as he went:

> Shadows stretch far from home, black claws sink into marble thrones.
>
> A tyrant seeks to overthrow, receives the magic, makes it glow.
>
> Escape his grip, when comes that day. Seek the guidance. Find your way.
>
> Be ye guided to this place, receive the blade that minds erased,
>
> and here a worthy man you'll find, the one who seeks to save mankind.
>
> The Kindling found in darkness thrives, sparks the Source to save your lives
>
> when by Pure Fyre it is released, the dragons live to slay the beast.

"Whoa," Pyram said, breathing heavily.

Some of what the poem said already made sense to him, but other things frightened him. The earliest people had seen this day coming, but they had seen more than he had yet witnessed. If he was reading correctly, Afor had taken the city, which wasn't much of a surprise, but it also wasn't comforting.

However, the talk of Pure Fyre being released gave him hope that Eofyn would soon realize his heritage and fulfill the destiny that had been written in stone long before he was born. That part gave Pyram a warm sensation of pride and confidence in Eofyn's ability to do what was necessary to awaken Cuman and Swelgan and bring Afor down.

But the lines between the first and the last were lost on him. He crouched down in the middle of the carvings and tried to relate to anything he could to decipher them. The more he knew, the more help he'd be to Eofyn when they finally got out of this mess, because if this message was to be believed, help was on the way.

A strange pulling sensation tugged Eofyn back through the bright, ethereal tunnel and back into his own body with a wave of relief from what he'd seen, both Pyram's safety and the message that had confirmed Eofyn's own insights from Bryta.

People were coming to help them. It could be any day, any minute now.

The panic threatened to consume his thoughts again. He took a few deep breaths and distracted himself with images of Lissa. She would know how to keep them both rational in a situation like this. That's why he had felt confident leaving Condel in her hands. He desperately hoped that Afor had done nothing to hurt her, but from what his father had told him about Afor's tendencies, mercy didn't seem likely.

So much for not panicking …

CHAPTER 20

Spyre's face was warm. He felt so rested. Nothing about him was even sore, except for a minuscule throb in his injured shoulder. He'd never felt this good before in his life. Even the air seemed was crisper and much less humid than it had been on the sea. He didn't want to open his eyes. This had to be a dream, and why in the world would he want to wake up?

He heard a giggle. "You can wake up now, sleepy head. You've been asleep half the day."

Spyre opened his eyes and lifted his head to look behind him. He was in the sand. He was damp, and there was a willowy-looking girl standing above him. She had pale, youthful skin and wavy, auburn hair. Her starry, green eyes glistened with contentment and joy. Instinctively, he smiled up at her.

"We figured you'd arrived when we heard that strange creature shouting from the water and the screams of the sea-maiden when the sands of our shores began to burn her for being out of her realm." Her voice was still sweet as a bell, but Spyre's smile faltered. The girl noticed. "Oh, no. She's fine. The human traps left behind by your army challenged her, but she prevailed and managed to save your possessions as well. She swam away. She's perfectly fine."

Spyre's smile returned. He must have been delirious. There was no other explanation for his being so complacent.

"The wisp wasn't so fortunate," the girl said, looking a little sad but still innocent.

"What?" Spyre exclaimed, bolting up and turning to face her. "What happened to Soru?"

The girl frowned and looked up at him through her eyelashes. "The wind caught the wisp and carried it too far inland." She fluttered a hand through the air like a leaf in the wind, showing Soru's fateful path. "It dissipated." She waved her hand with a small flourish and allowed it to fall to her side.

They both watched it with sadness as she said, "No one is really sure what that means. That's not to say its vapors weren't returned to the Cape of Eofot," she consoled Spyre, resting a hand on his arm. "It might be perfectly fine."

"How will we know?" Spyre asked softly.

The girl just gave a thin, regretful smile, bringing her shoulders to her pointed ears and shaking her head.

Spyre dropped his head, but he was more perplexed that this tragedy didn't bother him as much as he knew it should have. He just wanted to follow this girl wherever she wanted to go. He stood the rest of the way and noticed just how small she was. She was roughly the size of Faran, if not a few inches shorter, but she was more childlike and snowy skinned, where the elves had a constant crease of concern on their darker brows. Spyre wondered if her kind and the elves descended from the same race at some point in history, when the creatures of Curnen were not so divided.

"Where do we go from here?" Spyre asked. He knew he would have to travel inland, but beyond that, he was completely lost. Besides, if these sprites were anything like the elves, they'd have a hefty favor to demand of him.

The girl looked confused. "What do you mean?"

Spyre laughed, shaking his head. "I just figured that was the trend. I go somewhere, I meet the locals, they tell me what I have to do before they let me leave, or they speed the process of my going. So—"

Spyre gave her an expectant look, but she watched him, waiting for him to finish his sentence. Subtlety was obviously lost on her. "What do you need me to do?"

"Do you feel refreshed?" she asked, ignoring his question.

Spyre furrowed his brow, balking at the strangest thing he'd ever been asked. "Sorry, what?"

She tilted her head to the side, as if wondering what was so difficult for him to understand. "You've rested, but I'm sure you're still very weary. If you need more time, you can stay here until you feel strong enough to continue." Her voice carried the deepest sincerity.

Spyre didn't know what it was about this place, but he liked it. There was no pressure, no one rushing him along. For once, he was being asked how he felt, what he wanted. And it seemed like a wonderful idea to indulge in that.

"You don't have anything to eat, do you?" he asked hesitantly, not wanting to be rude but feeling famished.

The girl smiled. "We do. There's plenty of fruit back at the village. You'll love it. Just follow me." She turned on her heels and began skipping away.

Spyre happily followed. "What's your name, by the way?" He always got to that part late in the game. "I'm—"

"Spyre." The girl nodded. "The wisp was shouting your name. I'm Lif."

"What happened on the water?" Spyre asked, catching up and walking alongside her.

She looked up at him. "I don't know. By the time we got there, everything was over, and you were sleeping soundly on the beach."

Spyre knew it should bother him, but it just didn't. "Oh," was all he said in response as he looked around.

The trees were greener here, and flower-specked moss hung from the branches like draped curtains. The sunlight shone through the canopy, illuminating particles in the air. It was beautiful, enchanting almost. Spyre half-expected there to be ethereal singing coming from the trees.

"So Condel isn't far from here?" Spyre asked Lif. That was one concern that he hadn't lost.

She turned to him and smiled warmly, shaking her head. "You're almost there, Spyre. You're very close now."

He sighed, smiling like a child. It was so good to hear positive news. He was almost there. He was closer to Condel than he was to

Gaernod, and that felt fantastic. It was like he had finally cut the cord that connected him to the other kingdom.

Lif led Spyre through the woods and stopped at a rather large, old-looking tree. She turned to look at him, still smiling.

"Are you a strong climber?" she asked. She held up her hand, and a vine fell into her grasp.

Spyre followed the vine to see if someone else was there, but there was nothing.

"The trees welcome us here," Lif explained. "We understand each other, and we work together." Her smile grew smaller and faded away. "We lost a few trees recently, but fortunately, they know the difference between humans and sprites." She looked at Spyre, acknowledging his species with a brief lift of her eyebrows. "I hope they like you."

Spyre eyed the tree uncertainly. He looked high into its branches. "Yeah, me too." Did it see the wooden bow on his back? Was that considered murder? What about the arrows that poked out of small tears in his satchel?

"I'll tell you what," Lif said as she looped the bottom of the vine and knotted it. "We'll let the tree decide. It can let you up, or it can leave you here. It's more polite and less dangerous that way."

She held the vine out to Spyre, and he tentatively accepted, slipping his foot into the loop and holding on with both hands. Nothing happened for a moment, and he was about to step away, but it was only another second before the vine went taut and pulled him upward. He held on tight and looked down at Lif, whose eyes were glistening.

"He likes you."

Spyre nodded. The tree was a "he," and it liked him. As he entered the canopy of the pinewood, the first secret of the blessed land was revealed to him: There was a city in the trees, made by the trees. Branches twisted into buildings and bridges. Leaves and vines grew to cover doorways and windows, decorating the buildings with flower blossoms. It was gorgeous.

There were plenty of other sprites walking around, and none of them took notice of the stranger's arrival, which was a pleasant change to what he'd experienced in every other realm before this one. He took a few steps into the village, joined by Lif as she stepped up behind him.

She giggled and took his hand, leading him to a nearby treehouse and pulling the curtain of vines aside to reveal a series of three rooms with all-natural furnishings. Moss cushions lay around wooden stumps. The tree limbs even provided shelving. It looked like the trees viewed the sprites as their children and nurtured them accordingly. That would explain their incessant cheerfulness. It was weird.

"So you don't have a leader who needs to see me?" Spyre asked as Lif passed him a wooden bowl of fruit. He accepted it graciously and relished the taste of round, purple citrus fruit while he curiously peered into the next room, a bedroom.

Lif frowned at Spyre's suspicion. "You haven't been treated very well, have you?" she asked. "So many nervous assumptions. How many times have you had to fight since you left your kingdom?"

Spyre opened his mouth to respond, but it had apparently been a rhetorical question. She continued without pausing for him to speak.

"The trees are our caretakers," she explained. "They guide us. We do not have a king like Condel does. We do as the trees suggest, and we remained safe until Afor arrived. Even then, though, the trees provided our protection through camouflage." She lowered her gaze at him. "They'll take care of you, too, if you'll let them."

"So the trees can think." Spyre turned away from her eerie statement. He looked around him, eyeing the branches. "Can they hear us too?"

She smiled and nodded vigorously. "They hear everything."

"They're eavesdroppers ... or leaves droppers." Spyre laughed awkwardly, looking for a response to his attempt at humor.

Lif just smiled blankly. Who knew someone could have a blank smile? He glanced around the room again, wondering if the trees had a better sense of humor than the sprite, or would he suddenly receive a smack to the head from a sneaky tree branch?

Lif left Spyre's side and moved farther into the house. She knelt down in front of what looked like a fireplace, but Spyre could think of one or two hazards that would come of a fireplace in a treehouse. She took some dried leaves from a woven basket next to the fireplace and neatly placed them inside and then began lighting a fire.

Thoughts flashed in Spyre's mind that maybe all of this was indeed too good to be true and that she was about to escape through the window, leaving Spyre to be torched by the flames, but Lif simply used two small stones to send a tiny spark to the leaves, igniting them. The leaves gave off a flame that seemed to be strong enough to last for a while.

Spyre had never known leaves to sustain a flame without something more to burn, but he wasn't exactly in his comfort zone anymore, so he didn't bother asking. Smoke from the leaves rose and vented safely out of the house through a hollow tree trunk. The perfect system. The trees really did provide. He took a deep breath and felt happy again.

"There is nothing to worry about here," Lif said, stoking the flame with a charred stick. "Afor has already passed us by, and he has no intentions of coming back here for some time. Condel is on its knees, and he will establish a firm hold there before he bothers to return."

"Doesn't that bother you?" Spyre asked too casually, resting his chin in his palm.

She looked up at him and shook her head before tenderly going back to care for her fire. "You may take time to rest here, if you like," she said. "If Condel is there today, it will probably be there tomorrow."

"Why are you so calm about this?" Spyre asked, feeling paranoid at his own lack of emotion but remaining at ease, nonetheless.

Lif rose to her feet and walked over to Spyre, taking his hand in hers and looking deep into his eyes as she set the bowl of fruit back on the table. "This is Laefa Pinewood," she reminded him. "We are beyond the grayness of the sea, and we are not touched by the fickle dispositions of the humans in Condel. Here everything is good. We do not struggle with moral conflicts. The trees provide, and we accept and live in peace. In Condel, the people have found room for doubt. They question themselves, and that is ultimately what brought their downfall."

Spyre tilted his head to the side, finding a problem with her words in the haze that was clouding his senses. "Yeah, but don't you think you've become a little … I don't know, complacent?"

Lif looked innocently confused. "Is that a problem?" she asked. "We have everything we need here. What more could we ask for?"

"But when Afor decides to expand—and he will—you'll be vulnerable," Spyre insisted. His face contorted as he tried to convince

himself of the gravity of the situation as well, but his mind just wouldn't
be bothered by it. "If he removes the trees, what will you do?"

She looked to the side, thinking for the briefest moment. "I don't
think I should worry about that just now."

"When then?" he asked, brimming with a strange, childish curiosity.

She smiled at him. "Well, you're just full of questions, aren't you?
Is that why you couldn't find happiness in your own circumstances?"

Her words caught Spyre off guard. Happiness in Gaernod? Now he
knew something was wrong.

"If what you have does not satisfy you," Lif continued, "what will it
take to make you satisfied? What will be so different about Condel?"

Spyre paused. What wouldn't be so different was more like it. They
had better intentions; they treated each other better, and they were good
people who didn't want to conquer everything around them. He wanted
a peaceful life but not the one of blind bliss that Lif had. She was going
nowhere. She would discover nothing more than she already knew
because she had no questions. She was the polar opposite to Faran, who
never ceased asking questions, but then he had never asked the right
questions. There must have been a happy medium of inquisitiveness.
He would have to hope that the Condels had found it. Maybe having
the ability to leave his own realm also allowed for a broader sense of
exploration and curiosity.

Something about this place no longer seemed so magical. It made
his mind feel groggy. "You know, I really think I should move on," he
said, turning to leave.

Lif raised her eyebrows. "I don't think that's wise. You're still
exhausted. You should rest for a while."

Spyre felt his eyes growing heavy on cue. He frowned. Was he doing
that? He felt her take his hand and lead him into the bedroom, the size
fit for a child, which the sprites were compared to him, draped in tree
vines and branches that bent and curled to form the bed, as though the
trees embraced the sprites, even in sleep. He didn't stop her. His brain
just wasn't sending the distress signal to the rest of him. He lay down,
still feeling confused. She stood next to him.

"Sleep for a while," she coaxed sweetly. "You'll feel much better. The trees will provide the rest you need." Her voice sounded like an echo as the room blurred. "Just sleep."

Spyre struggled to lift his eyelids, but everything felt too heavy. "I don't—want to …" But that didn't matter. As if Lif had sedated him, he faded out of consciousness, head falling to the side, knowing with an intense feeling of dread that he was in trouble.

Hours later, Spyre bolted upright in the dark. His head felt much clearer, and he hated himself for not already being in Condel.

He'd had a dream. It was fuzzy, but he knew it had involved him standing amidst two feuding dragons. He knew his dream would naturally revolve around him, but the dragons? The only dragon he had ever seen was made of stone, and as far as he knew, Cuman was nothing more than an ornament to scare off the elves. Sure, there were legends of the dragon coming to life, bedtime stories to scare children, but they were to keep the kids of Gaernod suspicious of what others might try to take from them.

Spyre had hardly taken part in the dream, and there didn't seem to be a specific plot to it. The dragons stood on either side of him and stared at him as if waiting to see what he would do. He turned his head away from them and saw Condel, the only light in a void of black, but as he took a tentative step toward it, the dragons roared at him ferociously. He flinched, looking up to see both creatures glaring at him.

In Cuman's eyes, he saw the familiar countenance that was the default expression for most people of Gaernod. It was a fierce glare that seemed to say, "Don't you dare." Spyre swallowed the lump in his throat and turned to the blue dragon, who looked down on him sternly, as if challenging Spyre to enter Condel. Spyre had never felt so unworthy.

He froze, waiting to be devoured, but the dragons continued to stare, almost urging him to make a move. Following an impulse, Spyre bolted toward the blessed kingdom, and the dream swirled to an end. But if he was awake now, then that meant he would have a better chance of truly pursuing his course to Condel, and he had no intention of being held back this time. He crawled out of the pile of moss, which no longer seemed so quaint and inviting, and crept for the door, keeping an eye out for Lif. He crossed the main room, where the fire was merely embers, and reached to pull the vines aside to make an escape, but a small hand firmly caught his.

"It was the tree," Lif quickly explained before Spyre could pull away from her. She sounded much more normal, with a genuine air of concern to her matured voice. Her face had lost its childish glow and now looked youthful but wise. "The trees released mood-altering spores. They emphasized the effect of the sea-maiden's trick. They were testing your heart before they would allow you to continue your journey."

She smiled softly, a twinkle of remorse in her eyes. "I still have no desire to seek anything beyond what the trees give. That hasn't changed, but they have made me aware that you are not of the same inclination. You humans are so complicated."

She looked away, shaking her head.

"But you must continue. There is much ahead of you, and what held you back is behind you." She let out a small sigh. "You can thank the trees for that. They had you address your confusion while you slept. Your path should feel clearer to you now."

Spyre was about to request more information about the dream that the trees had given him, wondering what about his complicated journey was supposed to feel any clearer now, but Lif pulled the vines aside, revealing several other sprites waiting behind them. Spyre blanched at the group of small people staring at him and looked at Lif.

She explained. "They would like to see the man about to change everything in Curnen. You are not only attempting to save Condel; you're altering everything. Our lives will change just as much as yours is about to. This is a nervous moment for all of us."

"That's very ... awkward of them," Spyre said without thinking. "And kind, I suppose. I appreciate their, um, concern." He stood for a moment under the stares of a dozen sprites, but his nerves couldn't take much more of this. "I really should be going, though," he said, turning to Lif. "Maybe you can point me in the right direction so I don't mess this up before it starts."

Lif smiled warmly. "I will do better than that. I'll take you to Condel personally." Spyre's eyebrows rose in pleasant surprise. "I have never been there, but I can read the trees," she assured him. She walked past Spyre and through the small crowd.

Spyre stared after her for a moment, laughing to himself and shaking his head. "She can read the trees. Naturally."

More vines awaited them, lowering them to the forest floor. Spyre was half-surprised that they weren't swinging through the trees to Condel, but walking suited him fine. Part of him was thrilled to have his feet back on the ground, but the serenity of the morning had nearly faded as the images of Condel consumed his imagination. He would get to the town while it was still dark, and that would afford him better cover to sneak inside. Where he would go from there was yet to be determined, but again, he'd made it this far.

"It will probably please you to know," Lif said, sounding so much less like a disturbing little girl than she had before, "that Condel is only a fifteen-minute walk from here."

Spyre gawked at her, missing a step. "You're kidding." He looked up as though the people of Condel would be standing right in front of him, waving their welcome. Or maybe that dragon would be there, daring him to pass through the gates, but Spyre felt ready to accept that challenge now.

Lif tilted her face up at him, smiling genuinely, with playful sparkles in her eyes. "I kid you not. It's just through those trees. It only seems like such a distance because the trees have woven their leaves into such a dense curtain to protect us."

"About that," Spyre said, a finger in the air. "Do you really think trees are protection enough?"

Lif coyly narrowed her eyes at him. "If you are as impressive as you are meant to be, they will be more than enough protection."

"Ah," Spyre said, shrugging to mock Lif's carefree attitude. "Right. No pressure."

Lif giggled. "No, there is plenty of pressure."

Spyre looked at her, glad to hear someone finally admit it without framing it as a threat.

"But if you keep up what you've been doing, you should be able to squeeze by like you have so far. Have you planned anything ahead?"

Spyre laughed, shaking his head at the ground. "Nope. Nothing, which is strange. I'm usually good with sequences of cause and effect. You'd think I'd be looking at the next step."

"People are less predictable than wood and string," Lif noted wisely. "You're probably better off not trying, especially in times like these. The world has no experience in warfare, yet Afor seems unnaturally gifted."

"Probably because everyone is unnaturally petrified." Spyre looked into the distance with a sigh. "Can't say I blame them." Flashes of the dragons clashing over the shining city of Condel came back to him, and he had to admit that he was feeling considerably petrified himself as he remembered the blue dragon falling lifeless to the ground beneath the red dragon's claws—the claws of Cuman, of Gaernod. Of Afor, he assumed.

Lif nodded her agreement as they walked, yet Spyre noticed how unperturbed she was. The sprite honestly believed nothing could harm her or her people. It was all in her eyes. There was no sign of fear. More so, there was sublime disinterest. Her eyes were cloudy and passive, but they glistened with contentment. It seemed strange to Spyre, but he supposed it worked for her. She was happy. Then again, maybe it was the sight of someone who was genuinely happy that seemed bizarre to him.

"Have you ever seen Condel?" he asked. He realized visiting and seeing were entirely different things, but maybe some of her perpetual happiness had come from living next to the blessed kingdom.

"Yes," she said, staring ahead and still smiling softly. "On clear days, we can see it from the top of the canopy."

Spyre stared at her. "What does it look like?"

She finally pulled her attention away from the indistinct distance. Her eyes caught Spyre's with such intensity that he almost stopped in his tracks. She slowed her pace and came to a stop, leaving Spyre stumbling. He looked at her, waiting.

"See for yourself," she said, gesturing ahead of them with a sweep of her arm.

It was just the way he would have imagined someone revealing the Kingdom of Condel to him. Everything seemed to happen slowly, as Spyre followed her movements and looked up to see the pristine walls of the kingdom of crystals standing tall and proud, an advertisement more than a safeguard. It disappointed him. He'd expected a warm, welcoming haven of legend, but this was nothing more than an overdecorated, oversized garden. The walls were white, just as he'd heard, but the stories had always said the city glowed with the brilliance of the people's power. It was meant to light up the night sky like a sun nestled between the Pinewood and the desert. This city looked small and dim, with no majesty to offer.

The city was dark, only dimly lit in the shadows cast by the setting sun. There could only be two explanations: either the stories he'd heard were false, or Afor had already ruined the kingdom's power. He desperately hoped that Gaernod had exaggerated the glamour of Condel out of jealousy.

"What happened?" Spyre asked, staring, knowing his eyes might be the ones that were glistening now.

Lif looked at the kingdom and frowned, which would normally have drawn Spyre's attention. "The city sparkled before," she responded wistfully. "That has gradually faded over the past week." She looked up at him. "This is not the blessed kingdom, Spyre. This is a kingdom deprived of its life force. The crystals are part of the essence of the people. They merge with the citizens' physical selves. If the lights go out, then the people eventually go with them."

"They're dying," Spyre realized, staring at the darkened city.

Lif nodded. "Which is why you shouldn't be here anymore." She gave Spyre's bad shoulder a firm shove toward Condel.

He stumbled forward, wincing and grabbing his wound. He turned to her. She smiled, but this time, he knew it was out of sympathy. Not smiling himself, he nodded and turned to close the distance between himself and his ultimate goal, alone.

CHAPTER 21

Ness stayed in her blankets when the sun rose to flood the kitchen with the light of a new day; everyone else began to stir. She had slept well enough, but images conjured by the news she had received the night before plagued her dreams.

He's gone to Tir to find the source, Miss Ness. He and Pyram plan to return with it and use it to defeat Afor.

But will the source do anything to Afor if he's got a legitimate crystal? As far as she knew, the source could only enhance the strength of the Fyre. It would empower everyone, including their false king, but Afor was already so powerful. She didn't even allow the thought of his crystal glowing any brighter into her mind.

I … I don't know. Atelle sounded desperate and confused. *But the king had no way of knowing Afor would procure a crystal. He is doing the only thing he can to help. He'll find a way. He's braving the mysteries of Tir for the sake of his kingdom. That is very honorable, in my opinion. Someone willing to go to those lengths for the sake of his people can surely find Afor's weakness and exploit it, but I'm only sharing this with you because you're already in danger. Please try to keep this information to yourself. We don't want anyone getting hurt for knowing where the king is, okay?*

Ness couldn't believe it. King Eofyn had escaped into Tir to save Condel. Was this the same king who had spent an entire year allowing the morale of his kingdom to disintegrate? She tightly shut her eyes as her hand went to her forehead. She had spent so much time doubting her king that this new image of him was a challenge.

"Ness!" She heard her mother's voice calling from downstairs. "Why don't you come down here and help me make something for lunch?"

Ness groaned. In the cryptic tongue of her mother, that translated into, "Get down here where I can see you and make sure you know who's boss."

She begrudgingly threw her blankets aside and stood, blowing out a deep, frustrated breath before heading downstairs to her mother and Losian. When Ness hit the bottom stair, her brother looked at her and sneered, but their mother used her inhuman instincts to somehow read his thoughts and whipped him with a dishrag.

"You're in just as much trouble as she is," Elene reminded him. "You didn't tell us what was going on. That's incredibly irresponsible."

Ness smirked at Losian. It was a small victory, in her mind, that her brother had to share her punishment. Why else would he be peeling potatoes? Ness sauntered to the countertop, picked up a knife that was already laid out for her, and sliced the potatoes that her brother had peeled.

"I don't know why you insist on putting yourself in danger," Elene said after a long pause, which left Ness expecting her inevitable lecture. "You're not a part of the castle staff. You took your father's job as liaison upon yourself, and you misinterpreted it on top of that." She rested her stubby hands on rotund hips. "If you must do something, start in your own home, and leave the castle to the king."

Ness's eyes were wide with disbelief. She opened her mouth to ask her mother how she could possibly say such things, but Elene cut her off.

"Your job will one day be to visit the people, speak with them, understand their problems, share them with the king, and work with him to reassure the people. It will never be to get yourself killed for the sake of useless information."

"Useless? Are you serious?" Ness protested.

She dropped her knife. Her job was so much more than just listening to sob stories and relaying them to the king. If there was one thing she'd learned from watching her father before the invasion, it was that she should try to make sure that there was no call for fear and doubt. If she could prevent a catastrophe, wasn't that more useful than waiting to pick up the shattered pieces?

Elene gave her a stern look that silenced her, but she remained indignant. They stared at each other over Losian's head, making the room uncomfortable. It had been easy enough to imagine that the occupation and oppression hadn't been urgent until the arguments in the house had finally become centered on them. Afor had invaded not only the kingdom, not just the castle, but finally Ness's own home.

"There are fifteen people in this house," Elene said in a heavy monotone, breaking the silence. "That's quite a lot of potatoes to slice. You might want to pick up the pace." She turned away from Ness, face firm and uninviting, and marched wordlessly up the stairs to bed.

Ness was furious, but she knew she wouldn't get anywhere with her mother at this point. She wished she could tell her the importance of finding out more about Afor and his crystal. She wished she could explain that their king was off trying to find a weapon that might empower Afor rather than defeat him, but she respected Atelle's reasons and bit her tongue, taking her anger out on the potatoes.

She ignored the stare she was receiving from her brother, glaring at the potatoes instead and worrying over the burden she'd placed on her own shoulders by doing what she knew in her heart was right. From the corner of her eye, she saw Losian turn his attention to her steadily glowing crystal and then to his own unlit one as he toyed with it thoughtfully.

Miss Ness.

Ness's hands froze above the water she'd been using to rinse the potatoes. She cast a glance behind her, taking stock of the many people lounging in the room. Her eyes roamed the faces until she recognized Gesamne sitting at the table, whispering toilsome gossip into another neighbor's ear no doubt, but that meant Ness's bedroom was unoccupied. So she dropped the potato in the water, ignoring Losian's offended stare as the water splashed him, and strode to her room, shutting the door and locking it behind her.

How bad is it? she asked Atelle, her back pressed against the door, just in case.

She'll survive, Atelle assured her in a tense voice that hid too many truths from her.

That's not good enough. It took everything Ness had not to let her face betray what she was doing. Her mother would kill her.

Ness—

How can I get back in?

Are you insane? Atelle finally broke his usually accommodating tone.

I'm getting get her out of that castle, Ness insisted. *She'll die if they put her through this again.*

Ness opened her eyes in the twilit room. This was not the ideal time for her to get away. She had been talking to Atelle for several minutes; her mother had been resting more lately as her pregnancy drew on, but even she was probably not asleep yet. But Ness had to get to the castle. She needed a good plan. A smart person would wait until her mother was definitely asleep before attempting to sneak out, but Ness did not have that kind of patience. Afor would call for Lorette again soon, and by the sound of it, she wouldn't make it through another night.

Whatever, she thought, *I'm going for it.* She stood slowly and quietly crept to the top of the stairs.

"Really?" her mother snapped. Ness spun to see her mother leaning against her own bedroom's doorframe.

Ness loosed a defeated sigh. "Mom, I'm thirsty. I'm just going to the kitchen. Losian is down there, and he's your precious little guard dog. He'll never let me out of the house. He takes after you," she said bitterly.

Elene narrowed her eyes. "You've never been one for a glass of water before bed."

"Good thing I don't have a child's bedtime, then. Wouldn't want to break my streak."

"Young lady, I won't have you talk to me like that," Elene scolded, sitting up and looking at Ness with a Where did-I-go-wrong? face.

Ness dropped her head. She didn't really want to insult her mother. "Sorry, Mom. I just can't stand this. I have to do something. Can I please get a glass of water?"

Elene pinched the bridge of her nose and said, "Go on."

Ness briskly scaled the stairs. If she were just going for water, she wouldn't have to worry about Losian noticing. In fact, she might have tried her best to annoy him. When she reached the bottom step, as if by fate, the floorboard gave a whine of protest, and Losian's head spun her way, staring at her. She immediately pointed a warning finger at him, but he straightened anyway, responding with a single raised eyebrow.

"I don't want to go through this," Ness said dismissively, heading for the door.

Losian walked over to Ness, mirroring his mother's posture. "Are you really going to do this? What part of 'You'll be killed' don't you understand?" he hissed so the others wouldn't hear.

He looked so sure of himself. Ness almost pitied him. "We're already dying, Losian. Haven't you noticed your crystal looks completely normal compared to everyone else's now? You should be happy." Ness seethed through her teeth. "You wouldn't know because you can't feel it. You're fine, but anyone with a working crystal is feeling the strain of what Afor is doing to us, including Mom and Dad."

Losian's eyes widened, and Ness nodded.

"Yeah. Didn't know that, did you? I'm getting all kinds of grief for wanting to do something, but do you know the real reason I want to get out there? It's because if I don't do something, if somebody doesn't stop Afor, we are all going to die. And there's someone in that castle who's close to dead right now. I won't let that happen." She crossed her arms over her chest, challenging him to argue.

"But what can you do?" Losian asked, sounding only half-cynical.

She looked at him, not angry, but also not forgiving. "I don't know, but I've gotten in there before, and I'll have help to get in again. That's more than anyone else has got right now. Frankly, I don't see any other volunteers, do you?"

Losian stood in silence, his hand absently reaching for his useless crystal; Ness was never so happy that he didn't fit in to the norm of Condel.

Of course, she didn't really fit in, either. Losian was a boy without a glow, but Ness was a crystal without a cause, really. She was a purpose waiting for a reason, but the dream had chosen her, and that was reason enough for her to feel responsible for Condel's well-being.

After staring at the floor for a few moments, Losian sighed. "You should probably punch me," he mumbled.

Ness looked at him incredulously.

"So Mom thinks you got me out of the way."

Ness tilted her head. "Yeah, or you could just tell her I got out before you could stop me and that you're too smart to risk being outside at a time like this." She looked down at him and cracked a smile. "Or I could punch you. I mean, if that's what you prefer."

They smiled at each other for a very awkward moment that was promptly broken when Ness nodded toward Gesamne, practically holding court now with so many eyes on her storytelling. "Cover me," she said before slipping out the door and ducking around the corner, out of sight. She didn't turn to see if she'd been followed or if anyone had noticed. The sun was getting low, and she had no time to waste.

The street lamps had gone out. There was nothing but the smallest blush emitting from them. Ness looked down at her own dimly lit crystal. What good was promoting security and assuredness if there was no more Fyre left to use, and no one had the courage to step out of their homes (or what was left of them)? Afor had succeeded. It would be much harder to bring him down now because Ness knew the lack of light in the crystals also meant that his was burning brighter than ever.

It would take a miracle. But wasn't that what fate had given her? She had seen this coming, albeit vaguely. She had prepared herself, and because of it, she wasn't so afraid to do what she knew had to be done. There had to be hope left; otherwise, what was the point of anything?

There were still no guards on the streets, even though they must have known someone had taken her posters down. Why wouldn't they bother with their prisoners? Were they really that arrogant? She entered the castle yard and ducked behind a bush.

Go around the corner. Follow the water to the other side entrance.

There's another side entrance? Ness asked as she ran low to the ground.

Clearly, Atelle responded dryly. *Just go in that door. I'm waiting for you there.*

It was a short distance, and when Ness reached the door, it opened before her, revealing an agitated-looking Atelle.

"What?" she asked, walking past him and into the gloom. Even the castle was darker. It loomed menacingly like an abandoned temple rather than the head of a thriving kingdom.

"This is unnecessary," Atelle said, almost glaring after her.

He must have been getting used to life under Afor. Ness wasn't sure if it had made him stronger or corrupt.

"I understand your desire to help, Miss Ness, but we're already too close to losing one person in this. I can't stand the thought of you sacrificing yourself so needlessly."

"It isn't needless if it saves Lorette," Ness corrected him. "I'll be okay. I'm not going in with Afor. I'm just getting her out." She looked past Atelle and into the dark hallway. "Why didn't you just bring her here?"

Atelle looked downward, seeming defeated. "She isn't strong enough. It will take more than one of us to get her out of the castle."

"And none of the others would help you?" Ness asked, disappointed in their cowardice.

Atelle shook his head. "The guards would not hesitate to kill any one of them," he reminded her in their defense. "We have to get you to the kitchen quickly. I don't want anyone to know you're here." He turned and walked away quickly.

Ness followed, feeling in her gut that there was more danger in the castle now than there had been before. She could sense how bright Afor's crystal was. Her talent for measuring the strength of crystals apparently did not exclude him. She only wished that she could somehow use it to her advantage.

Ness was glad she'd kept her servant's frock on as they covertly navigated through the halls. Atelle checked around every corner before signaling for them to move, but they only came across a guard once.

"Why don't they give a darn about us?" Ness asked angrily. "They came here, invaded us, and just moved in. They completely ignore us like we're nothing."

Atelle stared as the guard rounded a corner. He grabbed her hand and tugged her across the hall.

"I imagine it's because we are not a threat to them," Atelle said as he scanned the next corridor. "We allowed them to conquer us with relatively no resistance, aside from the escape of the king, and the only one to make a move against them since then is you. They probably assume that the kingdom is so frightened that it's only a matter of time before someone does their dirty work for them by turning you in."

Ness cracked a cocky smile. "So I'm Condel's most wanted, huh?"

"Second," Atelle said, deflating her arrogance. "I imagine they'd much prefer to find King Eofyn." He lowered his head at her, eyebrows raised.

Ness's smile vanished, and reality rushed back to her. "Right. Keep your head in the game. Got it."

Atelle checked the next corner and waved her to cross the hall to descend the stairs into the kitchen. She followed his unspoken orders. They reached the kitchen and received unwelcoming stares from the seven maids huddled there. Most of them were the king's age, less than twenty-five years old, and had no concept of war, even from stories. They looked petrified to see Ness, but some of them looked annoyed.

"Why is she back?" one asked Atelle. "If they find her, they'll kill us all this time."

"She's only taking Lorette somewhere safe," Atelle explained. His voice pleaded with them to be patient. "It won't take long."

"Then who are they going to use next?" another asked from the corner of the room. "If it isn't Lorette, it'll be one of us."

Ness looked around, not believing what she was hearing. Not a single one of their crystals was lit, accounting for their strung-out nerves, but to turn on Lorette to spare themselves was beyond her comprehension. She moved to the pantry door while the ladies peppered Atelle with accusations. She grabbed the door handle and gently turned it to open the door with a small creak. The room was pitch-dark, where there should have been at least a faint glow from Lorette's crystal.

"Lorette?" Ness whispered delicately into the dark. "Are you here? Are you okay?"

Atelle was soon behind her, standing in the doorway. "She might be asleep," he said.

"You hope," Ness whispered, entering the room. She held up her own dim crystal for light and saw Lorette, sallow limbs, sunken eyes, and stringy blonde hair, standing in the corner, backed up against the wall, and staring at her in fear. "Lorette, I'm here to help you get out of here. You can come with me, and Afor won't be able to hurt you anymore."

Lorette's eyes were wide and seemed wild to Ness. She shook her head, curling into the wall as if she couldn't go any farther. "No," she said, staring at Ness's crystal. "No, that won't stop it." There were sobs in her voice, but her eyes seemed too wide to shed tears. "They'll take someone else, or they'll find me again, or they'll destroy the entire kingdom."

She glanced at Ness's face and then back to the crystal around her neck. "It's so bright. Brighter than yours. He's so strong now. I used to be able to last with him for several hours, but now just looking at him makes me die inside."

Ness's instincts were on alert. She backed out of the room, keeping her eyes on Lorette.

"Atelle, I think we should leave her alone for a while," she said in a low voice.

"No," Lorette screamed. She pushed away from the wall and lowered her shoulder, shoving Ness aside as she ran out of the pantry and up the stairs. They could hear her echoed cries for the guards as she ran toward the throne room.

"She's telling them you're here," Atelle said, eyes wide in shock and disbelief. "Quick, you have to hide." He reached out and grabbed her arm, running before Ness could prepare herself.

She stumbled after him as he dragged her up the stairs and down the opposite hallway than the one Lorette had used. They took several turns, none of which Ness could comprehend, and before she knew it, Atelle was pulling open a heavy door and forcing her inside.

"Stay hidden," he warned before running away.

Ness shut the door behind him and turned around to find cover, but she was not alone. She jumped and nearly yelled when she realized she'd been discovered, but Lissa hastily calmed her with a finger to her lips until Ness's senses returned to her.

"There's a niche behind the bed. Go. They'll be coming soon," Lissa said, pointing. She pulled her shoulders back and stood facing the door, preparing to deal with whoever came in next.

Ness didn't question her. She ran and slid under the bed, finding a space in the wall where several bricks had been removed behind the bed skirt. She rolled into it and covered the opening with the bed skirt just as the door creaked open.

"You're early," she heard Lissa say coolly.

There was no response, but Ness could hear the heavy footfalls of boots coming toward the bed. The bed shook as the guard lifted the skirt on the other side. Ness held a hand over her mouth, trying to control her breathing. The guard moved across the room, and Ness heard the closet door open. There was nothing for a few moments, and then the door slammed shut.

"If you see a girl that doesn't belong, you had better let us know," the guard threatened. He walked a few paces, and then Ness heard the door open and slam shut again. Her heart was pounding, and she really would have liked to cry.

"It's okay now," Lissa's voice said sadly. "Come on out. He won't be back for a while. They always think they get things right the first time."

Ness hesitated but rolled out from under the bed and onto one knee, looking up at the future queen. Lissa was smiling sadly, and Ness noticed that the guard had ransacked her closet, her clothes and belongings thrown everywhere. Ness slowly rose to her feet. Lissa's crystal, Ness noted with relief, still maintained a glow.

"Your Grace, I'm so sorry. I'll clean this up," Ness blurted, moving to pick up the strewn articles of clothing.

"Don't be ridiculous," Lissa said gently. "There's something else I need you to do."

Ness glanced up at her, a confused look on her face at such a sudden assignment. "What can I do?" she asked.

CHAPTER 22

The city gates. That wasn't the way Spyre would get in. For one thing, they were reduced to rubble, and someone would certainly notice him if he tried to pick his way through. But he liked the look of the small canal running out of the city that turned into a river leading back into the Pinewood. That was as good an entrance as any.

He scanned the rubble of the white gate and forced himself to focus on his mission and not the tragedy of the people's loss. These were the people he hoped to join, after all. If all went well—miraculously, exceptionally well—this would be Spyre's home too, and it had been laid to waste by people who looked too much like him.

There was no one patrolling the surrounding area of the city, but he kept to the edge of the Pinewood, just in case. If he knew Afor, all of his men would be in the castle, taking advantage of the amenities and awaiting their reward. He shook his head at their selfishness and hated that his own brother was somewhere among them.

How had they laid waste to the gate so easily, anyway? Afor hid things from his people, but when could he have tested something that would cause this much destruction? Had he really just conjured something and brought it here on the hunch that it would work? That didn't seem probable. Spyre knew in hindsight from Ryne's behavior that Afor had been working on this conquest for quite some time before he'd left Gaernod. But then, what was his secret?

Spyre was near the river now, running along the bank and stepping into the water momentarily to duck through the hole in the wall. He was officially in Condel, but the elation he'd expected to feel was not present. He looked around to see that half of the city was in ruin. He couldn't deny his curiosity at how Afor had managed this kind of destruction.

He trotted over to the closest crumbled building, someone's home, he realized with a wince. He stepped into the rubble and noticed the smell of ash still hung in the air. He saw something black in the corner of his eye. He knelt down and examined the charcoal residue on the white stone. He ran his hand along it and examined the dust on his fingers. It gave off a burnt scent, and Spyre suddenly had a flashback to the fireplace in his own home back in Gaernod. His eyes grew wide as he realized what this was: his own invention used as a weapon of war. This was the same powder he put in the pellets to light fires in his old house. Furious tears threatened Spyre's eyes as he stared at the carnage around him and the realization hit him.

This was his formula, he realized as hot tears stung the corners of his eyes. This was… His face dropped into his powdered hand as the guilt pummeled him in waves. This was his fault.

"Hey," a stern voice called in the distance.

He heard someone running toward him, but he froze under the weight of his guilt. The man grabbed Spyre under his arms and pulled him to his feet, staring him in the face. He didn't react. The soldier, stubble on his exposed face and ashy smudges on his cheeks, looked at him with confusion, noticing Spyre's tanned skin, dark hair, and blue eyes.

"Wait a minute. I know you. You're Ryne's brother, aren't you? What are you doing here?"

Spyre looked at him with emotionless eyes. He recognized the soldier from when his brother brought his peers home to gamble on each other's most valuable possessions. Spyre had lost a lot of his inventions that way, thanks to his brother's rotten poker face.

"You're a long way from home," the soldier observed suspiciously. "You're not cleared to be here." His mouth spread into a thin grin, as if he was suddenly very excited about something. "So you must really want to be here if you came all this way all by yourself, hmm?"

Spyre just stared at him.

The soldier shook him. "Come on, say something," he snapped. "I don't have to be so nice to you. No one will notice if you don't make it back home."

Spyre cocked an eyebrow at him.

The man's lips contorted in anger as he slapped Spyre across the face. "Ow!" Spyre yelled, rubbing his stinging cheek. He was getting tired of the abuse his body had continuously taken on this journey. Pain barely registered anymore, but the jolt of kicks and slaps and shoves was more than he could tolerate. "All right, yes, I want to be here. What do you—?"

He never got to say the last word. As soon as he admitted his desire to be in Condel, an invisible rope wound itself around Spyre's torso, and he was dragged through the dark streets of the formerly blessed kingdom, unable to catch his footing and regretting his words, without even knowing what they had done to him.

As the magical cord dragged him trippingly through the streets, Spyre tried to catch the rope or get a grip of anything that would help him keep himself upright, but he was at the mercy of the strange force that propelled him onward toward the castle. He passed a few bushes and entered a grassy area. The castle was directly ahead. It was rather majestic, except for a hole in the glass front, which appeared to be right where he was headed.

He tried to dig his feet into the ground to slow himself down, somehow, because it was becoming more and more plain that he was about to receive an audience with his own king. His immediate concern was that he didn't seem to be perfectly aligned with the hole in the glass. He was about to make it bigger. His focus went from his feet to his face as he threw his arms up, a little too quickly for his injured shoulder, to protect himself from the glass.

It didn't even slow him down. Spyre felt the glass bend and break against his arms and the sting of several small cuts on his face and forearms. He opened his eyes in time to see the person he'd been dreading, growing ever larger in his sight. Afor was smiling, and a brightly glowing crystal around his neck cast eerie shadows over his already sinister face. He held out a hand, closing one eye to measure Spyre's exact height. Spyre came to a painful halt when Afor's palm collided with his forehead, and he crumpled to the polished floor. Everything was sore, but especially his shoulder. It was throbbing, and he was seeing spots from his collision with the heel of Afor's hand. Spyre attempted to roll over, but a boot landed heavily on his chest, taking the air out of him and sending a searing pain through his shoulder.

"You're not one of my men," Afor said inquisitively, looking down his long, prominent nose at the man in front of him.

Spyre was too busy wincing against the pain to take in his king's appearance. The tear in Spyre's shirt drew Afor's attention, and he noticed the small piece of metal sticking out of his shoulder. He grinned and leaned down, putting a knee into Spyre's shoulder to replace his foot. Spyre responded with a small grunt of pain.

"Why are you here?" Afor whispered softly, sneering as he loomed over Spyre.

Spyre forced himself to open his eyes and saw the brightly glowing crystal dangling in front of his face. He had no intention of speaking. He looked Afor in the eye and blatantly denied him his answer. Afor narrowed his eyes and pressed harder into Spyre's shoulder until he could barely breathe through the pain. He'd never met Afor. The Gaernod king would have recognized Spyre's origins by the tanned skin and dark brown hair, yet this was how Afor welcomed one of his own countrymen, with no reason to doubt that Spyre supported his cause.

So Spyre said nothing to make his stance clear. Afor could piece the story together himself. "Your brother is in my service," he said, studying Spyre's atypical eyes. "So you must have noticed his prolonged absence. Is that why you came all this way?"

Okay, Spyre thought, *this is probably the opportunity I need. If I say yes, then maybe he'll use me rather than dispose of me.* Spyre nodded quickly, but Afor was already shaking his head.

"With absolutely no training, why would you bother coming such a distance only to check on your brother? I can assure you, he has no such level of concern for you." Afor smiled proudly. "He's one of my favorites—when he does the job correctly." The smile disappeared. "No, I don't think that's why you're here," he said, more to himself. He studied Spyre's face. "I think you're here to stop me."

"Well, how stupid would that be?" Spyre replied. "What possible hope would I ever have against you?"

Afor gave an agreeable nod. "But then why leave Gaernod?"

Spyre thought quickly. "I knew something … important had to be happening … since you were gone for so long," he began between panted breaths. "And I wanted to help. I'm handy with tools. I thought I could help with weapons designs or something."

The guard who had set him up to be dragged to the castle stepped through the broken window, saying, "He lies, Your Majesty."

Afor looked up, brows lifting in entertained intrigue, and Spyre craned his neck to see the stubbled soldier from before.

"I found him mourning the destruction of the city. He's not here to help. He's here to get in the way."

Afor looked back down at Spyre. "Any reply?" he asked.

Spyre knew to quit while he was ahead, and he also knew he'd never actually had a part in the race, so he tightened his jaw and maintained defiant eye contact with his king.

Afor smiled. "I admire your gall," he said. "And don't worry, as I'm sure you've seen throughout your journey, you have indeed been a great help to my cause." He sighed. "But your services are no longer required."

He looked up and gestured for a soldier.

"However, since you wanted so desperately to be here, you can enjoy your stay in the castle until death comes for you on its own time or until I see fit to make an example of you." He looked up at the guard. "Take him to a room with a view," he said, smiling.

He pressed his knee into Spyre's shoulder, grinning at his reaction to the torment, and stood, stepping aside for the soldier to grab Spyre's bad arm and drag him, stumbling, out of the room.

There were doors and tapestries and hallways and many usually awe-inspiring things on Spyre's journey to confinement, but he barely noticed any of them. The guard was more than happy to keep his thumb firmly pressed onto the arrowhead in Spyre's shoulder, causing his knees to give out with nearly every step he took.

The soldier took the long way to wherever he was taking Spyre, and when they finally arrived, he stood in the doorway and gave him a firm punch to the side of the head before closing the door and locking it. He fell to the floor, unable to move.

He was angry and devastated, and the searing, pulsing pain stabbed his shoulder in waves, drowning away the sting of his other scrapes, bruises, and sprains. So much for his opportunities. What was he supposed to do now? He had miraculously made it this far, only to be captured? It made no sense, but there was also no sign that he could get out of this room alive. He had come to aid a finished war. After all he had done, he was still useless. The only thing he had achieved was providing Afor with the devices he needed to hasten his victory. With that in mind, maybe this was how Spyre would prefer it all to end. He would just stay in this room and wait for it all to be over.

He felt something warm on his shoulder and knew without looking that it was bleeding. At least that would make things quicker.

What was he doing wrong? He thought back on the patterns of his journey and realized something: He had never been alone. In Tweogan, Faran had been his guide. In the Aforthian Mountains, he had partnered with Dugan, however unwillingly on both parts. Soru had helped him through both Eofot and the Sea of Modwen, and Rowan had saved his life, only for Lif to pick up the trail where they all left off. Was that really a coincidence?

No.

So what was it, then?

Design.

Right. Design. That made sense. Design had tripped him straight to his doom after a meaningless journey.

No.

Yes. If this was design, then where was his next guide, and how would he ever dream of getting out of this place?

Spyre opened his eyes to inspect the room he was in. The walls, like most other things in this kingdom, were white. It was rather beautiful, much nicer than anything in Gaernod, at any rate. He couldn't help but smile because he realized that he had made it. His original goal, or part of it, had been to make it to Condel, and here he was, in a better place. He hadn't completed the quest, but at least he had finished the journey.

He could take comfort in that. He stopped fighting the pain and allowed himself to just relax into the depths of his subconscious. It was all over.

A few hours later, Spyre's eyes popped open, and to his surprise, he was still alive in the same room as before. Apparently, the bleeding in his shoulder wasn't enough to kill him, though he was sure it would stain the wood floor. Was that a relief or a disappointment? He released a long sigh and stared up at the high ceiling, toying with the idea of trying to move.

As his body made the stubborn decision to stay put, something moved in the corner of his vision. He glanced over but didn't see anything. Had a guard come to finish him off? Was Afor going to make an example of him after all, and what did that even mean? But a soldier would be more vocal. He would rub Spyre's humiliation in his face. And he would probably have used the door instead of sneaking in. This was no soldier. He looked around, moving his head as much as he could without affecting his shoulder, but his breath hitched at the swell of pain, and he decided the effort wasn't worth the exhaustion.

Get up and find out what's going on, his mind scolded him.

Grimacing, Spyre rolled onto his good shoulder, his bad arm moving as if it were filled with sand. He pushed himself to his knees and turned to see someone in the shadows of the dwindling daylight. There was only the faint glow of a crystal to define them.

Was it Afor? He would be more likely to toy with Spyre like this. But why would he bother to hide his face? Spyre squinted, trying to make out any features he could. The silhouette did not look like Afor. It was too small.

Spyre slowly reached into his tattered bag for his carving knife as he dragged himself up to his full height. He pulled it out with one hand and took steps toward the intruder.

"What?" he asked the shadow bluntly. "What could you possibly want now?"

He knew his exhaustion was showing through his voice, but if they were going to kill him, couldn't they just do it already? He realized that he would never use the knife in his hand. He still wasn't over his kill in the mountains. He sighed, his whole body relaxing.

"Fine," he said as he dropped the knife. "Just get it over with, will you? I'm not feeling very patient right now."

A very confused-looking girl stepped out of the darkness; her brown hair was pulled away from her face, and she wore a torn commoner's dress over a pair of pants. She stared at the knife on the floor with wary green eyes and then glanced at Spyre.

He frowned. A girl? They would have him killed by a girl? And a Condel, no less. Oh, that was just cruel. Afor was making an example of him. He was using Spyre to corrupt the people of Condel. He had probably told this girl that Spyre was the mastermind behind the invasion. And that wasn't a lie.

"You," the girl started, stiffly pointing to the small blade on the floor. "You … dropped your knife."

Spyre rolled his eyes. "Yes. Yes, I did." His face softened its expression. "Did Afor tell you to come here? Is he forcing you to do this? Listen, I know what he's probably told you, but I didn't know he would do this. I didn't even know he'd taken my designs. I'm sorry."

"What are you talking about?" the girl asked, looking perplexed. He watched her eyes dart to the crimson on his shirt. "Fyre's light, look at you," she said, staring at his injury. "What happened?" Her eyes shot back up to his, glistening with curiosity.

Spyre stared at her, mouth open, but his brain was still struggling to decide which question he should ask. "Why—no, what … I mean, look, did Afor send you or what? I've been getting nothing but cryptic runarounds for days, and I'd really appreciate just one straight answer."

"Afor didn't send me," the girl replied, shrugging. She looked about ready to laugh at him. "I thought he'd planted you to catch me."

"What?" Spyre scoffed, laughing harshly. "No, I'm a captive, thank you very much. What did you do that Afor is after you?"

The girl furrowed her brow. "A captive?" she asked skeptically. "But you're one of them."

That stung. "Thanks," Spyre muttered, staring at the marble floor.

"Well, you are, though."

Spyre shot her an unappreciative glare. "I'm glad you told me that. I had no idea," he retorted.

"Sorry." She glanced around awkwardly and sighed, a blush dusting her high cheekbones. "Well, my name's Ness," she finally said. "The queen sent me to find you, but you're not exactly what we expected."

"What are you talking about?" Spyre asked. Whatever happened to straight answers?

Ness looked at the door. "Listen, you should come with me. The queen will explain it better than I can." She glanced down at the blood on his shoulder. "And maybe she can do something about that too."

Spyre wasn't sure how to feel about this girl, but she seemed nice enough, if a little awkward in the uncertain way she carried herself, as though she had to remind herself to stand up straight in the presence of a stranger. "How did you get in here?" he asked.

Ness pointed to a bookcase in the farthest corner of the room. "I came through that duct. This place has no windows. A lot of the rooms are like that, but they put in some little tunnels to the roof so there's fresh air."

Spyre raised an eyebrow. "Seriously?"

Ness looked at him innocently. "What? Don't you like fresh air?"

Spyre smiled and shook his head. "You're spoiled," he said, walking toward the bookshelf.

He stopped next to it and gestured for Ness to go first. She walked past him and easily climbed up the shelves and into the hole. Spyre followed, ignoring the pain in his shoulder, happy just to be getting out of his makeshift prison. Maybe there was still progress to be made, after all.

They made several wrong turns on their way to wherever Ness was taking him, and Spyre quickly realized that she was no trained soldier. She looked at least two years younger than him, possibly more.

She was making this up as she went along, just like he was, and he had to respect her for that, but on the fourth wrong turn, he said, "Do you even remember where you're going?"

"Hey," she quipped, "if you'd like to navigate, be my guest. We'll be there in a minute." She continued down the tunnel at a faster pace. "It's harder to do this when it's dark."

Excuses, excuses, Spyre thought, smiling.

Ness stopped, and Spyre fortunately noticed early enough to avoid bumping into her.

"It's this one," she said, looking back at him.

"You sure this time?"

"Yes, I'm sure," Ness said indignantly. "Just be quiet back there."

Spyre laughed at her, but it wasn't long before she rolled over onto her back and dropped herself out of another opening. Spyre followed her, landing on an elaborate carpet inside the closet of a bedchamber; he noticed the surprised eyes of still another, more regal woman. They were focused on him, and he could see the speck of distrust in them.

"So it wasn't the king," Ness said, stating the obvious, throwing her hand lazily into the air as she moved farther into the room.

Spyre looked at her. Wasn't the king? They had expected him to be the king? Why would the king have been recently captured? That was not something Spyre wanted to hear. The king should have been in captivity within the castle for at least a week now.

"I can see that," the refined woman said. She carried herself with grace and poise, her shining blonde hair falling past her shoulders. She wore a crystal too. It had a very calming blue aura to it while she examined Spyre's appearance. "He appears to be rather hurt," she observed.

A polite man would have said it was nothing and that he would be just fine, but Spyre was growing weary of having to cater to his shoulder everywhere he went, so he said nothing.

"Probably something Afor did," Ness grumbled. She stood next to the queen, arms folded, and studied Spyre with narrowed eyes. "He even tortures his own people."

Spyre squinted one eye in consideration. "To be fair, technically, I guess I did this to myself."

That earned him some confused looks.

"And Afor is fully aware that I'm not here to help him, so he isn't exactly in a hurry to make me feel at home. He doesn't work like that, anyway."

The distance between Spyre and the Condels became very noticeable as his natural acceptance of Afor's violence put a stunned look on their faces.

The second woman stepped forward carefully, hand outstretched. "My name is Lissa. I am King Eofyn's fiancée."

Spyre stared at her hand. To return her gesture, he would have to give her the hand of his injured left arm. Hadn't she noticed that? But she seemed kind, so he made the effort. He took her hand shakily, clenching his teeth against the stiffness of his shoulder. She tightened her grip on his hand and took a step toward him. Spyre tensed as the blue crystal around her neck glowed brighter. He stared at it with wide eyes, not sure if he should run or not.

"You've had this wound for a while now," she said, eyes closed. She looked as if she was reading something behind her eyelids. "It's an arrowhead." She opened her eyes and looked at him sadly. "What happened?"

Spyre stared at her, uncomfortable with her ability to know things she shouldn't. "It was a trap," he explained uncertainly. "I was in Tweogan Forest with an elf. He stepped on the trigger, and I, well, I sort of got in the way."

"You saved him, didn't you?" Lissa asked, lifting a knowing eyebrow.

Spyre shrugged and averted his gaze, feeling disconcerted under her constant stare.

Lissa looked into his eyes, leaning in to whisper, "I can fix this for you, if you'd like me to." Her face showed nothing but genuine concern.

Spyre frowned at the queen and eyed Ness, who gave a small, tight smile and nodded. He looked back at Lissa, more confused than ever, and slowly nodded. Lissa pulled a chair over and motioned for him to sit down. He hesitated but did as she asked. Then she knelt by him and placed her other hand over his wound. Spyre could immediately feel the heat radiating from her palm. He looked down at her hand in awe.

"Ness," Lissa said, eyes closed again and face serene. "I would like you to pull the arrow head out for me. Can you do that?"

Spyre blanched a little, his eyes darting to Ness, who also looked surprised. The girl didn't exactly seem prepared to be performing minor surgery today, and there was an eager gleam in her eyes that made Spyre nervous.

Ness nodded, speechless, as Lissa pulled her hand away enough to allow Ness to pinch the small piece of metal between her fingers. She slowly pulled it out while Spyre bit into the knuckle of his opposite hand and did his best not to make a sound. His eyes were closed, and he clenched his teeth, breathless against the pain. As they finally removed the arrowhead, Spyre's entire body relaxed with a subconscious sigh of relief.

Ness looked at the piece of metal in her fingers and gasped. Lissa looked sad, pressing her palm against the wound and breathing deeply. Spyre simply stared at her, his face relaxing more with every second, until Lissa finally released him and moved away. He pulled aside the two edges of his torn shirt and saw nothing but a well-healed scar. His eyes bulged, and he almost hyperventilated.

He looked at Ness in shock. "And what do you do, fly?" he asked, sounding slightly hysterical.

Ness smiled, chuckled, and said, "Nothing so impressive."

"Does it feel better?" Lissa asked.

"Is that even a question?" he responded, moving his eyes to her and then back to his shoulder. "It feels amazing." Then he remembered his manners. "Thank you."

Lissa smiled warmly.

"But …" His questions suddenly returned to him. "How did you know to come looking for me?" He looked up at the girls from his seat. "And why did you think I would be your king? Where is he? I thought he would be here. I came to help him."

"I had a dream," Lissa said. By the look on her face, that was supposed to be an acceptable answer.

Spyre slowly shook his head, waiting for more, and Lissa continued.

"Ness had it as well. We saw the two dragons of our kingdoms coming together in battle, just before Afor arrived."

Spyre wasn't following.

"In Gaernod, you have a statue of a dragon," Ness explained. "His name is Cuman."

Spyre nodded slowly. "Yeah, we do. So?"

"Don't you know the legends of the dragons?" Ness asked in disbelief.

Spyre shifted his eyes between the two women, but they appeared to be waiting for a more concrete response. He only knew of his own dream, but that had been a device of the Laefa trees to test his intentions. Had they stolen the images for his dream from these two women? He shook his head at Ness's question. It seemed the Gaernod version of the story differed from Condel's.

Lissa took over. "It is said that when Curnen falls out of balance, Cuman, the dragon of Gaernod, and Swelgan, the dragon of Condel, will animate to return order to the land. It wouldn't surprise me if Afor's family kept the legends hidden from your people. He wouldn't want anyone knowing he was planning to cause, let's say, a stir."

"I think I saw your dragon on my way into the castle," Spyre admitted, laughing a bit at how brief that glimpse was. "But that's kind of old news, don't you think? I mean, I'm not a dragon, so how did you know I'd be here?"

"I had another dream last night," Lissa said gravely, surprising Spyre with her tone. "I saw a man coming to Condel with a sword. He used it to defeat Afor and set the stage for the dragons to arrive." She looked to the side, puzzled. "I assumed, since Eofyn has gone to Tir to find the source of our abilities, that the man would be him, so I sent Ness to wait and see if Afor apprehended anyone. She must have heard the guards mention a prisoner. That's how she found you."

Ness nodded her agreement to Lissa's story.

Spyre's jaw dropped slightly, and he ran through Lissa's story in his head to make sure he'd heard her correctly. "Wait, so your king isn't here? He left?"

"My initial response exactly," Ness said, pointing a finger at him.

"He went to find a way to defeat Afor," Lissa said, defending her fiancé. "I expected him to return by now." She looked out her window with concern.

Spyre couldn't believe it. He'd come all this way, and the king wasn't even here. His hand went to his forehead as he attempted to rationalize the meaning of all this. Why was he led here? Why in the world was he brought to Condel?

"I'm sorry," Lissa said, interrupting his thoughts. "But we didn't even ask your name."

Spyre looked at her as if to say, "What good is a name now?" but he sighed and collected his composure. "My name is Spyre," he said bitterly.

"Well, Spyre, it pains me to ask you," Lissa began, unable to make eye contact with him, "but you must have come here for a reason—"

"You'd think that, wouldn't you?" he interrupted, frustrated with how useless he felt.

"I wonder if maybe," she continued, ignoring his cynicism, "you'd consider helping Eofyn find his way back to the kingdom?"

Spyre raised his eyebrows at her.

"I know it's a lot to ask, and you're probably exhausted—"

Spyre nodded agreeably.

"But this kingdom needs him. He is the only one with the gift of Pure Fyre. He is the one who can receive counsel from Bryta to help us defeat Afor."

"Bryta?" Spyre asked incredulously. He'd heard of the afterlife world before, but it was beyond him what the dead had to do with anything that was happening now.

"It's important," Ness reproached him. "I'll even go with you."

"No, you won't," both Lissa and Spyre said at the same time, Lissa admittedly more gently than Spyre. Spyre wouldn't have a liability with him. He'd been injured enough times to know the perils of leaving your own realm, and Tir was unknown territory, even by human standards. Ness was inexperienced, optimistic, and vibrant; he'd never forgive himself if something were to happen to her.

Ness gaped at them, offended.

"It's too dangerous," Lissa explained kindly. "You need to go back with your family, Ness."

"Exactly," Spyre agreed without Lissa's level of conviction, only glancing at the girl before returning his attention to the queen. "Where exactly am I supposed to go?"

Lissa looked at him, eyes full of gratitude. She put a hand on his healed shoulder and smiled up at him. Spyre, still unaccustomed to people coming near him without violent intentions, stared at her hand suspiciously and glanced up at her.

"Thank you," she whispered sincerely. "Just beyond Condel, there is a desert land called Tir." She grimaced a little, embarrassed. "Sadly, no one has ever journeyed there and returned to describe it."

Spyre rolled his eyes again, dropping his hands to his sides. "Oh, good. Is that all?"

"I don't think Eofyn and his guide, Pyram, lost their way," Lissa said, trying to comfort him. "But I fear that they may have met with trouble."

"And you want me to go save them and bring them back," Spyre finished for her.

Lissa nodded.

Spyre let out a short laugh. "I don't know if you've realized," he said, "but I'm not exactly well prepared for this kind of thing." He fished out his carving knife and dangled it in front him. "That's not exactly a sword like you saw in your dream, is it? I don't have a sword."

Lissa waved a dismissive hand at him. "The sword was most likely symbolic," she explained. "You are here for a reason. Something called you here, and I don't think you can deny that."

Spyre unwillingly agreed.

"You can do this. I believe you are meant to," Lissa said confidently. She placed a hand on Spyre's cheek, and his eyes grew wide.

He nearly backed away. The last time someone had done this, he had ended up half-drowned on a beach. But this queen seemed so sincere. That also scared him.

You can do this.

But could he?

Sure, why not? You've come this far. What are another few days?

He groaned. "Okay, but how do I get out of here?" He looked back at the door, wishing it could be that easy.

Lissa smiled at him and looked at Ness. "Ness has to be getting home before someone finds her, anyway."

Ness didn't look happy, but she also didn't argue. She let her folded arms fall to her sides and said, "I'll show you out."

"Are we taking the air tunnels, or can we use a door this time?" Spyre joked.

"What? Your shoulder is fine now. You can't handle a little crawling?" Ness asked, returning his wit.

"You know the way?" Lissa interrupted, frowning at Ness.

Ness blushed slightly. "I got a little lost on my way to find him." She tilted her head toward Spyre. "I found a hole that drops out near the side passage. I wouldn't be able to climb in from the door, but I can drop out of it with no problem."

Lissa smiled warmly at her. She walked over and pulled Ness into a hug, making Spyre feel awkward. "You get him safely outside, and then you go straight home, do you understand?" Her sweet tone didn't hide how serious she was.

Ness laughed and nodded. "As you wish, Your Highness." She looked at Spyre and nodded toward the hole in the wall, heading over to it as Lissa pulled Spyre aside by the arm.

"You're not going to hug me, are you?" he asked, shuffling back a step.

She laughed gently. "No. I just want to wish you the best of luck and thank you. Thank you so much." She looked almost proud. "I know you've been through a lot, and I don't know what lies ahead for you, but I am very glad you came here. I promise you a warm welcome into Condel when all of this is finished, if that's what you want."

Spyre smiled feebly and said, "Let's just see if I make it back first, hmm?"

She nodded, still smiling at him. He stepped away from her and followed Ness into the tunnel, feeling strange.

Ness was much more decisive about the direction to the exit. They took no wrong turns as they crawled in silence. Spyre marveled with every shift of his weight to his left shoulder. He could not believe he was back on his mission again so quickly, and that all his other wounds had finally been healed. He'd forgotten what it was like to be without pain as his constant companion. He would be alone for the rest of his quest, but at least now, he could move quicker without his energy being drained by his injuries, and he hadn't failed yet.

"It's just up here," Ness whispered back to him; her excitement made her eyes gleam in the dark of the tunnel. She jumped down and waved for him to follow, but as soon as Spyre's feet hit the stone floor, they heard shouting.

"You two," a guard yelled, grabbing his partner. "Get back here."

"This is it, huh?" Spyre growled cynically, glaring as he caught Ness by the arm and ran. "Which way is it, really?"

Ness quickly looked around. "Okay, so I was one off. It's just up there. The next left."

Spyre tightened his grip on her and picked up his speed, rounding the next corner and throwing the door open.

Not yet.

Ness moved to run through the door, but he yanked her back and threw her to the wall by both of her shoulders. He pressed them both against the stone and covered them with a thick hanging curtain that framed an elaborate portrait of some ancient king or another.

The guards caught up to them and ran through the open door, still shouting for them to give themselves up.

Spyre let himself breathe once their voices faded. "Sorry," he said to Ness as he pulled the curtain aside for her.

Her eyes were wide in surprise and stayed focused on him while she stepped away from the wall.

"That was brilliant," she whispered. "How did you think of that so fast?"

Spyre looked back at her. Questions? At a time like this? "Are you serious?"

She nodded, urging him to answer.

"I don't know," he let out frustrated. "Gut instinct, I guess." What did it matter?

"You really need to teach me—" Ness started, but Spyre cut her off.

"Oh, no, I don't. You really need to get home."

She looked at him as though he'd just spoiled her fun.

"Where do you live, anyway?" he asked, tugging her into the darkness outside. "I've got to get back through the city, so I might as well make sure you get back safely."

Ness's frown melted away at the idea that her adventure wasn't over yet. "I just have to go down that way." She pointed. "It's not too far. The soldiers don't go down there, either, so you should be okay."

"It's not me I'm worried about," Spyre said, taking her by the shoulders and pushing her forward before the guards could come back. The farther they were from the castle, the better.

He let Ness lead him back to her home. Her sense of direction was much better outside of the castle. She had clearly taken this path through the back streets of her neighborhood several times, and Spyre knew that meant she'd been getting herself into more trouble than she should have. This was the naivety Spyre expected of a Condel, but instead of the frustration he'd felt with the other creatures like Faran and Lif, he found Ness's intrepid spirit endearing, and he was happy that hers was not one of the crumbled houses. His inventions hadn't destroyed her home. He stopped at her door, waiting for her to go in, but she paused.

"Do you need anything?" she asked him, a feeble effort to prolong his leaving. "Food? Blankets? I don't know."

"I'm fine, thanks," Spyre said, nudging her toward the door. "I need to get out of here as soon as possible. Which is the fastest way to the canal?"

"On this side of the city, all you have to do is go down that way." She pointed around the corner and to the left. "You'll be there in no time."

"Okay. Got it. Thank you."

"Thank you," she said.

He looked at her as he adjusted his satchel, questioning.

"You're doing us a huge favor, and you don't have to. So thank you."

He nodded. "Yeah," was all he could think to say in response. "Listen, you should get inside. Take care of yourself." He didn't wait for her to respond before heading around the next corner.

His social skills were failing him in this city. The Condels made him feel uncomfortable, like he was something alien, which he sort of was. He skirted along the city wall until he came to another canal. He followed it and halted near the exit of the city.

Go now.

But what if someone was coming?

Just go. You'll be fine. Go now.

He rejected his body's urge for caution and ran into the water and out of the city, unnoticed.

Spyre was growing fond of darkness. It usually meant that he had a chance to rest and that nothing would threaten his life for a few hours, but tonight, he couldn't think of resting. His shoulder felt perfectly fine, and he knew he still had quite a way to go before he finished his journey. He was back in the game, and the confidence that the queen had in him made him feel like he might actually be capable of making a difference.

The king was in trouble, and Queen Lissa had seen Spyre as a hero, sword in hand, come to save her kingdom. It was believable enough. After all, wasn't he persevering simply on the notion that fate had lured him out of Gaernod? Was that so different from trusting the visions of a dream?

He was making decent time. The trees were fewer and farther between than they had been when he'd first left Condel, and he knew Tir couldn't be very far away. The thought of seeing a desert was sort of thrilling to Spyre. He felt wiser somehow, having experienced the many environments of Curnen, and he looked forward to completing the collection the land offered.

He felt privileged to be one of the few people ever to leave his own realm. It helped him better understand the difference between being a human and being a person. The elves, trolls, seafolk, sprites, and even the wisps were just as much people as the humans were. They all had feelings and opinions, even though they all feared each other. Granted, the brutish demeanor of the trolls didn't make it easy to like them at first, but once they relented and opened their own minds, a common ground wasn't hard to find.

He hoped that Faran and Dugan continued to work together. There was a lot they could learn from each other. There was a lot he had learned from them, and his fondness toward them made him realize that he was not only doing this for the sake of Condel. Spyre wanted to preserve the lifestyles of all the realms of Curnen from Afor's reach, like Lif had said. Where Afor had traversed the land to conquer it from top to bottom, Spyre had done it to connect them and spare them from Afor's selfish goals. It all felt very ironic.

He found himself at the top of a hill that would take him to the border of Tir and succumbed to the strangest urge to turn around. He saw Condel, a kingdom in the dark. It was still beautiful, and he tried to imagine what it would look like once the light returned to it.

But first you must take the light from Afor. The words formed clearly in his mind but felt foreign to him somehow, like they weren't his own thoughts.

What light?

His crystal, his mind offered.

That was a good point. How had he gotten a crystal to function for him, anyway?

The same way the people have a function in their own, his brain supplied. *The same reason they're losing it now.*

What reason was that?

Belief.

Belief?

Yes. They believe what Afor wants will happen; the thought sounded irritated. Could Spyre's own brain be frustrated with him? Was that even possible? *Therefore, when you expressed a want that coincided with Afor's intentions, their belief in Afor's strength brought you to him. The power is not his own but an unwilling gift given to him by the people's fear.*

Okay, now Spyre knew he hadn't come up with that one on his own. He'd heard this voice in his head since he'd entered the castle, and he'd assumed it was his own thoughts and instincts speaking to him, but this was ridiculous.

"Who is that?" he demanded out loud, to make it easier to tell the difference between the phantom voice and his own.

I thought you'd never ask.

"Well, I'm asking now," Spyre said defensively. It was hard not to feel vulnerable with a foreign voice inside his head. He glanced around, looking for any shadow that might be following him.

I've been with you since you left Gaernod, the voice explained. *I've never looked the same, but I've been there. You may call me Lateo.*

"I've only been hearing voices since I reached Condel. Don't lie to me," Spyre warned, walking faster as if the voice, Lateo, would have trouble keeping up.

First, I was small and affected, with the confusion of an elf. Then I was larger, with the suspicion of a troll, the voice explained in a tone that sounded like Spyre should catch on at any second.

"So … what? You were with Faran and Dugan?" Spyre asked. He felt lost.

Close, the voice said.

"You're kidding," Spyre said as the answer hit him. "You possessed them?"

I really wouldn't call it possession. This would always have happened, and they did nothing against their will. I merely enabled them to defy their nature enough to have the courage to guide you. It's not like they won't have benefited from it.

"Benefited?" Spyre scoffed angrily at the surrounding air. "What about Soru? How was what happened to it a benefit?"

The wisp was chosen because of its true desire to escape from its surroundings, Lateo explained calmly. It was the voice of a scholar, if Spyre had to put a title to it. Lateo's tone was clear, crisp, refined, more intelligent than Spyre's own internal dialogue ever sounded to him. *Soru had no intentions of returning to Eofot, just as you have no desire to return to Gaernod. The difference is you have the privilege of pursuing that option.*

Spyre could see the logic there, but that still didn't make it right in his mind. "So what are you, then? Are you supposed to be what lives in Tir? Your consciousness can reach across Curnen, but you live here?"

An interesting guess, but no. I exist in a world that is somewhat beyond this one.

"You mean Bryta, don't you?" Spyre asked suspiciously, not sure how ready he was to accept it.

You'll simply have to trust me, Lateo said. *I've gotten you this far, haven't I?*

"With more than a few close calls," Spyre pointed out indignantly.

Experiences of growth. You needed to realize what you're capable of.

Spyre shook his head. This was insane. He had gone insane. He scratched the back of his head, wondering which part of him had finally snapped. He looked skyward. "Okay, listen. I've been seeing a lot of new things lately, so it's easier to believe an abstract voice is guiding me from inside my head, but you must know how absurd this all sounds. There's a difference between trust and gullibility, you know?"

He looked back down to the ground and kicked a nearby stone, surprised when he heard it collide with something in front of him. He frowned and picked up his pace at the sight of a stone slab sticking out of the ground in front of him.

"A straight path has yet to earn its curves," Spyre read aloud. "What you seek is before you."

He stepped back and looked ahead of him. To his surprise, there was nothing but sand extending across the landscape in smooth dunes. He had reached Tir, and in the distance, he could see the faint outline of a towering building in the dark. That, he assumed, was what the stone implied he was seeking. Apparently, people didn't come to Tir for many reasons other than to find that structure, and who was Spyre to argue with that? If it was what he was seeking, it was probably also what King Eofyn had been seeking, which meant that it was what Spyre was looking for. Score one for the stone slab.

"This way?" he asked Lateo, staring into the distance. If the invisible being was going to tag along, then he might as well make use of it.

That way, the voice confirmed.

CHAPTER 23

Ness didn't like to lie, but she hadn't seen another option. As soon as she entered the door to her house, Losian was waiting for her, his hair rustling in the breeze from the open window behind the washbasin across the room. He looked over her shoulder and saw Spyre running away through the window. Even in the darkness, she knew he could tell that Spyre was not of Condel. His face had said it all: eyes wide, slacked jaw, the threat of a scream bobbing at his throat. Ness had quickly addressed it.

"It's okay," she said, putting her hands out toward Losian to gesture that he didn't have to panic. "He isn't like them. He's not a soldier. He's actually here for us." She smiled. "I'm going to follow him."

"Are you crazy?" Losian hissed. "Just because he isn't a soldier doesn't mean he'll think twice about killing you. And where is he going? Do you even know?"

Ness approached him, placing both hands on his shoulders. "Losian," she said calmly, "he's going to do something that will help stop Afor and save the kingdom. We need him, and he needs help."

"What will Mom and Dad do?" Losian asked. "They'll be devastated."

Ness had collected a few things to last her several days: a loaf of bread, some cheese.

"I'm safer outside of the city than I am here," she responded, remembering Lorette. "Just trust me."

"That's getting harder to do with the more ridiculous schemes you keep trying to pull off," Losian muttered.

He obviously worried about her, and Ness had to admit that she appreciated it, but she didn't have time to argue with him.

She discarded her gray frock in favor of the flexibility of her tunic. Then she threw her mother's shopping bag, food inside, onto her shoulder and gave Losian a curt smile.

"Take care of Mom and Dad while I'm gone," she meant to say, but an abrupt rapping that nearly sent their house's wooden door off its hinges startled both of them. Sounds of stirring filled the house as loud, angry men shouted to be let in by Afor's orders.

Ness caught Losian's eyes, so round with shock that they reflected even the dim light of the room, but she had no consolation for him. All she knew is they were looking for her, and everyone would be in danger if they found her here. Ness attempted one last, reassuring smile for her brother before running to the washbasin and slipping out the back window into the crisp air; she ducked around the corner, where she crouched and waited.

The uncharacteristic chill of night, probably due to the absence of ambient crystal energy, with the lights of the Fyre so dark now, seeped through Ness's clothes and into her bones. Or perhaps it was just the fear draining the blood from her limbs that sent cold chills all over her arms and at the crown of her head.

"I said open up," one of two soldiers sent to claim her shouted before kicking the door. "Out of the way."

Ness recognized her mother's delicate tone in a startled shout as the soldiers forced their way inside. The murmur of their fearful houseguests soon rose as everyone in the house must have emerged to investigate the noise, and panic ensued.

"Where's the girl?" a harsh voice demanded. "Where is she?"

Ness cast her gaze down the winding, cobbled street. She should run. To risk being seen would only incriminate her family. It was best they not be associated with her. Maybe if the guards thought they had the wrong house, they would leave everyone alone.

"You!" she heard one the Gaernods shout. Who? Who were they singling out?

Against everything in the core of her being, Ness ran to the window and ducked low, peering in so that her vision was half-windowsill and half the scene unfolding inside.

Both soldiers stood just inside the door, leering and proud of the fear they wrought, as no one dared peel themselves away from the wall to confront them. At the stares, she noticed her father trying to push through shoulders, but the others were too frozen with fear to budge. Her mother was in the tight, protective embrace of Gesamne, but Ness noticed she was struggling to free herself. Following her mother's desperately outstretched arm, Ness understood why.

The soldiers had caught Losian by the front of his shirt before he could retreat to the safety of the others. The boy struggled for a panicked moment, but his knees gave out and hit the planks of the floor, his eyes glazing over like an animal consigned to its fate in the clutches of a predator.

The grins that split across the soldier's faces showed they enjoyed Losian's resignation to his fate. The one with a grip on the boy's shirt yanked him to his feet and clutched him by the shoulders so tightly, Losian's feet only brushed the floor.

The soldier craned his neck to speak directly in Losian's ear. "King Afor requires your presence."

"No, wait," Darien shouted from the stairs.

The second soldier drew a sword; the sound of it leaving its sheath was shrill against the tense quiet in the room, and several people cringed away. "If anyone moves," the soldier warned, "I wouldn't mind having a bit of fun." He leveled the blade at Elene.

Darian stood still.

Elene shrieked as the soldiers laughed with each other and turned to leave, Losian unresponsive, save for his eyes darting to the window.

Ness's breath caught in her throat as their gazes met. Her brain erupted with panicked thoughts of what she had to do, how she had to save him, but her limbs knew better and did nothing.

I'll save you, her mind screamed for Losian, but she was not so talented as Atelle. Losian could only see that she wasn't coming to his aid. She had no way of relaying her promise or reassuring him that she would make things right.

The door creaked as the soldiers dragged Losian into the night air; as soon as his stare was cut away by the doorframe, Ness ran for the city gates. Her only option to save her brother from Gaernod was to bring back another Gaernod to face Afor. Spyre was more than a curiosity and an adventure now. He and King Eofyn were her family's—her kingdom's—only hope.

Fear, guilt, and disgrace numbed her legs, propelling her to the city gates and toward the rolling dunes of Tir before fatigue could catch up to her.

She caught sight of Spyre, the only figure moving toward the horizon, from the moment she'd left the city. Her heart leapt in relief, but she wasn't willing to join him until she was sure they were too far for him to send her back. She couldn't go back. It pained her to admit it, but she couldn't save anyone on her own, and a coiling tendril of shame in the pit of her stomach reminded her that she didn't want to face the evil within the city walls. She wanted denial and the daydream of helping the real hero save the day. She wanted joy, even if it was only to shield herself from reality. So she followed Spyre from a distance, watching him appear to mull things over while he walked through the night and gasping as they arrived at the border to Tir, where she stood now.

It was breathtaking. She looked out over the sand and couldn't believe how clear the border between the outlying Pinewood and Tir was. Grass quickly faded into sand, and trees just suddenly ceased to exist. Were all the borders this way? Spyre would know. She stared at him from a distance as he examined a large stone, imagining what he'd seen between Gaernod and here. She wished she could have traveled like that but under better circumstances.

She moved in closer so she wouldn't lose Spyre's trail in the sand, knowing full well that after traversing Curnen, he was in much better shape than she was, and that meant he would probably be moving faster as well. She couldn't wait to reveal herself to him. There was so much about the blue-eyed man from Gaernod that fascinated her.

CHAPTER 24

"It can't just be a straight line," Spyre said aloud, staring at the empty expanse of desert sand in front of him and remembering the consequences of taking the direct path in Tweogan. The enigmatic stone behind him had said as much. He hadn't taken a single step forward, convinced that there would be some kind of trap waiting for him. "Nothing is that easy."

It isn't, Lateo agreed, but he added nothing else.

"Helpful," Spyre quipped, kneeling down to examine the stone closer. "A straight path has yet to earn its curves …"

He straightened and glanced around. All he saw was sandy darkness on either side of him. No path. No curves. He looked back down at the stone.

"What you seek is before you," he muttered to himself. "I guess looking around here proves I have nowhere else to go, right?"

Just keep moving, Lateo urged him. *Time is not exactly waiting for you.*

Spyre sighed; he didn't feel fully confident, but he stood and moved forward, taking his first few steps gingerly, in case something collapsed from beneath him. Maybe the slab meant that he should continue to look around, like he should constantly make sure that the temple wasn't to the side of him.

No, that was stupid. This place was established long ago, and Spyre knew Afor's men, who would have undoubtedly been sent to find the king, just like Spyre had been, wouldn't have had time to plant traps for anyone foolish enough to try following them. Who might have followed them from Condel?

Spyre was just glad that Gaernod people didn't have magical gifts like the Condels, so Afor had no way of warning his agents that someone might pursue them. If he had, Spyre would surely have been killed by now.

Feeling confident of his security, Spyre walked on until the moon reached its climax in the crisp night sky, and Lateo interrupted his thoughts.

You may want to take some rest. It is late, and you may find yourself in a confrontation tomorrow.

"I'm almost there now," Spyre said dismissively. "I can make it closer. Why waste time tomorrow?"

You have unfinished business you need to take care of.

Spyre frowned, confused. "What business is that? And weren't you the one who said I should keep moving a while ago?"

You've come as far as you need to tonight, Lateo said briskly. *I needed you to get past your trepidation at the border. You've done it. Good job. Now sit and finish what you started.*

Spyre threw his hands into the air. "What did I start?"

The project you have in your pack, Lateo insisted. *Do you really want to end this journey without having finished that? It's so near to its completion.*

"It's a piece of wood," Spyre retorted, "a means to pass the time."

Suddenly, though, his legs felt exhausted, and the temple looked much farther away than he remembered. He heaved a childish sigh and dramatically dropped his bag to the sand, falling to a seated position next to it. He grumbled inwardly as he fished the piece of wood out of his bag. He looked at it in the light of the full moon. He really didn't know what he was planning to do with it. He'd fiddled with it so much that it seemed beyond anything functional.

It was now thinned out and rounded, two narrow grooves spiraling down the length of it to create a raised ribbon. The bottom had become somewhat bulbous, with small grooves making wide helixes all over it, and at the top, he had made a smooth, flat plate that curled in on itself at both ends. Intricate but useless. A mantle ornament, if anything.

He pulled out his knife and picked at the top of it, almost angrily, digging down through the center to create a thin opening at the top. Why couldn't he go find the king now? It was dark, and he hadn't brought any torches or anything that gave off light, like, say, a crystal from Condel, but that would do him no good anyway, and if he was honest, neither would entering a temple that must have been beyond ancient if no one had ever returned from it. Maybe it was a temple of advanced technology with some form of artificial lighting, and those who traveled there stayed voluntarily. Spyre laughed and shook his head at how naïve that theory was.

"Take some rest," he repeated, mocking Lateo's ethereal voice. "How is that even possible?"

Tomorrow, he would have to rescue a king who would see him as an enemy, but hey, no sweat. Where was Rowan when he needed her? Or, heck, he'd have even taken the spores of the Laefa trees to knock him out. Tonight promised to be a long one.

Spyre looked at his frivolous creation and wrinkled his nose. What a waste of time, he thought. But at least it had occupied his hands through his anxiety about tomorrow. He shoved the piece of wood into his pack, followed by his knife, and fell backward onto the sand.

He moved around until the sand beneath him fit the contours of his back more comfortably, and he looked up at the sky, glancing from star to star. He took in a deep breath and released it slowly, his mind clearing. If he was anything like the man that the Condel queen hoped he was, dumb luck would guide him through tomorrow, just as it had held his hand since Gaernod. He blinked, looking left and right, wondering if the voice in his head would remind him that the dumb luck had a name.

Lateo, his faceless chaperon, had been tugging him, tripping and stumbling, in the right direction. Creepy as that idea was, he knew he was lucky. Thinking about what he'd be doing right now if he'd stayed in Gaernod, Spyre couldn't have been happier to be alone in a desert on the eve of what would hopefully be a heroic conquest. He tilted his head back, releasing the tension he hadn't even known was stiffening his neck, serenity on his face. Honestly, he wasn't sure what he was so worried about. What did he have to lose?

CHAPTER 25

What a strange man Spyre was. Ness had followed him closely as he set off into Tir, but when he came to a sudden stop, she almost got too close. Without warning, the mystery man from Gaernod had simply stopped and sat down. He had worked on something, seeming very impatient about it, and then just flopped over. Now he was staring at the sky. She couldn't see his face, but he didn't seem so upset anymore. He was actually going to sleep.

At a time like this? They were almost halfway to the temple. She was hoping to catch up to him in a little while, but her paranoia told her they still weren't far enough into Tir for him to keep her around. Tomorrow would be better. For tonight, she would sleep in the sand.

Ness almost woke up too late. She had to keep up with Spyre if she had any hope of getting back to Condel in time to save Losian from whatever Afor had taken him for.

After she rubbed the sleep out of her eyes, she noticed that Spyre was already on the move. Thank goodness Tir was such an open space, or she might have lost his trail. She scrambled to her feet, feeling the toll of having slept in the lumpy sand as she stood. It took a few steps for the soreness in her back and legs to ease enough for her to move properly, but she caught up to Spyre quickly enough.

He was talking to himself again, shaking his head and making small gestures with his hands. Ness was questioning the man's sanity. Was he nervous? Lonely? Confused, most likely, but his pace was slowing, so she slowed too and paid close attention from the top of a small dune.

"Don't do what?" Spyre grumbled at the air around him, as though annoyed at being in the middle of a sentence she hadn't heard him speak.

Spyre paused and looked at the sand around his feet. He threw his hands to his sides in frustration. He glared to the side, puffing out his cheeks but then diverted his path, kicking the sand impetuously.

Ness watched him deviate from his path, even though the temple was right in front of him. He was full of senseless surprises. She tentatively stepped down the side of the dune to pursue him. This seemed like the perfect opportunity to quietly pass him and get to the temple ahead of him. He would be so surprised to see her that she should have no trouble convincing him not to send her back to Condel. Because there was no way she was going back now.

Smiling to herself, she marched down the side of the dune, but the smile was soon replaced by a gasp when the sand beneath her foot gave way. She threw her hands out for balance but only flung herself headfirst into a graceless cartwheel, sending her tumbling down the slope. She went down, heels swinging over her head, until she reached the bottom, conveniently landing on her feet, but she wasn't stable enough to catch her balance there.

She stumbled forward like a rag doll before finally tripping when her torso got too far ahead of her feet. With her next exaggerated step, her foot suddenly sank into the sand, which covered her leg up to her knee. She caught herself, one leg still on the sturdier sand and the other in the muck, leaving her in a very uncomfortable split position. She tried to jump closer to the edge of whatever pit she was in, but instead, she sank up to her thigh. She rolled her eyes. This was embarrassing. There was no way she was getting out of this on her own.

She stretched out, knowing she wouldn't be able to reach the edge of the pit and that even if she could, it would get her nowhere. But it was still better than the alternative. She cringed as she plucked up her gall and tried to ignore the shame of what she had to do. She desperately hoped he was still close.

"Sp—" She sighed, shaking her mortification from her mind and closing her eyes. "Spyre!"

Not too far away, Spyre's ears perked up at the sound of a girl's voice that didn't belong to either Lateo or himself. It was a welcome change, but who else would call his name in this strange desert, and a girl, no less? He looked over both of his shoulders before spinning around completely. The girl caught his eye and looked at him expectantly, arms hovering above the sinking sand. "Are you going to help me or what?" she called to him.

Spyre froze. What did she think she was doing? He didn't need keen vision to see who it was. He took his time, backtracking the way he had come, laughing to himself, fully aware at how annoyed Ness was becoming and enjoying it.

"So this is what you meant," he muttered to Lateo, earning a raised eyebrow from Ness.

He would worry about explaining that later. Now he could see a subtle difference between the sturdy sand and the quicksand. He slowly walked along the edge of the pit, aware of Ness's impatient eyes on him. He slipped his bow from his shoulder and extended it to the girl.

"Grab that," he instructed her.

She looked like she wanted to slap him but quietly took hold of the wooden bow. Spyre put his foot against hers on the solid sand and pulled her upward with the weapon, catching her hand in his when she was close enough and pulling her out of the soupy trap. He laughed more as she tried to brush the sand off her clothes.

"That's what you get for following me," he said. "And good luck getting those stains out." He gestured with a shallow bow to his own pants, still ruined from the Tweogan bog. "What in the world were you thinking?"

Ness scoffed at him. "Ha! You think I'd let you go alone?"

Spyre looked around at the empty desert. "Why not?"

"Because," Ness answered, but then she blinked and sighed. "Look, my home is at stake, and now they've taken my brother, and I can't go back without a way to rescue him."

"They took your brother?" Spyre curled his upper lip in an angry snarl. "See, this is why you should never have meddled in the first place."

Ness rolled her eyes. "That doesn't matter anymore. You're my only chance to save him now. And I just feel like I'm supposed to be here." She gave him a wary look before admitting, "I've been … connected to this from the beginning."

Spyre looked confused but felt intrigued; who was he to argue? It sounded no more insane than him having voices in his head. He held out an arm to her, waving her toward him. "Come on," he said evenly. "Walk and talk."

CHAPTER 26

"So you had a dream too, huh?" Spyre asked as they walked toward the temple.

He could have tried to send Ness back, but he knew by the look in her eyes that insisting would be a waste of time. He might as well argue over the meaning of life with Lateo.

Ness nodded.

"But that still doesn't explain why you're here. The queen didn't come along because of her dream."

Ness let out a short burst of breath. "The *queen*," she said with emphasis, "doesn't have an evil king trying to capture her and holding her family hostage."

Spyre nodded at her understandably defensive reaction.

"Besides," she added, shrugging, "I know I'm supposed to be here. I just do." She lowered her head. "Someone who spent the past few days talking to himself should know a little something about following instincts, I'd hope."

Spyre leveled his gaze at her. "Following and spying, hmm?"

"They're sort of the same thing, don't you think?" Ness looked up at him, eyebrows raised.

Spyre laughed. "I doubt it," he mumbled.

She had confused him, but not with her vague reasoning. Spyre was noticing the stark differences between the Condels and Gaernods beyond physical appearance. This girl was making him wonder if he might have social issues. Her ability to give the impression that she trusted him so quickly was not the welcome he was used to receiving from anyone, even the creatures he'd met on his way to Condel.

Suspicion or even eerie tests of courage were more like it, but now he felt that same sense of distrust he'd had such disdain for back in Gaernod. No offense to Ness. He liked her. With her blind spunk, she had reassured him that there was still such a thing as someone who was ignorant to the true evil of the world, even when she'd encountered him face to face. As she walked beside him, as if she belonged there, he couldn't help being just a little impressed by her.

"Why do you really think you had the dream?" Spyre asked, focusing intently on her as they walked.

Ness frowned, either confused or frustrated, but Spyre had a feeling she might actually be frustrated because she was so confused.

"I don't know," she said with a strain.

"Yes, you do," Spyre countered.

She looked up at him. Her eyes glazed with defensive insecurity.

"You have a theory." He held her eyes with his. "Otherwise, you wouldn't be here. You wouldn't have done anything from the start. You'd have stayed safely in your house like the smart people in your city." She folded her arms across her chest with a juvenile huff, but he held up a hand to calm her. "You think it's crazy," he conceded, looking into her eyes like he could see through her, "but you have an idea. So tell me."

Ness opened her mouth to speak, but only air came out. She shut her mouth and studied him for a moment. Spyre gave her an encouraging nod, and she tried again.

"I can't tell you why the dream came to only the queen and me," she began slowly, "but I can guess why we would be included in it."

Spyre nodded, impatient for her to continue.

"I can't give you a good reason, but I've always felt like I was meant to do something to help protect Condel."

Spyre frowned. "Was Condel in trouble before?" he asked.

"No," Ness admitted, sulking. "That was always kind of frustrating— not in a bad way," she amended quickly. "I just always knew something would happen one day, and then the dream came, and I saw the dragons."

"The statues," Spyre said.

Ness nodded stiffly. "Yes. Cuman and Swelgan. But the legends are real. They have to be. If all of this is happening, then I know those dragons will come to life sometime soon."

Spyre looked away. "Yeah, but why wouldn't they have just done it before Afor got there? He did a lot of awful things on his way to conquer you."

Spyre's fist clenched as he thought of the people of Curnen who had died for being too close to Afor on his way to Condel. What kind of protectors are they if they let that happen? "And the people who were killed when he first arrived at Condel—doesn't that bother you and your theory?"

"I think if we didn't suffer some losses," Ness said, choosing her words carefully, "then we wouldn't learn from this."

Spyre's felt his eyebrows rise to his hairline. "Oh, so you think all these people are suffering to teach us a lesson?"

Ness glared at him.

"I think things got this way because people on both sides were closed-minded and didn't ask enough questions."

One of Spyre's eyebrows returned to its original position, but the other was not yet convinced.

Ness rolled her eyes. "Do you think Afor would have the power to cause such a stir if your people questioned his authority when it got out of hand?"

Spyre's face fell.

"And do you think my people would be so utterly crippled if we'd have questioned whether we'd be eternally untouched by the outside world, even though we knew Afor existed and hated our previous king?" Ness looked to the sand. "We were ignorant," she said heavily.

Then she looked up at Spyre with fascination in her eyes. "But you came all this way because you did question Afor. You learned the lesson, and now you're helping us learn ours."

Spyre felt uncomfortable being given so much credit. He rubbed the back of his neck and looked away, escaping her constant gaze. He wasn't worth the fascination she seemed to have with him. He was human as much as she was, just from a different part of the world. Of the two of them, only she could wield a crystal and harness its power.

"I think once we've seen enough, the dragons will restore order," Ness concluded quietly, "but we have to learn to never let this happen again, if we can help it."

Spyre had no argument. It still didn't seem fair of the dragons to let so many innocent people suffer as a lesson for humans, but her point was a good one. "You never doubted it. Not once?" he asked her, raising an eyebrow.

She looked down her nose at him, lips in a thin line and chin jutted forward. She shook her head and glanced away. "Why would I? It's my birthright. One day, the confidence of the people will be on my shoulders, and I will make sure that no weakness will ever make them feel this vulnerable again."

"What's wrong with the current protector of the Fyre?" Spyre asked. Had he come all this way just because someone in Condel was underperforming at their special, crystal-given job? *Please,* he thought. *How complacent could they get?*

Ness looked down. "Nothing. He's amazing," she said, smiling. "He's just … too worried about what people think they are as compared to what they can be."

Spyre let out a short laugh. "You have an awful lot of faith in yourself and your people," he said, shaking his head, unable to relate. "You're really something special, you know that?"

Ness's eyes shot up to him, lit with gratitude. A bright smile spread across her face, and a soft blush dusted her cheeks. She glanced to the ground and took a deep breath. Spyre could only smile at her, glad he could lift her spirits in such a terrible time. It felt nice and reminded him of the importance of what they were fighting for.

"So let me ask you something." Ness poked his arm.

Spyre looked down at her, knowing there was a personal question in his future.

Ness's face went from cunning to quizzical. "Why were you talking to yourself so much on the way here? Are you really that confused?"

Spyre couldn't help but laugh. "No." He took a breath. "With your elaborate theories and ideas of dragons, how open-minded are you?"

Ness tilted her head at him, a sign for him to continue.

"Well …" He scratched the back of his head. "I wasn't talking to myself." He gave her a moment to piece it together on her own. She would process it better that way, and there would be fewer questions.

"Ever since I left Gaernod on a whim and a hunch," he began, remembering it as if it had been an entirely different man who'd set off into Tweogan, "I've met up with someone in each realm who helped me get through their land and to the next, with another guide waiting."

Ness nodded slowly, her mouth slightly open. He could tell she was trying, but not yet fully getting it.

"But when I got to Condel, I ended up on my own. The only person who met me there ended up sending me straight to Afor, and he was less than helpful."

Spyre smiled, looking down. He'd stopped walking, and Ness had stopped with him.

"And then you showed up." He turned his eyes to her. "I figured maybe you would be the next guide, but by then, I was already hearing strange things. Things happened too quickly for me to figure it out right then, so I went with it. Until I got out of the city."

"So …" Ness drew out, concluding. "You're being guided by a ghost now?"

Spyre shook his head at her absurdity. "No. At least, I don't see it that way. His name is Lateo, or so he tells me, and apparently, the only reason I've been fortunate enough to find a friend in every part of Curnen is because he was leading their movements so I would make it to Condel."

"What made you leave Gaernod in the first place?" Ness asked, genuine curiosity on her face.

Spyre focused his gaze on something that wasn't there, trying to think of a better answer than the truth. "Just an irrational impulse," he replied. "I don't know. I mean, one minute, I'm just a useless craftsman, and the next, I'm regarded as some hero led by destiny. What am I supposed to say?"

Ness shrugged agreeably. "Yeah, you certainly don't act like a hero," she said.

Spyre eyed her, wondering if he should bother being offended when he truly couldn't agree with her more. In the end, he couldn't help cracking a smile. He started walking again, and she followed.

They didn't need to have a debate about which of their stories sounded more absurd just now because the temple was right in front of them, tall and imposing. They'd come upon it without even realizing they'd covered the distance, but now it stood before them, ancient and foreboding cracks snaking along the stone facing in the afternoon light.

They stood, staring in silence. Then they looked at each other as if by one thought and back to the temple. There was an entryway that protruded from the main temple. This was the place to start. Spyre caught Ness's eye and held up a hand to show that they should proceed with caution. Ness shrugged and nodded her consent.

They approached the temple entrance slowly, both very aware that this was probably where King Eofyn had met his fate, whatever that had been.

After they found shelter under the entrance chamber, Spyre put a hand out to stop Ness, as he noticed something strange hanging from the ceiling. He took slow steps up to it and reached out to examine it between his fingers.

"Just string," he said thoughtfully.

Ness looked at it over his shoulder as Spyre's eyes traced it back to the ceiling.

"That's a trapdoor." He pointed upward. "Then what triggered ..." He looked around, remembering the stone from the beginning of the desert.

"Ah," he said, a little proud that he had figured it out. "Earn the curves ... Look around."

Ness did as Spyre approached a handprint on the wall. He placed his hand in the imprint and wondered, tracing his finger along the circular outline.

"Okay, easy enough," he said, leaving Ness a few steps behind. He turned back to the string, not quite satisfied. "There must have been something attached to this." He toyed with the string and then refocused his eyes on the temple door. He brushed the string out of the way and ran his fingers over the impression on the door. "Got it."

"What have you got?" Ness asked heatedly. "What is all of this?" She looked around the room as if she would find an instruction manual.

Spyre had nearly forgotten that she was there. The complexity of the mechanism was just too intriguing. "This," he said, placing his hand in the handprint, "gets turned in conjunction with the one on the other wall."

He turned and pointed at the print on the opposing wall.

"And when you turn them, they trigger a release of that trapdoor, probably as simple as removing a support piece that holds the door up. Lots of material but a beautifully simple design." He spun around. "And this," he walked over to the string, holding it up for Ness to see, "this would've had something attached to it."

Ness blinked at him. "Well, how do you know that?" she asked. "It could just be the tug rope for a doorbell or something."

Spyre stared at her with flat eyes.

"Or … you know, maybe something was tied to it," Ness recovered with a shrug as she crossed her arms and looked away, her cheeks turning red.

Spyre gave a sharp nod. "Yes, and I'll tell you why." He moved to the door. "You see this?" He framed the oddly shaped hole with his hands, looking back to Ness with excitement flashing in his eyes. "This is a keyhole."

Ness leaned in, looking at the outline. "Doesn't look like a key," she muttered.

Spyre gave her a blank stare.

She coughed. "Uh, continue," she said sheepishly.

"It's a keyhole," he reiterated firmly. "And the key would have been attached to the string." He stood tall, crossing his arms over his chest and smiling.

But Ness was still blinking at him.

"But …" she coaxed him with eyes narrowed at the ceiling.

His face fell.

"Oh, don't do that," she said finally. "Where is the key now? I'm thrilled that you can figure this whole thing out. Really, it's a lovely thing, but without the actual key, we can't get in there, so …"

Spyre exhaled with a much slower nod of his head. "Yeah," he said, accepting the flaw in his analysis. "That's a bit of a problem."

Is not, a voice in his head piped up.

Spyre shifted from curiosity to confusion in a blink. "What?"

Ness looked at him with a frown. "I didn't say anything," she said carefully.

He waved her off. "No, not you. Hang on."

"Oh," Ness whispered, looking around as if Lateo might be lurking in a corner. "Sorry."

Spyre closed his eyes, listening carefully for the inner voice.

What did I tell you before? Lateo asked, as if Spyre were some kind of child. *You have exactly what you need. You've already created it.*

Spyre's eye twitched as he thought about arguing, but he knew better than to try. Stubbornness surrounded him these days. Instead, he reached back into his satchel and rummaged for the thing Lateo was talking about. He pulled out his wooden sculpture and turned it over in his hands, not believing it had come to this.

This was just a stupid piece of wood he'd made an infantile bond with before he'd left his house. He'd taken it along because he needed to feel like there was hope for him to change and be sculpted, just as he had altered the fate of the wood. There was no way that this had been a product of design too.

Ness was standing next to him now, looking at his artwork. "It's very well done," she commented softly. "Did you do that yourself?"

Spyre nodded absently.

Ness paused for a moment. "And, you know ..." She shifted her weight from one foot to the other, looking at him intently.

He looked up at her, waiting.

"It does seem to be about the same shape as your keyhole over there." She glanced to the shape in the door.

Spyre looked at the keyhole and then down at his sculpture. He closed his fingers around it and walked up to the door, slowly inserting the wood into the impression to find that it was a perfect fit. He pushed it in and heard several metallic thunks. Two switches giving way, allowing two weights to fall, he assumed, as the door rose.

Ness and Spyre glanced at each other with mirrored looks of astonishment. But the moment quickly died away, and Spyre cringed when a man's terrible scream echoed from the darkness.

Ness started to run, but Spyre had already thought this through. She had nothing to protect herself with. He thrust out his arm, and she ran right into it. She looked at him angrily for stopping her. Spyre shook his head, slipping his hand back into his bag and detaching the arrows he'd made in the Aforthian Mountains. He slipped his bow over his head and handed it and the arrows to her, grabbing his carving knife for himself, just in case.

"Okay?" he asked gravely.

Ness's eyes were huge. For a moment, Spyre thought she might run away. Her hands reached for the bow, and she stared at it. Then she looked up at Spyre with fierce determination. "I'm with you," she said without a trace of doubt.

Spyre looked into her bright-green eyes almost apologetically for a second before he signaled their attack with a nod and ran into the darkness, Ness close behind him.

What they found was a clear hostage situation. A Gaernod officer stood over a bound and beaten victim. That would be the king, Spyre surmised.

The soldier held a knife in the air. This was about to end poorly for the bound man.

Spyre felt a whoosh of wind next to his face and heard a familiar whistle followed by an angry shout of pain. He spun to find Ness behind him, eyes wide and bow raised. He threw his arms in the air at her.

"What was that for?" he hissed.

"I was trying to figure out how to hold it."

There was no time. Their cover was blown. They had to move, so he prioritized the prisoner.

Spyre paused at the soldier who'd been shot with the arrow.

"I know your pain." He knelt down and picked up a rock, tossing it into the air and catching it. "But you're probably not going to be down for as long as I was." He weighed the rock in his hand and knelt down next to the cursing soldier. "I'm no professional at this, but I think I can manage. Really, I'm sorry. You'll be fine, I'm sure."

He hit the man in the side of the head with the rock in one quick motion, and the soldier slumped against the wall, unconscious.

Then he stood and looked around for Ness.

"I really don't know how long that will last, so can we make this quick, please?"

Ness wasn't listening. She'd just caught sight of the man on the floor.

"Here he is," she called to Spyre. "It's King Eofyn."

She ran to him and knelt in front of him, tears springing to her eyes. Her hands flew to her mouth as she took in a horrified breath.

Spyre noticed Eofyn had cuts everywhere. His clothes were bloodstained, and his eyes had lines of black and blue beneath them. They had tortured him, and the placement of many of the cuts, mostly on his shoulders and the backs of his forearms, were evidence of the impressive fight he'd put up for someone with such impaired movement.

Eofyn watched Ness as she set to work on his bindings. Spyre took hesitant steps toward the second soldier, who appeared to be knocked out.

Spyre leaned down to look at the guard, knowing who it was with no need of proof. "Ryne?" he asked, breathlessly. His head dropped. "This is awful," he said, earning the attention of both Ness and Eofyn.

"Because," he continued saying to the slumped soldier, "we've had plenty of fights before, and my punch was never enough to knock you out."

He held his knife up shakily, waiting for Ryne's eyes to open, but when they did, Spyre was still somehow unprepared. Ryne lunged forward, knocking Spyre to the floor but passing him by and heading for the Condel folk.

Spyre whirled around to see Eofyn desperately pulling against his ropes as he watched Ryne coming toward Ness, sword held back like a trigger ready to be pulled and aimed straight at her stomach.

Ness fumbled for another arrow but dropped it, with no time to recover. She turned and stared up into the man's eyes, waiting for whatever was to come next, but she recoiled, throwing her hands over her face.

Panicked, Spyre stumbled to his feet and grabbed his trusty rock, seeing an image of Dugan in his mind he was certain he hadn't witnessed. The strong troll had held a sturdy rock in his hand and drew it back over his shoulder, launching it and releasing at the perfect moment. Eyes closed, Spyre mimicked Dugan's movements until he felt the stone escape from his grip.

Shock washed over Ryne's face as his next step landed him at Ness's feet, eyes securely closed. Ness looked up to see Spyre standing where her attacker had been. Spyre looked pained, squatting beside the soldier and checking his pulse. He was somewhat relieved when he found it.

Looking up to Ness, he said, "They're both still alive. Let's just get him untied and get out of here as soon as we can, okay?"

Ness and Eofyn stared at him as Spyre stood up and walked to the center of the room, still listening. Ness returned to Eofyn's ropes with fumbling, shaking fingers, filling him in on their situation.

"Your Majesty, we've never met," she sputtered out hurriedly, focused on the ropes that bound his legs. "I'm Darian's daughter. My name is Ness, and the man behind me is Spyre. He's from Gaernod."

Spyre felt like he should apologize but decided against it.

Ness stepped in for him instead. "He came here to save you. Please, believe me when I tell you he's on our side. The queen-to-be sent him. I witnessed it personally."

Spyre noticed her struggling with the ropes, her hands still shaking from adrenalin. He dropped his knife and slid it to her with his foot. Ness looked down at the sound of metal on stone and quickly scooped the blade up to cut the remaining ropes from the king's hands.

As they fell away, Eofyn rubbed his sore wrists and looked at Ness. "I can tell you're Darian's daughter," he said, smiling. "You both have a surplus of words to share." He laughed a little, but the moment passed quickly.

"Listen, Pyram is still here. I know where he is, but I'm sure he won't be easy to get to. Will you help me?" the king asked, looking at Spyre.

Spyre turned around, stunned that the king had no questions about the fact that he was clearly from Gaernod. The Condels never ceased to surprise him.

He smiled softly. "Well, where is he?" he asked. "I'm not exactly a skilled warrior. These guys could wake up at any second, and I'm not sure if clumsy fighting really works more than once."

Eofyn gave Spyre an approving smile, standing shakily with Ness's help. "Both corridors lead to the same room," he explained. "Pyram is in there. They haven't left me since they captured us, so I'm not exactly sure what state he's in."

"He's fine," Spyre said distantly, frowning at the ceiling. "Come on, let's see for ourselves." He quickly set off toward the hallway to the right, leaving Eofyn to stare at Ness.

"About him," she said. "There's a voice in his head that tells him what to do." She looked after Spyre, smiling with excitement. "Long story. Or ridiculous story, really. We'll fill you in on the way back."

Eofyn seemed satisfied enough with that for the moment and obeyed Ness's gesture for him to follow them. They jogged down the curved hallway. Spyre examined the very large boulder that blocked the door and held his cheek against the stone, deciding how much force it would take to push it aside.

"Pyram," Eofyn called out next to him. "Pyram, are you in there?" They waited with bated breath for a very long moment.

Eofyn looked to Spyre, who smiled proudly. He nodded to the Condel king, and Eofyn said, "Yes. We'll get you out of there. Stand back."

Spyre, Eofyn, and Ness all put their shoulders into the boulder at specific points calculated by Spyre. It took several attempts for them to coordinate just right so that their combined force was enough to compromise its balance and gradually roll it away from the opening. As it finally gave way, Spyre and Ness sighed, but Eofyn climbed through without pause, searching the darkness for the owner of the other voice. Spyre jumped when he heard a loud "Oof!" in the king's voice, but Ness rested a calming hand on his shoulder.

"They're best friends," she explained, and from the darkness, Spyre heard confirmation.

"Fyn, I can't believe they didn't finish you off by now," Pyram said as Spyre helped Ness over the uneven ground and into the room. Pyram held his friend at arm's length. He appraised Eofyn's appearance. "Fyn, you look really terrible," he observed, as if he were commenting on a poor choice of outfit rather than the king's battered face.

Eofyn embraced Pyram, giving him a firmer slap on the back than Spyre thought was necessary. "Yeah, thanks. Better than dead, though, right?"

"Eh, I guess so," Pyram said with a smile.

Looking over Eofyn's shoulder, Pyram finally noticed Spyre hovering in faint light of the doorway. Pyram's eyes grew slightly, and his smile faded away as he pulled away from Eofyn.

"So you're the worthy man, I take it?" Pyram asked.

Spyre furrowed his brow, glancing behind him for another man and then looking back to Pyram in question.

Eofyn turned around and stared at Pyram. "What?" he asked, rubbing the back of his neck in the same way that Spyre was. "Pyram, I know it's been a lot of time to spend on your own," he said carefully, taking his friend by the shoulders. "Are you ... feeling all right? The darkness didn't ... you know ... get to you, did it?"

Pyram rolled his eyes, heading for the doorway. "No," he said curtly, "but thanks for the confidence."

He reached around the corner of the door past Spyre, who ducked out of his way, and grabbed an unlit torch, taking it back over to Eofyn and thrusting it into his hands.

It ignited, making Spyre and Ness take a surprised step back, shielding their eyes.

"Look." Pyram pointed to the floor now that they could see it clearly. "Read it."

They gathered around the inscription on the floor.

"Shadows stretch far from home, black claws sink into marble thrones. A tyrant seeks to overthrow, receives the magic, makes it glow," Ness mumbled. "Well, we know who that is. Afor's already got himself a crystal."

Eofyn and Pyram looked at Ness, thunderstruck.

"He's sucking his power from our people," Ness confirmed grimly with a nod.

"Are you sure?" Eofyn asked.

Ness glanced up at him. "Yeah," she responded shortly, absently reaching for her crystal. "I'm positive."

The king didn't question her any further. Instead, he looked back down to the passage on the floor.

"Escape his grip when comes that day. Seek the guidance. Find your way. Be ye guided to this place, receive the blade that minds erased," he muttered. He looked up and held the torch out toward the altar of rocks in the middle of the room. "So that's a sword?" he asked.

"Yeah," Pyram said, stepping to his side. "There's only one problem."

Eofyn looked at him, waiting.

Pyram continued, "See, I'm pretty sure that our key would have fit the blade perfectly to become its handle, but I haven't found it in here."

"You wouldn't," Eofyn informed him in a low tone. "They threw it into the sand a few days ago. Trying to make sure I knew there was no way someone could get in to find me."

The two men seemed to be hit by the same realization at the same time and slowly turned to face Spyre and Ness.

"But then, how did you ..." Eofyn began, suspiciously.

Ness cut in. "Remember the whole voice thing?" she asked. She jutted a not-so-discreet thumb toward Spyre, who dropped his head into his hand, shaking it at her silliness.

"No," Pyram scoffed.

"Yes," Eofyn drawled.

Ness looked from one man to the other. "Well, Spyre ended up carving this piece of wood on his way here, and wouldn't you know, it fit perfectly into the keyhole," she emphasized for Spyre's benefit, earning a smile from him.

Spyre was already reaching into his pocket, where he'd stowed his wooden creation. He held it out in front of him, jaw slack in disbelief. He looked to Eofyn and motioned to the blade. "May I?" he asked.

Eofyn nodded his stunned approval.

Spyre took a deep breath and walked over to the rocky altar, grabbing the loose stone that Pyram had previously used to make a fire as he crawled to the top. He steadied his footing on the rocks and tried to slide the carving onto the sword, remembering when he dug the thin slit into it just last night. It was too tight of squeeze, but Spyre had expected that and was actually encouraged by it. He used the stone as a hammer and gently tapped the rounded hilt into position, where it fit securely.

When it was fully attached, Spyre dropped the stone, allowing it to roll back to the floor. He took hold of the handle with both of his hands and pulled, nervous that it might slide right off and send him reeling backward.

Show a little confidence, would you? Lateo scolded him lightly.

Spyre breathed in, clearing his mind of doubt as much as he could and trying to fill it with positive thoughts of how removing the sword was entirely possible. Before the doubt could creep back into the edges of his mind, Spyre went for it and pulled the blade cleanly out of the altar.

It had come out much easier than he expected. He slid backward down the rock pile but kept his balance enough so he didn't end up landing on the sword and ending his journey right then and there. All clumsiness aside, the others still seemed rather impressed.

"I guess we have our worthy man," Pyram said, looking at Spyre approvingly.

Spyre gaped at the sword as though it would spring to life on him. He walked over to the rest of the group, carrying the weapon carefully. He looked at it for a moment, turning it every which way, and then handed it to Eofyn, but the king stepped away, hands raised like the shining blade would burn him.

"No," he said. "Actually, I think that's for you." He pointed to the words on the floor. "Says here that you're looking to 'save mankind.' I think you'll be needing it. Besides, you made the handle. You earned it."

Spyre eyed the king suspiciously. "If I didn't know any better, I'd think you were afraid of this thing," he said, lightheartedly.

Pyram stepped in. "Actually, I think Fyn is right. That line is still talking about you." He stared at Spyre.

"I'm not entirely sure I like the idea of an old floor talking about me," Spyre said absently. He gave the ancient stones a look of distrust.

"Well, you're not the only one," Pyram said. "Look." He took Eofyn's torch and squatted closer to the words. "Eofyn isn't mentioned again until the last line: 'When by Pure Fyre it is released, the dragons live to slay the beast.'"

"Those dragons again," Spyre whispered.

"Yep," Ness said confidently, leveling her eyes at him. "It's going to happen. And you and King Eofyn are both a part of it. Have you come to terms with that yet?"

Spyre looked at her. What did she want from him? He hadn't processed any of his journey yet. From the moment he left Gaernod, he'd been running away from his own rational mind as much as from his past.

"Actually, she's right," Eofyn added. "I had visions of you coming."

At these words, Ness's and Pyram's eyes lit up. Spyre listened, unaware of the significance. Everyone seemed to be seeing or hearing something lately.

"I got the impression you were someone important. You have a part to play in this, if you'll continue to help us."

Spyre didn't like the sound of this. The more they asked him to do, the more certain he became that he would end up as some kind of Condel martyr. But ...

"You're as hard to say no to as your queen is." He released the air that had been stuck in his chest. "Yeah. I mean, what else would I be doing?"

Eofyn smiled at him and gave him a firm slap on the back. Spyre guessed that was a good thing.

"There's just one problem," Pyram said, causing everyone to turn and look down at him. He was still looking at the words, his chin resting in a curled finger. "The second-to-last line: 'The Kindling found in darkness thrives, sparks the Source to save your lives.'" He looked up at Eofyn. "You said the source isn't here, and according to this, we need to find it."

"Where else are we supposed to go?" Spyre asked, exhausted with never reaching a final destination.

Eofyn studied the words. "Maybe I can find out," he said. "Give me a moment, would you?"

Ness and Pyram nodded, but Spyre was growing increasingly more nervous about his brother waking up. He wanted to urge the king to make it quick, but he knew he wasn't exactly in the position to be giving orders.

Eofyn walked to the corner and sat against the wall, breathing deeply and focusing. After a moment, the creases in the king's forehead smoothed away, and he smiled, nodding as if in thanks. He opened his eyes.

"We need to go back to Condel. It's there. I don't know where, but it's there."

"Good, good," Spyre said quickly. "Now, let's get out of here, okay? My—" He caught himself. "Those guys could wake up any minute."

Everyone else agreed, but as they began to leave the room, an increasingly loud rumble in the walls filled their ears. Spyre immediately looked to Ness, who was gazing at the ceiling. He wondered if she was shaking out of fear or if it was just the room itself.

"What's that?" she asked, her voice cracking.

Spyre stopped and listened keenly. "I think," he started, "that when I pulled the sword out, it triggered some sort of booby trap." His finger went to his chin as he scrutinized the pedestal. "They must have used the sand. I bet the blade was plugging some kind of hole, and now that it's gone, the sand is seeping through, and the temple is sinking." He shook his head, frowning as he thought. "But the structure isn't sound enough. This place'll start falling apart before it sinks."

Ness gawked at him in disbelief. "Give me strength," she snapped at the ceiling in frustration. "Enough with the device analysis."

She grabbed his arm and ran, a cue enough for the others to follow. "Let's just get out of here."

She yanked Spyre to the right as a large piece of the ceiling caved in, separating them from Eofyn and Pyram. Ness stopped. Spyre ran into her awkwardly. He caught her arm, trying to get her away from any more debris, but she pushed past him, calling out, "Your Majesty!" over the rubble.

"It's okay," Eofyn's voice called to Ness and Spyre from the other side of the rubble. "We have a way out. We'll meet you at the entrance."

Spyre and Ness exchanged a glance. It would have to be enough for now. Spyre waited for Ness to give a resolved nod before he took her hand, and they ran down the hallway, hearing the room behind them collapse further. They reached the main chamber first, Spyre taking the lead to find a very unwelcomed sight.

As soon as Spyre saw his brother standing, looking furious, he tightened his grip on Ness's arm without a thought or hesitation and shoved her into the next corridor, where she slammed into her king.

Spyre glimpsed the three Condels peeking around the corner at him. They were safe there, so he turned his attention back to Ryne, who was already circling him.

He put an open hand behind him, motioning for the others to stay where they were, but he kept his eyes locked on his brother. Ryne was everything Spyre wasn't. If gifts and talents were given in the womb, Ryne had raided the strongest traits before Spyre was a glimmer in their mother's eye, wherever she was now. Ryne stood a head taller than Spyre and was twice as broad at the chest. He conditioned his physique to emphasize his strength, and the contours of his scarred and bristled face added to the burly charm he always liked to flaunt back home. His eyes were a dark, deep brown.

They couldn't have been more different, and that's when Spyre realized that blood, be it spilled on the rocks of the Aforthian Mountains or coursing through his brother's veins, meant nothing. Spyre stopped circling and walked toward Ryne, sword uncomfortably in hand, not raised, because Ryne knew he had virtually no idea how to use a blade.

"Listen," Spyre said calmly, not sure what he could say to his brother, but fortunately, Ryne didn't give him a chance.

"You're a traitor," Ryne accused without preamble, directing the tip of his sword at Spyre's chest. "You should have stayed home. You were useless, but at least you were out of the way."

"I wouldn't say useless." Spyre glared, remembering the inventions he'd encountered along his journey. The pain in his shoulder swelled at the memory of his own design shooting him with an arrow in Tweogan. "Seems you put me to good use. I wonder how many times? How many lives?"

Ryne's face split with a sharp, toothy grin, and it was answer enough. More lives than just the man Spyre had killed on the mountain, but he couldn't let that paralyze him now. There were more lives, lives he could save, to repent for the crimes he'd unknowingly committed.

Spyre eyed the pointed blade, his breathing becoming shallower as he tried to think of a scenario that would get them all out of the crumbling temple alive.

The room shook, but they were too focused on the impending duel to notice. Small pieces of the ceiling fell like heavy snow around them, and Spyre couldn't encourage a dash for the exit without bringing Ryne's wrath down upon the Condels.

Spyre stopped, knowing silence was a waste of precious time, and shook his head sadly. "Who could I possibly have betrayed? You think Afor is worth your loyalty? You only work for him because you're afraid of him."

A pebble fell from the ceiling and landed in Spyre's hair. They had to get out of here quickly, but Ryne had positioned himself in front of their exit. Did he even know what was about to happen?

"And you're so brave?" Ryne snapped at him. "I fight for Afor because of the rewards he'll give me. Do you have any idea how he'll repay me for killing his competition?

"You and your tinkering," Ryne snapped. "And for what? What good did that ever do anyone?"

Spyre was getting angry now. "Apparently, it did you and the army plenty of good," he responded firmly, his face like stone as the betrayal consumed him. "You stole my designs and turned them into weapons. All of those people in Condel," he said, pointing outside, "they lost their homes and … and worse. Because of what you took from me."

"No, no, no," Ryne chided with a condescending smile. "Don't sugarcoat this for yourself. They died because of what you created. I hope you're proud of your hard work, now that I finally made it useful.

"And what are you going to do here?" Ryne asked, indicating Spyre's sword as it hung at his side. "You think you'll be able to take me on? You'd kill your own brother?"

Spyre winced as the truth was revealed for the Condels to hear. He struggled with himself as he looked at the only person he had ever been able to rely on in his entire life. This was his brother. Didn't that mean something? But there was more to this world than titles that carried no substance, wasn't there? There had never been any true bond between them, only one of self-preservation. What kind of loyalty was that? And was it enough to justify another life taken by Spyre's hand? His stomach churned against the thought. But would he have the strength to protect Ness and the innocent Condels?

"I will stop you somehow," Spyre replied, not sounding so sure himself, but he stood his ground as Ryne stepped closer, grinning. This was it.

Raise your sword, Lateo said calmly in Spyre's mind.

Spyre had almost forgotten about his faceless guide, but now he listened and held the ancient and shining blade up in front of him. More of the ceiling fell around him, but he remained patient.

"Is that a fact?" Ryne asked, sneering at Spyre's gall. "You know, you may have reservations about killing people, little brother," he said, checking his teeth in the dim gleam of his sword for effect, "but I've grown to enjoy watching the looks on people's faces as they realize they've reached their end. They're always so surprised." He looked Spyre square in the eyes. "But are you really surprised? You shouldn't be."

And swipe it down, Lateo instructed.

Spyre jumped to attention and waved his sword downward in front of him, hearing the clang of his blade against his brother's just as it passed over his chest, deflecting what would have been a deadly blow straight to his heart. Adrenalin kicked in, and Spyre could hear everything, even the sharp breaths that were coming from Ness in the hallway and especially the creaking around him as the weight of the temple gave way.

Ryne let out an impressed huff. "Interesting. You've been learning from someone. First the rocks, and now the swords. Tell me, have you had your first kill yet?"

Spyre's jaw was tight, his silence enough of an answer.

"Oh," Ryne confirmed, holding his brother at the point of his sword. "I'm proud of you. How did it feel? Was it an elf? That seems like an easy opponent for you. I doubt you could take on a troll, but a wisp maybe?"

He suddenly drew into Spyre's personal space, pulling him into an embrace with one strong arm tight enough that his smaller brother could not escape.

"Come on, make me proud," he said into Spyre's ear.

Spyre's lip curled in disgust.

"Who was it?"

"It was in the Aforthians," Spyre replied smoothly, hating himself as the image of his victim's eyes returned to him. Maybe this temple should bury him. Maybe that's what he deserved.

Ryne moved back, keeping his face only inches away from Spyre's. "A troll?" he asked approvingly. "Well?"

Spyre looked him in the eye defiantly. "No."

Ryne's face contorted into confusion. "Then what?" he demanded angrily, readying his sword.

Careful, Lateo warned. *Don't lose yourself.*

"He was a soldier," Spyre said, but his words were weakening as the guilt rushed back to him.

He was thrown roughly against the wall, Ryne pinning him so he could only brush the ground with the toes of his boots. Spyre wasn't resisting. He didn't look at Ryne. He wasn't proud. He wasn't even angry. He hated what he had done. He didn't even try to wriggle out of his brother's grip.

Over Ryne's shoulder, Spyre saw the shaky head of an arrow emerge from the darkness of the hall, but it quickly disappeared. Spyre quietly thanked Pyram for keeping Ness at bay.

"A soldier?" Ryne demanded, pushing his forearm into Spyre's throat and regaining his attention.

Spyre didn't move.

"You killed one of our own people?"

Spyre looked up at him, anger heating his face. "You weren't so upset when you were blaming me for the deaths of dozens of Condels," he accused through his blocked windpipe.

"You are not a Condel," Ryne roared angrily, choking Spyre further and drawing his sword back again.

Knee up, Lateo's voice said.

Spyre winced against gravity and brought his knee up firmly into his brother's stomach, making him stumble backward more from surprise than pain and dropping Spyre into a heap on the floor.

Pursue, Lateo urged.

Spyre dragged himself to his feet, trying to get air.

Wait for it.

He ran over to his reeling foe.

A simple shove will do.

Spyre pushed Ryne square in the chest, and he tripped backward over a stone, landing hard on his back.

Threaten, but do not act.

Spyre stood tall and held the tip of his sword to Ryne's throat.

Speak your piece, Lateo encouraged.

"You," Spyre rasped against his sore throat, "know nothing about who I am." He looked his brother in the eyes and saw genuine fear there, as more flakes from the temple fell on his face.

Spyre quickly shifted his hand on the hilt of his blade so he could kneel on one knee next to Ryne, pinning his brother to the floor with his free hand while still holding the sword in place.

"I don't know what drives you, Ryne," he said. "I don't know what you hope to gain or when you'll be satisfied, or who has to suffer until you finally are …" Spyre released some of his anger through his teeth, trying to keep his wits. "But it won't be them."

Well done, Lateo said calmly. *Now use your sword in the best way you know how.*

Spyre nodded, knowing exactly what Lateo meant. He spun the blade upright and knocked the butt of the handle into Ryne's head once more, keeping him alive but rendering him safely unconscious.

The tension in Spyre's head released, and he felt like clouds were parting behind his eyes, returning him to his more peaceful demeanor. With the rush over, Spyre's entire body relaxed to the point of weakness. He shoulders slowly fell. He breathed heavily as he looked down at his silent brother, shaking his head in disappointment. He started to lean on the tip of his sword to push himself up but then realized that Ryne had something he could use.

He undid the strap of his brother's sword sheath and found it to be a suitable fit for his own newly acquired blade. As the rumbling around him grew ever louder, he pushed his sword into the dust again, struggling to stand, but found that there were hands on each of his arms helping him to his feet instead.

When he was upright, he looked around and saw Pyram and Eofyn giving him concerned yet grateful looks. He stared at the ground, feeling uncertain, and was not prepared when Ness suddenly threw her arms around him, making him step back to keep them from winding up on the ground again. He cracked a smile.

"I knew we could trust you," she said to him in a wistful voice, holding him tight.

Spyre couldn't believe what he was hearing. He glanced down to the top of her head, but the rest of him was frozen. Still supporting her in his arms, he looked to Eofyn and Pyram. Eofyn nodded his agreement, and Pyram shrugged his approval before his eyes returned to the ceiling.

"I really think we should go now," Pyram said, pushing everyone to the door as the rumble escalated to a roar.

Ness and Eofyn went out first. Then Pyram caught Spyre's eye as if to say, "After you," and Spyre jolted back to reality, running through the door after the other two.

He couldn't believe it. Had they accepted him that quickly? What, no trial by fire?

CHAPTER 27

Outside, the world was much brighter, but the danger had not yet passed. The earth quaked as the temple behind them fell in on itself. Spyre saw Ness move to run away from the collapsing building, but he knew the mantle of the entrance would be the best shelter for them, so he quickly grabbed her arm. Red flashed in the corner of his vision as the sand beneath Ness's feet shifted, and Spyre looked up to see that Pyram had grabbed her other arm just in time to keep her from falling into a sea of moving sand.

Spyre and Pyram held onto Ness tightly as she slammed against the stone that had been buried in the sand. They pulled her up, back onto what was now a platform. As they pulled her to her feet, Ness shakily grabbed onto the front of Spyre's shirt and buried her face into it. He gently put his arms around her until she settled.

They all leaned near the edge, Ness not relinquishing Spyre's shirt, and peered down on a cobbled road. The sand continued to roar toward the horizon, as if the tide were going out to reveal rows and rows of pillared buildings beneath its grainy layers. Streets ran throughout the former metropolis with a plaza at the center, directly in line with the temple, the clear prominence of the city. With little effort, Spyre could imagine ghosts of people milling through the streets, leading daily lives, not knowing the future they were building each day.

Spyre stood with his Condel companions and watched in awe as an entire ancient civilization revealed itself.

"Nomads?" Eofyn asked Pyram.

Pyram looked at him, tearing his eyes away from their discovery, and shook his head, jaw slacked to its limit. "I guess not. They must have just guessed that part." He shrugged. "I mean," he gestured to the vast prehistoric city, "who knew?"

It must have been the original settlement of the people who would become the citizens of Condel, a large, linear city that stretched outward from the temple, similar to the layout of Condel itself, but with much straighter streets. The majority of buildings were perfect cubes, with no adornments or remnants of any decoration. Buried by sand, the city should have been well-preserved, but all that remained was stone.

The temple was a more Condel design, its rounded corridors insisting a journey before the destination, but the city must have been older. Even the support beneath the entryway where they stood indicated that their presence—and their need for sanctuary from the booby-trapped temple—had been expected. Had there been a talent for foresight among the early Condel people?

No, Spyre remembered, the ancients established Condel because it was the source of their crystals. No Condel, no crystals. This city was pre-power, and the temple was clearly a product of a revolutionized way of thinking; otherwise, the city would reflect the design of the temple, which, eventually, Condel did.

Eofyn, Pyram, and Ness stared at the city in wonderment, but Spyre was less impressed.

"Looks like Gaernod," he commented, earning stares from all sides as he leaned casually against the wall of the entryway. He noticed. "What? Our streets are stick-straight, and they lead right to the steps of the castle. A lot like this. Nothing flashy."

Eofyn and Pyram looked at each other, eyes widening. They turned to Spyre, staring at his darker skin and making him uncomfortable.

"It's like looking into the past," Pyram muttered, a smile twitching at the corner of his mouth.

Spyre frowned at Pyram in confusion before studying the excavated city. "But this was a Condel temple," he puzzled aloud, pointing to the ruin behind him with a thumb. "So …" His eyes blinked open wide as he realized the facts just a step behind the other men. "We—" He looked at Eofyn and Pyram for encouragement.

They nodded, urging him on.

"We come from the same ... the same group, or tribe ... or colony." He looked back over the city, scratching the top of his head as it sank in.

"What?" Ness blurted out, looking up at Spyre's astonished face.

But this was fantastic—for Spyre, at least. To him, it meant that he wasn't so very different from the Condels, and now, even their king had acknowledged it.

Feeling renewed and a little too bold, Spyre took his bag off his shoulder and tossed it down off the edge, hearing the soft thud of its landing a few seconds later. Pyram lunged for the bag with a gasp, turning to yell at Spyre as it fell out of his reach. Spyre held up a steady hand, urging Pyram to trust him. Pyram stepped back but continued to shake his head.

"We can make it," Spyre insisted. "Just be careful." He gently pushed Ness away from him and moved to the edge of the platform, calculating before he jumped from the ledge. Ness gasped in his wake.

He landed hard but safely on the archaic street, smiling at the small shout that had escaped from Ness as he'd jumped. He was soon joined by Eofyn and Pyram, who jumped easily, though Eofyn winced a little as the landing jarred him.

Spyre held his arms out as Ness closed her eyes tightly and leapt from the ledge. He caught her to lessen the brunt of her fall. They all turned to face the street before them. It would lead them directly to the edge of Tir. Smiling, they exchanged triumphant glances and walked on, Ness clinging to Spyre.

They walked among the houses and buildings, looking for signs of people having lived in them, but apart from the remaining layer of sand, there was nothing left in the small, mostly one-room buildings. The desertion of this city had been planned. There was nothing to see here. It was like walking among a city constructed with a child's building blocks. Spyre would have loved to investigate further, but time was not a resource they could spare. Maybe one day, once all of this was settled, he'd return to explore properly.

"So ..." Pyram said, glancing sideways at Spyre, whose arm was still in the fortified grasp of a visibly overjoyed Ness. "Voices?"

Spyre let out a small laugh. Conversation at a time like this? "Complicated," he replied.

Pyram raised his eyebrows for more.

Spyre acquiesced. "But, in short—"

"Someone named Lateo has been guiding him here all the way since Gaernod," Ness interrupted confidently. She glanced at Spyre, searching for his approval.

Spyre nodded. He was fine with allowing her to explain for him. Telling it made him feel insane.

"Lateo is apparently from Bryta," Ness continued, earning Eofyn's interest. "Spyre can hear him talking in his head." She looked at Spyre. "Is that what was going on back in the temple?"

Spyre glanced at her uncomfortably and nodded, averting his eyes to the identical buildings, as if they were suddenly more interesting, but Eofyn and Pyram seemed a little less on track.

"Wait," Pyram said, processing. "Isn't that like the Pure Fyre?" He looked at Eofyn.

"I don't think so," Ness said. She gestured with her hands and frowned in thought. "See, Spyre only hears things pertaining to him. Right?" She looked at Spyre. He shrugged but gave in and finally nodded.

"Uh, yeah," he said, feeling very awkward. "Far as I can tell. He—" He sighed. He felt like a liar for how ridiculous it sounded. "He tells me what immediate actions I should take, like fighting Ryne and avoiding the sand pit." He looked around, relieved that they wouldn't have to worry about getting stuck in the pit this time around.

"He also clarifies things to keep me on track when I doubt everything, but so far, that's it." He glanced into the doorways of the buildings that lined the street. They were still empty. Every single one. Their ancestors had lived simply and left cleanly, but that did little to help Spyre distract himself from this uneasiness.

Ness smiled. "Exactly," she said proudly, her eyes lit with excited determination. "See, this Lateo guy is more of a bodyguard for Spyre personally." She turned to the king. "I think His Majesty has a wider version of that, one that concerns everyone's well-being, making it the

Pure Fyre. Pure Fyre is selfless, as compared to everyone else's abilities that usually pertain only to them, much like Lateo does to Spyre."

She turned dramatically as she gestured back to Spyre. She tilted her head, frowning in thought. "That makes it seem likes Spyre might have some kind of connection to the Fyre, though. Maybe he was supposed to be born in Condel."

"Well, that's very good to know," Eofyn said, shifting the subject and receiving a grateful look from Spyre. "What I'm more concerned with right now is the source. It could be anything."

"Swelgan?" Pyram suggested.

Eofyn shook his head. "No, I don't think so. If all of this is to be believed, and at this point, I think it's beyond question, then Swelgan can't be the source, because he and Cuman will deal the final blow."

None of this seemed clear. Not knowing what the source was or where they could specifically find it was bringing back the tendrils of uncertainty from before. But Spyre refused to go back to that state of mind. Instead, he decided to trust that things were going according to plan and that he was on his way, with as much knowledge as he needed at this point. Lateo would tell him if something was amiss, right? It was out of his hands.

"When we get back," Eofyn said, drawing all eyes to him, but looking at Spyre in particular, "we will have to get into the castle without being captured."

Spyre nodded that he understood, though he knew it would not be a simple task.

"I accept that it's my job to find the source," the king said, "and do whatever it is that awakens the dragons. If it's the Pure Fyre that activates the source, then I'm the only one who can do it, which leads me to apologize ..." Eofyn's voice trailed off.

Spyre raised his eyebrows.

"Spyre, that means you're going to have to deal with Afor. You're the one with the sword and the instructor."

Spyre tightened his lips, glancing down and trying not to think about what he would have to do. Then a small hand slid into his. He stared at it before looking up to see Ness smiling softly and reassuringly.

"You won't be on your own," she said confidently. "I know Pyram will help King Eofyn, but I'll go with you."

"For the last time," Spyre sighed, rubbing his forehead with his free hand, "you are not going with me."

"Keep it up." Pyram laughed. "That seems to be working for you so far."

Ness smiled at him, and he responded with a small, good-humored bow.

"I don't think that's such a good idea," Eofyn said apologetically.

"With all due respect, Your Majesty," Ness said slowly. Spyre could tell from his limited experience that Eofyn's royalty was his only salvation from Ness's temper. "Afor is looking for me, and he'll be looking for my house. I'm staying away from there in hopes that he is lenient with my family, since they have no idea where I am. Most of them. I'm just as safe, if not safer, in the castle."

The king didn't look sympathetic.

"I'm not much younger than you," she said. "Only a few years, and I'm meant to be here."

Spyre knew she had a point as she filled the king and Pyram in on her own personal journey since Afor's takeover. While the king had been away and Spyre had been dragging his feet to get to Condel, Ness had been trying to protect her home, if only to buy them time, and she hadn't gone unscathed.

Eofyn seemed even more uncertain, especially when he heard what Afor had done to Ness's crystal, but then his face relaxed. He looked to the dark dusky sky, streaked with gray clouds, and breathed deeply. Spyre knew the king's thoughts weren't leaning in his favor. Ness would join him against Afor. He shook his head. It was just another piece of the puzzle he wouldn't understand until it fell more comfortably into place.

"We should probably stop here," Pyram said, having followed Eofyn's gaze skyward.

Spyre gave a frustrated sigh. "Can't we just keep going and get this over with?"

As Spyre looked peeved at the voice that piped up in his head, Ness ventured, "It's probably best to be well rested. You've done enough for today. You'll want to be at your best against Afor, right?"

"Yeah," Spyre said, rolling his eyes at the one who wasn't there. "So I've been told."

The other men looked quizzical, but Ness understood. She tapped the side of her head to explain Lateo in Spyre's mind. Eofyn caught on and nodded, while Spyre surrendered to the peer pressure and dropped his bag from his shoulder. They had stopped at what appeared to have been a fountain back in its time. Spyre walked up the three steps and examined the dried-up water feature.

"So this explains the sinking pit," Pyram said, sitting next to the edge of the empty pool.

Spyre gave a distracted laugh, thinking only of the sinking feeling in the pit of his stomach.

CHAPTER 28

Spyre knew the real reason Pyram had suggested they stop; it wasn't just the dimming light. He hadn't wanted to bring it up, because Eofyn was handling it well, but the king had been through torture. No one talked, and no one stared, but they were all very aware of the numerous cuts and gashes over his face and arms. That soldier had been trying to push him to ask for death. But now, he was growing too tired. He needed rest to give his body a chance to heal. Spyre was willing to bet that Eofyn was desperately missing his fiancée right about now.

Spyre dropped his satchel on the ground next to Pyram to draw his attention. He tilted his head toward Eofyn. Pyram accepted the offering with a nod of approval. He could give it to the king to use as a pillow. It wasn't much, but it spoke volumes. Then Spyre tugged at Ness's arm, moving them a few feet away but still within earshot to give Eofyn and Pyram some space.

"Took quite the abuse, didn't you?" Pyram said with laughter in his voice.

Eofyn chuckled. "What about you? They must have taken pretty good care of you too."

He nodded at the bruises on Pyram's face and shoulders, but his friend shrugged it off and tossed Spyre's bag onto the ground at the right distance for Eofyn to recline onto it.

Pyram wore a proud smile as Eofyn adjusted his head, finding the most comfortable spot on Spyre's donated satchel; he allowed his weary eyes to slowly shut.

Pyram gazed at the stars, giving Eofyn a moment to his thoughts, but when he glanced down to see his friend peacefully unconscious, he knew his protective duty was complete. From a few feet away, Spyre caught Pyram's eye and gave him a nod, confirming they were safe enough to not need someone on watch for the night. Pyram could take his deserved rest as well. Pyram blinked, feeling his own fatigue finally hit him as his brain shifted from alert to standby. He lay back, one vertebra at a time, and pillowed his head in his hands, sighing as he easily slipped away.

That's kind of you, but you should rest as well.

I don't want to, Spyre thought. *I'm not the one that's been tortured for days. And it was my family's fault.*

You know better than that, Lateo said simply. *He was born your brother, but there's nothing deeper between you.*

Spyre scoffed out loud, "Nothing but countless lives he's taken by weaponizing my designs."

The thought of it made his stomach roil. He turned his head, filling his lungs with the cool night air, and that's when he noticed Ness staring at him. His eyes glanced over her, seeing how awkward she was at the moment. She sat stiffly, trying to be discreet about her eyes being on him.

It was clear she was falling asleep where she sat, but pride or something like it must have kept her from abandoning Spyre to watch the night on his own. With a sigh, he stretched out in the sand, resting his head on his bent right arm and looking skyward. She followed his lead and curled up on her side, still facing him, but glancing up at the stars in thought.

Maybe it was a cultural difference, but Spyre felt uncomfortable under her stare. He caught her eye and looked away a few times to convey the awkwardness of the moment, but her eyes were glazed and unseeing. For a moment, he thought she might actually have fallen asleep with her eyes open, but then he felt something soft in his hand.

Glancing down, Spyre stiffened and darted his eyes to hers. She blinked, her own eyes round as her brain caught up with the rest of her. She looked down to see that she had reached out and taken Spyre's hand in hers, holding it as if to reassure him. She trailed her gaze back up to him guiltily, but his hand remained securely in hers.

Spyre stared at her with a stony look of confusion and a twinge of apprehension. Should he withdraw? Should he be still? His heart thudded with a similar rhythm as during his fight with Ryne, so should he fight or flee? Given Ness's apparent lack of weapon skills, he rationalized that fighting wasn't the answer. Instead, he sent her a question with his eyes. Did she need something from him, perhaps? Was this what giving comfort looked like?

With the same questions in her own eyes, she shook her head at him, mouth open, but nothing, not even a breath, came out. He looked down at their hands.

Let it be, Lateo encouraged him.

Spyre wasn't sure about this, but after a moment, the muscles in his forehead relaxed.

Ness stared at him, still looking slightly panicked on her own part. She was afraid of so many things, Spyre realized, but somehow, he wasn't one of them.

Spyre questioned himself for a moment but offered her what little reassurance he could by brushing her pinky with his thumb and gently squeezing her fingers. Then he turned his head back to the sky and closed his eyes, distracted enough to slip away from the threats of tomorrow and find one last night of peace.

CHAPTER 29

"What do you think?" Spyre heard Pyram's voice ask. "Should we wake them up or pretend not to notice?"

"Well, it could be worse," Eofyn's voice responded as Spyre's brain slowly woke the rest of him. "You know, it might be nothing. Do we want to blow it out of proportion?"

"That depends," Pyram said. "How bored are we?"

They never got the chance to decide, as Spyre stirred. He heard shuffling feet and opened his eyes to find Eofyn and Pyram acting like they had just been waking up themselves, as Spyre sat up with his back to them. Rubbing his bleary eyes, he looked down and jumped a little when he realized that his hand was still occupied.

Spyre delicately untangled his hand from Ness's, cringing in anticipation. When she didn't stir, he almost sighed, but the sigh caught in his throat when he turned around and saw the king and his right-hand man raising suggestive eyebrows at him. He opened his mouth to speak, but nothing came out.

"I was just … it was … I only wanted to … because she looked so confused, and …" He gave up.

Eofyn held up a hand, smiling. "No questions here," he said. "None of our business, right, Pyram?"

Pyram looked around him, mimetically searching. "Is there something here worth questioning?" he asked, though he still smiled slyly.

Spyre sat for an awkward moment but quickly settled into a smile.

"But we should get going," Eofyn said, glancing at Ness before looking back to Spyre.

Spyre jumped to attention, receiving the message. He gently untangled their fingers and gave her shoulder a shake until she stirred. Her hands brushed over the sand, and the world seemed to rush back to her in one swift motion.

With a sharp gasp, she sat up and smacked Spyre in the side of his head, toppling him over.

He curled on his side, clutching his temple and willing the buzzing in his ear to stop until he realized it wasn't buzzing at all but the sound of Eofyn and Pyram's laughter.

She gasped again, and he glared at her through squinted eyes. "I'm so sorry." She reached out to him, now fully conscious, but he flinched away from her. "It was a reflex, I swear."

"Was it, now?" Spyre asked in a dry tone.

Eofyn and Pyram were still laughing. "You okay?" Pyram asked between chuckles.

Spyre twisted to look back at them, a look of disinterest on his face. "Just fine," he said, his own smile finally breaking through to the surface. He looked up at Ness and waved away the anxiety in her expression. "No harm done." He stood up and shook himself off, looking around and measuring the remaining distance.

"Looks like we need to walk and plan," Spyre said. "We should be sneaking into the castle sometime tonight." He turned to them expectantly. "Everyone ready for that?"

The laughing stopped short, and the joy drained out of their faces. Spyre looked at the unamused looks. "What?" he asked cluelessly.

"Killjoy," Pyram muttered as he and Eofyn trudged past Spyre.

"I guess reality can be depressing sometimes," he said, receiving a sad nod from Ness, coupled with a glimmer of dread.

He frowned.

"But not for long," he said. "Let's go save the day." He smiled, holding out his hand.

Ness looked at it, eagerly accepting.

They all walked toward the edge of the mysterious, dry land with renewed determination.

"Plan," Pyram announced after an appropriate amount of time had passed, and they had worked up to a steady pace. "We need one."

Everyone was quiet for a moment, none of them feeling adequate to devise a successful strategy.

"You're the one with the street experience and the crystal to back it up," Eofyn said. "Why don't you tell us?"

"You're the king," Pyram retorted, laughing at the absurdity.

"Ness has snuck into the castle before, apparently," Spyre offered, throwing Ness a glance that earned him a backhand to the gut. The air left him rather quickly, but he only laughed.

"So have you," she countered. "Well, sort of."

Spyre held up a finger and wagged it. "On the contrary; I was dragged to the castle and smashed through the front window and then captured. That's not exactly a successful sneak-in."

Eofyn's jaw slacked a little. "You broke my window?" he asked in disbelief. "I love that window."

"He wasn't the first," Ness said, cringing and raising her hand before Eofyn could even ask who'd done it.

The king sighed, staring out at the city with sad eyes.

"It can be fixed," Pyram reminded him in a low tone. "Focus, Fyn."

"Right ..."

"So," Pyram said, getting them back on track, "there are only three viable entrances into the castle. The front and the sides."

"And the other windows," Spyre reminded him.

The others gave him blank stares.

"What? That's how I would sneak into somewhere if I had the backup to reach them. The windows."

The others nodded approvingly, but Spyre raised an eyebrow at them.

"Nothing has ever threatened you before this, has it? Not even your own people?"

"Why would anyone threaten each other in town?" Ness asked, eyes wide with innocence.

Spyre exhaled in disbelief. "Okay, now I see why I was brought here. Wow." He walked on as the other three trailed behind, exchanging confused glances.

"So we go in through a window," Spyre continued. "Which one? Definitely not the front, please."

Eofyn caught up to him, ready to make himself useful. "We can go in through the spare room on the first floor. There shouldn't be anyone in there. It'll give us a few seconds to breathe before we split up."

"Then, well, it will probably get a bit unpredictable after that, at least for us," Pyram said, gesturing to Eofyn, who nodded his agreement.

"But Spyre and I can plan for Afor somehow, right?" Ness looked at Spyre, but she might as well have held him at the point of a blade. "We know he'll be in the main hall," Ness encouraged. "We'll find him there, and while you challenge him directly, I'll watch your back."

"Some plan," Spyre muttered. "But it's what we've got."

"We have a little time," Pyram said. "Just run through all the scenarios you can think of, so we can be prepared for as much as possible."

"What about your source?" Spyre asked the king. "Aren't you supposed to unlock it or unleash it or something?"

Eofyn's face was blank. "They keep showing me the source as if it were a large crystal, and when it's activated, its glow spreads across Condel, touching everyone who wears a true crystal, and then it shatters, like it's just an empty vessel. The burst seems to be what revives the dragons."

Spyre nodded. "Makes sense, I guess."

Eofyn shrugged. "I just don't know how to find it or unleash it."

"You'll figure it out, Fyn," Pyram assured him with a clap on the shoulder.

The king smiled, but Spyre fell a step behind them. He wasn't so sure.

CHAPTER 30

The walk to the edge of Tir had been a relatively silent one, each of them taking turns to lighten the mood. They would all indulge in laughter for a moment, but it would soon fade back to silence. Even then, however, Spyre was growing more and more fond of the people around him.

They had such pure intentions, even if that made them seem like children in a few ways. He was happy to be fighting for them because he realized that he had little else to motivate him to take on Afor. He'd been raised to fear that man, and seeing him face to face had only supported his reasons for wanting to avoid him. The Condels had learned that lesson quickly enough, but as Ness knew, hiding would lead them nowhere. He glanced over to the girl, who was staring at her feet in thought, just as the rest of them were.

A girl. When an entire kingdom ran, a young girl was the one to step forward and foolishly defy the foreign king. Guided, maybe, but definitely stupid. He almost smiled. She sort of amazed him. He seriously doubted that he would have caught her looking as rugged as she did now at the beginning of this journey. Her long light-brown hair, so bright it was almost blonde, had once been secured by a ponytail, but many strands abandoned it now, framing her face, and she didn't bother fixing them. That was a sure sign she had her priorities in order. But what pleased him most about Ness and her people were their eyes. They were all bright with hues of blue or green, like his own darker blue ones. Spyre was often singled out for his brighter eye color back in Gaernod, but here, they didn't notice that difference about him. It was refreshing.

Ness looked up and caught Spyre watching her. He quickly looked away with no expression. She moved closer, and he feared she might ask why he was staring, but a jubilant shout from Pyram saved him from having to explain.

"Castle! I see the castle. We're almost there."

Eofyn and Ness ran to Pyram's side, staring at their home with light in their eyes. They would be there soon. Spyre was slower to approach the scene, feeling strange as he remembered that the two kingdoms that occupied that city had once been a single race. He marveled at the city, filled with people who were not as distant from him as he thought. With his new understanding, Spyre looked upon Condel as a younger sibling to Gaernod more than an estranged third cousin, but if they had been so close, why had his people been denied the magic of the crystals? Or had it started before that?

Yes, a voice softly encouraged in his mind.

Was it the king's ancestor?

Yes.

And he had that Pure Fyre epiphany. He must have been guided to leave Tir, but I guess not everyone agreed with that.

You're getting there.

So the crystals don't work for us, for Gaernods, because we never believed they would in the first place, before there were even crystals to have. And we evolved that way, didn't we? We remained stubborn until it was physically impossible for us to change.

There was silence in his mind, but Spyre knew he'd gotten it right.

He suddenly felt two hands tentatively grasping his arm, bringing him back to reality.

"Is everything okay?" Ness asked with faint concern.

He looked down at her and smiled warmly. "Everything's fine," he said with only a trace of doubt. "Let's get going, hmm?"

Ness smiled back up at him and nodded her agreement.

"They'll be watching the canal," Spyre reminded Eofyn. "That's how I got out, and I'm guessing that's how Ness followed me, so if they're not watching it, they're fools."

Eofyn nodded. "That's how we left too," he said.

"So you don't have some kind of back entrance?" Spyre asked, but the silent response gave him all the answer he needed.

"Oh, fine." He sighed. He stared at the grass as they walked, appreciating the sight of the green plants after a few days in the dust of Tir. He thought through what he knew about the city and what he knew about Afor and the inclinations of his men.

"Confirm something for me," Spyre said distantly.

Eofyn stared at him.

"Afor expects my brother"—he winced and changed his wording—"his men to have killed you by now, right? And Pyram should have either starved or suffocated or been killed?"

Eofyn rubbed the gashes on his arms. "Apparently," he replied quietly.

Spyre smiled devilishly at the ground as a thought occurred to him. "And they must know I went to save you, and they've probably figured out that Ness is gone by now."

Ness's eyes widened.

"Guys," Spyre said, looking up at each of them. "If you'll trust me, I think I might actually have a plan."

CHAPTER 31

Spyre fumbled his way over the rubble of the main city gate, standing at the top and struggling to keep his balance on the way back down. It was the only entrance to the city that might not be under surveillance, purely because it was nearly impassable, and anyone would be ridiculously stupid to try it, but he took the ruined city gate one step at a time, always keeping three points of contact with the rocks so he wouldn't fall and injure himself before the real pain could even begin. He found a secure hold for both of his hands and one foot as he moved the other and continued this slow pace until he finally reached the bottom of the other side and could jump the short distance to the ground.

He relaxed, exhaling as he looked around. He was back in Condel. It was dark, and the city looked awful from this perspective. Even where the houses were still standing, there seemed to be a painfully thick feeling of dread and hopelessness. But he would fix that.

Spyre walked cautiously along the main street before him, the only road, Eofyn had told him, that led directly to the castle, though it wound on its way. Spyre shook his head at the design of this city. For a blissful Utopia where nothing would ever go awry, that was a lovely little idea, forcing the people to mingle on their way to wherever they went, but how thick could they be? War had found them, and now look. It was a mess, and everything took longer than necessary.

There was movement to Spyre's left, and he reached for the hilt of his sword, searching the darkness for signs of his company. He would cross the bridge to the inner part of the city in a moment, which put him close to the canal exits, where he guessed the real trouble would start. Had they already noticed him? He hadn't made the quietest entrance over the crumbled gate, but he didn't think he'd caused enough commotion to draw attention. He wasn't exactly a pro at this. He continued forward warily, jumping at every little noise until one was finally worth the fear.

Spyre had reached the middle of the bridge when they surrounded him. Two soldiers at each end of the bridge, swords drawn, hands in their pockets, which he guessed were filled with the explosive pellets they'd stolen from Spyre's own designs.

Well played, he thought. He was nowhere near prepared to fight the men, but he was fully prepared to face them. He drew his sword. He would not be giving up.

He held on tight to the wooden handle of his blade with both hands as four men slowly closed in on him and backed him into the side of the bridge. They were light on their feet, watching Spyre's movement and ready to lunge for him if he tried anything foolish. But he wasn't foolish. He knew he wouldn't make it out of this alive if he fought them, and their eyes were gleaming with excitement.

Anytime now, he thought nervously, waiting for Lateo to spot him some moves that would at least prolong his existence.

But there was nothing.

Oh, of all the times for you to be quiet, Spyre thought, hoping the guide could hear him.

The guards were staring at him, waiting for him to make the first move for the sport of it before they finished him, but Spyre felt completely inadequate, and nothing came to his mind. He needed more time. He raised his sword, shifting his eyes from one soldier to the other, but their patience, like so many things about the Gaernod people, differed from his. The guard farthest to his right distorted his face, fed up with waiting, and took a jab at Spyre with his sword.

Spyre's blade instinctively flew up to deflect it. He smiled inwardly. He'd just blocked a soldier's sword without needing to be told to by Lateo. Not so worthless after all, huh?

But it was too soon to celebrate. The guard on the opposite end quickly filled the space of the first sword with his own.

Swing it, you fool.

He reacted by sweeping his sword to the left and blocking the attack, but he knew he wouldn't be able to keep up once they all went at him together. He hoped this had been enough.

Bringing the hilt of his sword down on a blade that had emerged from the center of the group, as ordered by Lateo, Spyre held his hands up in surrender, pausing the melee.

"Sorry, guys," he said, glancing around him and seeing nothing as he sheathed his sword. "I think your king is eager to see me. I shouldn't keep him waiting, because, truth is…" He leapt up onto the rail of the bridge and took a preparatory breath, closing his eyes in anticipation, "I'd really like to see him too."

No sooner had his admission left his mouth than Spyre felt himself jerked away from the group of soldiers by the same invisible rope from before; he surged toward the castle, dragged by the fear of Condel to meet his enemy and demand an audience with the dual king.

Spyre tried to relax as he passed through the streets, accepting that from now on, things would inevitably hurt. He distracted himself from that dreary truth by looking at the buildings painted with brighter colors, judging by the various shades of darkness that covered them now. It was quaint. He supposed he could get used to them.

Spyre looked up just as he reached the base of the staircase that led to Eofyn's favorite window. He glimpsed the stone dragon and glared at it, wondering what in the world Swelgan was waiting for. Fortunately, thanks to Swelgan, Spyre's head was curled against his chest when he smashed through the same hole he'd made days earlier, widening it a bit. He would apologize to Eofyn later.

He hit the marble floor with force and slid toward the center of the room, eyes shut tightly against the pain. *It's not that bad*, he told himself. He would be fine to fight, regardless of how sore he felt.

Face down on the floor, Spyre could tell that he'd already caused a stir within the main hall, knowing because he'd stopped here that Afor was present. Spyre pressed his palms into the floor next to his face and pushed himself upward, just enough to take in the scene.

Apparently, he'd interrupted something.

The first eyes he met were the sky-blue gems that belonged to the future queen. She looked shocked to see him, especially now that he was bleeding a little from the scratches he'd earned on his way in. He stared at her for a moment, trying to reassure her of something he could neither promise nor actually name.

Next to Lissa sat a young boy of Condel. He couldn't have been older than thirteen, and Spyre noted the boy's face resembled Ness's. They shared the same nose, eye shape, and rounded forehead, but it surprised Spyre to see that there was no fear in his eyes. In fact, the glint of them looked a lot like Afor's, and his crystal was blazing brightly. Spyre frowned in confusion as his eyes roved to where the boy was shifting his own glance.

He looked to his side, knowing who he would see if he looked forward and not feeling quite ready to face him. There was a young girl on her knees, shaking, with a crystal that looked like it was short-circuiting. It blinked in an erratic pattern, dimming and then surging before extinguishing for a few seconds and starting all over again. This must have been the nightly draining that Ness had fallen victim to. Anger flared in Spyre's eyes as he saw the pathetic state of the girl on the floor and imagined that it was Ness on her hands and knees in the agony of losing herself. His hands drew into fists.

No, Lateo chided.

Fine.

He took in a deep breath, preparing to meet the eyes of his enemy, but when he lifted his head, all he saw was a pair of feet standing dangerously close to him. He jolted backward, knowing what came next but unable to avoid it all the same.

One foot kicked Spyre's shoulder, reeling him backward. He mentally thanked Lissa for having healed it before. That blow would have ended him, otherwise. A hand caught Spyre by the neck before he could land on his back and drew him to his toes. He glanced down, straining for air and trying to meet Afor's dark eyes. It had begun, and it would definitely be painful.

"Would you help me, please?" Afor inquired of someone behind Spyre in the same way one might order a second glass of wine at the tavern, and Spyre quickly felt himself lowered into the grip of two more sets of hands that clamped around his arms and shoulders like steel traps.

He didn't even bother looking at them as he caught his breath. He remained defiantly focused on Afor. The false king smiled thinly and used his newly freed hand to drive a fist deep into Spyre's stomach, forcing away the air he'd only just taken in. Spyre's head fell to his chest as he gasped and fought to regain his composure, but a finger curled around his chin and drew his face upward before he had the chance to recover.

"Interesting to see you back so soon," Afor said. He tilted his head, narrowing his eyes at Spyre as if trying to read his thoughts. "Did you journey away to find the king, perhaps?"

Spyre didn't bother. Afor knew what he had been up to.

"I don't see him with you. Neither do I see the spark of victory in your eyes, boy," Afor continued, glancing around for signs of Eofyn. "What did you discover about the king?"

Before Spyre could work up enough moisture in his mouth to spit in the man's face, Afor said, "I encourage you to tell me. Did you find the king? Where is he? What has possibly come of him?"

The rage in Spyre's eyes faded away as they glossed over and closed tightly, his head dropping once more.

"Say it," Afor hissed.

"I was …" Spyre looked up at Lissa and held her gaze. "I was too late."

Lissa's eyes grew and filled with tears as she shook her head at Spyre, but there was nothing he could do to console her. Her face fell into her hands as the tears found their freedom, but she kept them silent. Spyre looked at the floor, hating to see her that way.

"So the boy did go to Tir," Afor confirmed happily. His eyes shot back to Spyre. "Did you happen to meet the men who dealt with him?"

"I saw," Spyre replied curtly. "I didn't stick around for a reunion, but I know who you sent."

Noticing that Afor's attention focused on the newcomer, the girl on the floor stood and ran for the door. She threw herself forward and burst through the larger door, racing away from the hall with a feverish shout.

Spyre stared over his shoulder after the girl in shock, as Afor's smile spread farther across his face. Spyre could only listen to the receding footfalls and glare at Afor for what he'd done to her.

"Isn't it an intriguing twist of fate that the man who betrayed his country to save an enemy's king got to see his own brother deal the final blow?" Afor asked.

"It's fascinating," Spyre said flatly, looking at Afor with hatred in his eyes.

Afor tilted his head, patting the side of Spyre's face condescendingly. "And I see you've found yourself a new toy," he said, reaching behind Spyre for the sword.

Give in, Lateo's voice rang in Spyre's head.

It was Spyre's turn to smile. He let his knees give out beneath him, dropping to the floor and partially out of the grip of the guards behind him. He remedied their hold on his arms by twisting and rolling once across the floor, moving directly to his feet as he drew his sword several feet away from an amused Afor.

"Impressive," Afor admitted, holding up a hand to the guards who ran at Spyre.

They stopped, looking at him with confusion. Afor turned and pointed to one guard's sword, curling his fingers in a "gimme" gesture. Uncertainly, the guard drew his sword and passed it to Afor. Afor's face fell into one of fierce wrath as he quickly sliced the blade across the guard's abdomen. The guard coughed as the air rushed out of his diaphragm and fumbled backward, grasping his wound as the other guard caught him and wordlessly dragged him to the side of the room, less out of concern and more as an excuse to distance himself from his king.

"That is for being dull-witted," Afor seethed before smoothly turning back to Spyre with renewed interest.

Spyre stared at the man in furious disbelief, reminded of what Soru had told him about the boat they'd used to cross the Modwen Sea and realizing how serious the wisp had been. The guard was bleeding profusely.

Noticing Spyre's distraction, Afor ordered the other man to remove his comrade, and now the two stared at each other, Afor looking disgustingly smug and Spyre glaring angrily as the door opened and shut behind him.

Spyre was waiting for directions from Lateo, trying to make the moment last as long as he could before Afor grew weary of him and attacked, when he heard a female sharply draw in a breath behind him. Spyre's narrowed eyes widened, knowing the sound of that gasp. Afor noticed the disturbance too and looked past Spyre to the door. Unable to resist, Spyre pivoted to see the door still cracked open, the point of an arrow aimed shakily at Afor. But the sea-green eyes behind the arrow were focused in another direction.

CHAPTER 32

This was the worst plan ever.

Ness had tried to argue, but as usual, she'd been overruled, even though Eofyn and Pyram had been reluctant themselves. And then the three of them had waited outside the city walls as Spyre clambered over the old gate. They kept themselves at a safe distance and angle from the small arch that admitted the canal into the city. Crouched low, they could see the feet of two guards standing at the side of the water.

They waited impatiently for their cue, Ness tapping her finger against the ground. How long could this possibly take? What was he doing in there? Was Losian with him or was he being held somewhere else in the castle? Was he even alive?

"Come on, come on," Pyram whispered restlessly, every muscle tensed and ready to run.

Then it came. The sets of feet turned slightly before slowly stepping out of view.

"That's it," Pyram said immediately. "Go, go, go!" He pushed the others in front of him impatiently, not willing to waste a second.

Ness went first, bent in half as she hurried to the water, stepping in to avoid splashing and drawing attention. She passed under the arch, followed closely by Eofyn and then Pyram, and she climbed out, looking up to see four soldiers huddled around something—actually someone— on the bridge. She heard a clang of metal and gasped, but Pyram gave her a small shove, reminding her that this was all according to plan. She nodded, refocusing and running low along the canal, heading for the closest houses and hiding among them as they covertly made their way to the castle, keeping one or two houses away from the canal to avoid any other guards.

Pyram had needed to grab her and yank her backward only once to avoid a passing Gaernod soldier. She'd looked back at him with a sheepish apology, but when she turned and noticed which street they were passing, her heart sank. It was hers, and there were three soldiers stationed at either end. She turned to him in protest, but he only calmly shook his head.

"We'll check on them later, Ness," he said soothingly. "I promise you'll see them as soon as we finish this. They won't be any worse off than they are now, not with so much commotion in the castle. A rebellious family will be the last thing on Afor's mind. And the soldiers could probably care less, let's face it."

That didn't satisfy Ness, but she weighed the lesser of two evils in her head, remembering that, though her family was probably huddled in fear inside her house, Spyre was being held at the point of a blade so she and the others would have time to get to the castle, and she couldn't let him down. She reluctantly nodded at Pyram, taking the lead once again, and they arrived at the castle rather quickly after that. Eofyn pointed to the window he intended for them to use, and they ran for it, flattening themselves up against the wall below it.

Ness's crystal flared in warning. She looked down, covering its light with her hand and accepting its message. She noticed the other two watching her patiently.

"Afor's gotten much stronger," she revealed to their dismay. "I don't know what he did, but it's like he's got a perpetual source of energy to feed off of."

"We have to get in there," Eofyn said, echoing their thoughts.

"Ness," Pyram whispered, cupping his hands and squatting. She stepped up to him and put a foot in his hands, bracing herself against the castle as he lifted her to the window. She peered around the room quickly, seeing it was empty as expected. She pressed her palms against the glass and pushed up, sliding the window just enough for her to wriggle her fingers underneath it and open it completely.

She grabbed the windowsill and pushed up off of Pyram's hands, using her arms to crawl into the small sitting room as quietly as possible before crossing the carpet back to the window to grab Eofyn's hands. They both jolted as they heard a small crash from the front of the castle. Eofyn's head fell back with a pained expression at the sound of his window shattering further. Ness gave him a weak smile, coupled with a shrug, as she helped him through the window. Eofyn leaned back out to help Pyram while Ness turned toward the room, stiffening as she noticed a shadowed figure in the corner.

Her breath caught in her throat as the man tentatively emerged from the shadows, and Ness exhaled, lowering her guard when she saw Atelle reveal himself just as Pyram made it through the window. He was holding broken pieces of clay in his hands, looking as if he was seeing ghosts.

Eofyn checked that Pyram was okay and turned to see the young man. "Atelle," he whispered happily. "I'm glad to see you're okay. What are you doing in here?"

Atelle looked shaky and nervous, and dread rose in Ness's throat as she tried to imagine what could have made him that way in just a few short days.

"I was just cleaning up after my—" He cut off, eyeing the others and looking like a skittish dog. Ness's heart shattered. "Forgive me," he intoned, keeping his cautious eyes on the trio, "but I believe a more productive question might be what are you doing here?" He turned to Eofyn with a deep bow. "Did you find the source, Your Highness?"

Eofyn sighed, shaking his head as he filled Atelle in on their new mission. "So I need to find it somewhere within the castle, and Ness will go help Spyre defeat Afor. He's already facing him in the throne room now."

Atelle pursed his lips in thought and nodded, folding his hands in front of his chest. "I'm not sure where you should start," he said to his king, "but if something that ancient were in the castle, I would assume it would be in the library."

"Our thoughts exactly," Pyram agreed. "We have to get to it as quickly as we can so Fyn can get it set up for the dragons to make their appearance."

Ness absently nodded her agreement. "While you guys do that, I'll head to the hall and try to help Spyre as best I can," she said, her hand drifting to her bow and the arrows she'd stored in the satchel Spyre had given her.

Eofyn stepped in front of her, placing a gentle hand on her shoulder, drawing her eyes to him. "Ness," he said, sounding every bit like a king, "I appreciate what you're doing for us. I can't thank you enough for your help." His eyes softened, making him look more like a friend. "But please, please be careful. Your father would be lost without you."

Tears threatened Ness's eyes as an image of her dad's face filled her mind. She wiped away the tears with her arm, swallowing hard as she gave a small smile and nodded.

They went to the door together, cracking it open.

"Miss Ness," Atelle whispered urgently, "I think there's something you should know before you go."

Ness looked back at him. "Is it my brother? Is he…?" She choked on the tears that threatened her eyes at the thought that Losian might be hurt or worse.

Atelle shook his head with dark, hooded eyes. "No, but he isn't safe, either." He cast his eyes toward the hall. "There's no time to explain here, I know, but you need to understand that your brother has taken to Afor's mind-set. He's been at Afor's side from the start."

Ness gaped at Atelle, repeating his words in her head but sure she'd misheard. Losian was annoying, but he wasn't a traitor. What could Afor possibly have offered him to …

Of course. Afor had a crystal when he shouldn't have. He must have offered Losian the talent her brother had been missing. Afor had exploited his insecurity and offered him an easy way out.

Ness's fingers curled into angry fists, and she turned away from Atelle. "Thank you for telling me," she said in a dull tone. Then she darted from the room, heading left where Eofyn and Pyram had gone right and leaving Atelle to shut the door behind her and go where he would.

Ness knew her way from this point. They were close to the kitchen, and she'd made the trip from there to the main hall before. The corridors were empty, and she wondered why, hoping that Spyre wasn't being ambushed. She took the corners by planting her outside foot and pivoting in the direction of the hall, not stopping for anything. As she went, she drew an arrow from her satchel and pulled the bow over her head, ready to use her weapon with more accuracy than she had back at the temple in Tir.

She rounded the last corner and dropped to one knee when she noticed that the doors were open. She crawled closer, quickly grabbing the door in front of her so she wouldn't be exposed as two men went down the corridor, leaving droplets of red in their wake. She forced herself not to think about it, afraid of who had dealt the blow and who else might be in worse condition than the injured soldier.

Feeling safe, she pushed her door closed so she could catch the other just before it sealed the entrance, leaving about an inch for her to prop it open with the toe of her shoe. She drew the bow and found her target, relieved to see that Afor was sword to sword with Spyre, who seemed to be holding his ground well against his former king.

Afor was directly in front of her, only partially blocked by Spyre's slightly shorter frame, and Ness's arrow was prepared. She glanced at Spyre, waiting for him to make a move, when a familiar face came into focus over Spyre's shoulder. She saw a new throne on the raised platform, gasping as she recognized the boy sitting there to be her little brother.

Her breath echoed into the cavernous room, and both of the dueling Gaernod men looked her way, Spyre looking pained.

With Spyre momentarily distracted, Afor bludgeoned him in the ribs with the handle of his blade, forcing him to stumble away while Afor stepped toward the door where Ness was frozen.

"Another familiar face," Afor exclaimed in sadistic surprise as he bent to peek around the door at Ness.

The pain she'd experienced before returned, clouding Ness's senses as Losian finally realized her presence and sat forward, looking concerned. Ness caught his eye and saw the radiant glow of his crystal, realizing the color and hating Afor all the more. She stood defiantly and pushed the door open, seeing no more point in hiding. Bow raised, she regarded Afor with a contemptuous glare.

"You took my brother?" she demanded, no longer caring who he was or how strong his stolen power could be.

Losian leaned forward in his seat, a flabbergasted look on his face in response to Ness's nerve.

"Ness?" He made to stand, but Afor held up a hand, not turning to face his apprentice.

"Don't let her fool you, child," Afor said. "She would take you back to who you were. Do you want to lose your power so soon?"

Jaw firm, Losian sat back. Ness gaped at him.

"Losian," she said firmly, returning her gaze to Afor and seeing Spyre slowly approaching him from behind, eyes fixed on the back of Afor's head and sword poised to strike. "You can't honestly think that he's given you the real Fyre that you deserve, do you?"

Losian remained silent, and Ness rolled her eyes. Losian hated being treated like a child. It was her favorite way to irritate him. Now it almost seemed like their sibling rivalry had been divinely ordained for exactly this moment so Ness would know what to do.

"I thought I was the family disappointment," she said, trying to anger him.

It worked.

Losian stood up sharply. "I am not a disappointment," he argued.

"Not what it looks like to me." She tutted at him, shaking her head slowly. "What would Mom say?"

Afor waited to see Losian's reaction.

"You don't have to worry, boy," Afor said soothingly, keeping his eyes on Ness's bow. "What parents wouldn't be proud to see their son become such a powerful prince?"

Losian sat down, still eyeing Ness as the gears in his mind continued to turn. Afor smiled with pride.

Ness wanted to vomit. She pulled her bowstring, preparing to shoot, but a wave from Spyre's hand in the corner of her vision stopped her. He was trying to calm her, pleading with her to hold back. This was not how it was supposed to be, and she trusted that Lateo was the motivation behind him stopping her. With every muscle arguing against it, Ness lowered her bow, and Afor's eyes flashed with victory. He turned back to Spyre, who was already staring at him.

"So I see you've made friends." Afor sneered at Spyre, gesturing to Ness with a small wave of his arm, clearly not regarding her as a threat. "Was she with you when you journeyed into Tir?"

Spyre didn't alter his expression. He stared at Afor, waiting for the fight to continue. Then a glint passed in Afor's eye, and suddenly his sword was slicing toward Spyre's gut.

Ness's stomach clenched, but Spyre waved his sword in front of him, catching Afor's blade and bringing it to the floor. He looked as surprised at the move as Ness was, and then she realized Spyre wasn't fighting alone. The voice from Bryta must be guiding him.

Afor yanked his sword away, and Spyre fell back a step, but Afor quickly rebounded with another attack, raising his sword above Spyre's head as if he were about to split a block of wood in two. Afor smirked at Spyre as he forcefully swung his sword downward.

Spyre's eyes grew wide, and he hurriedly thrust his sword up, supporting it with both of his hands as Afor's heavy strike came down on him. The side of the blade dug into Spyre's fingers until they bled, but Afor still pushed, and Spyre's arms inched downward until Ness feared they'd give out under Afor's strength. Ness watched in horror; all she could do was pray that the voice in Spyre's head found a way to save him.

CHAPTER 33

Relax.

Spyre hesitated but allowed his arms to weaken for a moment, exhaling calmly and taking in another breath as the blade dipped dangerously close to his face.

And push.

Spyre's eyes flashed with a renewed tenacity as he gathered his strength and shoved his sword upward, sliding Afor's off of it and causing the false king to lose his composure for just a second before coming at him again. Spyre blocked it, and the two began a duel, Afor dealing offensive blows while Spyre countered, waiting for the go-ahead from Lateo to retaliate.

From the edge of his vision, Spyre caught movement as Ness took this chance to run to her brother's side, crouching next to his throne.

"Losian," she said urgently, "you've got to get out of here. Go through the window and get back to Mom and Dad. It's too dangerous here." She looked in his eyes, expecting to see her little brother, slightly defiant but at least a little sensible, but what she saw was a Gaernod soldier in a boy's body. He looked at her angrily and pushed her away from him, causing her to sit back on her heels, looking astonished.

He glared at her and said, "No. You're just upset because I finally have a purpose. My crystal is finally glowing, and it's stronger than yours—than anyone's. You want to rob me of what's mine." His voice was shockingly low for someone of his age. He sounded nothing like himself, and Ness's eyes reflected that in fear.

She grabbed his arm and tugged on him as the duel drew closer to them. Lissa was pressing herself into her seat, turning her face away but unable to tear her eyes from the scene.

"You have to go," Ness insisted, pulling him to his feet, but he yanked away from her.

"No!"

Lissa and Ness both looked at him, surprised by how loud and demanding his voice was; Spyre was so surprised, he lost track of Afor for a moment, but one moment was enough for him to take advantage of the distraction. He lunged, and Spyre felt a sharp, searing pain in his shoulder he hadn't forgotten but hadn't missed. Looking down, Spyre saw blood seeping through a slice in his shirt, and upon seeing it, the pain swelled even more. Spyre shouted as the blade slid back out. His sword hung at his side as his sleeve was slowly dyed red.

Spyre glared at Afor resentfully as the king smiled, swinging his sword in a circle to show off.

"This was fun." Afor sighed, running his eyes over his colored blade. "But I have things to do, and I think we should wrap this up."

Spyre followed the tip of the blade as it rose above his head, hearing nothing but his own labored breathing and feeling nothing but pain when he attempted to move his arm to his defense. A strange light graced Spyre's face, glaring in his eyes. He blinked against the blinding glow to see Afor smiling maliciously, his face illuminated from below. Spyre glanced downward just long enough to see the sickly glow of Afor's crystal burst as though a small explosion had erupted inside; the light breached the confines of the crystal, traveling up Afor's arms and into the shining metal of his blade.

The other three in the room could only watch as the culminated fears of Condel lent themselves to Afor's strength, promising to make Spyre's punishment both quick and painful. Spyre looked to the ceiling, realizing that help would not come, and he tightly closed his eyes in anticipation.

"Afor!"

Spyre's eyes popped open in confusion while Afor turned to see Ness, arrow poised and ready to shoot him in the head. Spyre's confidence was low, remembering her lack of accuracy at the temple, but Afor took no chances. His sword lowered slightly, and its gleam faltered as his face reflected a small twinge of anxiety.

His arms tensed to bring his sword down completely when he smiled, and the glow came back full force. He raised his sword at Spyre once more.

Frowning at this turn of events, Spyre followed Afor's eyes to see that a man had quietly stepped through the hole in the window behind Ness, his own unsheathed sword ready to attack if she made a move to shoot.

It was impossible. Spyre shouted for Ness to move as he left Afor and ran to intercept his brother's sword with his own. Startled, Ness ducked to the side as their swords collided. They pushed against each other, faces inches apart, teeth gritted as one struggled to overpower the other.

Spyre looked into his brother's eyes, feeling no familial compassion and no remorse as he received the same expression from Ryne.

"How did you get out of the temple?" Spyre strained, pushing harder against Ryne's blade.

His brother smiled ruefully. "Another one of yours," he said.

Then Spyre remembered his invention that the army had used to explode the gate and surrounding houses. He almost cursed himself for not having checked his brother for the powder before he left the temple, but there just hadn't been enough time.

"And it's a lot quicker to get out of the desert when there's no sand to slow you down," Ryne remarked, his sword gaining ground between their faces, scraping against Spyre's blade.

Spyre felt his upper lip twitch in anger. He moved instinctively, ducking and spinning to his left, away from where Ryne's sword came down, but his brother was quick to recover, far more experienced in battle, and spun himself, dragging his sword across Spyre's chest and eliciting a loud yell from his younger sibling and a horrified shout from Ness.

Spyre recoiled, gasping for breath, the pain increasing every time his chest rose and fell. His eyes were hooded, and his jaw slacked as his breathing became more ragged. He eyed Ryne angrily, waiting for his next ruthless move.

What he didn't expect was to see Ness recklessly jump onto Ryne's back, grabbing his forehead and yanking it backward. Spyre appreciated her attempt, in a half-thought before the fear for her set in, but this was child's play for his brother.

Ryne allowed himself to fall backward on top of her, smacking the back of her head off of the arm of her younger brother's throne on their way down.

Ness's head lolled to the side as she slumped against the chair. Spyre let out a shout as he ran to her aid. He didn't care what it took. He would get past his brother and help her.

Ness groaned as Ryne approached her, raising his blade without hesitation. She yelped and rolled to her side, narrowly escaping the swing of Ryne's sword. Spyre watched his brother prepare another blow and broke into a run to shoulder him away from her. Ryne spun to the side, and Spyre levelled the point of the ancient sword, glaring in fury at Ryne's gall.

"You leave her alone," Spyre growled in a low, no-nonsense tone, but Ryne continued to smile annoyingly.

"Spyre, behind you," Ness called from his left.

He ducked again, barely avoiding another blow from Afor's enhanced blade. As it contacted the marble floor, the glow dispersed, its power spent, but not before sending a large web of cracks across the floor.

Spyre stared wide eyed at the damage, but the trance shattered when he heard his brother cry out in pain; Ness had stabbed Ryne in the thigh with one of her arrows. She looked up at him as he turned to her angrily, and the color drained from her face.

Ness's jaw dropped, and she bolted away, out through the opening in the window, running behind Swelgan before Ryne could emerge.

Spyre stole every glance he could and listened keenly as Ryne stepped over the broken glass, looking around for Ness. Ryne held his sword at his side and broke the arrow off with his free hand, wincing and seething, but handling the pain better than Spyre ever had. He walked along the steps to the other side of the stone twin, to the dragon of Gaernod, swinging his sword as he rounded the corner of the statue, but only igniting a few sparks as the metal of his sword collided with nothing but stone. Ness recoiled at the sound.

"Come out, little girl," Ryne called in a singsong voice that made Spyre's blood boil and fueled his anger against Afor's continuous onslaught. "Your precious Spyre will be gone soon, and then what will you have to fight for? He's from Gaernod, you know. He's just like me. Same blood. How long do you think he'll last before he returns to his right mind and follows in his big brother's footsteps?

"He'll never truly belong to your people. And he'll never belong to you, if that's what you were hoping for."

Spyre flushed at his brother's words, deflecting Afor's sword and trying to catch his breath as Ryne continued.

"He'll either join us, or you can stay out here and listen to him scream when we take his life away from him. Then we'll do the same to your precious queen. That should draw your king out, don't you think?"

Spyre shoved Afor away and turned fully toward the window, to find Ness perched on Swelgan's massive stone head. Ness took silent aim with her bow and let loose an arrow into Ryne's shoulder, just barely making her target. A little more to the left, and she'd have given herself away. Instead, she left Ryne bent over, clutching his shoulder the same way he'd left Spyre reeling from the slice to his torso. Spyre's chest swelled with pride, even as he noticed Afor watching along from the corner of his eye.

While Ryne was still hunched over, Ness jumped from her hiding place and landed on him, buckling his knees and pinning him to the ground in an awkward position. She stumbled to her feet, reaching into her satchel for another arrow, but Ryne grabbed her ankle, jerking her to the ground. She tried to catch herself, but Ryne tugged her backward just as her palms hit the ground, dragging her across the stone. Spyre lunged forward but found a cold blade at his throat.

"Ah-ah," Afor chided him, even as Spyre glared in his direction. "I think this is something we'll all want to see." He nodded toward the scene, and Spyre followed his gaze, not because Afor suggested it but because that was Ness out there.

Ryne flipped her over, grabbing the front of her tunic and lifting her almost to her feet. He pulled the arrow out of his shoulder, keeping her eyes locked on his own with a piercing stare.

"No one is going to save you," he reminded her as Spyre gritted his teeth against Afor's steady sword.

Afor chuckled next to Spyre's ear, too close for him to make a move, and Lateo had abandoned him.

Ryne didn't give Ness time to realize her fate before he shoved the arrow into her stomach, widening his eyes to mock her own shocked expression.

"See?" he asked conversationally as he lowered her first to her knees and then lightly pushed her to fall onto her back, with her legs positioned awkwardly beneath her. He left her gasping for breath and staring skyward, but he turned his own face to look Spyre in the eye through the broken window. "They always look surprised."

Spyre unleashed a broken scream at the sight of Ness, gasping on the ground. Consequences or no, he threw the hilt of his sword into Afor's gut, forcing the false king to stumble back enough for Spyre to dip around his blade, but not without a flailing slice to his leg as Afor recovered. Spyre hissed, shifting his weight to his uninjured leg as the two men from Gaernod closed in on him.

Ryne's grin split wider across his face as he ran back into the throne room to engage in the battle, while Afor looked on, recovering.

Spyre found himself in a standoff between two men: his brother and his king. His breathing was weak, and his body was torn, blood seeping from his arm, torso, and the opposite leg to complement countless bloody scratches.

"The girl is dying," his brother goaded Spyre, who tried to keep his bleary eyes on both of his enemies at once. "Nothing will fix her now. I hope you're happy. You failed to protect her."

Spyre's head filled with a pressure so immense he felt it might explode, and he'd have welcomed it as he alternated pointing his sword from Ryne to Afor, his arm quivering.

"What do you have left to fight for, now that the girl's blood is painting the castle red?" Afor asked in an innocent tone, sounding genuine yet acidic as his crystal blazed the color of burned rust. Spyre stared in horror at its brilliance. "The king is as good as dead, and you've lost your little Condel pet."

Spyre felt in the pit of his stomach that Afor was right, and he could only think of one place to look, the only eyes in the room that could offer him any comfort: the mossy green eyes of the boy who was leaning forward in his seat, staring at the men in fright, but unmoving. Ness's brother, Losian. Spyre didn't miss the glow of his crystal around Losian's neck that matched Afor's own. This was not of the Fyre, which meant that Afor had corrupted this boy, and now Spyre was furious.

"If you wish," Ryne said, breaking Spyre from his thoughts, "we can pause this fight so you can have the opportunity to watch her fade. That will surely set your priorities straight."

"Shut up," Spyre finally shouted at his brother, brashly slicing his sword through the air in anger, but his strike was interrupted by a blow to his gut and a swift kick to the side of his head, knocking him to the floor.

The two men pursued him, and Spyre staggered up the few steps toward the thrones, bracing himself against the largest as he caught his balance and held his sword in front of him in shaky defiance.

He nearly jumped out of his skin when he felt someone grasp onto his ankle. Turning, he looked beneath the empty throne to find King Eofyn hiding there.

"Shush!" Eofyn hushed just loud enough to reach Spyre's ears.

Spyre glanced downward, shaking with adrenalin while Afor and Ryne advanced toward him, but still giving Eofyn his chance to explain. Eofyn hesitated, brushing Spyre's skin through a tear in his pant leg.

But nothing happened.

"What in the world are you doing?" Spyre hissed at him from the corner of his mouth. Then the realization hit him. "No. I'm not your source. Get out of here!" He jerked his leg away from Eofyn in time to defend himself against a strike from his brother as Afor watched, his crystal gaining strength.

Eofyn scurried backward while Spyre distracted the others. He hurried for the window again while Spyre lured his enemies to the opposite side of the room, drawing Ryne and Afor as far from the king as possible. Once safe, Eofyn leapt through the window toward where Spyre knew Ness lay.

If the king had thought Spyre was the source and was now with Ness, then he assumed the source was still unidentified and Ness was, for the moment, still alive. Suddenly, the swords, and the pain, and the bleeding, and the kingdom didn't matter to Spyre anymore. If Ness was still alive, and he had the chance to say goodbye to her, he would take it.

Spyre caught Ryne's blade with his own and knocked it out of the way. He ducked and whacked him in the stomach to knock him off guard before spinning around to slam the wooden sword handle into his brother's temple, watching Ryne's tense muscles release as he fell unconscious to the throne room floor.

He should have checked Afor's reaction, but nothing within Spyre cared. If Afor pursued him, he'd do what he must to get around him and out to Ness, so to avoid giving Afore the chance, Spyre simply pivoted on his heel and ran for the window, sliding around the sharp left turn toward Swelgan's statue, where he found Ness surrounded by Lissa, Eofyn, and Pyram.

They all wore bleak visages, apologizing to Spyre as he dropped to his knees next to them. He opened his mouth to ask what could be done, but it was pointless. Lissa has already done everything she could. Words were a waste of time. Spyre dropped his sword, both hands planted on the cold marble, and forced himself to face Ness, expecting pain and the glazed look he'd seen on the soldier in the Aforthian Mountains just moments before he ...

But Ness was smiling. In the last seconds of her life, she still found cause for joy, though Spyre had no idea what it could be. Her eyes remained fixed on the sky, like she was watching a scene play out before her eyes. It made her smile so Spyre kept quiet, allowing her this moment.

Then surprise washed over her features, even as the color began to drain from her face.

"Me ..." she rasped out.

They all drew closer, mirroring the same frown at what she could mean.

"You what, Ness?" Eofyn asked with a gentle hand on her arm. "What do you need?"

A single tear rolled down Ness's cheek, and her chest heaved in what Spyre couldn't decide was laughter or sobs. "It's ... me ... Your Majesty."

"What?" Eofyn leaned in closer. She reached out to him and he sighed, taking her hand and smiling at her bravery, but a second later, her words became clear, as a bright aura emanated from the center of her crystal, spreading to encompass her entire body in seconds.

Air rushed into her chest, and her hooded eyes opened completely as she looked at Spyre with golden light swirling in them, complementing their green hues while he and the others leaned away from her in shock.

"It's me," she said breathlessly, more strength behind her melodious words.

For a moment, she looked so alive and radiant, almost as if she could stand and run free, but she didn't rise. She held on tightly to Spyre's hand, smiling sadly as they watched her Fyre spread across the marble to grace the base of Swelgan's statue, igniting the dragon as well. A shock wave rushed out over the city, expanding beyond its walls as far as the eye could see.

"They're coming," she confirmed, bright tears rolling down her cheeks. She tugged on Spyre's hand. "Please," she whispered, "you have to save my brother. Please, save him. He's not lost yet." She looked toward the broken glass behind the dragon statue that was now pulsing with light. "And tell Spyre …"

Spyre leaned in, listening carefully as Ness lost her strength and sense of self, the glow receding.

"Tell him … that he meant everything to me. I wouldn't be this without him." Her whispered voice carried an echo like the chime of a bell, as she blinked new tears away. "He has to hold out." Her eyes returned to Spyre's as her breathing turned more ragged.

"Hold out," she told him. "The Fyre is returned. The baby is born. They're coming." She quickly shut her eyes, bracing herself until her face slowly relaxed, and the air left her lungs for the last time. Her crystal darkened and expired, looking dark and hollow. She was gone.

Spyre clutched Ness's hand, bending over her and resting their entwined hands against his forehead, thinking of how loyal she'd been to her kingdom and how worthy she was of being the Source of the Fyre. His face collapsed into sorrow as he brushed stray strands of hair away from Ness's face, folding her hands across her chest while the others knelt silently by her side.

Ness was the first casualty of this battle, and with Cuman and Swelgan approaching reality and Spyre still with a fight to finish inside, he was determined she would be the only life lost.

CHAPTER 34

As he re-entered the throne room, a blow to the temple from Ryne sent Spyre sliding across the floor. Spyre rolled onto his hands and knees, feeling the knob forming on the side of his head to complete a set of bumps and bruises across his face, now including a very large black eye that threatened to impair his vision. But he could see well enough that both of his enemies were on the approach. He spit on the floor, seeing a splash of red and realizing that, of all things, he had bitten his own tongue. Shaking his head tiredly, he looked out the window, drawn to the breaking light of day.

But it wasn't the sun that shone so brightly.

Spyre's eyes rounded as he saw the frighteningly bright glow of the dragon just outside the window. Ness was right. They were coming. And she was really gone.

Yes. Lateo confirmed sadly, speaking for the first time in too long. *I'm so sorry ...*

"Sorry isn't good enough," Spyre growled, moving his hooded eyes up to his opponents, who paused at the determination in his glare.

Not caring about the danger or about Afor's stupid crystal, Spyre stood and firmly walked over to the light that poured in through the window.

Take it, Lateo agreed. *It's time.*

Spyre held his sword out, soaking it in the light of the Fyre's source. As soon as the metal left the shadows, a golden glow coursed down the blade, even brighter than Afor's had been, like a wave reclaiming the land, stopping at the wooden handle.

Spyre slowly turned to face Afor and Ryne, eyes dark and piercing.

Ness was dead. The source that had silently guided them all as its incarnation fought on the home front had been released. The pure light that had called him from his own kingdom, followed him, saved him, and frustrated him to no end was extinguished, but not before she'd had her final swan song and had given Spyre one last glimmer of hope. He had nothing—nothing left to lose.

In the glow's warmth, Spyre felt that Ness was somehow fighting at his side, urging him forward from the same dimension Lateo had called to him from. He would fight for her. He would die for her, but first, he would destroy the scum who had overrun her city, completing her mission in her name.

Spyre swung the blazing sword up, holding it tightly with both hands, seeing only Ness's face and feeling nothing but pain. He gave no warning. He charged, the tip of his blade focused on Afor. He heard Lateo's urges in his head to not lose himself, but he pursued his target anyway. With less than a second to spare, Afor raised his sword in defense as Ryne dove away, not willing to accept the assault in his king's stead.

"Some bravery," Spyre grunted through his gritted teeth, his voice dripping with sarcasm as he forced Afor's sword away. "Very loyal."

"Ryne," Afor called out, keeping his eyes on Spyre, who narrowed his own eyes in return. "If I die, you will be captured and killed. You will lose everything you have, including your freedom."

For the first time in Spyre's life, he saw neither anger nor pride on Ryne's face. He saw fear. Ryne dashed from the hall with a nod, running for backup while Afor's thin smile returned.

"Ready to face an entire army, are you?" he goaded, but Spyre would have none of it.

He followed Lateo's instruction and swiped his sword in front of Afor, slicing a thin cut along his neck, sending him reeling back toward the thrones, clutching the nearly fatal wound in fear, but the king was not ready to surrender. He charged after Spyre, intent on returning the favor with a matching scar but a much deeper one.

Their swords met as they stepped lightly across the room, Spyre maintaining the defensive advantage over Afor, lunging and swiping but never intending to truly injure the tyrant. That honor was reserved for someone else, as he recalled from the temple. He wanted nothing more than to ignore the temple floor and finish Afor off himself, but the image of Ness's disappointed face in his mind would not let him pursue it. Condel would never trust a killer, even if he was their guided hero.

Spyre ducked under a high swipe from the king and quickly elbowed him in the chest. Afor fell backward onto the steps of the thrones. They stared at each other, both breathing heavily. Spyre stood over Afor, taking in the cold air from outside that filled the open room, keeping himself focused on the extent of the role he was to play, but Afor did not miss his chance.

Desperate anger in his eyes, Afor quickly jumped to his feet only inches from Spyre, reached out, and grabbed Spyre's arm, squeezing where he had cut into him earlier and sapping Spyre of his strength. Afor pushed him, following up with a strong kick to his side, and sent him to the floor, where he slammed into the wooden thrones, one of them still occupied by a now-petrified young boy.

The boy tumbled to the floor as his chair toppled onto its side. He picked up his head to see Spyre gasping for breath.

Spyre quickly tried to get to his feet, but Afor's crystal flared as he thrust his left hand out in Spyre's direction. An invisible force slammed into Spyre, forcing him onto his back while emphasizing the pain of every wound and simultaneously depriving him of air. Spyre struggled, trying to kick and push and breathe, deaf to the sound of his own agonized screams until, finally, he no longer had enough oxygen to breathe or strength to fight. His body fell silent, and he stared blankly at the ceiling as the force removed itself, leaving him with nothing else to give.

Above him, Losian looked down at Spyre's broken form and then at his own crystal. He touched it lightly, recoiling as though it burned him.

"Is she...?" he asked, not meeting Spyre's eyes.

Spyre released a sardonic laugh. "Yeah. She's..." He clutched his ribs against a muscle spasm. "She's gone." He struggled to catch Losian's gaze. There was something he needed to know. "She wanted me to save you. Her last words …"

With angry tears brimming in his eyes, Spyre watched Ness's brother clutch the crystal tightly and yank it off, casting it out through the broken window and crawling closer to Spyre, shaking him back to his senses.

"You fought for her, didn't you?" Losian asked as Spyre's glossy eyes trailed upward, meeting his. "You want this kingdom to be free?"

Spyre winced as he tried to move but nodded.

"How do you find the courage?" Losian asked, almost sobbing the words.

Spyre wheezed but offered a weak grin that was meant to be a laugh. He wiped a trail of blood from the corner of his mouth with a trembling hand. "It's easy." He choked, still laughing. "I'm just more afraid of what will happen if I don't."

He moved his half-lidded eyes to Afor, who was already approaching them. He looked back at Losian. "Don't let her down," he said as sternly as he could, causing a veil of calm energy to fall over them. "Get yourself out of here."

Scared as a young boy should be, Losian stared at Spyre for only a moment before fumbling for the window, barely making it to his feet by the time he rushed through the broken glass.

Spyre exhaled in relief. At least the boy was safe. With that consolation, he slowly turned his head to meet Afor's gaze, noticing that his crystal had suddenly lost much of its intensity. Spyre smiled, realizing that Losian's desire for the Fyre had incidentally fueled Afor's own strength, but that had just been stripped away from him.

Spyre stayed on the cool marble for a moment, feeling useless and spent. Even with the Fyre in his blade and the blow to Afor's power, Afor had weakened him beyond the chance of victory, and now the Gaernod king was about to succeed. He kicked Spyre down the platform steps and delicately placed his boot on Spyre's neck, pushing just enough to hinder his breathing.

No, Spyre thought. *Not like this. I might go down, but I will have my dignity.*

Directing all of his remaining strength to his left arm, Spyre leaned over and drove the tip of his sword underneath the leg of the closest throne and used the step as a fulcrum, catapulting the chair at an angle to send it crashing into Afor, forcing him to stumble. Spyre moved with a sudden burst of triumphant energy, not strong but no longer useless.

Dragging himself over to his enemy, he smashed the hilt of his sword into the side of Afor's knee, hearing a few sickening cracks as his former king fell away from him. Spyre moved as fast as he could, pushing himself to his feet. He hunched over, dragging his sword on the floor. He limped toward Afor, hearing the thunderous roar of multiple footsteps coming down the corridor toward them. This would be the end. What more could the Fyre or Bryta or those ridiculous dragons possibly ask from him?

Nothing, Lateo assured him. *Your work is finished.*

Feeling both relieved and terrified, Spyre nodded his head at the invisible entity. One more thing, then, he decided. One more shot.

He stood next to his enemy, sword hanging lazily at his side. Afor looked up at him, anger cloaking only a speck of fear as the older man stood with difficulty, leaning on his own sword.

"I won't say this twice," Spyre said wearily, raising his sword toward Afor but unable to lift it higher than waist level. "Leave now. Go away and be happy with your pile of filth back home."

The door behind Spyre opened, and he watched Afor grin widely at the number of men who had come to their king's aid, all seeking the promises that Afor never intended to make good on. Afor looked Spyre in the eye, but Spyre well knew of his situation and maintained his defiant glare.

"You think you can possibly succeed now?" Afor asked, laughing at him. He caught his balance on his good leg and raised his sword, sending a glance to his soldiers to wait a moment.

Spyre thought about lifting his own glowing sword, but it seemed so pointless. If he fought back, an army would kill him. If he didn't, a king would kill him.

Then it occurred to him. Why on earth not?

A shadow passed over the room as Spyre summoned everything he had left in him to make his last stand. He could see Ness's proud smile beaming at him.

"You," he said with reckless confidence, pointing his blade at Afor as steadily as he could manage. "You're going down with me." He gave a cocky, crooked grin and raised his sword to meet Afor's in the air above their heads.

The moment Afor lost the upper hand, the army would descend upon him, so Spyre decided he might as well make his last act count. He tightened his arms, getting ready to bring both of their swords down before quickly piercing Afor through the chest, knowing he would probably do the same thing.

But it was not meant to be.

The shadow over the room grew larger, stretching even farther, and it was only now that Spyre registered that the light from the stone dragon had disappeared. That couldn't have been good. A large, heavy object collided with the back of Spyre's knee, crumpling his legs from beneath him. Foul play from one of the soldiers. They had slung a stone at him, and they had been accurate about it. Spyre caught himself on the floor with one arm, but when he looked up, Afor dominated his vision.

"Die slowly," Afor whispered venomously, bringing his sword up with both hands and forcing it downward, where it would pin Spyre to the marble floor through his ribs.

Spyre closed his eyes, preparing for the pain and ordering himself not to give them the satisfaction of hearing him scream.

A second later, Spyre felt himself shoved flat on his back by a large, blunt object that struck him between the eyes. The air rushed out of him as he hit the floor, surprised that no one had jumped at him yet. He frantically looked back to Afor, sitting up on his forearms and coming face to face with the weapon that had disarmed him.

Afor's eyes were wide and glistening. They stared directly ahead of him, level with Spyre's eyes but looking through him. A small trail of blood brimmed at the edge of his mouth, and Spyre, gaping and forgetting to breathe, glanced down to see that something he couldn't even identify had ripped a large, round hole, not only through Afor's chest, but essentially removing it.

Afraid of what had done this, Spyre looked back to Afor's eyes, almost wanting to save him, but the king who was now nothing more than a corpse was dragged backward by the massive, curved claw hooked through his chest. Spyre trailed his eyes along a very large and thick crimson-scaled arm that was attached to an even more massive torso, topped off with a head that Spyre was both familiar with yet unaccustomed to, though he'd never seen Cuman alive before.

Do I bow? Should I stand? Spyre wasn't sure he had the wits about him to do either of those things. Instead, he stared at the large crystal eyes until, finally, something came out of him. "Cuman?" It sounded like a question, but really, who else would the imposing red dragon be?

Cuman lowered his large head, two horns curling on either side of his slitted yellow eyes, meeting Spyre's gaze over his long snout. Spyre took in a quiet, slow breath, unable to hold it anymore but also unwilling to move too much in front of the massive beast. The sword in his hand suddenly stopped glowing, as if its power had been blown away by some divine wind.

Cuman would like to thank you for your patience and endurance while he followed the Fyre of your sword to find you.

Spyre jolted at the sound of Lateo's voice in his head, sounding more reverent than he was used to. So the glow wasn't added strength; it was a beacon. Took him long enough …

Your work is done, Lateo continued, sounding much more enthusiastic than the last time he spoke those words just minutes ago.

The dragon slowly turned, moving on his four legs with much more effort than it must have taken him to arrive. He tucked his wings close, lowered his swooping tail, and flung Afor off his claw with an effortless flick of his wrist that sent the false king flying into the wall.

Spyre released his breath as his shaky arms collapsed beneath him. He stayed on the floor for a few brief moments, letting the rush subside. Then he tilted his head upward, seeing an upside-down view of the army behind him. They were staring at the lumbering dragon, frozen in fear.

He laughed. Here was the entire army of Gaernod, which had been fully prepared to gut him without hesitation just a moment ago, now gawking, not a closed jaw among them. It was truly entertaining. But then Spyre remembered just who they were, what they'd done, what they'd been willing to do, and what they'd taken from him. As they stared at him, his face distorted from laughter into grim accusation, and he stood to face them.

"What?" he loudly demanded of all of them, raising his arms, sword still in his hand. He shook his head at them, arms dropping loosely as they continued to stare at him. "Get out of here."

He gestured them away with the sword, chastising them as if they were obstinate children.

"Get out of this city. Go home. I don't have time to deal with you." He turned away but spun on them again on a second thought, pointing the blade in their direction and spearing the air to emphasize his words. "And you think about what you've done." His voice was low and demanded their attention. He turned his back on them, no longer caring about what they were thinking or what their motives had been.

He caught up with Cuman in a few long strides, sheltering himself underneath his long tale as the dragon crashed through the only part of the grand window that had survived the invasion intact. Grinning, he dared Eofyn to say something to the dragon about breaking his precious window, but he couldn't bring himself to relish in the moment, because there she was.

Another smaller dragon, blue in color, was sitting, staring at Eofyn with intensity, probably sending a message of his own to the king. Spyre solemnly followed Cuman, passing him to stand next to Eofyn at the foot of Ness's lifeless body. He winced at the sight of her pale, quiet form, choking back tears and quickly turning to face the two dragons at the king's side. Neither of the men were happy.

They couldn't even muster up enough joy to be enthused. They just stared blankly at the beasts, waiting for their declarations.

From the bottom of the steps, a mournful wail reached their ears as they turned to see Ness's parents; her mother, clutching a small bundle, collapsed against her father's embrace. They had seen her.

Eofyn glanced at Spyre with a dulled look of confusion. Spyre was emotionless and disinterested, no longer impressed in the least by the dragons before him and numb to everything else.

Spyre turned at the sound of glass being disturbed to see a thunderstruck man emerge from the broken window and bend down to pick something up from among the glass. That would be Atelle, based on what Spyre had learned from Ness. He hurried to Pyram's side, never taking his awestruck eyes off the dragons.

"I saw the guards retreating through the halls," he whispered to Pyram out of the corner of his mouth. "So I told Darian to come find his children."

Spyre saw Atelle's eyes fall on Ness and immediately glisten. Then they shot up to her younger brother, crystal missing and tears streaming down his face. Atelle held out his hand to Losian, taking the boy's hand and carefully placing his discarded crystal back in his palm. A soft hue of emerald green pulsed through it.

The boy scoffed at it, shaking his head with a look of bitterness on his face. He stared at it and then ignored it, focusing on the more grave matters at hand.

Now, they were all gathered. Everyone who had directly suffered and fought—including Darian and Elene, carrying her brand-new baby daughter—stood before the dragons, silently pleading for an explanation or some direction. How would they ever rebuild not only the city but themselves?

"I can sense your pain," a booming voice echoed around them.

Spyre glanced to his side, seeing that Eofyn heard it as well and knowing they were all privy to the dragon's words.

Swelgan's ocean-deep eyes scanned them sadly.

He lowered his head, regarding Ness's silent form lying among those who'd been blessed enough to know her. She was the connection between them all. Suddenly, everything about the emotional, passionate girl made sense.

"But you've gained your freedom." He lowered his eyes to Spyre, but the man was less than impressed, waiting for what he thought was sure to come.

"With the removal of Afor, balance is restored. None of you carry the weight of his death on your shoulders. You carry no blame."

The towering blue dragon looked to his crimson twin. They nodded slowly to each other in mutual understanding.

"We leave you now to rebuild an era of peace and of wisdom."

Spyre knew the message had been intended for Eofyn, but it was he who spoke out.

"Wait, what?" he asked, stepping forward with an incredulous look on his face as Eofyn took his chance and retreated to finally take hold of his beloved fiancée, pulling her close.

"That's it?" Spyre demanded. "You're just going to leave?" He stepped to the side, gesturing at Ness with both hands. "A few words of consolation and motivation, and you're just going to leave without bringing her back?" He lowered his voice. "You really are made of stone."

Cuman tilted his head to the side, as if confused by Spyre's dissatisfaction. "She was the source. She was always meant for this," he explained. "She was not meant to return. Her life force was released to the people of the kingdom."

Spyre tried to speak, but he was too disgusted. He held up a hand, turning away from the beasts and forcefully pushing heated breath out before turning back to them. "I'm sorry," he said, not the least bit apologetic, "but you're trying to tell me she was nothing more than some Fyre vessel? She wasn't even her own person? She doesn't deserve the right to her own life? What kind of reasoning is that?"

"Not everything is fair," Cuman countered evenly. "You've seen enough in your travels to know that." The dragon lowered his gaze, acknowledging Spyre as a child of Gaernod.

Images of Soru, Dugan, Faran, and Rowan flashed in Spyre's mind, but he waved them away, not willing to be swayed by some magical manipulation. "That's not good enough," he spit out. "Not for her."

Swelgan lowered his head to Spyre's level. "Each of you had a part to play in the development of this plot," he said soothingly. "You played yours well, and she did the same. Brilliantly." He raised himself to his full height, turning to Cuman.

"No," Spyre shouted after them. The creatures were several times his size, but he would make himself heard. "I will not accept that. No one here can consider this a victory with a loss like this." His head almost turned toward Ness, but he couldn't bring himself to do it.

"Would you have preferred Afor to have won?" Cuman asked, losing his sage composure and sounding angry. The Condels all fell back a step at the rumble of his voice, but Spyre stood firm.

"Personally?" Spyre asked in challenge. The dragon could kill him where he stood, for all Spyre cared. If it was a match of anger, he was certain he could exceed any sort of rage even a giant dragon could muster in this moment. He realized his brashness and sighed, his whole body falling weak. "What do I have to do?" he asked. "Can I replace her? Do I have to go somewhere—travel from Gaernod to Tir and back again? Circle the globe ten times? What can I do? I will do anything to bring her back to these people."

"Just to them?" Swelgan questioned. "Are you so devastated for their loss and not your own?" He lowered himself back to Spyre's level.

Spyre twitched under the ancient stare but stood his ground.

He remained silent for a moment, his jaw firmly in place. Finally, his will broke, and he averted his gaze. "I want her back," he confessed, his eyes glossing over, as he no longer had the will to fight. He dropped to his knees, looking at the guardians. "I've seen too much to take her for granted," he said between heavy breaths. "Please." He clutched his dizzy head in his hands before dropping them to his knees and staring upward.

He tried to listen for any sign of Lateo's support in his mind, but with the introduction of the two dragons, his guide had taken his leave, retreating into the untouchable realm of Bryta. Spyre felt utterly alone, devastated, and confused. There was nowhere to look, no one to turn to, but he needed something. There was nothing left but surrender.

"Bring her back to me," he pleaded, eyes shut tightly against the emptiness that filled his chest.

The dragons exchanged glances as everyone else present watched. Spyre was reduced to nothing but shock. The mythical beasts looked sad but resolved, returning their gazes to Spyre's pleading eyes. He had broken. After everything, this young girl had broken him. But without another word or gesture, Cuman disappeared into a jet of red light, shooting over the city and out of sight as Swelgan returned to his pedestal with one final apologetic glance to the company gathered at his side. He froze from his claws to his eyes back into stone. Spyre stared as his only hope for a miracle abandoned him. This was not how victory was supposed to feel.

With an angry shout, Spyre pounded the marble as tears escaped against his will. He pressed his forehead to the cool stone, trying to contain himself while the others behind him held onto each other, mourning in their own way as the sun finally rose.

The light slowly crept up the streets of the ruined city, climbing the stairs one at a time and covering them all in its warmth, but Spyre wanted nothing to do with it.

CHAPTER 35

No one knew how long they'd stood there, but the sun was making progress across the sky by the time Spyre felt Pyram's hand on his shoulder as he crouched in front of the lifeless statue.

Spyre threw it off and determinedly stood of his own accord, not facing them. He lowered his head, speaking to them over his shoulder.

"I'm sorry," he said, wiping a hand across his heavy, burning eyes. "I'm just so sorry."

His hand lowered slowly as he turned around to finally face Ness head on. No one stood in his way as he walked over to her; he knelt by her side and stroked her messy hair with his tear-soaked hand, smiling despite himself.

"You are so special," he whispered to her, leaning down and gently kissing her forehead; he pulled away and pushed himself up from his knee.

He looked up and saw Darian first. He was holding onto his wife, who held onto their newborn daughter protectively as she buried her face into his shoulder. They exchanged an understanding glance as the others slowly moved away, heading back into the castle to give them privacy.

"I've got her," Spyre said to Darian. "You go inside. Get some rest, or eat something," he said, but his eyes sent another message, giving Darian permission to tend to what remained of his traumatized family.

Darian hesitated but relented, giving Spyre a grateful nod before ushering his wife, baby, and son through the ruined window.

Spyre turned away from the castle, staring down at Ness. He cast a hateful glance at the slumbering dragon to his left and bent down to gently slide an arm under the girl's knees and another under her head, lifting her into his arms. He carried her like a child, walking her over to Swelgan.

"The dragons came," he said lightly. "You did that." He laughed, trying to avoid the alternative.

He walked to the edge of the steps, looking out over the kingdom. It felt so cold and uninviting now. The welcoming atmosphere he had dreamed of was nowhere to be found in his mind. The city held nothing for him.

"Yeah, I really don't know what I'm going to do from here, but it's safe, Ness. You protected them." He looked down at her peaceful face as it rested against his shoulder. "I could've gotten used to this."

He laughed hollowly.

"And you've got a sister. Oh, and your brother's crystal is glowing a normal color now. Good news there." He dropped his head with a frustrated sigh, unable to pretend any longer. His pent-up frustration seethed from him in a low growl.

"It wasn't supposed to be this way. Leave Gaernod, get to Condel, help the king save the day, and—I don't know—find a way to just blend in. That's how it was supposed to be."

He tipped his head, considering the luster of the crystal street lights. "But then Eofyn had to run off to Tir, and you just had to follow me. Why did you do that?" But he knew why. "Next time, maybe you'll listen," he said, allowing himself to pretend for just a moment before his eyes closed against rebellious tears.

"Not likely," he could hear her voice say.

He smiled, eyes still closed, remembering her tenacity as he held her close to him and blindly found her forehead, pressing another small kiss to it.

"After all this, that's all I get?" the strained yet vibrant voice said.

He frowned. That's not the response his mind would have given Ness. It was like meeting Lateo all over again, except this ripped his heart out of him. Then the worst happened: hope sparked in his chest, and the earth seemed to quake beneath his unsteady feet; Spyre didn't want to open his eyes for fear it wasn't true. He felt four fingers drumming against his shoulder impatiently.

"You're kidding, right?" the tired voice droned. "I just came back from the dead here. You could at least be a little impressed."

His eyes slowly opened, and in that moment, nothing else in the world existed but those bright sea-green eyes. His breath was gone. The strength in his knees only remained because he refused to risk hurting her if he fell. Instead, he allowed himself to quickly sink into a crouch, setting her on the ground and holding her in front of him, but after a moment, the awe faded from his face, and his features shifted into a cocky smirk.

"Prove it," he dared.

Ness's eyes widened at him in frustrated disbelief. "Don't you think I've done enough work for one day?"

Spyre only gave a thin smile, his eyes glistening with what he would never admit were tears of joy, but he knew she noticed. She smiled at him, a mischievous glint in her eye.

"All right, then," she said before quickly grabbing the front of his shirt and pulling him in for what she considered a real kiss.

She held him close with a hand at the back of his neck as his hands drifted to support her back.

It didn't take long before the first spark of real and pure joy had Spyre pulling Ness in closer, reminding himself that she was there in his arms, breathing and alive. This was the feeling he'd expected as his reward for helping to save the blessed kingdom.

When they finally pulled away from each other, they were content to just stare into each other's eyes, but only for a moment.

"I can't be selfish," Spyre blurted, standing quickly and pulling her to her feet. He forgot any pain he had and grabbed her hand, leading her through the window, reveling in the sound of her full-throated laugh when she saw the new damage and remarked at how furious the king must be.

The others were still in the throne room, Afor's body no longer present. When they saw Ness, no one moved. Then Elene broke free of Darian's arms and rushed forward. Spyre put a supportive hand on

Ness's back, bracing her for the impact as Elene ran to embrace her daughter, still causing her to take a step back to steady herself.

Darian was close behind, followed by Losian, Atelle, Pyram, Eofyn, and then Lissa. Lissa reached forward gently to a spot on Ness that wasn't being smothered by the others and allowed her crystal to gleam brightly, healing Ness of anything and everything she could as her crystal blazed at its full potential, no longer dampened by the threat of Afor. She then moved onto Spyre, placing a hand on his shoulder and sending her power through him to mend every cut and bruise. It still spooked him, but this time, he smiled in gratitude.

After a few moments of an elated reunion and Ness fawning over her new baby sister and her brother's legitimate glow, Spyre watched as the group spread out and related their own stories of the past week to one another.

"You were stunning," Eofyn said, taking Lissa's face into his hands and kissing her deeply, holding her close.

"I missed you," she whispered, resting her head on his shoulder and relishing being in his arms.

"What are you going to name her?" Ness asked whimsically, touching her sister's tiny nose with her finger.

Elene looked to Darian and smiled. "We were thinking maybe Wena."

Ness looked up and smiled approvingly, cooing to the baby. "Hi, Wena. Welcome to the family. There's no way you're going to be normal, but that's okay. It's sort of our thing to be strange. Just ask your brother," she said, casting a sly glance to her brother, who returned the insult with a playful jab to her side.

"Nothing's changed," Darian said, shaking his head and pulling Losian in sharply with one arm, gathering the rest of his family for a hug.

But Spyre stood away from the others, arms folded across his healed chest, staring out at the sunlight over the city until Eofyn stepped up beside him, a broad, proud, and relieved smile on his face. Spyre shuffled his feet, looking forward.

"Sorry about the window," he muttered, suppressing a laugh.

Eofyn looked down, smiling. "Windows can be replaced," he said, looking meaningfully over his shoulder to Ness.

Spyre nodded his agreement, and Eofyn turned to him.

"You didn't have to do anything," he said. "You didn't have to come here, and you didn't have to save Pyram and me." He paused. "And you didn't have to face Afor."

Spyre could feel himself growing red at the ears under the uncomfortable attention, and Eofyn smiled, placing his hands on Spyre's shoulders, one curled into a fist.

"But you did all of those things. And then you stood up to the dragons in Ness's defense. That took courage." He released Spyre and joined him in looking out the window.

"It's not courage," Spyre said, still believing what he'd told Losian. "I was just more afraid of what would have happened if I didn't."

Eofyn smiled with an understanding glance toward his betrothed. He looked back to Spyre. "You know, if there's anything you need, a place to stay, something to do, just ask. I think it's fair to say I owe you one."

Spyre turned his head to Eofyn. "Those things would be great," he admitted, "especially considering the alternative." He was not going back to Gaernod. "I mean, I could always camp out with the sprites, but I've developed this strange aversion to trees." He shuddered a little at the memory of the events in Laefa Pinewood.

Eofyn tilted his head and frowned, mouth open in question, but then he shook his head and sighed instead. "There is something else I'd like to give you, though." He held out his clenched hand, and Spyre curiously held out his own, ready to catch whatever Eofyn was hiding.

Eofyn's fingers released, and a chain with a crystal attached fell into Spyre's hands, lighting with an orange glow almost immediately. Both of their eyes widened as the crystal sparked in Spyre's palm, drawing the attention of the others. They drew closer to see him take on a portion of the Fyre as his own. Ness squealed and jumped as she hugged him close, staring down at his crystal.

"Orange," Losian observed. "Wonder what that means." He toyed with his own yet-to-be defined light.

Spyre looked down at him, still at a loss for words. "I ..." He smiled. "I guess we can find out together." He put his arm around Ness, pulling her close as he stared at the very thing Afor had lusted after but could not rightfully own.

"Welcome to the blessed kingdom," Ness said, excitement still in her voice as she pressed her forehead to Spyre's. "Welcome back to where you belong."

Spyre smiled, realizing the truth behind her words as he thought about who he'd been in Gaernod, who he'd become on his way to Condel, thanks to the many guides that had aided him, and the lineage they'd discovered in Tir. He did belong, because somewhere in the desert, eons ago, they had been the same.

He turned to Ness and pulled her close, never wanting to let go.

"This is where I belong," he said, resting his chin on top of her head as she smiled against him. "You know, I think I'm going to like it here."

Over the top of Ness's head, Spyre caught Darian's glance. In his eyes, he saw joy, relief, and the remnants of pain but also a hint of a challenge. That was Darian's daughter Spyre held in his arms, and Spyre had best respect her if he knew what was good for him. He returned Darian's good-natured warning with a weak and crooked smile. Message received.

It was then that Spyre realized that he had faced the kings and leaders of every nation between Gaernod and Condel. He'd been threatened and beaten and saved, only to be abused all over again, somehow surviving through to the end. But it was here, standing in the light of a new era, he saw the truth culminating in Darian's eyes. The real adventure was just beginning.

Spyre grinned. Bring it on.

ABOUT THE AUTHOR

KristaLyn is a certified holistic practitioner, author, and intuitive coach who helps people attract the lives they want to live with the one thing they can't control: divine timing.

For her thirteenth birthday, KristaLyn's mother took her on the first of many mission trips, showing her how a single person can make a large impact on the world, one fellow human being at a time. Thanks to this, KristaLyn has spent more than a decade serving others through coaching and holistic therapies. She is certified in life, spiritual, and health coaching and follows various holistic modalities including reiki (master/teacher), crystal healing, advanced integrated energy therapy, and advanced ThetaHealing, with additional certifications in Hellenistic astrology and chirology.

After graduating from Susquehanna University with a BA in English, KristaLyn wrote several books with motivational themes of being your own hero and serving the world through your unique talents and gifts, which she knows everyone was born with.

A paragon of the millennial generation, KristaLyn entertained a variety of jobs, ranging from amusement park showgirl, coordinator of the Group Mission Trip Week of Hope Program, and cast member at Disney World, as she pursued her dreams of sharing her message with the world.

KristaLyn lives in a treehouse in Elysburg, Pennsylvania, with her husband and corgi, Jack, and cooperates with her family to help revitalize the coal region of Pennsylvania to a new, sustainable glory.

Website: www.KristaLynAVetovich.com
Email: info@KristaLynAVetovich.com
Social Media Handle: @AuthorKristaLyn

Printed in the United States
By Bookmasters